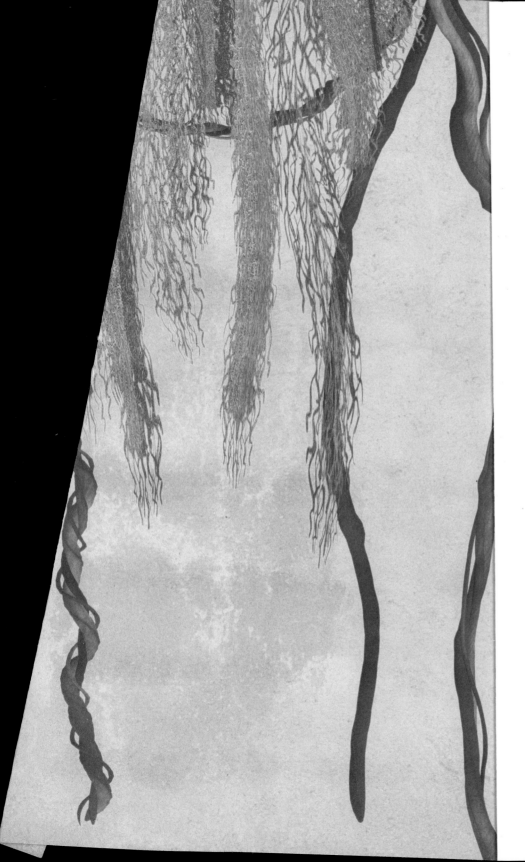

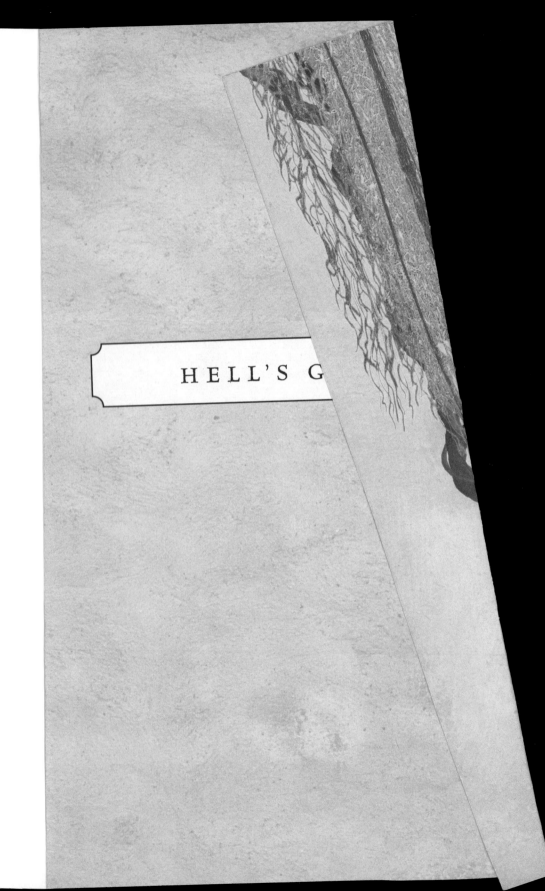

HELL'S G

Hell's Gate

BILL SCHUTT
& J. R. FINCH

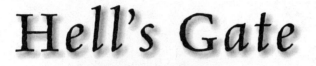

WILLIAM MORROW

An Imprint of HarperCollins*Publishers*

HELL'S GATE. Copyright © 2016 by Bakk Bone LLC. All rights reserved. Printed in the United States of America. No part of this book may be used or reproduced in any manner whatsoever without written permission except in the case of brief quotations embodied in critical articles and reviews. For information, address HarperCollins Publishers, 195 Broadway, New York, NY 10007.

HarperCollins books may be purchased for educational, business, or sales promotional use. For information, please e-mail the Special Markets Department at SPsales@harpercollins.com.

FIRST EDITION

Designed by William Ruoto

Illustrations courtesy of Patricia J. Wynne

Title page illustrations courtesy Shutterstock/KathyGold (vines);
Shutterstock/Maximus256 (map)

Library of Congress Cataloging-in-Publication Data has been applied for.

ISBN 978-0-06-241252-2

16 17 18 19 20   OV/RRD   10 9 8 7 6 5 4 3 2 1

For our families,

and for Colonel Percy Harrison Fawcett,

who was there

HELL'S GATE

Blood Bright and Bible Black

God has no power over the past
except to cover it with oblivion.
——PLINY THE ELDER

February 16, 1944
Along the banks of the Gniloy Tickich River, Ukraine
Soviet-German Front

An early thaw.

That is how it began.

The air was peculiarly humid for this place at this time of year. The hard freeze that usually set in around December and lasted until March had never arrived. The river, usually a sluggish stream, was now a freezing torrent.

A light breeze blew hair into Viktor's eyes. Brushing it aside, the seventeen-year-old stopped momentarily to admire the view. The countryside was beautiful—even peaceful, especially if one discounted certain facts: the muddy tank tracks in the snow, the constant engine noise, and the smell of black fumes.

The gray packhorse turned his head toward the boy and chewed wetly on his metal bit.

You're hungry, Sasha. Me too.

Viktor loosened Sasha's bridle, then reached into his coat pocket, withdrawing half a handful of grain. Sasha took it eagerly, then nudged the boy's shoulder.

"That's all there is," he said, giving the animal an exaggerated shrug.

The horse, a small Russian *panje,* was native to the Eurasian Steppe and not much larger than a donkey. Viktor had known the breed for most of his life. They were Russia's answer to the knee-deep mud trails that were referred to only by mapmakers as roads. This particular horse was strong and steady, although he was pulling a sled piled more than a little too high with wooden crates. For three days, the cargo had not left young Viktor's sight. At night, he had slept on it. The boy knew that although many of the crates his countrymen were hauling through the mud contained ammunition or even guns, this one held only shovels and pick axes. *But they are as important as guns,* he reminded himself. *Maybe more important.*

Viktor was right, although he was as ignorant as the next man when it came to the specifics of their mission. As they had been for many of his countrymen, his only orders were to "go forward" and to "kill them all." For his part, Viktor had never actually seen a German, but more and more of late, he wondered how he would react if he did. The boy gave an involuntary shudder and focused on removing a small burr from the horse's withers.

As he stood comforting Sasha, he had no idea that he was one of nearly half a million soldiers converging from almost every point on Russia's compass. They were gathering along a front more than two hundred miles long, their commanders hoping to disintegrate, beyond all hope of recovery, the last German offensive capability in the East. With the help of the weather and local partisan units, the Soviet forces had driven Hitler's armies steadily back through

Russia into the Ukraine. Only the generals knew that sixty-five thousand German soldiers were now nearly surrounded in a salient that bulged deep into the Russian lines. To historians it would become known as the Cherkassy Pocket. To those trapped there, to the ones who survived, it would always be known as *Hell's Gate.*

Within the salient, sleet, mud, and melting snow had combined to immobilize the once-unstoppable invading force. The Luftwaffe had finally dropped supplies and ammunition but unfortunately for the Germans, the materials landed behind the Soviet lines. Equipment and even lines of communication were breaking down—although the beleaguered Germans did learn that their "inadequately lit" drop site had been blamed for the Luftwaffe's error. Unknown to the Axis troops was the fact that the 24th Panzer Unit, after slogging north to relieve the German forces, never even came close. Instead they had inexplicably turned back—in accordance with a direct order from Adolf Hitler. Nearly encircled at Cherkassy, the Germans knew that their only hope for survival would be a massive breakout; but now even this had been postponed.

The Russians, meanwhile, continued to strengthen their positions in what was shaping up to be a classic pincer movement. Russian historians would record that some 200,000 Soviets formed the enveloping arms of the pincer. The German high command believed that it contained twice that number—and, for a while, it did.

Viktor stroked the horse's neck, then tightened up the bridle. *If we dig in deep enough, for long enough, you'll be food.*

He tried to push the thought aside, but could not, until a strange sound distracted him. A loud rumble was not unusual in a war zone. But with this rumble the sky itself seemed to have exploded, somewhere in the distance.

Seconds later, the sound came again—louder. Overhead now, like a thunderclap . . . on a cloudless day. The boy's ribs absorbed the shock wave and they vibrated like twelve pairs of tuning forks.

And then there was silence. Cold silence.

Men and vehicles stopped. As they had done in the past under a variety of circumstances, the shell-shocked and the inexperienced looked toward their officers and to the older soldiers for an explanation. Fresh conscripts turned expectantly toward men who had lived through the Blitzkrieg and the Siege of Leningrad, where starvation, cold, and round-the-clock bombings killed a million of their countrymen. Surely these battle-hardened survivors, the *frontoviki*, could tell them what had just happened.

But even they had never heard a sound like this before. No one had.

It was the boom of a supersonic object decelerating.

A palpable sense of confusion, mingled ever so slightly with fear, moved through the Soviet ranks. Hundreds of soldiers stopped whatever they were doing to search the sky, shielding their eyes against the sun's glare. Those with the best eyes, or who happened to be looking in the right direction, perceived a faint metallic glint, moving with unnatural speed against the heavens. Some of the men instinctively raised their weapons but by then the plane—or whatever it was—had already disappeared from view.

Aleksey Karasev was a master sergeant in the Red Army but with three gold war stripes he commanded as much respect among the soldiers as any general. Karasev blew a cloud of smoke from a cigar that resembled a mummified finger. *Can't be artillery,* he thought. At last report, German tank divisions were more than seventy miles away. *It hadn't sounded like artillery either.*

"Ёб твою мать!" the sergeant cursed, "Keep moving!" But

there was already a commotion up ahead. *What now,* he thought, striding toward the source of the problem—a cargo truck that had stopped in the road. Karasev knew that his weary men would use any excuse to catch a few moments of rest—and if left to their own devices some of them would settle in, like homesteaders, right there in the mud.

The truck was one of the newly arrived American models. A Dodge, they called it. The driver of the canvas-sided vehicle, a young Russian woman, hung out the open door, pointing excitedly at the sky. The grizzled sergeant never noticed that she was extremely attractive, with long black hair that hung down the thickly padded *polushubki* she wore. Now, though, she let her truck's engine stall. A little knot of soldiers, clustered near the truck, was tracking a path from her index finger into the sky.

"There! There!" she shouted.

Several of the men stood by mutely, while others, having caught a glimpse of the truck driver, puffed themselves up to full height.

One of the girl's new guardians fired a single round into the air. It was immediately followed by several more from the man's companions.

Sergeant Karasev could see that they were taking aim at two parachutes that had appeared above them—white circles with a red marking of some kind—incongruous against the blue sky.

There was another shot, this one from farther up the convoy. Karasev squinted into the unnaturally bright sky. There were more parachutes—perhaps half a dozen that he could see—and more rifle fire.

Returning his attention to the closest chutes overhead, Karasev saw that there were no men hanging below them. Instead, there were black canisters.

Supply drop? Karasev wondered. *Another botched attempt by the Luftwaffe?* But another thought intruded, bothering him remotely: The canisters seemed too small to be carrying very much in the way of fuel or supplies.

One more shot cracked the morning air and Karasev's thoughts refocused. Not only were these idiots wasting ammo, they were probably alerting the enemy.

"Who gave the order to fire?" he barked, but something kept his eyes focused skyward, even though his neck was beginning to ache badly. "Damn you! Cease—"

The containers suspended below the two nearest parachutes exploded, simultaneously.

A cheer went up and a few of the shooters turned back toward the girl seeking approval or perhaps just a smile. Instead the gunfire, the bursting canisters, or both had startled the partisan, and she retreated into the cab of the truck and rolled up the window.

Karasev was not thinking about the woman. He was thinking about the accuracy and range of the Mosin-Nagant rifles his men were carrying: the supply-drop containers were too high off the ground when they exploded. *Far too high.*

His men seemed to realize this as well, and Karasev saw that his was not the only face now creased with concern. He looked skyward again but there was nothing left to see except the wounded parachutes, one of which fell near the convoy. Before he could stop them, two of the shooters were tramping their way through thick, wet snow.

The men were out of breath by the time they reached the chute, though it had landed fewer than a hundred steps ahead—strangely beautiful, in its own way: stark white and crimson against the mud.

"Draja, this silk is priceless."

"And it's ours. Now, grab it before it decides to fly off."

Draja and his friend Marius took hold of the material, stretching the fabric between them.

"You're crazy, Draja. They'll never let us keep—"

The men froze, the lament over proprietary rights wiped from their thoughts by the insignia seemingly painted onto the silk: a red circle and within it a black swastika. The circle was enclosed by another symbol: the wide gape of a strange skeletal mouth.

Marius released the parachute as though it had stung him, and at precisely that second a gust of wind blew under the fabric and lifted it toward Draja until it clung to his face. The silk vibrated with a low, chilling moan.

I'm being swallowed! Draja thought, as he kicked and batted at the billowing chute. Logic had dropped dead. His instincts were turning toward panic.

Sergeant Karasev saw none of this. Nearby, an elderly soldier with Asian features had let out a shriek. The man had been leaning against the truck's grill to warm himself when Titania gunned the engine to life.

"Private," Karasev snarled, and the man snapped to attention. "How do you expect to protect the motherland with a load of shit in your pants?"

The man looked down at the ground, shamed, and for a moment the sergeant felt shamed himself, as if he had just shouted down his own father. Now Karasev noticed how thin the man was, even through his thick clothing. He appeared to be more a bird than a man, so recently and so horribly malnourished was he. And yet he had stiffened his spine and come voluntarily to the front lines. The sergeant bowed his own head briefly, then turned and called out to the two men who had chased down the fallen parachute. The idiots were struggling with it—and the parachute seemed to be getting the better of them.

"Bring it!" the sergeant shouted. "Clowns! What are you doing, making this your life's work? Get back here!"

Karasev turned again toward the elderly, red-faced foot soldier and did not see the two men as they stopped struggling and sat down in the snow. Addressing the private, his tone softened. The sergeant noticed that the man's face bore an irregular pattern of shrapnel scars that had become known as "German kisses." He had also lost several fingers, probably to frostbite.

"Let's go, soldier."

But instead of falling in as ordered, the old man remained at attention. Cocking his head slightly to one side, he gave the sergeant a quizzical look.

I can't believe this. Now what? Karasev wondered. *These easterners—yellow Russians. So many dialects.* "Where are the translators when you need them? Go! Go!" he said as firmly and respectfully as he could. But his words and gestures seemed futile.

The old man slowly raised his arm and pointed a trembling finger at him. The expression on his face sent a shiver down Karasev's spine and made his knees feel suddenly loose. He looked down and noticed that a yellow film had coated his white-quilted pants and field jacket.

"What . . . ?"

Karasev sampled the gritty substance with a finger. *It smells like flowers.* He looked up at the sky, then at the private, whose clothing appeared to have been similarly misted. A trickle of blood ran out of the old man's nose.

The sergeant sniffed loudly and tasted copper. His own nose was bleeding as well. He wiped at the flow with his sleeve and recoiled at the size of the red smear.

For a moment Karasev's world went completely silent—no engines, his men no longer cursing or quarreling. It was as if someone had poured wax into his ears, so that the only sound he could hear was the rapid pounding of his own heart. Then, as quickly as the sensation had come upon him, it was gone. Karasev gave an involuntary flinch—for now his world was full of sounds.

No more than forty paces away, a horse reared up and overturned the crate-laden sled it had been pulling.

"Easy, Sasha—easy, boy!" the young sled driver cried but the animal's eyes rolled back into its head and it let out a surprisingly human cry that startled its driver and anyone else near enough to hear. The boy tried to utter more words of comfort to his horse and was rewarded with an immense sneeze that hit him squarely in the face. As the sled driver wiped his eyes, Sergeant Karasev watched him stiffen with fear, unable to comprehend what had just occurred and unable to utter any more words.

The boy's face and hands were covered with blood. In shock and stunned silence he stepped back, just in time to avoid being crushed by his horse as it collapsed in a red gush and the sickening wet sound of ribs snapping. Dying, the animal whipped its head back and forth—blood and pink lung tissue spraying out of its nose in great arcs.

Sergeant Karasev turned away, his eyes widening under a surge of adrenaline . . . until he saw the rest of his men, and closed his eyes. They too had started to bleed—all of them—out of their noses, from their mouths. *"No!"*

The roar of an engine alerted him now and he spun toward the sound. A T-34 tank veering wildly off course, throttle open. Its broad treads threw mud and blackened snow into the air. Several of Karasev's men dove out of the way just before the war machine struck the side of the truck they'd been standing next to only a moment earlier. The tank toppled the lighter vehicle and without slowing, rode up and over the cab. In the time it took Karasev to snatch a single breath, the driver's compartment was compressed, from roof to floor, into a space too small for anyone to fit even a hand. Within that space, the sergeant knew, the girl must have died even before she realized what was happening.

She was the lucky one.

In every direction, men were staggering and turning red, bleeding from every orifice. For many, their last voluntary movement was something they never dared do in public—their trembling fingers making the sign of the cross—forehead . . . lips . . . and breast.

Along a path five miles north and five miles south, wherever the scent of flowers had descended, snow was stealing heat from fresh-fallen blood, and melting. The field on which Sergeant Karasev stood smelled suddenly like the floor of a slaughterhouse.

Karasev's oxygen-starved nervous system misfired, sending wave after wave of spasm through his body. The sergeant's vascular system was degenerating into a maze of hemorrhage. Blood normally routed to the brain poured instead into his intestines, which swelled until the rising pressure blasted the hot liquid past an ineffectual muscular valve and into his stomach. He vomited an enormous quantity of blood onto his boots, then followed it down when his knees gave out.

As he lay weeping and groping at the mud, Karasev discovered that his vocal cords had slackened and that the musculature around his mouth was now numb and beyond conscious control.

My lips are dead and I must pray . . .

He surveyed the battlefield through a red filter, for his tears were blood. And his last conscious perception was the sound of ten thousand people dying.

CHAPTER 1

Who Goes There?

Let us not go over the old ground,
Let us rather prepare for what is to come.
—Marcus Tullius Cicero

Trinidad, West Indies
One month earlier
January 19, 1944

The wings of the great bird painted a shadow on the rainforest canopy. In the trees, a male capuchin monkey shrieked a warning and the members of his troop reacted instantly. While younger males mimicked the bitonal call, a dozen females knotted together and shielded their young. Juveniles that had lately begun to explore their arboreal habitat now clung shivering to their mothers' hair with both hands and feet. The adults shifted position on the branches, craning their necks to see the jagged patches of sky that showed through holes in the ceiling of foliage. After reaching a terrifying pitch, the cries of the winged hunter faded quickly. The bird was moving off. There would be no attack. The juveniles braved a look upward, then scurried away from their parents, posturing and chattering to send a message that they hadn't been frightened at all. The adults in the troop ignored them; they had already resumed their incessant search for fruits, nuts, and flowers.

As the dual-engine Bobcat followed the Aripo valley south, the mountain forest of Trinidad's Northern Range gave way to savanna, with its scattered assortment of shrubs and stunted trees. In the cockpit, and nearly five hours out of Havana, Captain R. J. MacCready gripped the controls of the camouflage-colored Cessna with aggravated impatience, unaware of the havoc his plane had caused for the capuchins living below.

The C-78 Bobcat was a light personnel transport, with a cabin capacity of five, but on this trip there was only one passenger—a Major Fogarty, who seemed content to sleep through the entire flight. As a result, MacCready hadn't spoken for several hours—which might have been a record, had anyone bothered to keep track of such things. Although zoology was his favorite topic of discussion, MacCready was known to range at a moment's notice from the mechanics behind kangaroo jumps to what might have existed in the seconds before the birth of the universe. Whether he was debating the existence of the Loch Ness Monster with someone he had bumped into on the street, or lecturing a classroom full of sixth graders on the wonders of the new injectable antibiotics, it did not matter. *It was all so interesting.* But recently not everyone appreciated the breadth of MacCready's knowledge or his oratory skills. "The man's sense of wonder has been replaced by something darker," said an anonymous academic, quoted in the press. The article went on to call him "an oratorical and conversational sniper." Outwardly, MacCready referred to his new title as a strong aversion to bullshit. Inwardly though, he would have given up all of life's triumphs and titles, including his Ph.D. from Cornell, if even one person he truly loved were still alive.

As they began their descent toward Waller Field, MacCready radioed the tower for clearance. Fogarty was finally showing signs of life, pressing his face against the cabin window as the Army Air Forces base loomed nearer, eating up more and more of the horizon.

To MacCready, Waller Field resembled a series of ragged scars torn into central Trinidad's Caroni Plain. He wondered how long it would take for the savanna to reclaim the base once the war ended and the Allies went home. *Too long, probably.*

MacCready received his landing clearance, but as he took the Cessna down for a final approach, something thudded against the starboard engine, splashing the cockpit window on that side with streamers of red. Simultaneously, the plane was yanked hard to MacCready's right. He glanced over his shoulder, but his view of the struggling engine was partially obscured by blood.

MacCready reacted automatically, feathering the starboard propeller. The blades angled into the wind, reducing drag, and he gunned the port-side engine, simultaneously slamming hard on the left rudder. The Cessna responded—pulling back to port until finally, it was holding a straight line toward the runway. The entire episode had occupied all of five seconds.

"Now *that's* something you don't experience every day," Mac-Cready called back toward the cabin.

There was no response, so he shot a quick glance at his passenger—and while he could not be absolutely sure, it appeared that Fogarty had somehow curled himself into a fetal ball.

"Never mind," MacCready said to himself.

•   •   •

C rew chief Eddie Dykes knew that the wet season was end-ing because his men had stopped bellyaching about the rain and mud and started bellyaching about the heat and humidity. His ground crew at Waller Field had staked out the available shade around the landing strip and now the game was to see who could remain out of the sun the longest. Although it was only 10 A.M., the temperature at the base—a center for American military oper-ations in the South Atlantic since 1941—had risen to 90 degrees Fahrenheit, with humidity to match. As the Cessna banked and circled the landing strip, Dykes had been alone on the tarmac, shielding his eyes against the glare.

"Uh-oh," he said to himself; then he whistled loudly to sig-nal his crew. The Army's "Bobcat," known less affectionately as "Rhapsody in Glue," or "Flying Formation of Cessna Parts," was struggling. The drone from the starboard engine had suddenly shifted from a high-pitched whine to a sputter, and it appeared that the plane wanted to sway and stagger in its course. Keeping his gaze skyward, Dykes sensed someone approaching from behind.

"Sounds like he's comin' in with a bum coffee grinder." The drawl belonged to Private Redding, who had been stationed at Waller Field for a year but was still known as N.G.—New Guy.

Dykes ignored the man and kept his eyes on the plane, which seemed to have straightened itself out. "N.G., who's the flyboy?"

Redding fumbled with a clipboard before pointing to a spot at the bottom of a sweat-stained sheet of paper. "MacCready, sir."

Dykes glanced at the flight manifest and relaxed a bit. "They'll be fine."

A flash of movement caused him to look up. It was accompa-nied by the sound of another engine in distress. And this one was bearing down on them at unnatural speed.

"What the—?" Dykes cried, and the two men dove off the runway and into the brush, barely avoiding being run down by a speeding jeep that blew past them.

Rising to his knees, Dykes could see that he'd been right about the landing; the pilot had managed to ease his bird down. He touched the ground lightly, despite the engine trouble, and despite the vehicle that had lurched onto the blacktop and threatened to clip the pilot's wings if he needed more runway.

"Who's the asshole?" Dykes asked, rolling his eyes again as the terminally puzzled Redding scanned his clipboard of papers for an answer. *Yes, this was going to be a long war.*

The driver of the jeep was Corporal Frank Juliano, whose short stature and hangdog expression gave him an uncanny resemblance to comedian Lou Costello. Having scattered Dykes's ground crew, Juliano brought the jeep to a skidding, gear-grinding halt, before running to intercept the plane's passenger, who had flung open the cabin door and was racing away from the Bobcat as though it were on fire.

Corporal Juliano held a large envelope in one hand and saluted with the other. He backpedaled quickly, speaking in a high-pitched voice: "Good morning, Captain MacCready. Welcome to Trinidad, sir. Major Hendry has been expecting—"

The officer jerked a thumb over his shoulder and toward the plane. "You got the wrong guy, buddy," he said, brushing past the puzzled corporal without breaking his stride.

Juliano hurried to the plane, clutching the envelope. Struggling up onto the wing, he peered into the five-seat cabin. It was empty, so he backed up, slid to the ground, and turned toward the pilot. The man was examining one of the engines and whistling Bing Crosby's new hit, "Junk Ain't Junk No More."

"Captain MacCready?"

"That's me," the pilot replied into the seven-cylinder Jacobs engine. "Hey, have a look at this."

Juliano hesitated, glanced past the open cabin door a final time, and took a few tentative steps toward the man, "Sir?"

"Shit, that's hot," the pilot said, his face streaked with grease and something else Juliano could not identify. MacCready shielded his eyes against the sun and scanned the buildings nearest to the runway. "Hey, you haven't seen the ground crew anywhere, have you?"

Juliano glanced around, but the landing strip was deserted, except for two men, plastered with dirt and briars. They were walking away at a brisk pace, pausing only long enough to flip Juliano their middle fingers.

MacCready smiled. "Friends of yours?"

"No, sir," the corporal replied.

Returning his attention to the engine, the pilot reached into the air intake with a gloved hand and began wrestling with something. Grunting and cursing, he yanked out a glistening red mass and held it out to Juliano.

"Corporal, meet *Eudocimus ruber*!"

Juliano took a step back and grimaced. "Eudo-see-*what,* sir?"

"It's a scarlet ibis. My vote for national bird, once Trinidad shakes loose from the Brits."

The scent of engine-seared flesh and feathers was overpowering in the thick, humid air; the corporal could feel his breakfast shifting uneasily. "Gets my vote, too, sir. It's . . . a beaut . . . a real beaut."

Juliano had been about to hand over a large envelope; but

instead he hesitated, swallowing the gorge that was rising in his throat like a sour tide.

"Yeah, but this one has definitely seen better days. Those papers for me?" MacCready asked, reaching for the manila envelope. But the corporal was either unwilling or unable to let go of the envelope, even as he held it out, arm extended.

"Thanks a lot, Corporal." MacCready tugged again, harder this time. Juliano finally relinquished his grip. With one eye on the corporal, MacCready tore the envelope open with his teeth and withdrew several sheets of paper. In one oil- and blood-smeared glove he still held the prop-shredded remains of the bird.

He took a deep breath. "Good morning, Captain MacCready. Welcome to Trinidad, sir. Major Hendry has been expecting you. I'm supposed to drive you to the meeting room on the double."

MacCready looked up from the papers and acknowledged him with a nod, strolling to the far side of the jeep.

"Say, you're the explorer guy, aren't you, sir?" Juliano said, before easing himself behind the wheel.

The pilot tucked the papers into his field vest and climbed into the back of the jeep. "I've done some bushwhacking. But I'm really just a tropical zoologist, although *was* a tropical zoologist might be a better description."

"Why's that, sir?"

"Not much call for that kind of gig since they decided to throw another war."

Corporal Juliano punched the stick shift forward, jerking the vehicle loudly into gear. The jeep shuddered, then started to pick up speed.

"You'll wanna try out that clutch one of these days, Corporal. Some folks say it makes shifting easier."

Juliano shot MacCready a look in the rearview mirror, but any reply he might have made was lost in the metallic death throes of second gear.

As the jeep lurched through the camp, MacCready noted that Waller Field was even larger than it appeared from the air. *More like a small city than an airfield,* he thought as they passed row after row of prefabricated buildings. Each had been elevated off the ground by a series of eight-foot wooden beams. There was a baseball field as well, and MacCready could have sworn he saw two officers carrying golf clubs. Strangest of all, though, was the fact that Waller Field appeared to have been built upon (and primarily of) asphalt. Runways, roads, even rooftops were tarred. Men, buildings, and mountains of crated supplies were shimmering in waves of late morning "mirage air." MacCready guessed that the ambient temperature had to be fifteen degrees higher than the already tropical surroundings, and because of this, most of the soldiers were stripped to the waist.

MacCready shouted over the sound of the jeep. "Jeez, they built this place outta tar, huh? I'd have never thought of that."

"Got it all for free, sir," the corporal shouted back. "Pitch Lake—three hundred feet deep."

MacCready shook his head. "Now there ya go, Corporal, military intelligence at work. Lucky it wasn't Dog Shit Lake."

The driver made no reply and so MacCready turned his attention back to the handful of burnt bird. He carefully separated several of the brilliant, though slightly singed, primary feathers from the bloody connective tissue—flicking the grizzle out the side of the jeep. Looking up, he noticed that the corporal was watching him out the corner of one eye but the driver quickly shifted his attention to the road and gripped the steering wheel ever more tightly.

"Nice furcula," MacCready said to himself, holding the wishbone between his thumb and index finger as if it were a miniature divining rod.

Juliano took another peek backward, feeling increasingly uneasy as he wondered whether MacCready was complimenting *his* furcula?

"And what the hell is a furcula, anyway?" he muttered.

CHAPTER 2

Missing Cargo

*Hell's Gate, I think, is the most damnable place I
have ever visited, and I'd willingly have paid ten
pounds not to have seen it.*
—GEORGE BERNARD SHAW

The land upon which Waller Field had risen
was still British-owned, but as part of the
Lend-Lease Program, the United States was
allowed to construct a strategically located base in the Caribbean.
In exchange, Churchill's shell-shocked and grateful government
had received fifty outdated American destroyers. In its largest,
hottest building, R. J. MacCready found Major Patrick Hendry
standing in a haze of cigar smoke beside a floor-to-ceiling map of
Brazil. The room was sparsely furnished and uncomfortable. The
dense smoke made it feel like hell warmed up.

MacCready saluted. "Pat."

Hendry waved off the salute and extended his hand, which
MacCready took. "How long's it been, Mac?"

"Eight months."

"New Guinea, right?"

"Solomon Islands, actually. The canoe search for that rich
Massachusetts kid."

"Found him, though, that's all that matters."

MacCready winced. His right leg still ached from the spear-head the medics had dug out of his calf. "Yeah, kid's got a brass pair. Reckless fucker, though."

Hendry laughed, "Reckless? That's a hoot comin' from you. But I'm glad you could squeeze in some R-and-R back home after that one." The major hesitated. "I was really sorry to hear about your sister and your mom."

"Thanks," he said, quietly.

"If I'd have known—"

MacCready held up his hand, "Save it," he said firmly, feeling suddenly claustrophobic.

"Any word about your cousins?" Hendry asked, gently. "I suppose that even behind the lines, they might have heard about—"

"No!" MacCready responded, more forcefully then he'd intended. He shot Hendry a quick glance, then dialed it down. "But then again the Wehrmacht were never any good at sending Christmas cards."

MacCready moved toward an open window and, without thinking, removed the ibis wishbone from his pocket. After flexing the Y-shaped bone between his fingers like a spring, he held it up, inspecting it in the sunlight. "Not many people know this, but birds need a lot more oxygen than we do."

"All that wing flapping, huh?"

"Very expensive—flying. Energy-wise, that is. The furcula works like a fireplace bellows. Helps to pump more air in and out. Incredible adaptation."

"I'll remember that . . . next time my kid wants to use one to make a wish."

Major Hendry turned toward the map, letting his index finger follow the curve of the Amazon River from its source. "You know,

Mac, I keep thinking about something you said last year when we were in London."

"About Marlene Dietrich and those GIs?" MacCready tucked the bone back into his pocket. "You think I made that one up?"

"I'm *talking* about that stuff you mentioned about injured or trapped animals . . . you know . . . being the most dangerous kind."

"Oh, that one. And?"

"And, I don't like it. In fact, I don't like it *a lot*."

"Well, I wouldn't take it personally, Pat, but you know as well as I do. Those guys are all on the road to extinction. Hitler, Mussolini, Hirohito."

"What's so bad about that?" Hendry asked. And even though he agreed with MacCready, right now that didn't matter. What *did* matter was the carefully baited hook he'd just cast.

"Of course it's not bad," MacCready replied. "But the point was—*is*—that the world's a burning house now. And this one's filled with carnivores. They're wounded, pissed-off, and dangerous. And if we forget that—even for an instant—if we get complacent . . . we're dead."

"So, complacency is the enemy?"

"You got it. And now you're a believer, right?"

"Sure I am," Hendry said. Then he set the hook. "That's why you're here."

MacCready realized at once what the major had done, and now there was nothing to do but wait for the real story.

"Mac, we've suspected for a while now that the Jerries were up to something in the Brazilian interior. At first it was only a hint here and there. Never anything solid . . . until four weeks ago. That's when a fisherman came across an I-400-class sub that had run aground. And that's when we *all* started to believe."

"I read about it," MacCready lied, tapping the manila envelope he'd withdrawn from his field vest. "But I don't understand what the fuss is about. There are U-boats all over the Atlantic right now."

Hendry's face suddenly brightened, but MacCready, who'd found his orator's rhythm, didn't notice. "Heck, you can practically walk across the Caribbean without getting your feet wet. Why, last year on Aruba, four Dutch guys on a beach got blown up by a—"

The major snatched the envelope out of MacCready's hands, withdrew a cutaway drawing of the I-400, and grunted. Had the scale bar at the bottom of the drawing not been covered by grease and what appeared to be blood, MacCready would have seen immediately that the sub was more than three hundred feet long. It wasn't like him to miss such an important detail.

Hendry handed the drawing back with the same awful expression of a mentor disappointed by his prize student. "You're slipping, Mac, and this is no time for complacency *or* slipups."

MacCready looked at the paper—more closely this time.

The major continued, "The I-400 is no U-boat. It's a new Jap design. And while it's no news that they've been using subs to exchange supplies and technology with the Krauts, this vessel is a different kettle of fish. It's got a huge cargo hold and a sixty-five-foot hangar right below the conning tower. We think it was built to carry up to three *Seiran*s—single-engine, floatplane bombers."

"Shit."

"Yeah, shit. And here's the kicker—they found this thing on the upper Rio Xingu.

"But that's—"

"Seven hundred and fifty miles inland."

"They ran a three-hundred-foot sub seven hundred and fifty miles upriver and nobody saw anything? How the—"

Mission or not, the major took a measure of pride in surprising MacCready—which wasn't very often. There were few living Westerners who knew the South American tropics better than the zoologist. Coupled with his fearless daring and his ability to do almost anything—fly a plane, embed himself in a hostile tribe, help remove the spear point *they'd* embedded in him—if there was anyone capable of untangling the current cluster-fuck, it was, Hendry knew, Mac—even in his present, darker state.

"We don't know how they did it," Hendry conceded. "The region had a serious rainy season last year. That much we do know. Anyway, the boat was half-sunk."

"Pat, that's a big boat. How much rain are we talking about here?"

"Not quite enough I guess. The sub is hung up tighter than General Montgomery at an intel briefing. Our divers said the cargo hold was clean as a whistle. No nothing. Just some strapping and padding."

"So . . . let me get this straight," MacCready said. "You think somebody hauled some heavy equipment out of this sub."

"A shitload. The cargo crane on this thing would be right at home on a Jersey City dock. No sweat gettin' their planes back on board with that thing."

"And what, they just . . . left?"

"Like I said, the sub wasn't going anywhere, so yeah, they covered the whole thing in brush and abandoned it."

"How long's it been there?"

"Tough to say. Two, three months. We can't tell for sure."

"Nobody could figure out when that brush had been cut?"

"Um . . ." The major shifted uncomfortably. More than he liked besting MacCready, he loathed when the adventurer pointed out his own mistakes. "Not that I know of."

"Right," MacCready said, with a mirthless laugh before turning his attention to the map.

The dismissive laugh troubled Hendry, but not nearly so much as his friend's sudden focus on the map. The Old MacCready would have spent fifteen minutes explaining *exactly* how small changes in slashed wood could be traced over days, weeks, and months—until he had to be grabbed by the shoulders and forced to study the map.

"Well, they couldn't have gotten too far," MacCready ventured. "What about a trail? They must have cut a pretty wide swath through the forest."

"Our scouts found no trail. No abandoned cargo, either, and no reports of Jap seaplanes." Hendry hesitated, watching MacCready. If he could hook him in through his insatiable curiosity, the major could forgo the inevitable order to send his friend on yet another suicide mission. "Who knows? Maybe they hauled it off with porters and covered their tracks."

"Porters? I don't care how clever these guys were. They would have left some trace." MacCready turned to Hendry. "Something . . . ?" he added, hopefully.

"There was *nothing*. It's like they levitated out of there."

"Well then, forget porters," MacCready said, turning back to the map. "They must have used the river—rafts, maybe."

Hendry, who had never cared for real fishing, began to reel in his catch. "You think so, huh?"

MacCready nodded his head, very slowly, and the major saw a glimmer of excitement rising in the man, something of the delight one might see on a child's face if he had been given a new puzzle to solve.

"If that sub's as big as you say it is—"

"It *is*," Hendry emphasized.

"With enough storage capacity to hold planes?"

"That's right."

"*Damn!* That's a handy toy to have in your arsenal. And not the sort of thing you'd want to lose." MacCready was talking to himself as much as he was to Hendry. "So what the hell were they doing so far upriver? They must have known that they'd never get back out of there. And what were they carrying that was so risk-worthy?"

"Good questions, Mac. And like you said, whatever it was, it was important enough for them to sacrifice a world-class submarine. Hell, it was too damned important to risk leaking in their own coded messages."

MacCready turned from the map. "So, we've broken their latest code?"

Hendry looked away; suddenly interested in a gecko that was stalking a cockroach across the ceiling.

MacCready didn't take the hint. "Who was it? Not those Limeys at Bletchley Park?"

Ignoring the question, Hendry drew hard on his cigar. Exhaling, he pointed to a spot on the map. "Working on your theory that the sub was brought within range of a few days' rafting, and taking into account the most likely river routes, we think they were headed here: Portão do Inferno."

MacCready smiled. "*My* theory, huh?" Squinting at the location on the map, he continued, "Hell's Gate. Where that British explorer went in the twenties, looking for El Dorado, or whatever he was calling it?"

"That would be Colonel Percy Harrison Fawcett and his City of Z," Hendry answered, a little too quickly.

The zoologist continued. "There never was any city, and Fawcett and his men never came out."

"Right," Hendry said finally, and blew a puff of smoke at the map. "Well, this 'Hell's Gate' is actually a canyon below the Mato Grosso Plateau. The cliffs are roughly two thousand feet high and the valley floor is perpetually shrouded in mist. That's where *I'd* be if I wanted to hide something from Allied recon."

MacCready remained silent, his eyes focused at a small point along the river.

"So . . . what do *you* think, Mac?"

MacCready cleared his throat. "Great effect with the cigar smoke."

Hendry let the remark pass without comment, and especially without showing any signs of bristling. It was something he'd learned to do with his friend: try, try, and try never to let him know if he's scored.

Mac turned back to the map. "Perpetual mist, two-thousand-foot cliffs, sounds about right. Have you got anybody in there?"

"Three weeks ago, we sent in a squad of Rangers. Tough fuckers."

"And?"

"We haven't heard a word from them. Nothing."

MacCready remained silent.

Hendry picked up a lead paperweight from his desk. It was shaped like a stack of cannonballs, and the major flipped it slowly from one hand to another. "I realize now . . . maybe it wasn't Rangers we needed to send in there."

"And what? Now you want *me* to go in there?"

Hendry banged the paperweight down like a gavel. "First guess, Mac. Not bad!"

MacCready never flinched and his eyes never left the map. He shook his head. "I can't believe you guys," he said, quietly and to himself.

As Hendry puffed more smoke, he opened a file cabinet and withdrew a bottle of Jack Daniel's and a pair of shot glasses. "You know, I remember talking to this fellow a couple of years ago. He was going on and on about how the Age of Adventure was dead." The colonel paused, taking his time as he unscrewed the bottle. "Guy sound familiar to you?"

MacCready finally turned toward the other man. "Yeah, I know him. Damn fool."

Hendry poured a pair of stiff shots, then offered one to his friend. "Big pain in the ass, too. But still, I'd never ask him to do something like this if—"

"—if it wasn't absolutely necessary," MacCready said, and took the glass.

"You got it." Hendry tossed back the sour mash and Mac-Cready followed.

The scientist approached the map again—closer this time. Slowly, he drew a finger across the plateau, the valley, and a knot of river tributaries so hopelessly tangled that he knew the map-maker had to be guessing. *Had to be.*

"Pat, not even the Brazilians know much about this place. Except that it defines remote. A quarter of a million square miles of wilderness—and shit for roads, where you can find 'em. We could go in with a hundred men, a thousand, and still not run across anybody. The bad guys could be anywhere. And those Rangers you sent in . . ." He trailed off into thought, trying to dredge up everything he knew about the region. It wasn't much. In fact, no one really knew anything. It was a blank spot on South American maps, as inaccessible as any place on the planet.

Hendry pressed on: "I don't know if our men ran into that I-400 crew, but it's only fair to warn you, the alternative's not pretty, either. One of the tribes living in Hell's Gate may be a real problem: the Xavante," which he pronounced "zhah-vahn-thee."

"I've heard of them."

"Then you know these babies are no good from way down deep. In fact the last recorded meeting with the tribe happened around the time the Conquistadors were working over the Inca for their gold. Story has it that the Xavante chieftain promised to satisfy, once and for all, the newly installed governor's appetite for the shiny stuff. The Portuguese thought they'd finally gotten a peace offering, you know, out of sheer desperation. Well, at the feast of the treaty signing, the Xavante grabbed the governor and bound him. Then they propped his mouth open and poured molten gold down his throat. Just to make sure *everybody* got the message, they slaughtered every white man for a hundred miles around."

MacCready grimaced. "Lousy party."

"You can say that again. Since then, just about the only thing they know about these Xavante is what their arrows look like. Kids swim out and recover 'em from the backs of guys who come floating down that river."

"Sounds like effective advertising. The mist, the river, friendly Indians."

"Right: 'Stay the fuck out!'"

"And just the kind of place you'd want to bring a three-hundred-foot submarine into, if . . ." MacCready's voice trailed off, unable to fill in the blank.

Hendry slammed the empty glass down on the desk. "Exactly, Mac. And that's why I need *you* to find out what those Axis bastards are up to. And while you're at it, find out what happened to our men."

The major drew in a mouthful of cigar smoke, held it, then

blew it past MacCready's face. The blast of smoke impacted on the map, downriver; and Hendry pointed to a small dot marked "Chapada dos Guimarães." "Jesuits built this town in the late 1700s. Now it's mostly farmers: half-breed Caboclos. But there's a fine assortment of scumbags there, too—gold miners and the like—so watch it. We're dropping you just outside of Chapada. You'll hook up with an old friend of yours: Robert Thorne."

MacCready, who'd been wondering what the gold looked like once it hardened inside that Portuguese governor, did a double take. "Wh—what?"

"You heard me, Mac."

"But Bob Thorne disappeared five years ago in—"

"—the Amazon. Yeah, yeah—we know all about his *disappearance*."

"They found his campsite in ruins. There was blood. They said he'd been—" MacCready paused for a moment at the memory. Things had already started unraveling back home, and the loss of a close friend made it even worse. "Are you *sure* we're talking about the same guy?"

"Brooklyn boy, right? Leaf-head."

"Botanist," MacCready corrected. "But that can't be." Then his voice dropped, almost inaudible. "Everyone said that Bob was—"

"They're right. He is dead. And he's working for us now."

Hendry saw MacCready's head come up. "*There* you are," he thought, aloud. "Oh, and before I forget, Thorne says to bring him a dozen packages of cigarette papers. So, I figure not only is he dead, he's growin' his own tobacco. Now if I was a hotshot scientist like you—that'd be *my* theory."

MacCready shook his head, then smiled broadly. It *was* Bob Thorne. "Jesus, Pat . . . I spoke at his memorial service."

"Well, now you can tell him all about it. And I betcha folks'll be streaming out of the bush for miles around, just to be on hand for that historic reunion."

"Bob Thorne," he said to himself, drifting.

"Captain MacCready, are you quite finished?" Hendry said, not bothering to mask his growing annoyance.

"Yes, sir."

"When you get to Chapada, pick up any new information you can from your dead friend. He's chummy with the natives—big-time. And if anyone is going to notice signs of an incursion by Axis assholes, it'll be the locals. Get that information, then hike into Hell's Gate and figure this out. You'll be going wheels-up as soon as you pull your gear together. Corporal Juliano will assist you."

MacCready said nothing, but the major knew that wouldn't last.

"You got something to add?" Hendry asked.

"Yeah. Well, besides the fact that this whole thing sucks, that would be a hypothesis you have about Thorne and the tobacco. Not a theory. Everybody gets those two terms mixed—"

"*Fuck* your hypothesis!" the major barked, then paused and added calmly, "That's an exclamation, right?"

"Right."

"That's good, Mac. Because I'm always gettin' that one mixed up, too."

Now it was MacCready who looked annoyed. "Is there anything else, *Major*?"

"Yeah." Hendry stared into MacCready's eyes. "It's good to have you back."

The zoologist transitioned from annoyed to embarrassed.

The sentiment hung awkwardly in the silence that followed. Hendry straightened his back and cleared his throat. "Just be sure to leave the mission brief on the plane when you jump, and don't get killed down there. *That's* an order."

MacCready snapped off a perfect salute. "Yes, sir."

Sure thing, the zoologist told himself.

Japs.

Xavante.

And Bob Thorne.

What could possibly go wrong?

A ctivity had slowed down as the heat of midday descended upon Waller Field, but the steady pounding of a sledge-hammer shaping metal continued apace. A shirtless black teen stopped hammering and looked up as MacCready and Juliano passed by. Slick with sweat, the kid had been banging indentations onto the bottom of an empty fifty-five-gallon fuel drum. Now he had stopped in mid-swing. MacCready was puzzled, but as he passed, they exchanged nods.

"What's that all about, Corporal?" he asked Juliano.

"Right up your alley, Captain MacCready. Guy's name is Sparrow."

"Yeah?"

"That's a bird, sir."

"Thanks, Corporal. I've seen them. But why's he banging on that can?"

"Sir, Sparrow's a kind of musician—calls himself a calypso man."

MacCready had a flash of recognition.

"'Bout a year ago, some of these local guys started scroungin' oil drums. Only when they got done with 'em, they weren't oil drums no more."

"Pan drums, right?"

"You got it, sir. Pan drums. Steel drums."

As they moved off, there was one more sharp bang—followed by a beautiful, repeated tone. MacCready stopped and turned. Juliano continued walking. The pan tuner was striking the heat-tempered steel with a wooden mallet and the ringing, clanging rhythm was like nothing he'd ever heard before.

Without looking up, the kid seemed to sense the presence of an audience and began to sing.

> *This war with England and Germany*
> *Going to mean more starvation and misery*
> *But I going plant provision and fix me affairs*
> *And the white people could fight for a thousand years*

As he finished, Sparrow turned toward MacCready and smiled broadly. MacCready nodded and gave the teen the "A-okay" signal. He was about to stop and exchange pleasantries but before he could the corporal began gesturing frantically toward the supply shack.

"We *got* to get you going, sir."

MacCready gave Sparrow a last wave before catching up with Juliano. "Nice job if you can get it, Corporal."

"What's that, sir?"

"Turning the Army's junk into music."

"It ain't bad, sir," Juliano replied as they entered the shack. "It ain't bad."

Twenty minutes later, the zoologist had finished drawing his field equipment. As he pulled hard on the canvas straps of his jump pack, he thought about a line in Sparrow's song.

"Fighting for a thousand years. Let's hope not," he said, turning as Juliano entered from a back room. The corporal was carrying something and his smile was as broad as the musician's had been.

As MacCready watched, Juliano unwrapped a leather pouch that smelled of gun oil, from which he withdrew a strange-looking weapon.

"Sir, you are gonna love this. It's a PPSh-41," he explained. "Two pounds lighter than a Thompson."

"A Russian grease gun. Now Corporal, why would I want—"

"It's got a drum mag that holds seventy-three rounds," Juliano continued, ignoring the interruption. "Accurate to about a hundred yards. And here's the kicker, sir. She'll give you nine hundred rounds a minute with almost no recoil." He scanned the room, then lowered his voice. "It fell off a tanker, if you know what I mean?"

"Tanker must have been headed north," MacCready said, noting the incongruent white and black markings on the sling—obviously meant for snow-country camouflage.

"Just rub some mud on that sling, sir," Juliano replied. "You'll find plenty of it where you're going."

MacCready, who would rather have been picking out a pan drum, was suddenly interested. He flashed back to a Ford assembly line he'd seen near Detroit and remembered reading somewhere that the PPSh was one of the first examples of mass-production techniques applied to automatic weapons.

MacCready pointed to a small switch in front of the trigger. "What's with the lever?"

"Push it forward, it'll fire a burst; pull it back, single rounds."

Unexpectedly, the corporal flipped the gun around and gripped the muzzle. He took an imaginary cut with the weapon, then another, as if he were swinging a baseball bat. "Sir, you run out of ammo—you can always use this thing as a club. It's *solid*."

Juliano held the gun out stock first. "All in all, sir, a top-shelf weapon."

MacCready took the machine gun and hefted it. "I don't know. Seems like a load to drag around." He handed it back to Juliano.

"Captain, Major Hendry wants you to carry something besides a sidearm. He was quite insistent. I figured you might find the PPSh kind of interesting."

MacCready had to admit—it *was* kind of interesting. "And what happens when it gets dirty or wet?"

Juliano responded by demonstrating a record-time field strip that reduced the gun to a layout of parts. After he finished, he picked up the barrel and peered into one end, holding the other up to the light. "Sir, you could shit down this thing and it would still fire."

"I'll take your word on that one," MacCready replied quickly.

Satisfied that everything was in order, the corporal began to reassemble the gun. The zoologist's eyes never left Juliano's hands. "Just think, Corporal: Before the war, we used to worry about what type of tent we wanted to hump into the field. Now it's which machine gun."

He paused, waiting for some response from Juliano. He got none, so he responded to himself, "That's *not* what I'd consider progress."

The corporal examined each part, looking for defects and dirt. "I guess you're right about that, Captain . . . But you're not going to scare too many bad guys swinging a tent pole—now are you, sir?"

Once again, MacCready found himself agreeing with the man, while another part of his brain screamed, *This cannot be good!*

• • •

The C-47 had been idling on the runway for ten minutes by the time MacCready returned Juliano's salute, hauled his gear up a portable ramp, and stepped into the twin-engine transport. There were two rows of folding seats that ran down the length of the cabin, room for twenty-eight paratroopers and their gear. But the plane seemed to be empty. He took a seat near the tail.

MacCready watched Juliano's jeep pulling away from the plane and he winced as the transmission was submitted to another round of "corporal punishment." But soon the slam of metal on metal was lost in the roar of twenty-eight cylinders of supercharged Pratt & Whitney.

MacCready's departure from Waller Field was less eventful than his arrival. Once the plane had leveled off, a flight-suited figure ducked out of the radioman's compartment. Mac was immediately reminded of a circus clown emerging from an absurdly tiny car. He appeared to be at least six and a half feet tall, all arms and legs, but he could not have weighed more than 160 pounds. The man made his way aft, saluted, and spoke over the engine noise. "Afternoon, sir. I'm Richards. Tex Richards."

MacCready returned the salute. "MacCready . . . R. J. Mac-Cready."

"We know, Captain," Richards said, and MacCready caught a hint of annoyance in the man's drawl. "Y'all make yourself at home. S'gonna be a long ride—twenty hours, not counting a fuel stop. There's a cot back here. Toilet, too. And some sandwiches."

MacCready nodded. "Thanks."

"Just give a yell if ya need anything, sir," Richards called back over his shoulder, before smoothly folding himself back into the tiny, equipment-filled space.

MacCready suppressed an urge to see what the man looked like, jammed into his cubbyhole. Instead he double-checked that his gear was securely stowed in the starboard baggage compartment, settled into his aft window seat, and fastened the seat belt.

Thirty minutes later, the Skytrain was cruising west-southwest at five thousand feet.

He peered out a small rectangular window, and as if on cue, the green forests of Venezuela disappeared under dense, unbroken cloud cover that stretched to the horizon.

Bob Thorne—alive.

MacCready turned forward and let out a long breath. *What if he's changed? What if he's pulled some kind of Kurtz act?* He had often wondered what czarist demons had driven a Ukrainian named Józef Teodor Konrad Korzeniowski to write about the malarial backwaters of Africa. *Very strange . . .*

MacCready's head slowly ratcheted down toward his chest.

very . . . st . . .

Sometime later, the C-47 hit turbulence and MacCready came awake for a few seconds. He'd been dreaming about the summers of his childhood on Long Island's South Shore. It was a time filled with sun-drenched beaches and books and baseball. And never any talk of Japs or Nazis.

Jesus. Seems like a thousand centuries ago.

As the drone of the engines faded once again, R. J. MacCready had a final thought before drifting back into sleep.

Nazis. How on earth did people turn into Nazis?

For most people, after the age of sixteen, the perception of time's passage seemed to speed up. Yet for MacCready, the past twelve months were so crowded with new and unprecedented events that it felt to him as if twelve years had passed—maybe twenty. He sometimes wondered if his mind itself, and not just his perception of time, had started to become unhinged.

Nazis, how on earth did people turn into Nazis?

Whenever this question intruded upon him—whether sleeping or awake—the pictures in his head shifted easily backward in time, to childhood summers on rural Long Island. Mac's two cousins were as innocent as any other children then, and brighter than most. Together with Mac, they were the three stellar children on an Irish-German family tree, each seemingly destined to go far in whatever fields they chose.

Recently, though, it seemed that every time he slept, his wonderful childhood memories morphed into an ever-worsening series of nightmares. His cousins now slithered into his dreams, mutated from boyhood pals into goose-stepping monsters, even as the end of the Nazi parade was within sight. And the face of his little sister flashed brightly, then dissolved to air. With each passing night, it became harder to recall what she looked like.

And the worst horror of all was the never-ending haunting by the two words MacCready wished no one had ever put together: *If only.*

If only I hadn't been overseas when my family needed me most.

If only having a son fighting against the Axis had weighed more heavily in Mom's favor than having nephews who became part of that evil.

No one would have believed, before it actually happened, that the same American president who had damned the Axis powers as "apostles of racial arrogance" was condoning, along the entire west coast, the forceful relocation of almost anyone with Japanese or Italian ancestors. Along the east coast, Italian-Americans received a special dispensation from such intrusion, after Charles "Lucky" Luciano's crime family volunteered to protect New York

City's waterfront from Axis saboteurs. However, along that same waterfront, German-Americans were not faring much better than west coast Italians.

MacCready, who was German on his mother's side, had been on an assignment with some indigenous allies in the Solomons. And as he came within a gnat's breath of losing a leg to a poison-tipped lance, thousands of miles away, rogue elements of the government back home brought unspeakable calamity into the MacCready household.

Ostensibly in the name of "protecting children," some newly empowered faction of New York's wartime bureaucracy decreed that any American child adopted into the family of a German-American should be returned to its "natural" family. Mac learned that it mattered not at all that his father was an American veteran who had recently suffocated from the long-term effects of mustard gas—thanks to the Germans he'd fought in World War I. Nor did it matter that his mother had been born and raised on Long Island. During what turned out to be more of a condemnation than a hearing, the court sat idle while Amelia MacCready was referred to as "the Führer." Soon after, Mac's thirteen-year-old adopted sister, Brigitte, was removed from their loving home and forced back into the snake pit from which she had been rescued a decade earlier—half-starved, with the fingers of one hand broken. This time, the girl did not survive. Mac's mother soon followed her down, slowly and agonizingly; and since then, the "if onlys" gnawed at him, day and night.

If only I'd heard of this atrocity in time to return home. To try to stop them from taking Brigitte. To call on favors from the people I knew in high places. To remind Mom she still had something to live for.

Instead, Mac lived now with rage and regret, guilt and solitude. For him there seemed nothing left to think about except the death of the innocent, the death of a mother and child.

If only the telegram had found me sooner.

If only Mom had been just a little bit stronger.

In the end, they had given Mom shock therapy. "The most effective treatment for nervous breakdowns and schizophrenia," the doctors had said, though none of them could agree on a diagnosis.

"Experimental quackery!" MacCready called it, after he first read about it in a telegram from home, a month after it had been sent.

If only I'd been there to stop it.

If only.

In Mac's current dream, his mother's face screamed and screamed until it shifted into something grotesque and strange— which revealed itself to be a hideous hand puppet pushing toward him, snapping and biting, at the end of his little sister's arm.

Brigitte, Mom—I'm sorry. So sorry!

MacCready awoke on the verge of a shout, willed it to stay inside, then looked around the cabin. However uneasy his dreams, he had not been loud enough to stir Richards from his compartment. It was a very small blessing, but he'd take it.

He looked out the tiny window for a few seconds, then dozed off to face the next round of nightmares. On the world below, an immense carpet of trees spread from horizon to horizon.

CHAPTER 3

The Hidden

I ran to the rock to hide my face,
But the rock cried out, "No hiding place!
"No hiding place down here!"
—"No Hiding Place Down Here" (African-American spiritual)

Portão do Inferno, Central Brazil
January 19, 1944

In the forests of the night, nothing existed except life and death in nature's extinction lottery.

Nothing more.

And nothing less.

A half-billion years of scurrying monstrosities—of entire empires hidden underfoot—had led, here and there, to thoughtless existence. The mind of a tarantula was as close to nothing as anything could be and still *be* something. The spider, poised to strike at a cricket, was no more thoughtful than a bundle of mechanized neurological responses, no more aware of itself than the digi-comp machines that the Allies were using to break Axis codes. The arachnid had come this far, and not a step closer to sentience. But this was enough. Her kind had been walking across the planet five hundred million years before the first human footprints entered the fossil record; and they would still be here five hundred million years after the pyramids had turned to dust.

Down on the forest floor, even when something enormous moved suddenly into the spider's field of vision, there was only an instantaneous summoning of limbs and fangs to a defensive posture. The intruder descended with astonishing rapidity, but there was nothing in the predator-turned-prey that could have been called either astonishment or horror.

For the coati, however, there *was* something that might have been called a sense of self. He was a leaner, sleeker rendition of the American raccoon, and although he'd lived these past three years alone, he felt nothing like regret. An arthritic hip had begun to slow him down, but even the fastest responses of a spider were all too predictable. The coati's meal reared up on four hind limbs, projected its fangs, and waved its forearms menacingly.

In five ticks of a stopwatch, confrontation flared and died. Feinting with his right paw, the coati distracted the spider just long enough to blindside it with a crushing blow from the left. To the coati, tarantulas were a rare and satisfying delicacy—as fine in texture as the yolk of a freshly broken egg.

In the forest surrounding the little clearing, something watched, and waited.

The coati was more focused than usual on his meal, and for this reason more careless than usual. Ordinarily, he might have felt a faint vibration, might have sensed that in the surrounding tangle of vines and twigs, crickets had stopped chirping and even the delicate lacewings no longer stirred. In the trees only the tiniest creatures—springtails and mites, mostly—registered

any change at all, in their unseen empires of bark and leaf. Had
they been sentient beings, able to communicate, they would have
sounded the alarm. But they too were creatures of mechanized
instinct. So instinct waited, silent and deep in the night, waited
for the shadows to shift, and to move away.

Unmindful of shadows, the coati was finishing its meal when
there came a new sound—a whoosh of air, followed by the crack
of bushes or brambles being snapped by a pair of large animals
approaching. They moved with all the grace of a tree fall—large
enough, the coati sensed, not to care about moving so clumsily
and attracting attention. The coati stood up on his hind legs,
facing the sound, trying to assess the danger. He was unfamiliar with these animals. Reckless and lumbering, they emitted an
alternating sequence of calls, birdlike yet at the same time quite
unlike a bird. The sounds brought a surge of fear and adrenaline,
and the coati lost all sensation of pain in his arthritic hindquarters. Seemingly without effort, his legs springboarded him away
from the threat, and from the last few morsels of a favorite meal.

Having closed within striking distance, the shadows in the
trees waited, silent. They had been tracking the old coati for almost an hour. The game, and it was a game in every sense of
the word, was to get as close to the creature as possible without
alarming it. But the unexpected and strange new sounds had put
an end to all of that.

Now they turned their attention to a new set of calls.

The two soldiers had set off on patrol from *Nostromo* Base in
daylight; but deep within the river valley, the sun's rays never
quite burned through the ever-present blanket of mist. Now they
had lost the light altogether. It had taken the better part of fifteen

hours to find the parachute, and now the Germans were staring up through a drizzle of rain at a tangle of white cloth. The fabric was hung up on a tree limb about ten meters off the ground. They could just make out the nose-cone-mounted camera housing and its harness, dangling alongside the rest of the chute.

"I can't climb," one of the men said, throwing up his hands. "My back is shot."

"That's just great," his colleague mumbled. Private Wilhelm Becker was already squinting up into the rain, searching for the lowest branch that might support his weight. "Well, you'll need to give me a boost, bad back or not."

Private Karl Fuchs let out a loud sigh, then stomped over to the tree trunk. Leaning against it for support, he clasped his fingers together. "Come on, then," he said with a distinct lack of enthusiasm.

Becker used Fuchs's boost to get a grip on a horizontal branch only a little higher up than he was tall. Deftly, he swung his legs upward, twisting his body around and over the limb. He sat for a few moments, catching his breath and shaking his head. The incessant heat and humidity seemed to turn even the simplest of physical tasks into a sweat-drenched struggle.

"You taking a break already?" Fuchs asked.

Becker responded by standing up. Holding on to the vertical trunk with one hand, he feigned pulling down his fly with the other. "Open wide, Karl," he called down, but the other man ignored him.

Carefully, Private Becker made his way up a ladder of branches.

On the ground, Fuchs squinted into the forest. Feeling queasy, he reached into his tunic, extracted a cigarette, then lit it. He remembered his first impression of the place—with its strange, never-lifting cover of fog. He had been standing on

Nostromo's deck after the seemingly interminable submarine voyage.

His first thought had been that it was a mist that only Poe could love, and he soon discovered that he wasn't alone in this regard.

"If this is what London is like," his friend Auerbach had whispered, "then that fat fuck Churchill can keep it."

No, this was *not* London. Nor was it anything like what he had expected.

Fuchs had convinced himself that their assignment to the enormous Japanese submarine was the start of a fantastic Jules Verne voyage. Soon after their brief stopover in Peenemünde, rumors began to circulate about a secret base in the tropics, which served only to stoke his imagination. There would be an idyllic lagoon, ringed with white sand and palm trees. There would be butterflies as well, swirls of metallic blues and reds against a cloudless sky. And there would be no war.

But as they emerged from the humid belly of the *Nostromo*, Fuchs saw the other men, officers and those they commanded, standing motionless and silent. Twenty meters away, and appearing to surround the boat on all sides, loomed the forest. Occasional breaks in the fog revealed dense stands of trees, and Fuchs's image of butterflies dissolved into a vision of dark-hooded sentinels, their dead skeletal branches reaching out through the mist, crowding in on what had suddenly become a tiny patch of deck.

Fuchs thought it couldn't get any worse than the bad air and cramped quarters of the submarine. By then, of course, their sister boat had run aground. To say that anything felt more confining than the inside of the *Nostromo* was saying a lot, especially after the double jam-up of crew spaces they'd suffered through after the grounding of *Demeter*. But somehow, this fog-cloaked wilderness was even more claustrophobic, with the rotten egg scent of swamp gas (methane, he was informed) adding to the displeasure.

Demeter. Shit. Hadn't there been a fictional ship with the same name. And why would they rename—?

"Karl!"

Above, in the tree, Private Becker had reached the level where the camera hung, an arm's length away. "Will you shine that light up here, for Christ's sake."

Resembling a giant mechanical eye, the nose cone swung gently from a tangle of braided cotton.

"Looks like this thing held together," Becker called down.

"Well, that's good news," came the reply. Neither man wanted to tell Dr. Sänger that they couldn't find his precious movie camera, or that it had been smashed to bits upon landing.

Below the canopy, Fuchs was becoming more and more uneasy. The forest had come suddenly alive with night sounds—layer upon layer of chirps, buzzes, and clicks, all of them set against the incessant drone of mosquitoes. Just once, Fuchs thought he felt a vibration brushing over his spine and ribs, barely perceptible. But the feeling passed as quickly as it had come, so he shrugged it off and tried to think about something else, anything else.

When he first came ashore, Fuchs had sought to calm his fears by trying to identify the night sounds. Unfortunately, his effort to make familiar what he could not understand had left him with nothing but a serving of crow for breakfast. His mistake was a suggestion that the mechanical *toc-toc-toc* they had all heard while on patrol might have been produced by a woodpecker.

"Fuchs, whoever heard of a woodpecker at night?" Sergeant Vogt had said mockingly. The SS sergeant made a point of waiting until there were several other sentries gathered round. "That was a frog, you ass."

The private had shrugged his shoulders, his face reddening. "Sounded like a woodpecker, Sergeant."

Several of the others present also thought they'd heard woodpeckers, but they'd decided to follow Vogt's lead, and they feigned disappointment at Fuchs for such an obvious mistake.

A sudden return of the *toc-toc-toc,* impersonal and jarring, brought Private Fuchs back to the reality of *tonight's* sounds. The mist seemed to have settled a bit lower than it had been just minutes before.

"Toc-toc-toc," Fuchs called to the dark, shining his light into the fog.

"Toc-toc-toc," he called again, not caring if Willy heard him and mocked him again.

He stopped for a moment, wiping a sweaty brow with his forearm.

And then the forest called back to him.

Fuchs stiffened. His *toc-toc-toc* had been returned by a series of musical tones—almost metallic but unlike anything he had heard before. Yet "heard" was the wrong word. It was as if the sounds had passed *through* his body, more felt than heard.

What . . . Where did that come from? He whirled around and the flashlight beam swung into the trees, shadows shifting in the tangled foliage.

"You imagined that," Fuchs told himself. Without thinking, he quickly called out into the dark again. "Toc-toc-toc."

But this time there were only night sounds and the intermittent patter of rain that had begun to fall. He pointed the beam upward but now the light did not reach the canopy. The settling mist seemed even more dense than usual.

"Willy, did you hear that?" he called up into the tree, nervously. "It sounded like . . ."

"Don't tell me—woodpeckers," came Becker's voice. "Never mind that. I've got Sänger's camera. I'll lower it down to you."

"All right, then. Hurry up," Fuchs called back.

From above, there came the sound of a branch shaking— *Willy, finally freeing the camera,* Fuchs thought, more than happy to finish their chore and get back to camp.

A single leaf spun down and landed on his shoulder.

Suddenly, he heard a loud crack, and something was falling out of the tree—seemingly aimed straight at his head. Fuchs jumped back just in time to avoid having his skull fractured by the falling camera—which came down in separate pieces, the larger one trailing a streamer of exposed film.

"Jesus Christ, Willy, you've broken it!" Fuchs cried, staring down at the shattered camera. "Who's going to explain this to Sänger and the colonel? Not me!"

There was no reply.

"Willy?"

Fuchs realized that the forest had gone silent—as if the encroaching mist were swallowing every sound. Even the hum of mosquitoes had ceased abruptly, as had the rain; and yet somehow, this was as startling as a grenade blast.

The private shivered and grabbed his machine gun, clipping the flashlight onto the barrel of the MP-43. With trembling hands he flicked off the safety and squinted upward. "Willy? Willy, get down here right now!"

Silence.

An almost imperceptible rustle from behind caused the private to swing the gun barrel toward the sound. The flashlight was of no use. If it was possible, the mist was growing even thicker— reflecting everything back at him. From only five meters away, the world was a shapeless glare.

"Who goes there?"

Dead air.

"God damn it Willy," he called again, his voice high-pitched and cracking.

Backing up against the tree trunk, Fuchs flinched as something thorny pinched him below the left shoulder blade.

What do I do now? he thought, but before he could come up with an answer, the dead air was broken by a vibration. It penetrated his chest and rippled outward to his limbs and head. For an instant, his teeth buzzed and he felt as if someone had just peered deep inside of him. The piercing filled him with fear—a dread such as he had never known.

He was probed again, this time more strongly and from two directions at once. The thought that gripped Fuchs was instinctive, and unbreakable. *You are not imagining this.*

Get away from here, he thought. But what held him in place was a third piercing, this one from a new direction.

RELAX

Instantly, the private felt calmer. Something had begun vibrating through his skull, deeply like an X-ray, as if somehow that mysterious . . . *something,* was systematically turning on and off specific regions of his brain—which, in fact, it was.

GENTLE

"Who's . . .

RELAX

" . . . there?"

In a brain-soaking release of endorphins so calming that it all but paralyzed him, Fuchs's mind formed a picture of his mother. She was basting a fat Christmas goose and turned to him, smiling.

"Where . . . where are you?" he called into the mist.

GENTLE, his mother seemed to say, her reassurance vibrating through his body like a song—a lullaby.

Inhuman. The thought reached up from Fuchs's subconscious, and his heart rate spiked. "What do you want?"

GENTLE, came the reply from within, and Fuchs felt the muscles in his left shoulder relax. The bite there had been painless enough to be mistaken for a mere thorn prick.

It's all right now, he thought. *I will see my family again. I will make it home.* He tried to smile but only the right side of his upper lip moved—drawing upward, then freezing in place.

Now his mouth seemed to be filling quickly. Filling with . . .

Fuchs reclined against the tree trunk, and began to slump. *Everything is all right.*

Time was getting away from him.

The machine gun fell from the private's wet hands and he reached to retrieve it, but it seemed too slippery to hold. He fumbled for the tiny silver crucifix he kept in his tunic pocket, and his fingers entwined around the chain, by accident.

His head lolled to one side and his body followed it down. The MP-43 seemed to fade out of focus.

"Mother?" he whispered—although anyone else present would have heard something very different.

GENTLE, came the reply.

Then one last time. RELAX.

Fuchs responded with a whimper that turned into a choking wet cough. From what seemed very far away, he thought he could hear a wet thump as something hit the ground. Private Becker had returned.

But that did not matter now for there were new signals. And there was nothing gentle or relaxing about them.

HUNGRY

HUNGRY

BE STILL

Fuchs tried to raise his arms, and he discovered that his limbs did not respond, *could* not respond.

His scream started as a gargle but rose in volume even as he felt hot breath on his face. In response, the creatures stopped feeding and stepped back to listen—cocking their heads sideways. One of them seemed momentarily distracted by the small silvery object that had fallen into the mud.

Fuchs could see their faces now—their curiosity, eyes like glistening black marbles. One of the creatures hissed at him. Then, for a moment, the private's scream became strong and clear, spiraling up, and up, and up into the night, until it was lost in the mist.

CHAPTER 4

Someone to Watch Over Me

I know of no part of South America about which so little authentic information is available as this central plateau.

—COMMANDER GEORGE M. DYOTT
Leader of the 1928 expedition (unsuccessful) to find Colonel Percy H. Fawcett

Northern outskirts of the Pantanal, Central Brazil
Sixteen hours later, January 20, 1944

The ancient kapok tree was dead now, but its lower half was still anchored to the thin tropical soil by four giant buttress roots, radiating from its base like triangular fins. Assailed by fungi and wood-boring insects, what remained was a hollow shell. Gray and skeletal, it had resisted rain and wind to stand fifty feet above the forest floor. But no birds flew near this kapok anymore and even the insects seemed to avoid it. The sentinel stood silent against the approaching fall of night, its interior blacker than a mine shaft. Yet deep within the dead tree, the darkness had begun to shift.

•   •   •

S everal miles away and at an altitude some five hundred feet above the hollow tree, R. J. MacCready gripped the parachute's static-line hook in his left hand. His right hand lay across the chest pack of his reserve chute.

A red light went on above the jump door.

"Hook up, Captain," Richards called, reemerging from his cubbyhole. This was the first Mac had heard from the radio engineer since the order to "gear up for drop," and it was the first he'd seen of him since their refueling and leg-stretching stopover. "Sixty seconds to go."

MacCready rose from the bench seat and attached the metal clip to a steel cable that ran the length of the aisle just below the ceiling of the plane. He shuffled toward the jump door feeling like an eighty-year-old man under the weight of his gear and the bulky T-5 parachute. Why couldn't he be like other academics, content to spend their lives among mountains of library books and museum specimens rather than mountains of trouble? Three times before, he had resolved, "This is the last time I will jump out of an airplane that is not on fire or coming apart at the seams."

And yet here he was again.

This time, though, the forest canopy below was whipping by too fast and too close. *High pucker factor,* he thought, squinting against a warm blast of air. A green mat of trees stretched, unbroken, to the horizon. "Where's Chapada?" he shouted back to Richards.

"Forty-five seconds, Captain." Either the man hadn't heard the question or he'd chosen to ignore it.

MacCready tried again. "Where's the town? Major Hendry said I was getting dropped just outside Chapada."

Richards shook his head and moved up to stand behind him.

"Captain, we can't very well drop ya right into the town." Mac-Cready could feel the man conducting a final check of his main parachute. "Wrong person gets a look at this plane or you jumpin' out of it—who knows *what* could happen?"

Richards had a point, but MacCready gave him only the slightest of nods as he scanned the terrain below. "Well, where *are* you dropping me, then?"

"It's marked on your map, sir," the radioman replied, and Mac-Cready could hear the impatience returning to his voice. "There's a village down there and a road. Y'all should avoid the village and get on the road. Head north for three hours—you're in Chapada." Richards checked his watch. "Fifteen seconds, Captain."

They were still flying over lowland forest but MacCready could see that there were a few patches of open ground. He probably should have reviewed the game plan in the plane, but he'd needed the sleep. *Preparation is overrated,* he'd reassured himself. In the distance, the terrain began to rise into a maze of soaring rock formations that would have looked at home in the American Southwest—Utah, perhaps. But there was still no sign of a village *or* a road, and MacCready was becoming extremely skeptical about his chances of finding either.

"I am extremely skeptical, Richards!" MacCready yelled, noticing that the red light above the jump door had gone off— replaced by a green light.

"Time to go, sir."

MacCready braced himself in front of the jump door. "Are you *sure* there's a—?"

"Knees to the breeze, Captain!" the radioman shouted.

"What?"

"Go! Go! Go!" Richards said, pointing out the door.

MacCready shot the man a final dirty look, then stepped off

with his right foot into nothingness. He concentrated on keeping himself in a tight, semifetal position, which he knew would prevent him from getting in the way of the chute deployment. The blast of the slipstream spun his body toward the rear of the airplane, and a split second later the fifteen-foot-long static line reached its full extension. It seemed to MacCready as if someone were trying to jerk the parachute off his back from above. He knew this was the static line tearing away the canvas lid on the main pack.

So far, so good.

"One . . . two . . . three . . . f—" MacCready felt a tremendous jolt rip through his body—as if a giant had snapped an enormous bullwhip—with him at the end of it. Unfortunately, it also felt like the big guy was trying to yank the parachute saddle harness that looped from his crotch to his shoulders, right up through his ass.

So far, so good.

MacCready looked up and felt an instant rush of relief at the sight of the billowy, silk canopy. He checked the suspension lines. None of them appeared to be twisted.

Perfect. He pulled on his rucksack release tab and snapped into the prepare-to-land position.

But where the hell am I landing?

The opening shock had sent his body into a wide swinging arc, which made it difficult to get a good look at the ground. He'd hoped for a few seconds to scan for the village or better yet, the road, but the forest was rushing up even faster than he had expected.

Relax, he told himself. *Don't tense up. Don't—*

Before he could complete the thought, the giant was back, this time flinging him into the trees.

•   •   •

C *an we try that again?* MacCready thought, as he stared through the canopy and lengthening shadows at what was still a clear blue sky. But the only "aircraft" he would be seeing were mosquitoes, gnats, and pium flies. Richards and the C-47 were long gone.

He stood at the edge of a turgid brown stream, on a narrow tongue of silver sand—compass in one hand, and map in the other. MacCready looked at the map from four different angles, none of which provided him with the slightest information about his location.

Not far from Chapada, MacCready thought. *Yeah, right. Make that miles away with two hours of sunlight left.*

He used the compass and the last bright shafts of true afternoon daylight to estimate the direction to Chapada or at least the road that would supposedly lead him there. It was a frustrating task from where he stood, beneath a humid ceiling of greenery, next to a stream that no one had charted. Finally, he seemed satisfied, until he looked up from the compass to his projected path, across the stream.

"Shit," MacCready muttered, as he waded into the murky water. *It's going to take some real thought and a whole lot of creativity to pay Hendry back for this one.*

S logging into swampy terrain, Mac tried to keep his mind from focusing too much on the impossibility of his mission. Just two weeks earlier he had been on leave, eating hot dogs at Nathan's, and now he was deep in the Brazilian interior looking for a needle in a haystack—a group of Japs and Nazis who implausibly had submarined their way deep into the middle of nowhere, and whose unknown pursuits *had* to be a threat, in ways he and Hendry could not yet fathom. Mac hoped he would get some important clues from Bob Thorne and his native buddies. A happier thought. *Bob is alive.* That too seemed impossible—as impossible as his cabin mate Richard's directions to Chapada. He checked his compass, tried out a colorful curse on the Texan, and charted a new course to hopefully bypass the mud. *Maybe this route will be easier.*

Two hours later, filthy, wet, and mumbling about "Conquistadors and gold-filled intestines," MacCready pushed his way out of the dense undergrowth into a clearing. He felt like a moth that had just escaped a jam jar. He was also wondering if that young pan tuner in Trinidad needed an assistant.

Okay, everybody off, MacCready thought, certain in the knowledge that his hump through the dense brush had attracted a variety of bloodsuckers, from ticks to terrestrial leeches, each of them now swelling to hundreds of times their unfed body weight, gorging on his blood.

You guys should just drop off now and save yourselves some tr—
He froze.

At the center of the clearing lay an Indian village. There were four rectangular huts—each one a framework of poles draped with palm fronds. The huts were supported ten feet above the ground on wooden stilts. The surroundings looked fairly typical: There were pots and baskets scattered about and a rack that held several dried skins—capybara and coati, by the look of them.

"Avoid the village," Richards had said. *A little late for that,* MacCready thought, but nevertheless he began to back quickly and stealthily out of the clearing. *Get on the road.*

Yet just as he was about to turn his back on the village, he stopped.

Something's wrong.

MacCready scanned the area again.

No people. No dogs. No fire. No movement at all.

With my luck, the remnants of a Xavante raid. He drew his Colt .45 from its holster, then stepped out of the brush and into the open.

The silence was strange and unnerving. Even the insects were quiet.

"Bom dia," he said, softly. "Hello."

There was no reply.

The forest seemed to have crept in closer and the light was going fast.

He checked his watch. *It'll be pitch black in ten minutes,* he thought. *And that's gonna be fun.*

Back home, darkness came in stages. But in the tropics, Mac-Cready knew, twilight was fleeting, almost momentary. Something told him to find the damned road before it was too late, but instead he approached the nearest hut. Sheets of dirty fabric hung like dead skin across a large screenless window flanking one side of the doorway. The entrance seemed to be gathering shadows.

Seeing that he would need to maneuver up a wooden ladder to enter the hut, he holstered his pistol, then silently, carefully, he began to climb. A faint odor was wafting from within, almost sweet, and he recognized it as the last stage of extreme decomposition. MacCready poked his head over the top rung, and into the hut.

Are those——?

Suddenly, something hugged his face, like a veil, vibrating wildly. MacCready stepped back and fell halfway down the ladder, bruising both knees as he released his grip to claw at a membranous shroud that clung to his cheeks and brow.

MacCready felt something buzzing and pulsating in his hair and he batted at his own head for several seconds before regaining his composure. Looking down at his hand, he saw several silk-entrapped creatures. *Insects . . . flies. It's a spiderweb,* he thought, shaking his head. *A spiderweb and I'm pitchin' a goddamned fit.*

But it wasn't the spiderweb and the flies that were the real problem. It was *something else. Something else inside this h—*

As if on cue, from within the dwelling came more buzzing, rising in volume like radio static. And before MacCready could move, a thick cloud of flies rose from the floor, swirled through the doorway, and engulfed him.

"Shit," he cried in disgust, swinging his arms wildly. More insects became entrapped in the remains of the organic veil still clinging to his face—more and more of them. A half dozen found their way into his mouth, tasting faintly of their last meal. Mac-Cready tore at the webbing, spitting and coughing.

S everal minutes later, his pack at his side, his lips wiped clean of webbing and flies, R. J. MacCready stared up at the door-way. *Well, that could have gone better.*

I should be on that road by now, he thought. But there was *something* about this hut—for starters, the flies and the smell—which told him, *You're not going anywhere just yet.*

"Let's hold the flies this time, huh?" MacCready announced, hauling himself back up the ladder, this time using a flashlight.

The first thing he saw was the body of a man, sitting with its back against the far wall. MacCready was reminded of a balloon that had lost most of its air—and he also knew that this was not far from the truth. He had once seen a water buffalo collapse and die in the tropical heat. For whatever the reason, rather than removing the huge carcass, the villagers merely stepped around it, most of them giving the putrefying meat pile an increasingly wide berth as the days passed. Some of them, however, had not paid attention and one day the water buffalo paid them back—with interest. After swelling with internal gases for seven days, the buffalo exploded like a bomb, spraying several horrified villagers with a slurry of liquefied flesh. In the tropics, the special effects of death were often more than even a biologist could bear. Mac-Cready knew that something similar had occurred in the hut. The man's torso, inflated by bacterial gasses, had popped. *About a week ago,* MacCready guessed. *The explosion phase was over, thankfully.* These days, the Balloon Man was sinking quietly into himself.

He peered into the man's mouth, locked now into a silent scream—gums drawn back, teeth blackened from an eruption of blood that appeared to have gushed onto his chest. The scientist knew that the Balloon Man's mouth had taken on a new role—as a convenient portal for the insects that came and went and laid their eggs.

Ten days. Definitely.

Even the scent of death had become more subtle—a cloying mixture of decayed meat and vegetables that the zoologist hated more than any other smell. And yet, beneath this stench, there was something else—something familiar.

It smells like flowers, and he was momentarily reminded of his mother's favorite scent, a perfume called Field of Gardenias.

MacCready aimed his flashlight away from the corpse, but the rest of the room looked no better. The man's entire family lay dead on woven pallets. *No sign of struggle. Killed in their sleep? Is someone experimenting with poison gas?*

But the bodies were lying in pools of black, tarry matter. *Glued to the floor in their own dried blood. No. Not poison gas. Something else.*

MacCready shivered. "Is this bad ju-ju, or what?"

He was answered by a barely perceptible rustle, like parchment, fluttering in a breeze. He glanced up at the nearest "curtains." There was no breeze.

The rustling ceased, and there came to him a grim certainty that the sound had come from the far end of the hut. *From the dark.* Instinct told him that if he aimed his flashlight there, whatever it was would be gone. *Would that be so bad?* The scientist resisted the urge to stare, an ineffective means of viewing objects in the dark. Instead, he watched from the corner of his eye—the closest thing to "night vision" that humans possessed.

Something moved: a shape barely discernible from shadow, accompanied by a dry scuttle across the wooden floor. Then silence.

Now MacCready did aim his flashlight. The beam partially illuminated a wall of simple bamboo shelves tucked into a recessed corner. Too small for a hiding place but still, an inner voice screamed, "Ambush!"

MacCready backed slowly out of the doorway and down the ladder.

I'm being watched.

On the ground, he kept the light aimed at the doorway and slowly lowered one hand toward the holstered Colt.

The moment his hand touched the gun butt, something shot through his body—a vibration. *An energy burst,* MacCready thought, even as an adrenaline rush prepared him to face a threat—whether real or imagined.

GO, something told him. An unstoppable message that spread through his nervous system like a wave.

MacCready backed away from the hut, aiming his pistol alternately at each of its two openings, pausing just long enough to pick up his pack, just long enough to—

GO!

He tightened his grip on the strap and ran—dangerously fast if he wasn't careful. But in those seconds, his only concerns lay in obeying the *GO* command and in putting the greatest possible distance between himself and whatever had been watching from the hut.

GO. The word repeated itself again. *Is it only in my mind, or is this real?*

The forest was a maze of shadows, and he strode quickly over fallen trees and through thorny scrub that clutched at his pants as he went. Yet something drew his gaze upward. *Watch the canopy,* he told himself.

MacCready shook his head. *Yeah, and fall on my ass.* But the feeling would not go away. *There's something up there—watching me.*

Once, when he stopped for a sip from his canteen, he *did* look up—and swore that there were shapes peering back at him. He even drew his flashlight and turned the beam upward—but whatever had been there was gone.

An hour later, he still had not found the road to Chapada but he stumbled into a smaller clearing—a tree-fall gap. No huts. No bodies.

MacCready went down on one knee and tried to catch his breath. *What the fuck was that all about?* he thought. *First the spiderweb, then a mad dash through the forest.* The scientist realized that he had lost control—twice.

Is this how it starts? Madness?

"Shit," he said, quietly.

Then, as he had done on hundreds of other nights, R. J. MacCready lit a small fire. Yet on this night, for the first time, he sat awake beside it until sunrise with his pistol drawn. And he did not look up.

•   •   •

Outside Chapada dos Guimarães, Central Brazil

JANUARY 21, 1944

After bushwhacking for the better part of a day, MacCready climbed a muddy embankment on all fours and stood atop what was clearly a raised dirt road. The fact that it looked more like a raised streambed than a road didn't bother him at all—relieved as he was to be standing in the open, and in sunlight.

His entire body ached, and he thought about how sometimes, out in the wilderness, no matter how beaten up his body might feel, he actually enjoyed the aches and pains that came with fieldwork. Clearly, though, this was not one of those times. It wasn't fatigue, nor was it the insect bites, ticks, and thorns—it was what had happened in that village. And surprisingly, it wasn't the image of the flyblown bodies or even the taste of the flies themselves that kept coming back to him. It was the deep, interior shriek—a command to get away from there. Too loud, too powerful, to be his own imagination. Something had come from *outside* of his own mind.

GO

Have I inherited my mother's illness? Does schizophrenia really be-gin like this?

"All right, *next!*" MacCready said out loud, forcing himself to concentrate on something else—*anything else.*

Bob Thorne is alive, he thought, and gave a small laugh. He was still getting used to that one. MacCready pulled a hunk of *rapedura* out of his pocket and began munching on the toffeelike sugarcane product. As he ate, he thought back to Thorne's sudden departure from the States. Only a few weeks later, word had arrived about his disappearance. Missing and presumed dead.

What do I tell him if he starts asking about things back home? MacCready shook his head. He had to admit, after five years, *he* still didn't know what had sparked the shit storm at Manhattan's Atlantic Tech.

MacCready tucked away his snack and recalculated his bearings. He had always viewed being lost (which he reluctantly admitted was now the case) as a puzzle, one that could be easily solved. In this instance, Bob's town was *somewhere* in the vicinity, and soon it would reveal itself through human activity. He could see for miles across a rocky vista to remote blue cliffs. Terrain-wise, the region was as different from the Amazonian rainforest as the rainforest was from midtown Manhattan. It definitely reminded him of the American Southwest, except that here, towering rock sentinels formed natural shelters for a variety of microclimates. Without climbing more than a hundred feet, he could move between the stunted and gnarled trees of the drier flatland, the Cerrado, into a patch of stratified forest thick with ferns and broad-leaved evergreens.

Then there were the birds. They seemed to be everywhere, toucans and parrots of every size and color. And he'd never seen so many raptors.

Yeah, plenty of birds, he thought, as a flock of emerald-green parakeets burst from the trees calling to one another. As he watched them land at a new gathering place down the road, he noticed a thin plume of smoke in the distance.

"Ta-da!" MacCready said, quietly. *That must be the place.*

He took a few unsteady steps in the direction of the smoke, which appeared to be about five miles away; but then he stopped. The last of another day's sunlight was going, and MacCready felt as if someone had arc-welded his vertebrae together. *Too tired to head in there now,* he told himself. *And no sense getting everybody riled up.*

MacCready found a patch of flat ground on the overlook that faced the blue cliffs, started a small fire, and spread out his blanket. Within minutes, he was drifting off toward sleep beneath the first starlight.

When he opened his eyes, there were a million stars overhead.

MacCready had never believed in ghosts. But just the same, he was, this night, afraid that he no longer entirely disbelieved in them, either.

"Go!" MacCready said to the night.

But there were only the stars, and the forest—only the hunters and the hunted . . . And the living.

And the dead.

And madness.

CHAPTER 5

Reunion

*The doors of Heaven and Hell are adjacent and
identical.*
—NIKOS KAZANTZAKIS

Maybe this world is another planet's Hell.
—ALDOUS HUXLEY

Chapada dos Guimarães, Brazil
January 22, 1944

The first thing MacCready noticed about
Chapada dos Guimarães was the stone
archway, from which hung a pair of sev-
ered human legs. Two boys, who appeared to be about eight years
old, were taking turns shooting arrows at the legs with a small
bow. They stopped as MacCready approached, then turned to
face him—silently.

MacCready forced a smile and purposely avoided looking at
the legs. *"Bom dia. Meu nome é MacCready. Alguem fala ingles?"*

The children said nothing. Then one of them dropped his

bow and they both bolted under the arch, disappearing into the dusty plaza.

"Muito obrigado," MacCready called after them with a wave. *Don't forget to put your legs away, kids,* he thought of adding, but knew that he'd never come close to working out the Portuguese translation.

Common logic told him that the best thing to do was wait around until someone else showed up, but the severed legs, which dangled from bands of rough leather cord, were giving him a serious case of the creeps. So he decided to enter the plaza and look for Thorne, or maybe some breakfast—making certain not to walk under the fermenting limbs.

In the center of the plaza, a magnificently dusty old church stood in faded elegance. Jesuits had built the Igreja de Senhora Sant' Ana in 1779 with the help of local Indians. These days, it appeared that the congregation had dwindled to a couple of dejected dogs and some scrawny chickens, scratching around in the courtyard. Most of the buildings surrounding the square weren't much more than huts, and the town exhibited the same casual squalor to which MacCready had become accustomed in the tropics. In fact, he'd come to like the peace of such places. But the silence of Chapada was unusual, and would have been unnerving even without the legs, and the slow circuit of vultures that rode the thermal currents far above the stone arch.

Mac climbed the steps to the church, shrugged off an odd feeling that he'd been through this sort of thing before, and stepped inside. The daylight streaming through the glassless windows fell obliquely onto wooden pews. There was no one inside—the only movement was from the dust that swirled into and out of the light—a shaft of motes. MacCready turned to leave but stopped, after one of the statues caught his eye. It was Joseph, his face appropriately benevolent. Oddly, though, the carpenter from Nazareth was wearing a pair of heavy modern work boots.

Suddenly there were voices calling from the courtyard and MacCready quickly moved toward the door and peered outside. A group of about ten serious-looking locals strode purposefully in his direction, followed by the two squirts he'd seen earlier. What alarmed him most, initially, were the children, who seemed too hyperactively gleeful as they danced behind the advancing adults. Simultaneously his eyes were drawn to the glint of finely honed metal being carried by some of the members of what was apparently his welcoming party.

While the sympathetic division of R. J. MacCready's autonomic nervous system had already begun the chemical preparations for "fight or flight," the tiny sliver of his brain that dealt with concepts related to "optimism" valiantly tried to offer up alternatives: *Maybe all these guys just happened to be working with machetes when they got word of a visitor—in which case, in their haste to greet their guest, they've simply forgotten to put their tools away.* MacCready's decidedly reptilian midbrain responded with the electrochemical equivalent of *Not fucking likely!* The response was so definitive in fact that all other positive alternatives (*Maybe they always bring machetes to church?*) were neurochemically circumvented. As adrenaline and tunnel vision began to hold sway, MacCready could sense something else about these men—from their body language and from the way they kept themselves bunched together. *These guys aren't just pissed-off—they're scared shitless.* And fear made them even more dangerous. *Especially,* MacCready thought, *if you happened to be a stranger attached to a fresh set of legs.*

"*Bom dia. Meu nome é MacCready. Alguem fala ingles?*" MacCready repeated, stepping into open daylight, moving slowly and showing both empty hands.

"*Vá embora!*" one of men shouted angrily.

"*Nao entendo*," MacCready replied. *I have no idea what you just said.*

"*Vá embora!*" the man repeated.

Oh, right: This time I understand, MacCready thought, as he shook his head and raised his palms upward in what he hoped was the universal sign for "peaceful guy." But as MacCready again saw the metallic flash of sharpened steel, he started thinking less about peace and more about the .45-caliber Colt strapped to his right hip.

Damn, I'm gonna have to shoot somebody.

"This mook is requesting, and with no little emphasis, that you make tracks immediately."

The Brooklyn accent was unmistakable. *Bob Thorne.* He seemed to have stepped out of nowhere, between MacCready and the arriving mob. His hair was longer—*a lot* longer, and even though the killing might start at any second, MacCready could not help laughing at his friend's hair. *A ponytail!*

Thorne spoke in rapid-fire Portuguese to the one who looked like the point man. Although this particular local seemed to be vibrating at a slightly lower frequency than the other members of what MacCready would later refer to as the Chapada Dismemberment Commission, it was apparent, through the language barrier, that the only decisions left to be made at the moment of Thorne's arrival were *where* they were going to hang MacCready's carcass and *who* was going to do the prep work.

MacCready tried to make out what Thorne was saying but he could only register a phrase or two—"*Todo bom!*" (Everything's fine!) and something else that either meant "I'd like another pillow" or "He's a scientist, not a *chupacabra*."

I've been called a lot of things in my life, Mac thought. *But not goat-sucker.*

The arm-waving and loud discussion went on for three long minutes, during which MacCready smiled and tried to appear as nonthreatening as possible. *Pay no attention to the Russian submachine gun slung across my back,* he thought.

Finally the *jefe* shot MacCready a look of disgust, then mumbled something to Thorne before turning away. As the group dispersed, MacCready could sense their disappointment as easily as they could sense his relief.

Thorne watched the group warily—as if not quite convinced that they had at least postponed hacking his friend into easy-to-string pieces. "Now, Mac, you have put the kibosh on this mook Raza's entire day. So in that regard it appears that you ain't changed a bit."

"You call that a ruined day? I almost kneecapped Señor Raza. Now *that* is what I call a ruined day."

Thorne gave a grudging nod of agreement. "Granted, but you *still* have a way with people."

"*I've* got a way with people?" MacCready jerked a thumb over his shoulder. "What's with the legs? And *what* are you doing alive? I spoke at your funeral."

"Yeah, well, I'm glad I missed that one."

The two men grabbed each other simultaneously in what turned out to be a bear hug instead of a handshake. Thorne's bearded face was suddenly an inch away from the muzzle of Mac-Cready's machine gun and he motioned toward the weapon as they pulled away. "Interesting new gear. Let me guess, all the zoologists are wearin' iron this year."

MacCready shook his head. "Yeah, this one makes a nifty club *and* you can shit down the barrel."

Thorne shot his friend a puzzled look, but MacCready waved him off. "Don't ask. I've got other problems."

"So I hear."

"Oh yeah, Jap subs, maybe Nazis, early-stage schizophrenia. The normal stuff." He motioned toward the arch. "Those legs are an interesting touch."

Thorne let out a nervous, high-pitched laugh that MacCready hadn't heard in five years, instantly recalling a time that now seemed to be part of someone else's life. Before Thorne's sudden disappearance, he had been one of America's most brilliant young botanists. They'd met as graduate students and, though they attended different schools (MacCready at Cornell and Thorne at Atlantic Tech), it was a mutual love for the Neotropics that brought them together at a scientific conference in Manhattan. But while MacCready had put much of his attention into verte-brate zoology, Thorne split his time between Brooklyn and the Brazilian Amazon, investigating medicinal plants at both locales. He'd actually written and passed the defense of his Ph.D. thesis ("The Urucu Plant as an Insect Repellant with Comments on Possible Psychotropic Effects"). Then, at the age of twenty-four, he was on the verge of taking an assistant professorship when, as his mother, Ashley Thorne, later put it, "He saw something shiny and got distracted."

Thorne sat down on a stone bench outside the church and pat-ted the space next to him. "So, answering your second question first. Let's just say it started out as a little tax problem."

"A *little* tax problem?" MacCready said, sitting down next to his friend with a laugh. "I heard they wanted to boil you in oil."

"Yeah, well, it's all relative—if you're reading your Einstein. A double sawbuck actually, from a student grant. Seems I somehow forgot to declare it. Big fuckin' deal, right?"

MacCready shook his head. *That can't be right,* he thought.

"That is what I was thinking, too. But for *some reason* the

feds start squawking like it is some nut-crusher of biblical pro-
portions."

"And . . . ?" Mac said, still shaking his head, doubt sliding
into disbelief.

"And . . . a nut-crusher is what it turns out to be."

A double sawbuck? "Only twenty dollars?" *This could only happen to Bob Thorne.*

"Now *that* is what I call relativity. So *I* says, 'Hey let's talk
about this.' And the fed says, 'Yeah right,' and he heads like an arrow straight for the rest of my grant money—the chunk he could
lay his mitts on, that is."

"What did the school have to say about that?"

"Hah!" Thorne said, throwing up his hands. "They were a
big help. Their response was something along the lines of 'You're
lucky we are letting you into the school in the first place—*Jew!*'"

That was it, Mac thought. *That's why they rescinded his Ph.D.
credits. The fuckers had even downgraded his master's degree. Now
it made sense. All of it.*

MacCready had heard of this type of thing happening to
other Jewish-American students, in colleges across the United
States, about the time his friend had turned up missing. He knew
how the public groundswell that raised the Nazis to power had
not been entirely unique to Germany. And despite proclamations
against the Axis powers overseas, a number of prestigious American academic institutions began writing their darkest chapters.

Shaken by his friend's response, MacCready decided that *this*
was not a good time to tell Thorne what had happened to his
academic credentials.

"Now this is a nice long story with exciting escapes and this
and that," Thorne continued, "but I now give you the much
abridged version. Basically, I got to thinking about it. And before

these feds could get their hooks into the entire head of lettuce, or worse, toss me in the canaroo, I decided to skip."

"To Brazil?"

"I figure, *Hey, Brazil has got plenty of plants to study and less than a few Jew-hating universities.* Now at first I'm thinking this will only be temporary, you know, to allow some time for the shit storm to blow over. But as time goes by—which is a great tune, by the way—the more I think about being dead, the more I like it. And all things considered, is anyone as free as a dead man?"

MacCready paused. "I'll give you that one, but I still think you're tying your ponytail a bit too tight."

"Yeah, well . . . dead or not, eventually the feds found me down here anyway, and now it seems I am working for them on something they will not tell me more than half about."

"Everybody's doing his part, I guess," MacCready said. He jerked a thumb over his shoulder. "Speaking of machete-wielding mobs, what the hell's going on with the legs?"

Thorne avoided looking at the flyblown limbs, which were twisting synchronously in the breeze. "Mac, this is no time for 'information please' unless of course you wanna swing with the locals—if you catch my drift."

"I'll pass."

"I figured as much. Personally, I am thinking more in terms of breakfast. Jeet?"

MacCready shook his head.

"In which case, we should head back to—"

"And what's Joseph doing with boots on in your church?"

Thorne gave an embarrassed shrug. "Yeah, that would be the less than subtle influence of the gold miners on the artist they commissioned to do the sculpture. Seems that after a night of much *pinga*—which is the local bug juice—these guys all decide that boots would be a nice touch. Funny thing is, after they start talkin' up the benefits of premature burial, the artist gets all enthusiastic about it, too. Now, personally, I think he got the laces all wrong but what do I know from sculptures? So, did you bring those cigarette papers?"

Mac could not suppress a laugh. His friend might have gone native, but the basics had apparently remained unchanged. Thorne had always been a congenial guy, yet even his friends acknowledged that he was also a guy whose brain had some "unique rewiring." MacCready knew this was primarily due to the botanist's legendary penchant for smoking or eating most of his subject matter on a regular basis. He also knew that Bob Thorne had learned many things as a graduate student in New York—most of which had very little to do with being a graduate student in New York.

"You'll get your papers, but not until you answer *the leg question.*"

Thorne shook his head. "The legs, huh," he said quietly. "Ya know, Mac, I'm not sure I know how to Begin this Beguine but believe me, this is yet another long story. Let's talk about it somewhere safer—like my place—over breakfast and a smoke. And speaking of which, there is someone I am very pleased to have you meet, which is the real reason I'm stayin' here."

As they crossed the plaza, Thorne threw an arm around his friend's shoulder, "So tell me all about my funeral—was it cheery-like, or was it heavy on the waterworks?"

CHAPTER 6

Yanni

God gives all men all Earth to love,
 But, since man's heart is small,
  Ordains for each one spot shall prove
Beloved over all.
—RUDYARD KIPLING

Chapada dos Guimarães, Brazil

Bob Thorne had indeed settled in. His house was simple—a single-level, wooden construction that was almost impossible to see through a blanket of flowering vines. MacCready noticed that, in addition to the brilliant colors, there was movement everywhere. Hummingbirds would suddenly appear, hover over a flower for a moment, and then, just as suddenly, disappear. There were butterflies as well—dozens of intermingling species that formed a swirling dance of blue, yellow, red, and black.

Stepping onto the porch, MacCready saw that it too was full of flowering tropical plants of seemingly infinite variety—each contributing to a captivating smell that managed to avoid being overpowering. Most surprising of all, the place was spotlessly clean. Housekeeping had never been one of Thorne's strengths, but his habits were apparently changing. MacCready was about to discover why.

A young woman stepped out of a back room. She had waist-length, shiny black hair and moved with a strange grace that MacCready found to be vaguely feline. As Thorne rushed over and took her arm, Mac noticed that she was at least three inches taller than the botanist.

"Mac, this is Yanni. Yanni, this is Mac, my old friend from New York."

The woman stepped forward and bowed slightly. She was dark-complected, with features that seemed distinctly Asian, clearly those of some indigenous Indian tribe.

And her eyes—were they really violet?

Thorne cleared his throat and Mac realized, too late, that he had been staring. *"Bom dia,"* he blurted out, returning Yanni's bow, while mentally running through his list of Portuguese phrases.

She seemed to be examining him as he might examine some new species of insect. MacCready glanced down at his filthy jungle attire.

Great first impression, he thought, deciding to charm his way out of it. "Yanni, *meu nome é Mac,*" he pronounced slowly.

"Yankee fan, right?" Yanni replied. The accent was one hundred percent Flatbush Avenue.

MacCready's double take nearly caused him to pull a neck muscle. *Did I just hear that?* he thought; but the broad grin on his friend's face all but screamed "setup." He decided to play along. "Yep, Bill Dickey's number-one fan," the zoologist announced.

Yanni waved her hand as if shooing away a bothersome fly. "Dey stink even more den you," she said, before turning away with a smile that only her husband could see.

"Now, of course, Yanni prefers da Bums," Thorne said, struggling to keep a straight face. "So Mac, about these cigarette papers."

The two men sat down for breakfast on a layered mat of multi-colored cotton, both of them occasionally glancing at Yanni, who was in the kitchen area, slicing fruit.

"I am dizzy with the dame, Mac," Thorne said, passing his friend a cup of fresh-squeezed juice. "Here, dip your bill."

"Seems like a dilly," MacCready said, noting just how much of an understatement that really was. In fact it was hard to believe that this was the same guy he'd known in college. (Back then, it was said that Bob Thorne would have screwed a snake and that he'd have screwed a pile of rocks if he thought there might be a snake hiding in it.)

Yes, things have changed, MacCready thought, stretching out somewhat uncomfortably in a set of his friend's too-small clothes. Soon after his arrival, Yanni had passed his own filthy jungle gear off to a teenage girl who did not bother to hide her disgust at the task ahead.

Yanni finished up, then nonchalantly flipped the knife toward a tin washbasin, where it stuck into a small block of wood.

"Good with a blade, too," Thorne piped in, taking the fruit from his wife.

"Yeah, that seems to be a real plus round here," MacCready replied. "And speaking of which, where do you think my clothes are by now?"

"You need to relax, Mac. At least they are not hangin' in the square—with you in 'em."

He's right about that, MacCready thought, managing a smile.

"Of course I am right," Thorne replied, reading his friend's expression once again. "And speaking of which, you need to lighten up before we get to the serious talk, and I am just the man to light you up."

With that he produced an herbal cigar that seemed as thick as his index finger. "I know you don't like coffin nails," he said, referring to MacCready's odd dislike of cigarettes. He struck a match. "But this is . . . how do I put it? Something unique."

MacCready waved him off, watching as Thorne drew hard on the dangerous-looking stogie. "Thanks, but I'm on duty, remember?"

After holding his breath for what seemed to be a perilously long time, the botanist released a lungful of blue-gray smoke toward the ceiling. As MacCready watched, several house geckos were momentarily enveloped by fog before disappearing under a wooden beam, presumably compelled to seek out something eight-legged and crunchy.

"So this mission of yours," Thorne wheezed, "spill it, because I know a little less than jack shit."

Although the Army had apparently worked out some kind of tit-for-tat deal with the botanist—allowing Thorne to remain in Brazil as long as he functioned as their eyes and ears in the region—it became apparent that much of the information Mac began to relay to his friend was new to him, including everything about the stranded Japanese submarine. Evidently, Army brass hadn't wanted to provide any more than the barest, "need to know" details to a civilian. Mac learned that Thorne had met with the Rangers on their way in, but they had not told him what they were up to. To Mac, that level of secrecy was foolish given the circumstances. *Maybe if the Rangers had relied more on the advice of a local—even one from Brooklyn—they would have made it back out.*

Mac finished his tale just as Thorne finished rolling another magic cigarette. "And here I thought I was supposed to pump information from you," he said to Thorne.

"You want information? Not for nuttin', Mac, but there is definitely *something* goin' on out there near the plateau—strange sounds and such."

"What type of sounds?"

"Rumbling, like thunder but not really. Starts right before those Rangers passed through here."

"So what was their response when you told them about this rumbling?"

" 'We got it covered,' one of them tells me—all smart ass-like. Then in two shakes they are heading off into the valley."

"These sounds . . . what else can you tell me about them?"

"Well, at first they were like once every few weeks. Now, more like every other day."

"Artillery?"

"No . . . more sustained. Like thunder . . . but . . ."

" . . . not really."

"Exactly! Although I will tell you, this shit will get you on edge but it's *not* what had Raza and his machete crew so distressed today."

"Huh?"

"About a month ago, something starts knockin' off their livestock at night."

Mac looked puzzled, "Come again?"

"Croaked. You know . . . iced."

Mac nodded. "And?"

"So the local brain trust decides to tie their mutts out—to keep an eye on these potentially former livestock."

"Let me guess: The watchdogs ended up dead."

Thorne gave a funeral laugh. "Without so much as a bark. And Mac, we are talking serious watchdogs here."

While MacCready's thoughts drifted back to the dead village in the woods, his friend continued: "Now at first, these guys blame the mess on the Xavante—which is no great surprise since this tribe generally takes the rap for everything from missing laundry to constipated chickens. Now, personally, I find this accusation more ridiculous than slightly—especially since most of the locals would not know a Xavante tribesman from Carmen Miranda. Their ancestors eventually drove these Xavante deep into the forest, and from what I hear they were *not* pleasant about how they went about it. Anyway, once the Xavante took a powder, it also seems they took on a new role."

"What's that?"

"As boogiemen. You know, 'eat your peas or the Xavante will get you.'"

Always hated peas, Mac thought.

"Yeah, yeah, I know. Peas—bad example. So for a while things stayed quiet—until recently, which is when the locals started seeing these boogiemen in the flesh."

"Is that whose legs were strung up from that archway?"

"No, that was what we call an unlucky stranger. *You* on the other hand are a lucky stranger. Now, you gonna let me finish or what?"

Mac nodded.

"So now Raza and his boys are thinkin' these Xavante are being flushed out of the woods by the *chupacabra.*"

Chupacabra? MacCready remembered the name from his run-in with the machete crew that morning. "Any chance we could we be talking about Japs here, or Krauts? Whatever assholes brought in that sub?"

Thorne shook his head. "Not possible. According to local legend, these *chupacabra* are night demons—now busy killing livestock and scaring the Xavante out of the bush. And whatever these things are, they are not Japs or Krauts. Apparently, though, they do not take lightly to people squattin' in their backyard— which, if you have not noticed, is exactly where we squat."

"So what's your take on all this?"

"No soap, Mac. But for what it is worth—and that has always been a lot—Yanni says these locals are on the right track."

"Not for nothing, Bob, but I think Yanni's on the right track, too."

"How so?"

MacCready described his "stroll" through the dead village, and the condition of the bodies he'd seen there. He left out the part about the shriek that had driven him away in a near panic, keeping that to himself for no reason that he could consciously explain.

"Sounds like we could be looking at the same killers," Mac said. After pausing for a moment, he added, "The day isn't getting any younger. Let's go take a look at these dead animals."

Thorne held his unlit cigarette, unable to hide his disappointment. "Now personally, *I* am thinking more along the lines of munchin' mangoes and weightin' down those hammocks over there—you know, so they do not fly off their hooks and all. But if you would prefer to look at dead animals . . ."

MacCready nodded.

Bob Thorne grimaced.

After breakfast, Thorne led his friend across town. MacCready kept alert for a reappearance of his welcoming party, but except for a few dismal-looking dogs, the streets were nearly deserted.

"Probably inside, sharpenin' their machetes," Thorne mentioned, cheerfully.

"Swell," MacCready mumbled.

Thorne stopped in front of a rough-hewn stall, connected to a simple wooden home that appeared to have been recently abandoned. The buzzing of flies reached the men just before the sour smell of spoiling meat.

"This happened last night?" MacCready asked.

Thorne nodded, holding his nose. "It is the main reason you got such a warm reception this morning."

Mac swatted at the air as he stepped through the doorway of the stall. "Well, this is getting good already," he said.

"Huh?"

"Flies. I am *really* starting to hate flies."

"Well, we are lousy with flies—mangoes we got, too—but *somebody* wanted to see dead animals."

Before MacCready could protest, Thorne waved him off. "Yeah, I know, I know . . . the mission. Although I see no connection between strange thunder and this shit."

Thorne shook his head, still holding his nose, before following his friend into the stable.

A blackened crust of slowly drying and coagulating blood covered the dirt floor. In the center of the gore lay a dead donkey, on its side, mouth open. As MacCready approached, a cloud of flies emerged from the gaping mouth.

Even the zoologist had to turn away, and as he did he saw the body of a dog—a big one—something like a German shepherd. Like the donkey, its eyes were wide open, the white scleras barely visible behind a black film. Both animals were cemented to the ground by what appeared to be buckets of blood. And what hadn't spilled on the floor had been sprayed across the nearby walls.

"Do you smell that?" MacCready said.

"Of course I smell that. And I am less than envious of the guy who cleans up this horror show," Thorne said.

"No, Bob . . . something else. I'm smelling something more . . . flowery."

"Flowery? I am smelling something more . . . shitty."

Mac ignored his friend, instead kneeling to examine the dirt at the edge of a tarry-looking blood pool. "These scratches—there's something very odd here."

"Now *that* is a relief, Mac, because I am just thinking about how normal all of this is."

"Look at these," the zoologist said, pointing at a spot on the floor. "They're animal prints—very strange animal prints."

Thorne squinted, peering at the seemingly random scratches in the dirt floor. Mac continued. "See how they're squared off perpendicular to the puddle. It's almost like—"

"—like animals gatherin' round a watering hole," Thorne finished for him.

"Just what I was thinking."

"But there *is* no animal that feeds like this, correct?"

"Right. Except this one does—and there's more than one of them."

Then MacCready did something that even his friend didn't expect. He waded into the dark paste and squatted down next to the dead donkey. "A blunt probe would be helpful," he said, with an actual hint of hope in his voice.

"Yeah, well, unfortunately, my dissection kit was traded some time ago . . . for some, ah . . . research material," Thorne said.

"Then get me something pointy. I need to get a better look at this."

After leaving the stall for about thirty seconds, Thorne returned—proudly holding out the six-inch twig he'd managed to scrounge up. "Ta-da!"

Mac gave the stick a skeptical glance then took it. Leaning over the donkey's hindquarters, he prodded its flesh with the wooden point. "Look at this!" he said, probing a craterlike divot on the back of the donkey's left thigh.

"That is an awful lot of blood from such a little wound," Thorne observed. "What coulda—"

"I *almost* want to say—" MacCready hesitated, using a thumb and index finger to measure the wound. It was about a half-inch long.

"What?"

"Never mind. This bite is all wrong. Too long, too wide, too deep."

"So what is it?"

"I'm not sure, but *something* initiated massive systemic hemorrhaging."

"The bite, maybe?"

"Yeah, maybe, but that'd be a first." MacCready stood. Having finished his assessment he stepped out of the gore puddle then turned toward his friend. "Fun way to get your ticket punched, huh?"

"*Chupacabra,*" Thorne muttered. Mac threw him a puzzled look before realizing that Thorne had answered his earlier, half-completed question.

"Yeah, whatever the hell *they* are. You know, Bob, we could be looking at a new species here. Damn! Maybe a new genus or even a family."

Thorne saw that his friend had been jacked into zoology overdrive. "You are right, Mac. This is all very wonderful and exciting. So I'm thinking . . . you wanna buy a farm down here? Because coincidentally, mine is now up for sale."

"What, and give up your great new job with the—"

Just then, a loud rumble—actually more of a prolonged hiss—reached down from the sky. Stepping outside, the friends saw that there were people in the street now—men, women, and children. And they were all looking up.

"Now *that* is what I call timing," Thorne said. "Since this is precisely the thunder we keep hearing."

"You got a phone in this town?"

Thorne answered with a laugh. "Nearest phone or telegraph is in Cuiabá, 'bout fifty miles from here."

MacCready followed the track of several pointing fingers and saw a long, thin streamer of smoke, trailing up ten miles, maybe more. At its front end he thought he saw a spark of light. *The flare of an engine burn?* And then it was gone, leaving nothing but a smoky contrail.

No mistaking it. A fucking rocket. "Shit," MacCready whispered under his breath. His mission was still a needle in the haystack, but the haystack had just gotten smaller.

Thorne shook his head. "So this is the other reason those local guys snapped their caps when you showed up." The botanist was deadly serious now, gesturing toward the sky. "And five'll get ya ten your pal Hendry expects you to sniff out those fireworks."

MacCready continued to watch the thread of smoke. *No bet,* he thought.

CHAPTER 7

To Hell's Gate, Demeter

I will give to anyone his weight in gold who can tell me where to find Eugen Sänger.
—Vasilli Stalin (Joseph Stalin's son)

As a high school freshman, Maurice Voorhees had once written to a relative, "If the devil could teach me how to reach the moon and the planets, I would gladly become his pupil."

In the winter of 1942, the devil had come knocking at his door and the twenty-three-year-old propulsion engineer pricked his finger and signed on the dotted line without taking pause to read the small print. Like most of history's great misadventures, the sojourn of Maurice Voorhees, from Peenemünde on Germany's Baltic Coast to Brazil, had begun with tragic blindness, and was fated to end with tragic vision.

Presently, Voorhees stood with another man at the bottom of a long, long thread of solid rocket booster smoke. The base of the trail had started out horizontal and, though originally hidden, was convecting up through the surface of the Hell's Gate "fog lake," as a kilometer-long stain of muddy, scalding mist. The horizontal exhaust trail followed an ancient paved road, recently refurbished and onto which a wood-cased monorail track had been built.

"Your track won't take much more of this, Dr. Sänger."

The older man waved, as if shooing away a fly. "Once the two ships are launched it won't much matter what happens to the launch rail, will it?"

Voorhees knew that Sänger appreciated the strategic significance of his design simplifications. It seemed like the flight director's prior worries about using the last of the base's concrete and rebar before his "*Silverbirds*" could be launched had gone down proportionally with each of Voorhees's material-saving improvements.

"Still, I wish we could have launched that last sled with a water-filled, full-scale model," Sänger lamented, utilizing an annoying and whiny tone that had unfortunately become a trademark.

"Trust me on this," Voorhees countered. "A fully weighted mock-up is not worth the extra wear-and-tear on the track—not to mention the risk. I can do all the relevant calculations from the launch results of a 'naked' sled."

Voorhees gazed up into the decks of mist as if he could peer straight through them. "The only difference, here, is that the sled left the rail sooner and flew a lot higher."

He glanced at his stopwatch. "I'm betting it reached thirty kilometers before starting back. Drogue chute will have deployed by now."

"Where's your aiming point for the return impact?" Sänger asked.

"Right here."

"*Scheisse!* Tell me you're joking."

"Don't look so concerned, Dr. Sänger. Your gyros are good, but not *that* good. We'll never get a direct hit on the aiming point," Voorhees said. "And besides, it's a good test of your guidance systems for the reentry vehicles."

Not for the first time that day, he found himself grinning at the thought that his logic had prevailed once more. It felt strange to be smiling again; strange to be feeling enthusiastic about anything.

Sänger had reminded Voorhees on several occasions that two officers literally had to drag him from a bomb crater the morning after the RAF had attacked the rocket facility at Peenemünde. "They found you digging on all fours like a dog," Sänger added, seeming to relish this portion of the tale if only for the pain he knew it would cause.

Up until the night of the bombing raid, Voorhees's thoughts about *Demeter* would have been amazement over the engineering foresight that had gone into a submarine nearly half as long as the *Hindenburg*. But the man who used to dream that one day people would look down from the new oceans of space had stepped from the bomb-blasted pit into a vessel in which he was afraid to dream—and, to one degree or another, even ashamed to dream.

On the long transatlantic voyage, Sänger had arranged for Voorhees to be bunked in a closet of a room that, in accordance with the standard of confined crew spaces aboard submarines, qualified as luxurious officer's quarters. It was equipped with a pull-down bed, foldout table, and tiny chair. There was no door; only a canvas curtain through which he heard constant activity outside his cabin. Some of the voices were German. Others, though, had spoken Japanese.

Initially, Voorhees had felt like a prisoner. But no one blocked his way when he went outside in search of the nearest toilet—which looked as if it had been wedged into a maze of copper pipes and multicolored valves almost as an afterthought. He received no orders. No one bothered him. Meals were delivered in silence by a Japanese galley assistant—dried fish and rice, mostly.

Although the man smiled and bowed each time he entered the cabin, he never spoke, never tried to communicate.

Voorhees liked that about the man.

He barely touched his food.

He tried to avoid sleep.

Voorhees had lost track of the days, when he heard a voice calling his name from the doorway. Eugen Sänger did not wait for a reply.

"We thought you could use some rest," the unwelcome visitor said. "And in that regard I do hope you are finding the accommodations—"

"Why am I here?" Voorhees asked. He was lying on his back on the fold-down cot.

"You have been through much," Sänger continued. It appeared that he was trying to sound sympathetic, but even in Voorhees's post-Peenemünde physical and mental state, he could see through the act: The man might just as well have been commenting on the lumps in someone's oatmeal.

"You haven't answered my question," Voorhees said.

Sänger's voice was cool and controlled. "You are here, Dr. Voorhees, because *I* requested that you be here. May I sit down?"

Once again, the young rocket scientist said nothing. And once again, Sänger did not wait for permission. Instead he unfolded the small chair and sat intimidatingly near to Voorhees's face.

"Maurice, I wonder if you are aware that you and von Braun's friends at Peenemünde were not the only group involved in a major rocketry program for the fatherland."

Voorhees continued to stare upward at nothing in particular and, noting this, the older man unfurled a set of drawings and spread them out on what little space was left on the cot.

Voorhees glanced down at the figures, then sat upright. His first thought was that this must be Sänger's idea of a joke.

"*There* you are," said Sänger, sounding like someone who had just hooked a prize-winning fish. "Shall I continue?"

Voorhees said nothing, but sensed the older man reading the answer in his eyes. "Yes, I'll continue, then," Sänger said. "As you can see, these craft will be piloted. The best guidance systems our engineers have come up with are too heavy for—"

"What is it that you want from me, Dr. Sänger?"

"Maurice, we wanted you here . . . *I* wanted you here because of your expertise with rocket engine design and control—and because of your ability to redesign at short notice. Your talents have become vital to the success of our mission."

"You mean, now that Dr. von Braun is missing?"

Now Sänger moved uneasily in his chair. "I don't care where von Braun is. Your idol had become a liability. An increasingly unstable liability."

A strange expression passed across Voorhees's face. At another time, seemingly a lifetime ago, his beloved Lisl, a bright young woman with glasses and a warm smile, would have laughed at the thought of von Braun or any of the rocket men being characterized as anything *but* unstable.

"There is something funny, Maurice?"

"No, I was just thinking, back to—"

"Peenemünde. Yes. Your attachment to von Braun's project is . . . admirable. Now, though, you must face the facts. Peenemünde was a dinosaur even before the RAF forced our hand. Now you must deal with the future, not von Braun's future, Germany's future!"

Voorhees shook his head. "Dr. Sänger, Peenemünde wasn't the dinosaur. It's our so-called government that will soon be extinct. And you and I, and everyone on this boat . . . just a pile of bleached bones."

Sänger sat in silence for a moment. "That's an interesting hypothesis. Perhaps the *Reichsführer* would—"

"But now, what? Let me guess? You want me to help you build your new rocket?"

"No. That won't be necessary," Sänger replied with nonchalance. "You see, we already have a fully functional rocket—two, in fact—sailing with us."

Voorhees flashed him a puzzled look and Sänger returned it with the slightest hint of a smile. "Maurice, I want you to build me a sled."

F or nearly twenty thousand years before *Demeter*'s arrival, the hoatzins had been nesting in trees along the banks of the Rio Xingu. The chicken-size birds were ancient survivors who, during their first years of life, possessed a set of claws on their wings, making them uniquely adapted to a riverine lifestyle. At the first sign of danger, nonflying juveniles would dive like a flock of penguins into the water, reemerging once the danger had passed, and using their wing claws to climb back into the trees.

Because the hoatzins were highly specialized, and therefore not particularly adaptable, they were the first creatures to feel the change when a series of early winter earthquakes and earthquake-generated landslides began to alter the shape and even the course of the Rio Xingu. The quakes were relatively minor, but their impact on the hoatzin colonies was enormous. Trees that had recently overhung the water were now completely submerged, or had been thrust upward with the shoreline and were standing far back from the river's edge. Hunting parties of flesh-eating monkeys took quick advantage of the birds' confusion. Fast-moving troops of big-brained primates made deliberately loud approaches from the trees, while others hid in the muddy underbrush, waiting for a rain of disoriented birds, whose familiar escape routes no longer existed. Six weeks after the first earthquake, half a generation of Rio Xingu hoatzins had been eliminated. By the time the *Demeter* approached Brazil's Atlantic coast in September 1943, they were extinct along the entire length of the river.

Although few humans had felt these natural rumblings, the landscape was changing with such increasing frequency that previously navigated and mapped river bottoms were being reshaped into the first drafts of the broad, white-water interrupted passages that would become familiar to future cartographers. Even the unusually intense rains of the previous season could not raise the waters high enough to ensure safe passage—and especially not for a craft over one hundred meters long. And so, inevitably, the river bottom reached up, subtly at first, until at last it snared the *Demeter*, ever so lightly, some 1,200 kilometers inland.

As the hours and then the days passed, every attempt to reverse or to drive forward succeeded only in miring the vessel more deeply, until it became, as Sänger finally summed it up, "Hopeless. We are like a fly, trapped in a spider's web."

Eventually there was no choice left but to anchor the sister ship, *Nostromo,* in deeper water nearby, and to transfer fuel and equipment from the *Demeter* to the second boat. Voorhees had been caught by surprise when *Demeter*'s cargo cranes pulled the prefabricated sections of two heavy-lift helicopters out of the hold.

The two men stood silently, which was itself a testament to the spectacle that was unfolding. Once the craft were assembled, they could see that each was powered by a single engine, driving two three-bladed rotors. Nearly twelve meters across, each rotor was mounted on twin tubular steel outriggers on either side of the planelike fuselage—the forward section of which was rounded with a fully glazed cockpit. Voorhees thought this last feature would provide the pilots with a panoramic view of their own deaths. The "chosen" pilots appeared to be a slender, feral-looking man and a pixy-like woman with short blond hair.

"What are those machines?" Voorhees asked.

"The builders, Heinrich Focke and Gerd Achgelis, call them *Drache*."

Voorhees gestured toward one of the "Dragon" pilots. "And is that who I think it is?"

"Hanna Reitsch," Sänger replied with pride. "Do you know her?"

Voorhees winced. "Unfortunately."

As the young engineer watched the insectlike flying machines rise into the humid air, it was immediately apparent to him that the *Dragons* were inherently unstable at slow speeds. Annoyingly, the older man seemed to be reading his thoughts.

"If you think the challenges of controlling a rocket-plane are large, just imagine the skill Reitsch and Lothar need to control *these*. If they lose control for an instant . . ."

Voorhees tuned out the rest of the lecture, instead envisioning Hanna Reitsch's expression turning from surprise to terror as her mechanical dragonfly began to wobble, then spin out of control, then smash into the river, one of the blades severing—

"Maurice?" Sänger's voice was a mixture of exasperation and annoyance, especially as he noticed the wry smile his reluctant protégé was now wearing.

Although the current project had proceeded with great haste, there were no crashes. The two helicopters covered the corpse of *Demeter* in downpours of vines and branches. Yet Sänger was far from satisfied and the theme of his next and most oft-repeated monologue was an expression of fear that all too soon, after the last useful pieces of equipment were gutted from *Demeter* and airlifted out, the wreck would be discovered—by someone.

"Not much time," he told Voorhees. "We must hurry."

On the same morning MacCready and Bob Thorne examined dead animals, pasted into drying pools of their own blood, Voorhees had watched the bright glow of his latest test sled rapidly diminish, then vanish into the mist. Proper flight test analysis required that the rocket sled, despite being designed as a throwaway booster stage, had to be brought back for study. Recovery would have been a simple affair if only Voorhees had been permitted to attach a radio transponder to the sled. But more than a year's work had gone into planning and preparing the base for the arrival of the two space-planes. And even without the greater chance of discovery arising from the grounding of the *Demeter,* the base commander had insisted that the fog-shrouded compound remain radio silent. Because of this, more primitive methods were required for the search and recovery: A team of four would locate the sled and helicopter it back to base for a final examination.

It had gone like clockwork the first time around. The recovery team for the earlier test rocket launch had located the sled's landing spot in less than a day, sending back a runner to report that it was being prepared for airlift. Hanna Reitsch flew *Dragon I* four kilometers north to the spot indicated on the runner's map—zeroing in on a tethered red balloon that suddenly appeared through the fog as she hovered. Reitsch lowered the helicopter's payload cable, the terminal end of which had been modified with a set of heavy-duty straps. Minutes later, when the female pilot took her craft higher, Voorhees's rocket sled came with her.

Although examination of the sled led to slight design modifications, in concept the intricate launch vehicle worked perfectly. Despite the purpose to which he knew this great new science was being applied, Voorhees was able to draw some small consolation from the knowledge that the door to space had been kicked wide open. For a fleeting moment he had wanted to shout about it, but he knew that there were people around him who did not want to hear of such dreams.

Now, though, the nightmares were taking over.

After the next sled test, things did not go according to plan. Two days passed without word from the recovery team, then two more, then a week. It was as if the forest had simply reached out and snatched them. Three nights ago, two more men had gone out in search of cameras from one of Sänger's stage separation tests. They were two days overdue when a local tribesman found their bodies—drained of blood.

"*Phantoms.*" That's what the German and Japanese crew members began calling the unseen enemies that had descended upon their men. The native workers had their own name for the attackers: *chupacabra.*

"Phantoms" or *chupacabra*—the names made no difference. The Axis workers were becoming as downcast as the locals. First, the river had reached out and wrecked the *Demeter.* Now the forest itself was reaching out, causing men to do what Voorhees was beginning to suppose humans did best: bleed and die. During the very same seconds in which R. J. MacCready and Bob Thorne watched the last test sled scratching fire straight up into the sky, Maurice Voorhees, in a rare metaphysical moment—the kind of moment he would more have expected of Lisl than of himself—started to wonder if it was possible that nature, aroused by the ravages of techno-violence, was beginning to lash back consciously, with her own very strange style of violence.

CHAPTER 8

Whistling in the Dark

In nature there are neither rewards, nor punishments;
There are only consequences.
　　—ROBERT B. INGERSOLL (1833–1899)

Chapada dos Guimarães, Brazil
January 22, 1944

The rocket launch, as Bob Thorne would have put it, was somewhat less than a good sign. What it had done was to remove from R. J. MacCready's mind even the slightest doubt that the enemy force he had been seeking was large and well equipped. The nature of their mission remained unclear, but whatever it was, the bad guys had been at it for a while. Even worse was their proximity to the American mainland. *Close. Too close.*

They were testing something. Mac had watched it blaze a nearly vertical path, trailing a clear thread of smoke back to the launch site. By comparing notes and using basic geometry, he and Thorne had been able to narrow down the launch site to a degree that Hendry's Rangers could not have known previously. It was at most, only thirty miles away.

There's no time to waste.

MacCready mapped out a simple plan. First, he'd send Thorne and Yanni to contact Hendry with the approximate coordinates of the launch point.

"Let Hendry's bomber boys take it from there."

Unfortunately, it would take days for the news to reach relevant parties and for the brass to mobilize a response. In the meantime, Mac would head into Hell's Gate, find the Axis fireworks squad, and attempt to better pinpoint their launch sites. Of course he'd look for signs of the missing Rangers along the way, although he considered their prospects to be poor at best.

What Mac needed first, but somehow knew he'd never get, was a good night's sleep. For as much as he abhorred the possibility of blundering bleary-eyed into "enemy territory," what he hated even more was the idea of leaving a good mystery unsolved—especially a zoological mystery.

"I want to check this out tonight," he told Bob Thorne.

"What, mangos? We got them."

"Yeah right, mangos or maybe what killed those animals. I'm going to set up a little observation post tonight and try to catch our messy friends in the act."

"Now, Mac, you know I love a dead donkey crusted in shit and blood as much as the next guy but you cannot be serious about this so-called plan. You need to bunk in tonight, pally."

MacCready held up his hand. "Look, I appreciate your concern but what I *do* need is for you to help me get some stuff together. Can you rustle me up a goat and some rope to tie him up with?"

Thorne knew the argument was over. "Jeez, Mac, really?"

"And I'm gonna need a ladder and blanket as well," Mac continued. And before Thorne could turn that one around, he held up his hand again. "Don't make me have to kill you, Bob."

The botanist gave his friend a "who me?" shrug. "Hey, it's your party," he said.

Soon after, MacCready had his supplies, and the two men stood in an orchard on the outskirts of town. The scattering of fruit trees dead-ended at the top of a two-hundred-foot bluff. They were a hundred yards from the nearest farmhouse and, for whatever the reason, the owner of this particular *fazenda* seemed to have hauled up stakes and gone into hiding.

"This is the spot," MacCready said, surveying the orchard and the place he had selected, before letting his gaze settle on the spectacular view of the valley below.

For a long time the two men said nothing, but only stood watching the sunset. Then Thorne picked up a piece of rotting fruit and pitched it toward the pile of rocks at the foot of the bluff. "Now, Mac, if it were me wandering off to take a leak tonight, I would watch that first step."

MacCready acknowledged his friend with a nod.

Behind them, the goat shook its head and tested the strength of the ten-foot rope that had been secured around its neck. Thorne gestured toward the animal. "Are you sure you two don't want to rent a room?"

MacCready ignored the comment. He was looking at an ancient and gnarled tree that rose above the citrus grove. "What's that tree, Leaf Boy?"

"Bertholletia excelsa."

"Show-off."

"Brazil nut to you zoologist types."

"Any thorns?"

"Nope."

"Poisonous sap?"

"Negative."

"That'll do."

Within five minutes, Thorne had used a tent peg to stake out the goat near the base of the great tree. By the time he'd finished, MacCready was settling atop a thick horizontal branch situated a dozen or so feet above the ground. Satisfied that it was sturdy enough to hold him comfortably, he smiled down at his friend, "If I'm not back by zero three hundred, send Yanni with some *pinga* and a couple of glasses. That ought to perk things up."

Thorne replied with a new rude hand gesture he'd learned from some Italian guys who had passed through Chapada the year before. "You like that one?"

MacCready waved him off. "Old one. You need to get out more."

"Yes . . . well, just be careful, huh?"

The two friends exchanged nods, and Thorne headed back toward town, picking up speed as he went. Any guilt he felt about leaving Mac behind was being quickly overridden by a desperate need to outrace the rapidly approaching darkness.

MacCready scooched himself backward until his back rested against the tree trunk. Unfolding the blanket he'd brought, he used it as a cushion. The goat, which had apparently given up on yanking out the tent peg, glanced up with apparent interest at the proceedings. MacCready gave the animal a quick wave, then checked his watch, his flashlight, and the Colt .45 holstered to his side.

There was something theatrical about how night fell in the tropics—the suddenness of it. And now the curtain had fallen.

Mac squinted into the encroaching dark, somewhat surprised at not being able to see the edge of the bluff, though it was less than a hundred feet away. *Watch that first step is right,* he thought.

Although the zoologist had set up camp in rainforests on many occasions and in many odd places, *including* tree branches, once he clicked off the flashlight his thoughts turned, as always, to the overwhelming, alien blackness. He was acutely aware that the trees themselves were alive and covered with life, and this awareness brought with it a mild claustrophobia that was impossible to describe and which never entirely went away.

He concentrated on the night sounds: the steady din of cicadas . . . the occasional sharp click of an insect he had yet to identify . . . the sporadic peeping of a male frog. Unlike the incessant chorus of frogs inhabiting more temperate regions, MacCready knew that the song of *Physalaemus* was subtle, brief, and infrequent. *He's looking for a mate. But he doesn't want to get eaten.*

Another sound came to him, tinny and incongruent but somehow reassuring. In the distance, a gramophone was playing Frank Sinatra's "Embraceable You."

The music wafted from the direction of what he'd *thought* was an abandoned farmhouse, lulling the exhausted scientist, and momentarily—*only momentarily,* he was certain—he dozed . . .

MacCready was jolted instantly awake by an agitated bleat from the goat. *How long have I* really *been asleep?* The music had stopped and, strangely, so had the noise from the insects and frogs. As the moon emerged from behind a cloud, the staked-out goat and the surrounding stand of trees were illuminated. MacCready's imagination, too, seemed illuminated, and in ghostly silence, he saw shadows everywhere—and deep within the shadows he sensed movement . . .

Phantoms?

Ghosts?

Chupacabra?

No, he told himself. *Figments of my imagination. Nothing more.*

I n the darkness of the forest, four "figments" reacted as the biped stretched, yawned, and, after a long look around, relaxed again against the tree trunk. Honed by more than fifty million years of evolution, the creatures in the trees employed an ultrasonic equivalent of night vision, through which they created acoustic images of their mammalian prey—both species. MacCready's body, even his slow, rhythmic breathing, was analyzed at unimaginable speed, simultaneously visualized and heard through a chorus of rapid-fire clicks. Communicating in the language of sonar, the mother and child identified the biped on the branch as the same one they had encountered in the straw cave several days before. He had been more alert then—dangerous to the mother and, more important, to her child. But now the biped was slowing down, becoming more relaxed . . . almost asleep. Now, she decided, he would serve as the next step in her child's education.

The largest of MacCready's ghosts transmitted what to human ears would register as a barely detectable streamer of clicks. The child received the message and understood: food.

The young creature tensed and actually vibrated with anticipation.

Then the command.

KILL

In the clearing below MacCready and his phantoms, the goat shifted uneasily. The animal was completely oblivious to the blood that streamed from a pair of incisions above each of its rear hooves. Two dark shapes crouched behind the goat's hind legs—but the twins, a year older than their brother, were anything but oblivious to the warm flow.

As the mother observed, the youngest crept—suspended below the branch on which the biped slept. The child moved cautiously but true stealth came only with experience, and as the predator neared MacCready's right leg, the claw on his elongated thumb snapped a thin, dry twig.

Jerked instantly awake, MacCready blinked into the moonlight. *Can't see a thing.*

He swiped at his eyes with a sleeve, and then looked down, searching for the goat.

Two black forms, resembling nothing more threatening than mounds of leaf litter, flanked the goat on either side. Then, reacting as one, the mounds came alive. Raising their bowed heads and, with long incisors glistening like tinsel, they glared up at MacCready. And then, in an instant, they were gone.

Whathefuck?

There was a faint rustle of parchment—*Just like the sound in the Balloon Man's hut*—and the scientist knew that he was not alone in his tree. Strange shapes were moving toward him—ever so slowly, keeping to the shadows; and he understood that the darkness itself had come alive. Overcome with a sudden sense of claustrophobia, MacCready snatched a deep breath and pressed his back firmly against the tree trunk—trying to put more space between himself and the phantoms. Now, if he could only convince himself that the faint scuttle, more felt than heard, came from his imagination and not from directly behind him, on the opposite side of the trunk. *If only—*

Craning his neck to one side, MacCready glimpsed—or thought he glimpsed—a shadow, adjusting its position, keeping the vertical trunk between itself and its prey's line of sight. Only by accident did he discover that flesh-and-blood shadows and not phantoms of his imagination actually did surround him—only by accident. Three feet away, on the branch that supported him, he sighted a dark bump that hadn't been there before.

I'm dead . . .

For long seconds, MacCready watched the tightening perimeter of shapes as if in a trance, and for the first time within memory he retreated into himself—squashing panic with what he expected would be his last scientific observation: *Incredibly cryptic morphology and behavior. No wasted movement. These are pack hunters at the peak of their evolutionary game. Black fucking ju-ju! These are the creatures that—*

Something like a wave pierced his body, vibrating. It instantly reminded him of the *GO* sensation from the dead village—but this time, it was different.

GENTLE

"What the—"

GENTLE, came the message again, and immediately an incomparable sense of peace crept into him, *seized* him.

You're not losing your mind, MacCready thought. *Everything is all right, now.*

RELAX

And suddenly he was dreaming of his mother's face. *It's been so long. So long since I've seen you smile.*

On the ground below, the goat jerked spasmodically, as if it were lying in electrified water. The animal let out a wet cough that sounded astonishingly human.

MacCready's eyes widened. He could *still* see his mother—but now she was swallowing a handful of pills. Now she was about to—

"No!" he screamed. *It's some type of sonar. They're in my head— buzzing and whistling inside my head and they're trying to kill me.*

"No!"

MacCready tried to make a grab for the Colt, and within that first part of a second he sensed a flinch within the shadows and, still within that small part of a second, he was certain that the shadows would be upon him before the gun was drawn. And it would have ended that way, had MacCready's haste not cost him his balance and pitched him out of the tree.

He sensed another flutter of dry parchment before slamming, side-first, into the ground. Keeping his back to the earth, he aimed the .45 in alternate directions, searching for a target. But the shapes were gone—and a moment later, so too was the long, forbidding silence, broken now by the reemergence of insect-and- frog song. It was as if someone had pushed the night sounds "on" button.

MacCready remained on his back, taking several deep breaths—never lowering his weapon.

"Gentle, my ass," he said, carefully rising to his feet.

He used the flashlight to examine the goat. The collapsed an- imal continued to twitch, less frequently now. Blood seeped from every body opening, and as a slight breeze began to spread the scent of death and gardenias, a new sound spread with it. The dogs in the village had begun to howl. But this was not the wail of watchdogs straining at their leads. These were animals howling in fear.

Standing atop the bluff, MacCready stared off toward the horizon, making his best guess at the direction the creatures had fled.

Straight over the cliff, he thought, as his mind began snapping all the puzzle pieces together.

Seen from this spot, at this hour, the forest's treetops were illuminated below him—their shadows deepening in contrast as the moon began to climb down the sky, shifting the angle of light, minute by minute. Mac's gaze settled more than fifteen miles away, where the cliffs of the Mato Grosso Plateau were blazing out ghostly white against the backdrop of space. They towered over the valley into which, tomorrow, he would descend.

CHAPTER 9

Departure

Now and then, though I rarely admit it, the universe
projects itself toward me in a hideous grimace.
    —H. G. WELLS

January 23, 1944

MacCready entered the Thorne residence quietly, not wanting to awaken anyone, and not particularly eager to speak about his all-too-close encounter. His friend had set out a hammock in a screen-enclosed front room, and the zoologist fell into it with an audible sigh. Although deeply shaken by his experience in the orchard, and even more so by what he had *nearly* experienced, he fell asleep quickly.

Sometime later, MacCready had a dream, born in the dark recesses of the Balloon Man's hut and in the branches of a haunted Brazil nut tree. And once again, it was a dream about his mother.

She was bent over a dark shape, back turned . . . beckoning him . . . needing his help.

"*Gentle.*"

But there was something wrong, something very wrong, and in-

stead of approaching his mother, he took a step back. He could still smell her favorite perfume.

The camera in his mind pulled back even further . . .

Far enough to reveal her entire body,
rotting flesh draped in tattered rags,
crouched over the dead goat.
Then his mother's head came up, slowly. And she began to smile.
Her teeth glistened like tinsel.

MacCready's scream woke the Thornes, and Bob stumbled into the room where the hammock had been strung. The sun had not yet risen.

"Mac, wake up," Thorne said, shaking his friend's shoulder gently. Yanni stood behind him, holding a candle.

"No!" MacCready cried, grabbing Bob's arm violently. "Please, M—"

"Relax, buddy. It's only a nightmare."

MacCready sat up in the hammock, steadying himself. He looked around the room, searching the shadows. Finally, he focused on Thorne, who was taking a candle from Yanni. The botanist managed a small wave and something like a smile.

"Hey."

Mac acknowledged him with a nod.

"I warned you to lay off the goats," Thorne said, watching him, gauging his response.

MacCready gave a small laugh that broke into a cough.

Yanni watched her husband's shoulders relax slightly. Reading Bob's body language, she saw that he had it under control, and headed toward the kitchen.

"You wanna talk about it?" Thorne said.

Mac rubbed his eyes—which felt as if they'd been sandblasted. "Not particularly."

"Then humor me. What happened?"

"Well, let's just say I had a little run-in with some of your neighbors last night."

"Raza's crew again?"

"No, these were decidedly nonhuman."

Thorne paused, waiting for a punch line that never came. "You're serious, right?"

"Oh yeah."

"So spill it. What are they?"

MacCready swung his legs off the side of the hammock but remained seated. "They're pack hunters. They're arboreal. And they're smart—*real* smart."

"And by 'they,' you mean—?"

"Vampire bats."

Thorne held his thumb and index finger about three inches apart. "Vampire bats?"

"No," Mac said. Then he held his cupped hands almost three feet apart. "*Vampire* bats."

Thorne pointed toward the space between Mac's hands. "You're talkin' wingspan, I suppose?"

MacCready shook his head, "No, I am talkin' body length. Significantly larger than any bat species I've ever heard of. Living species, anyway. And sneaky? Shit."

"You *saw* these things?"

"Yeah, I saw them! Well . . . barely."

Thorne looked alarmed. "But . . . how is this possible?"

"Good question. Sometimes species we *thought* were extinct . . . *aren't*." Then, almost to himself, he continued. "And these bats can . . . they can—"

—make you think things . . . do things, he left unsaid.

"Now wait a minute, Mac, by 'significantly larger' you mean—?"

"Picture a bat with a body as big as a raccoon and a wingspan of about, I don't know . . . ten feet?"

"But you . . . you said these things are extinct?"

"I said we *thought* they were extinct. Anyway, there were at least three of them—probably four, and they were hunting me last night. Just like they were hunting the animals in that stall and those people in the dead village."

"Bats with ten-foot wing spans—alive? Today? *Here?* How is that possible?"

Yanni returned from the kitchen with two cups of something hot and aromatic. As she handed one of them to Bob, her calm presence seemed to soothe him immediately. Quietly, she handed the second cup to Mac and sat down beside her husband.

"Thanks," Mac said, nodding to Yanni, before turning back to his friend. "Like I said, I don't know. But giant vampire bats *did* live in Brazil, and recently, too!"

"How recently?"

"I don't know . . . couple of thousand years. Guess we can revise that number, huh?"

Although Thorne said nothing, Mac could tell from his friend's expression that the man was definitely not fully sold on the idea of giant winged mammals. "Look, Bob, I know how this must sound . . . but I think this is them."

"And who is *them?*"

"*Desmodus draculae.*"

"Dra-coo-lay?" Thorne repeated. "And what the hell are these dra-coo-lay doing here in 1944?"

Yanni broke her silence. "The *chupacabra* have always been

here," she said, and the two friends straightened their spines, as if they had been touched at the same instant, by the same live wire.

"Jesus," Thorne whispered. "This is not possible."

MacCready stood up. "Think about it, Bob. It makes *perfect* sense. These creatures aren't myths, they're survivors—living fossils."

"You mean, like that butt-ugly fish everybody thought was extinct for eighty million years?"

"The coelacanth? Yeah, kinda like the coelacanth, I suppose."

"But why the dead livestock all of a sudden—and that village you wandered into? If people think you're extinct, why not just stay hidden?"

"Excellent questions," Mac said, moving to a window. *It'll be dawn soon,* he thought, focusing on the outline of a fenced-in chicken coop. "Maybe it's about food. Maybe they're starting to run low on natural prey. Along come your cattle farmers—your chicken pluckers, and, 'Bang!' Before you know it there are new blood banks open all over town."

"Yeah, could be, I suppose," Thorne replied. "Or, assumin' you haven't flipped your wig, maybe these *draculae* got driven out of the woods by the same guys who stirred up the Xavante."

"You mean whoever ran that sub upriver?"

"Sure, maybe the Krauts riled them up. *Everybody* hates those fucks, so why not a bunch of extinct bats?"

"Bob, let's not forget, that was a Jap sub that ran aground."

"Japs, Nazis, same shit, different uniform."

MacCready smiled at the imagery.

"But I don't know, Mac. This still seems like a bit of a stretch to me. I mean, what do I know from bats?"

"Enough to take Yanni and get the hell out of here." Mac answered. "I need you to get to Cuiabá, anyway. Contact Hendry and tell him about those rocket contrails and the new coordinates we figured out. But for shit's sake—do *not* mention giant vampire bats. Last thing I need is for him to think I've gone crazy."

"Leave . . . here?" Thorne sat down as if his legs had given out. "I know what I said yesterday, but maybe there is another—"

"There *is* no other explanation! Believe me, Bob, I've seen these things, and whatever kept them at bay for all these years . . . well, they're not shy anymore. And right now the two of you need to find yourselves a new paradise, because this one's got a serious downside."

Thorne seemed to be waiting for another alternative, and realizing that there would be none forthcoming, he buried his head in his hands.

Mac turned toward Yanni, looking for support, but she was gone.

Thorne rose without another word and shuffled slowly back toward his bedroom. Mac carried his cup to the window. He was hoping he'd done a good enough job convincing his friend to leave Chapada, when a strange sound came to him from somewhere outside the house. It was familiar somehow, but at the same time completely unique.

Without a word, Mac picked up the candle and began to follow it, stopping as he reached the back door.

Extending his arm, the candle flickered against the predawn breeze, animating the boxes and gardening tools that cluttered the Thornes' backyard.

MacCready edged a couple of steps farther, then paused again. Though he was only a few feet from the house, he could already feel the immensity of the forest—a living thing that waited beyond the tiny plot of cleared earth on which he stood.

The sound came again, and he knew where he'd heard it before.

He was back in the orchard.

The Brazil nut tree.

The branch.

GENTLE

It sounds like—

MacCready squinted into the darkness. There was a figure in the flickering candlelight.

Is it . . . Yanni?

It was, and he could just make out her back. She was standing absolutely still, her silhouette barely visible against a forest backdrop. For a moment MacCready thought she was listening to the strange song, until he realized that the sounds were coming from her.

MacCready sensed Thorne's arrival beside him. "What is it, Mac?"

"It's Yanni." The zoologist nodded toward the silhouette, which continued to whistle and click into the forest. Her attention appeared to be focused on the dense stands of trees that began barely five feet from where she stood.

Abruptly, the whistling ceased but Yanni remained motionless.

For several seconds, there was absolute silence . . .

. . . and then the forest answered her back.

An hour later, Thorne watched nervously as MacCready rearranged the contents of his backpack on the porch. Yanni was seated beside him, her face full of concern. "You should come with us instead, Mac."

Although his silence said no, MacCready knew that if he were to be totally honest, he would have much preferred to go anywhere with his suddenly resurrected best friend and his mysterious wife. *Anywhere but that valley.* Instead, he began pulling items out of the backpack—looking for anything that could lighten the load.

A Brazil nut hit him in the back and he flipped Bob a middle finger without bothering to look up.

"Yeah, Mac," his friend chimed in. "Porto do Inferno, what a shithole."

Now MacCready looked up from his *un*packing job. "Are you guys finished?" he said, shaking his head.

The Thornes shrugged, simultaneously. Then Yanni rose and went back into the house.

MacCready decided to change the subject. "So Yanni talks to these things, huh? That's interesting."

"Hey, that was news to me," Thorne said.

"Bob, we're talking about your wife here. You must have some inkling of what all that whistling and clicking was about?"

"And I am tellin' ya, Mac, I am clueless. But Yanni has always been kinda . . . you know, spooky."

"Spooky?"

"Yeah, 'woooo-wooooo' and all that supernatural shit. It got her kicked out of her own tribe."

"Really?"

"Yeah, the assholes 'round here think she is some kinda witch."

"A witch?"

Thorne shrugged. "Hey, everyone just leaves her alone, which is fine by me. But witch or no, she is currently mum on any topic related to conversations with giant extinct vampire bats."

Mac shook his head. "Well, that's real helpful Bob. In any event, it'll give you both something to chat about while you're packing up for the big move."

Thorne looked away. "Jeez, this whole relocation thing . . . where are we supposed to go, anyways?"

"I don't know. After you contact Hendry you can look for an apartment in Cuiabá."

"That dump?"

"Why not go back to Brooklyn? Yanni's certainly primed for it."

"Brooklyn?" Thorne said, with a laugh. "And how do we get there—yellow cab?"

"Look, all I'm saying is that you've gotta get out of here."

Before Thorne could respond, Mac pushed the Russian submachine gun and a sack full of cartridges into his hands. "And speaking of getting out of here, I need to travel lighter. Can you hold on to these for me?"

Yanni returned from inside the house and noticed a new and uncomfortable look on her husband's face.

MacCready turned to her for support. "Hey, Yanni. It's gettin' dangerous around here. I'd like to leave this grease gun with you guys. It's a beaut, huh?"

Yanni took the gun from her husband with one hand and the sack of shells with the other. "You shred it, wheat!"

MacCready smiled at the slang and his tone became more gentle, "So, now that you're both well armed and all, there's a question I've been itching to ask Yanni since last night."

"Spill it, Mac," Bob said.

"What's all this about you talking to these things? Singing to them."

Yanni stood silently.

"Your people chased you out, exiled you because of it . . . didn't they?"

Yanni shot her husband a dirty look and he responded with a shrug of his shoulders.

"There was another like me . . . exiled," Yanni said, finally. "She went toward the cliffs, like you will do. Her mother followed. I don't think you'll find them."

"I see," Mac said. "But do the *chupacabra* put words in your head? Thoughts?"

Yanni nodded. "They can make the people we lost talk to us again. By listenin' to their voices I learned to speak to the *chupacabra*. What you call singing."

Mac's face brightened. "Yanni, that might be the best news I've heard in years.

"Why's that?" Bob asked, noting the puzzled look on his wife's face.

"Because I just might not be losing my mind after all."

"Well, I suppose that's good news. But why do you figure these vampire bats are doin' all this croonin'?"

"It's an adaptation, Bob. It's how they get you to do things. 'Relax' and become their prey. Or 'go' and leave them the fuck alone."

"But how do they—?"

"Bats echolocate, right? Well, I think this species can do something more, much more. These creatures were scanning me, and I'm betting those scans can trigger the release of specific—"

"—neurotransmitters." Thorne finished the thought for him.

"Bingo."

"And what are those?" Yanni asked.

"Chemicals in your brain, Yanni," her husband answered. "Some of them cause emotions."

"Like fear or a sense of calm," Mac added. "In this case, I think the bats have found a way to use these emotions, as a tool—a hunting technique."

"The *chupacabra* . . ." Yanni turned to her husband. "They *e-volved* this, right?"

"You got it, Yanni!" Thorne replied. Then, flashing his proudest shit-eating grin, he addressed his friend. "So last night in that Brazil nut tree, is this what they did to you?"

"Yeah," MacCready replied, shifting his stance to suppress a shudder. "They tried to set me up by making me remember things."

"Like the people you lost?" Yanni asked, quietly.

Mac let out a sigh. "Like the people I lost."

Twenty minutes later, having shown the Thornes how to operate the Russian weapon, MacCready stood with them on the outskirts of Chapada. Although the sun had been up for nearly an hour, there was little activity in the village. The pigs and poultry were nowhere to be seen, and even the dogs were quiet.

"And speaking of careful," Thorne said, "having to speak at *your* funeral would cause me no little embarrassment. So let's avoid that scene—if you catch my drift."

"I catch it," Mac said, as the friends embraced. "Just remember, Bob. Two things. One, tell Hendry about the rocket and the coordinates. And two, get the hell away from here, at least until this shit blows over."

"Of course, Redundzel, although I also heard you the first sixteen times."

Mac laughed at the reference to his old nickname. He *did* have a tendency to repeat what he considered to be important concepts.

"And don't make me and Yanni have to come in there to rescue your skinny ass."

"Gotcha," Mac said, throwing his pal a salute.

Mac never used the word *goodbye*. In his family, and at this kind of time, *goodbye* was considered bad luck.

"See you soon, Yanni," he said. "Maybe at Ebbets Field."

As the woman approached him, Mac thought he was about to be kissed on the cheek. Instead, Yanni produced a strange-looking necklace and placed it over his head.

"Wear this, Mac," she said.

The thin band of leather was attached to a tiny, stoppered bottle, sealed with something rubbery. *More local juju,* MacCready supposed.

Yanni spoke two or three sentences in her native tongue and Thorne translated: "She says, if you go into the swamp, be sure to rub this stuff on yourself first. It will keep you from getting bitten."

Mac gave her a slight bow. "You got it, sister!" he said.

Then the friends exchanged nods and Mac turned away, setting off at a brisk pace for the tree line. He knew there was a canyon somewhere beyond those distant trees, a canyon they called Hell's Gate.

CHAPTER 10

Predator

*We hang the petty thieves and appoint the great ones
to public office.*

—Aesop, Greek slave and author

Chapada dos Guimarães
10 A.M. *the next day, January 24, 1944*

Jesus Raza belched as he reached for a half-empty bottle of *pinga,* nearly knocking it off the table—*again.* "You should have seen that gringo," he slurred to his wife.

Maria was sixteen—some forty years younger than her husband—and although she had not told Raza yet, she was two months pregnant with his child. She had been forced to marry the *jefe* for one reason only. It certainly wasn't his manners (*there were none*) or the fact that even on his best days Raza was a drunken bully. He was simply the most powerful man in Chapada dos Guimarães. Everyone feared him.

Maria sometimes wondered how Raza had become so important. She remembered him bragging about a youth spent in a place called Mexico where he had ridden with someone named Zapata.

But Maria, who, in her entire life had not traveled more than five miles from her village, had never heard that name before.

And he bragged about so many other things, she thought. It seemed he had made a career inventing imaginary friendships with famous people, none of whom she had ever heard of.

What she *was* certain about was that Raza was a killer. His victims were strangers, mostly. Some were unlucky enough to have crossed him, while others had simply wandered into Chapada at the wrong time. She also knew that with the recent livestock killings, this was *definitely* one of those "wrong times."

"The gringo nearly wet himself when he saw me," Raza said, between swigs of cane liquor, proudly regaling Maria with yet another rendition of his encounter in the church courtyard. He would have killed the stranger, Maria knew, but that other gringo, Thorne, had promised him two tubs of liquor if he'd go away. And if there was one thing Raza liked better than bullying, it was drinking. She also knew that he didn't want Thorne's witch of a wife to cast a spell on him.

Maria smiled, trying to remember if this was the third or fourth time that he had repeated this very same story. She nodded her head and made sure to continue smiling. *It was four— definitely four.*

"You should have seen his face," Raza said, finishing the brag with another belch that reminded her of a sick cow.

Maria nodded again. *And fortunately, you had a dozen of your machete-carrying friends with you,* she thought. Then she flashed her very brightest smile. *I am getting good at this.*

"He's just lucky I was feeling—"

Someone kicked the front door into the room, landing a section of the frame beside the table where Jesus Raza sat.

The *jefe*'s *pinga*-soaked brain registered Maria's scream and a flash of movement; but before he could rise from his chair, there was a gun muzzle pressing against the back of his head and another jammed into his right cheek.

Raza froze, keeping his hands on the table. Only his eyes moved.

Someone was dragging Maria into the back room. "Nooooo—" she cried, until her voice was cut off by the closing of the bedroom door.

Now the room was silent—so silent that Raza was able to hear the quickening thump of his heart, inside his own chest.

"Who killed my men?"

The voice had come from behind him. It was calm and measured, almost gentle in tone. The speaker was definitely a foreigner but his Portuguese was fluent.

Raza tried to turn toward the voice but a painful increase in pressure from the twin gun muzzles prevented any movement at all.

"I . . . I don't know what you mean," Raza replied. "What men?"

More silence, but five seconds later a bone-chilling scream sounded through the walls of his bedroom. *I have heard her scream before,* Raza thought, *but not like this.*

Her cries stopped as abruptly as they had begun.

"Who killed my men?" The voice had come again, still calm, still measured.

"This is a mistake," Raza blurted out. "But you know . . . mistakes happen. So *take* the woman. I . . . I *give* her to you."

There was another pause, then a sudden ease in pressure from the gun barrel that had been pressing into the back of his head.

That's better, Raza thought. *Now—*

Something smashed into the side of his jaw. Raza felt an enormous bolt of pain shoot down his neck and arm. It felt like electricity dipped in fire, and his right arm straightened in something that resembled a salute. Pieces of hard and sharp matter were clattering in the bottom of his mouth, and when he slid his tongue along the place where four teeth had been only a moment before, he felt cold air behind warm blood.

Unbeknownst to Raza, the man with the calm voice had instantly recognized the involuntary arm movement as a muscle spasm resulting from a damaged nerve. He also recognized the expression of startled surprise in a man who had just pushed his tongue through his own cheek and into open air.

Raza slumped to the floor and one of the guns followed him down, the muzzle resting uncomfortably close to his right eye.

"Who killed my men?" The tone of the man's voice had not changed at all.

"I . . . thon't—" Raza's mouth was full of hornets. He spat them out, hard and wet, and waited for another blow—which did not come. For some reason, this scared him more than anything else the last few minutes had wrought.

Ask me again, Raza thought. *Ask me the question!* But there was no question—only excruciating pain and even more excruciating silence. His mind was racing. *Maybe a bullet this time.* And Raza flinched at the image of his head, mostly gone above the eyes.

But the room remained silent.

Then Raza's mind fixed on something else. Something important. *Yes. Something that can save me. The gringo.* He willed his mind to clear.

"Stran-ger . . . choo days . . . ag . . . o . . . Amer . . . Amer . . . can." The hinge of his jaw was not working right. Still, his only concern was getting the words out.

"Witch . . . esss . . . housh . . ." Raza spat again. "Witch anner cra-zzee hush-ban. Liv . . ." He paused. The clicking of the hinge and the dribble of fresh blood was making him dizzy, so he pointed: " . . . ne . . . rrrr . . . edge . . . town."

Instantly, the gun muzzle was withdrawn.

The pain was coming in dull waves now, but with great effort, Raza raised his head. A tall figure had materialized in front of him. He had a narrow face, with a thin mustache.

Something familiar, Raza thought, squinting as if trying to remember the name of an old acquaintance.

Was he a movie actor? His mind flashed to a film he'd seen in Cuiabá.

Raza could see that the thin-faced man was smiling. But the smile wasn't making him feel any better at all. In fact, Jesus Raza suddenly felt his bowels churning.

The smiling man nodded slightly.

Suddenly he knew. *It was—*

Raza's head was jerked back by a powerful hand and in that same sweeping motion he was thrown forward onto his knees. He kicked backward with one foot and tried to stand but his hands slid on something hot and wet. His whole world tilted into dizziness and irrational calm, tilted like the deck of a sinking ship, leaving him puzzled that his fingers seemed to be resting under a warm spray.

The roof is leaking, he thought.

Raza called out to his wife. *The bitch can clean it up.* But his bisected trachea only let out a long, bubbling gurgle. Calm and a descending dreamscape were gaining dominion over his thoughts—a dreamscape in which shadowy figures stepped out of the corners, their hands lengthening toward him, as if seeking to drag him into the earth itself. The shadows and his own wet croak snapped the toughest man in Chapada to hyperconsciousness. And in that moment he saw two men in black uniforms.

As the shadows stepped closer, the image flickered like a candle in a draft.

But why are they upside d—

Jesus Raza's consciousness blinked off like a light switch, and he toppled backward, landing on his own contorted face and rolling sideways.

The smiling shadow with the thin mustache kept close and silent vigil, counting off the seconds between dying and death, between Earth and Hell. The shadow looked at a pocket watch, noting the moment Raza's eyes stopped searching, recording the exact instant that life had gone out of them.

"Thank you." A voice addressed the dead man, in German. "You have been most cooperative." Then he tucked his watch into a tunic pocket and calmly stepped over Jesus Raza's freshly severed head. It mattered little to the shadow man that the two dead privates, Fuchs and Becker, deserved their fates. They had been fools. Even worse, they had broken Sänger's movie camera in their deaths. The important thing, the *only* thing that mattered, was that they were German soldiers—his soldiers. In the process of tracking down their killer, this dirty, drunken local, as highly as he thought of himself, was utterly dispensable.

The SS officer was quite proud of his own perceived place in history, though unaware that posterity would reduce him to a stereotypical boogieman. But this too would have brought a smile to Colonel Gerhardt Wolff's face.

At the table, Sergeant Vogt used the last of the foul-smelling alcohol the dead man had been drinking to clean his stiletto, and now he was wiping the blade on the homespun tablecloth.

The colonel appreciates the beauty of those cuts, Vogt thought, watching as Wolff opened the door to the bedroom and entered silently.

From inside the room, he caught a faint whimper and a whispered response. "Ssssshhhhhhh."

And then . . . silence.

Like a spider, Vogt thought, and grinned. *Just like a spider.*

CHAPTER 11

Extinction

The universe is not only stranger than we imagine, it is stranger than we can imagine.

—Arthur Stanley Eddington, paraphrasing J.B.S. Haldane

January 25, 1944

It was midafternoon and MacCready had been trying to figure out where he'd experienced a worse combination of heat and humidity before. *Bangkok? Maybe. August in Port Arthur, Texas?* He winced at the memory.

Currently, he was taking a breather beside an algae-choked watering hole rimmed by a few half-dead trees. *A mud puddle with aspirations,* he thought. But he needed some shade and he needed a safe place to hole up.

The forest was fragmented here—islands of clustered trees, scattered across a sea of tall grass. Right now it was the "tall-grass-in-broad-daylight" part that concerned MacCready most. He took a swig from his canteen. *Hendry'd probably blacktop this place.*

Though tired, and certainly ready for a nap, MacCready also

knew that there were several pressing issues to consider. Finding the missing Rangers without getting skewered by the Xavante was currently in the lead, but for some reason he couldn't shake the image of Yanni staring into the forest—and sounding just a little too much like the creatures he had encountered in the Brazil nut tree, the same creatures that had nearly killed him, *twice*.

They were actually stalking me, he thought. And in spite of the heat, he gave an involuntary shiver. *And what? She was calling them?*

As if interested suddenly in MacCready's dilemma, a caiman surfaced nearby.

A big'un, he determined. *Ten feet long from nose to tail tip.*

A single sweep of the reptile's tail sent it three feet closer to where MacCready sat. The zoologist knew that the caiman's brain hadn't changed much since the Age of Dinosaurs, and as a consequence its cerebrum was about as big as a gnat's ass. *Well, maybe a little bigger.* But although the crocodile cousin couldn't paint the *Mona Lisa* or start wars, its kind *had* survived unchanged through whatever had killed its brawnier, brainier cousins, the dinosaurs.

Maybe nature's trying to tell us that brains and brawn don't always count for much, MacCready thought.

He bounced a pebble off the caiman's back, then glanced around for another bit of rock. *Survivor or not, this guy's getting too close.*

"How *does* Yanni do that?" MacCready mumbled under his breath. He watched as the scaly body submerged below a layer of green, then gave it a dismissive wave. But another question, a more important one, had been forming since his departure from Chapada and had finally come to the fore. "In all this time, why haven't the *draculae* killed her?"

The caiman's eyes resurfaced, black and unblinking. Mac-

Cready held out a bigger, heftier pebble. *Don't make me bonk you with this,* he thought.

With one eye on the reptile, his mind drifted back to Yanni and her formerly extinct pals. *Well, whatever the answer is, it's no wonder Thorne's chipping in with the housework.*

MacCready was about to carry out another preemptive pebble strike when he heard a slight rustle off to one side in the tall grass. Instinctively, he went as motionless as the caiman, but his right hand eased down toward the Colt. Feeling a presence as much as hearing it, he sensed something creeping by, keeping low to the ground and passing him on the left side less than ten feet away.

MacCready squinted, trying to identify the newly arrived visitor. But whatever it was, it had stopped—its sun-dappled profile all but invisible against the tall stalks of grass.

Then, without any warning or shyness, it stepped into a narrow clearing at the water's edge.

The zoologist's eyes widened. *You are not there.*

He resisted the urge to blink—half-fearing that if he did the tiny creature would dissolve like a mirage.

You are definitely not there, MacCready's mind repeated, leaving him feeling uneasy this time. He was, until now, just getting used to the idea that maybe, *just maybe,* he wasn't following his mother into the perpetual, uncontrollable dreamscape of insanity. *Time to reevaluate.*

The animal standing at the edge of the watering hole looked *something* like a horse. And as the animal dipped its long snout to drink, MacCready could see that it behaved something like a horse as well—gold-colored eyes scanning the surface of the water, alert for any sign of movement.

Beyond appearance and mannerisms, though, calling this species a horse was a stretch. For starters (and *just* for starters) it stood no more than three feet tall at the shoulder and, incredibly, instead of a single hoof, it had toes—*three of them* by the look of it.

MacCready concentrated on keeping his jaw from dropping open, while another part of his brain slipped easily into paleontology mode—working through everything it could dredge up about the evolution of prehistoric equids.

He knew that the granddaddy of all horses had been a short-snouted forest browser, with four toes on the front legs and three on the hind legs. As North American climates changed around twenty million years ago, humid forests gave way to grasslands, and new horse lineages developed longer legs, fewer toes, and, on one surviving offshoot—single hooves.

MacCready watched the animal paw at something near the waterline.

Mesohippus?

No, this guy's a little larger. Parahippus.

But that was a North American species—supposedly a long-extinct intermediate between woodland and grassland horses.

Well, this little fella is going to throw a real monkey wrench into what we thought we knew about the ancestry of horses.

As if overhearing MacCready's thoughts, *Parahippus* raised his head, cocking an ear. MacCready held his breath.

Suddenly there was a horselike cry from the sea of grass bordering the far side of the watering hole.

Unknowingly, the scientist's body reacted with the slightest twitch. *There are more of them,* he thought, *maybe a whole—*

The tiny creature turned its head and looked directly into MacCready's eyes.

—herd.

MacCready never bothered to stifle the smile that had begun

to spread across his face. But even before he could complete the grin, the crack of a gunshot sent him sprawling into the mud.

Mauser, MacCready thought, reaching for his sidearm and catching a glimpse of the tiny horse as it flew across the muddy pool in a single leap. A split second later, there came an explosion of green-streaked water. Even before MacCready's gun arm could spin toward the new commotion, a toothy reptilian snout stabbed upward and closed only on open air. With a measure of relief, MacCready saw that the frightened *Parahippus* had already vanished into the grass.

Reptilian reflexes pitted against mammalian ones had become the horses' good fortune, and MacCready's misfortune. The caiman landed with all the grace of a fat kid belly-flopping into a pool, a noise that was certain to be heard by whoever had fired the gun. MacCready rolled into cover, alert for any hint of someone approaching through the grass.

About a minute later, there came another gunshot, farther away this time. *Definitely Mauser. Definitely Krauts, but they're not shooting at me,* he thought, his relief tinged with annoyance. *Leave it to the Master Race to take pot shots at a herd of animals that've been extinct for fifteen million years.*

By the time his adrenaline rush wore off, MacCready began to realize just what exhaustion combined with a decision to press forward in broad daylight had nearly cost him. Now he would wait for dusk before leaving cover.

Three long hours later, the zoologist skirted the waterhole in a semi-crouch, taking a moment to appreciate a perfect set of *Parahippus* toe prints in the mud.

I'd give a million bucks to make casts of these, he thought. Then he shot a glance into the grass where the animal had disappeared. *And another million to track that herd.*

But he pushed his explorer impulses aside. He had a civilization to save. His own. MacCready turned resolutely toward the stark cliffs of the Mato Grosso Plateau. Rising out of their lake of mist, and far closer now, the stony guardians of Hell's Gate looked impossibly steep and just as inhospitable.

Jesus, MacCready thought. *Don't make me have to climb those fuckers.*

CHAPTER 12

From the Mist

God is in the details.
—Freeman Dyson

The devil has a better press agent.
—Lewis Abernathy

January 26, 1944
An hour before dawn

The vampire bats hung like ten giant black teardrops beneath the gnarled branches of the great tree. For uncounted millennia this had been an especially rich section of their hunting ground, until the strange sounds and a sudden swarm of bipeds had driven most of them away.

Now they had come back to investigate.

Just beyond their roost, it was as if a strong wind had blown through the forest in a straight line, sweeping away every tree and every sign of life. The lead male sent out a stream of ultrasonic clicks that beamed along the clearing in a clean, straight line, unimpeded.

Puzzled, he repeated the call, this time casting a wider beam of energy that painted a sonic picture of the dense foliage bordering both sides of the clearing. The return information was processed instantly. A long stretch of forest had disappeared.

From her position at the center of the cluster, the mother could already sense the combination of fear and anger in the pheromonal response of her mate. Hanging from the same branch, she felt the twins stirring uneasily in response to their father's chemical message.

The lead male's body vibrated for a moment, then his jaws snapped open. A pair of specialized salivary glands swelled, filling the front half of the bat's mouth. The creature let out a long audible hiss that was accompanied by a thin, aerosolized spray, and from behind the mother, several subordinate males, including the male twin, responded immediately, mimicking his call.

Before, they had taken the new bipeds only when they encountered them by accident. Now they would hunt them.

Moments later, the branches of the great tree were empty. The creatures who had been roosting there were now returning to the cliffs, racing the coming dawn, and leaving in their wake the scent of gardenias.

MacCready peered down from a thickly vegetated ledge of rock into the valley of Hell's Gate. Dawn was only moments away, and a hundred feet below his perch, a sea of fog stretched unbroken across the miles.

He had arrived the evening before, deciding that the high ground would reveal the best possible routes into the valley. Thankfully, he'd also been able to catch a few hours of sleep, but Mac was still feeling exhausted as he looked out across the surface of the mist.

His first impression was that if it weren't for the treetops poking up here and there, an observer might have been fooled into thinking there was water under the fog instead of a lush forest. *Indian Lake, at sunrise,* he thought, smiling as he remembered the early morning view from a hilltop cabin in the Adirondack Mountains.

The squawk of parrots, moving from the high ground into the valley, brought him back to present reality. Like clockwork, the birds noisily left their nests each dawn, descending into the lowlands to feed. At twilight, the same loud commute took place in reverse. There were other sounds as well—insects mostly, and frogs.

Suddenly, as if a switch had been thrown, there was only silence.

MacCready's brain barely had time to register the change when the earth began to tremble. A second later, he felt a low rumble.

It's coming from under the mist! MacCready thought, and with this realization, he saw a small patch of fog begin to glow, about a half mile away. Almost simultaneously, from the center of the glow, the missile appeared. From this distance it seemed to measure around twenty-five feet long and maybe three feet across, with four backward-sweeping wings located mid-body. Reddish black exhaust trailed behind the engine and MacCready watched it ascend, accelerating rapidly.

That's not what I saw in Chapada, he realized. Then his eyes caught another object coming onto the scene, barely visible because of its great height.

MacCready strained to hear the engines. *It's Allied photo recon—gotta be. A B-24 by the sound of it.* "Shit," he whispered.

The rocket's exhaust trail took a sudden, sharp turn, and for a moment MacCready thought that it had been thrown off course, but only for a moment. And in that moment, he knew he was watching an antiaircraft missile, one that was headed directly for the plane.

Somebody is controlling that thing, he thought, and in the same instant, missile and reconnaissance plane merged in the flash of a fireball.

The sound of the explosion reached him several seconds later and MacCready's body jerked in response. Stunned, he allowed his gaze to drop back down into the valley, but now there was only the fog and a scattering of skeletal branches, pointing skyward like accusing fingers.

I need to contact Hendry with these exact *coordinates,* he thought. If only Thorne hadn't already left. As his mind sought the fastest way to get this new information back to civilization, something bit him just below the right ear.

It's—

MacCready neither heard nor saw anything. All sense of danger, all sense of time, all conscious and subconscious thought, all sense of self, had simply ceased to be.

Far above MacCready's prone form, the jagged scar of a missile contrail was already fading against the blue sky of morning.

CHAPTER 13

Maruta

The legacy of cruelty, pain, and fear left behind by the Japanese Chemical Weapons Division under General Ishii Shiro still haunts the world today. There has been little effort to make restitution to the victims' families who suffered through his barbaric experiments. Ishii Shiro is gone, but the results of his work are a threat to disrupt the free world today.

—GREGORY DEAN BYRD, "GENERAL ISHII SHIRO: HIS LEGACY IS THAT OF GENIUS AND MADMAN," M.A. THESIS, 2005

Nostromo Base
January 26, 1944

W ho killed my men?" Colonel Wolff asked in perfect but accented English.

The prisoner stood on unsteady legs, his hands bound tightly behind his back. "Has anyone ever told you that you look like that actor?" the captive asked. Then he turned to Wolff's hulking right-hand man, SS Sergeant Schrödinger. "You know who I mean, right? Tall guy, like you—only human."

The giant's face betrayed no emotion.

"Who killed my men?" Wolff repeated. His voice held no malice. It was almost soothing.

The bound man turned back to face the black-clad officer. "This actor I'm thinking of—really strange excuse for a romantic lead. I'm thinking he'd be better off—"

There was a flash of movement and the prisoner dropped as if he had been deboned. Like the Indian dart that had taken him down four hours earlier, the lightning-fast punch that Sergeant Schrödinger just landed to his temple went completely unseen by Captain R. J. MacCready.

Wolff stood over the crumpled man for a moment, then shot the sergeant a look that was half exasperation and half annoyance.

"An interesting way to end an interrogation," came a voice from behind the colonel. The man was Dr. Kimura, one of the project's latest additions.

"Can this one be responsible for the killings?" Kimura asked in passable German. He was wearing a lab coat, but beyond that his choice of attire fell apart quickly. The bespectacled scientist wore short pants, and on his feet—some sort of platform-elevated sandal. A paper surgical mask had been pulled down and now served to barely conceal several of his ample chins.

"I think not," Wolff replied. "Clearly he was sent here to locate his missing friends."

"Good, then I can use him for—"

"Before you do *anything*, Doctor, *I* will spend some time with our guest." Then, without further explanation, and before Kimura could respond, the colonel turned and strode off in the direction of the *Nostromo*, Schrödinger at his heels.

"You probably weren't so haughty when you hung up our other

submarine," Kimura muttered to Colonel Wolff in Japanese, and under his breath.

Satisfied that the colonel and his goon were not around to observe, he prodded the prisoner's body with a *geta* clog. Further satisfied that the prisoner was at best only semiconscious, he nodded to a pair of Japanese soldiers who were standing by at attention. The men gave no hint that a minute earlier they had been snickering at Kimura's eccentric attire.

The doctor's order consisted of a single word: *Maruta*. But it was all the pair needed to hear. They watched their superior hobble off, trying hard to mask his limp. They'd all spent their childhoods in the shadow of polio.

The two soldiers hauled the prisoner's body up by the arms and began dragging him away—his boots digging a pair of shallow troughs that ended as the men approached a hangar-shaped building, roughly the size of a truck garage. The rounded roof of the corrugated structure was streaked with reddish brown rivulets—the metal panels corroding after nearly four months in the hothouse climate. One of the men kicked open the door and they disappeared inside Dr. Kimura's "woodshed."

Akira Kimura wished he were still in Manchuria, or anywhere else for that matter. *Anywhere but here, where savages fly their colors on our prized submarines—and have the impudence to rename them. What is a* Nostromo, *anyway?*

My work there was far from finished, the doctor thought, as he peered into a microscope. *"Maruta,"* he said to himself. It was a word that caused him to chuckle, in spite of the heat, humidity, bad food, and worse company. Back in Harbin, even Dr. Ishii had gotten a laugh out of that one. *Maruta.*

Kimura was a trained microbiologist, with a doctoral degree from Kyoto Imperial University. He'd stayed on after graduation, working at the army's medical hospital and winning the favor of the senior officers there. The young researcher had identified himself with the National Socialists, adopting their goals and aspirations, as well as their hatred for all things capitalistic, bourgeois, or liberal.

Kimura's life changed by accident in 1928, after he read a document from the Geneva Disarmament Convention. It was a report that banned chemical and biological warfare. But the young scientist was not dissuaded.

"If they took the trouble to outlaw it," Kimura reasoned, "it must have great potential as a weapon."

Using his connections with several ultranationalists in the War Ministry, Kimura began to lobby for the creation of a program to develop pathogenic weapons. Knowing that their military was greatly outnumbered by the Bolsheviks, Kimura's superiors were all too eager to promote the development of weapons that could be used to counter the Soviet advantage in any upcoming conflict. Kimura savored the memory of how his stature rose during construction of a massive research complex in occupied Manchuria. By the time of its completion in 1939, and under the supervision of Lieutenant Colonel Ishii Shiro, the Ping Fan facility consisted of more than seventy structures. In addition to the state-of-the-art labs and dissection-autopsy facilities, there were twenty-two dormitories, a large Shinto temple, eight restaurant-bars, and brothels serviced by young Chinese and Korean "comfort girls." Kimura always found it amusing that the fifteen thousand Ping Fan construction workers, illiterate Chinese mostly, died from the work-to-death directive, without ever knowing what they were building.

Even less fortunate were those housed in buildings 7 and 8, who were surprised at being given ample food and warm cells in which to sleep.

"My patients," Dr. Kimura had called them, but he knew that the comforts lavished upon these men were akin to those lavished by Kobe cattlemen on their well-fattened herds. In hushed tones, the program was referred to as "Unit 731."

Most of Unit 731's "patients" were Chinese but there were Russians and Koreans as well. There were even a few dozen English and American prisoners of war. Although all would eventually meet horrible deaths, the method of their murder varied greatly. Some were staked to the ground in gridlike patterns, then "bombed" with a broad spectrum of disease agents, ranging from plague-infected fleas to anthrax. Kimura and his crew would then calculate the effective killing distance of the pathogens from the epicenter of the blast.

In the occupied villages nearby, children were spared the bacterial bombs; instead Kimura's men handed out chocolates that had been filled with anthrax and cookies smeared with plague.

The scale of experimentation had grown so large that bodies could not be buried fast enough, or deep enough. Indeed, the decay of so much accumulated flesh had produced emissions of methane gas in such quantity that in some places the ground ballooned upward almost a full story. Kimura and Ishii had noted, with more annoyance than concern, how attempts to disguise the burial ground as ordinary farmland were doomed to failure. "The farmers said that the ground was poisoned. All the plants died and not even pigs would go there."

But the toxic earth wasn't the only horror-show detail for the locals to ponder and Kimura to smile about. The Ping Fan facility itself was foreboding—140 acres—surrounded by a five-meter-deep moat and a series of high brick walls, either electrified or bristling with barbed wire, and, in each of the camp's four corners, a machine-gun-equipped watchtower. He'd ordered commuter train crews to draw the curtains on all passenger car windows as their trains neared the Ping Fan station: "Those fool-hardy enough to risk a peek will see the complex from a far less comfortable vantage point."

A continual source of pride for Kimura was the realization that, by comparison to the German death camps, the efficiency of Unit 731's commanders was absolute. *Not even rumors escape.*

Locals knew better than to take an interest in the "special transport vehicles" that roared into the facility at all hours. They had learned that whenever the blare of police sirens preceded these large trucks, they must never be caught within viewing distance.

The situation had reached a point at which even regional ad-ministrators in the puppet Manchukuo government were con-cerned about maintaining the cover-up.

"What should we tell the people?"

Kimura would always remember Lieutenant Colonel Ishii's contemptuous reply. "Tell them we have constructed a lumber mill," he told his subordinates, and they in turn had informed the Manchu ministers.

From that day forward, the "patients" at Ping Fan would have a new name—*maruta.*

From that day forward, they would become "logs."

Inside the "woodshed," which had no visible windows and only a single vent near the ceiling, the heat of the day had made the conditions even more oppressive. Beyond the temperature and humidity, there was the unmistakable smell of human excrement, and something else—something indescribable. One of the Japanese soldiers began gagging even before they had dumped R. J. MacCready's unconscious body into the first of a line of steel-barred cells. The sickened man gestured toward the cell door, then fled quickly, without uttering a word.

The soldier who remained, a private named Yamane, locked the cell as quickly as he could. He wanted to follow his sickened friend's hasty retreat and was surprised, therefore, to find his dash for the exit thwarted by hesitation.

Strangely, suddenly, there was something about this place that brought back a memory of Yamane's youth and the butcher shop where his father worked.

It certainly isn't the horrible smell, he thought. But just then, and only for a moment, he could almost hear his beloved father's voice.

JENTORU

Yamane shook his head. *Not something my father would have said,* he thought.

There was a hiss of air, and the private's hand moved instinctively toward the sidearm he carried. But it was only the stirrings of the new prisoner, beginning to regain consciousness. Yamane relaxed a bit, watching as the American groaned and half-rolled onto his back.

The newest permanent resident was quiet again, but just as Yamane turned to leave, there was a rustling sound from the far corner of the room. *Like two pieces of old rice paper sliding past each other.*

The private squinted into the darkness. Something was there—something odd and barely visible—a black shape suspended near the ceiling. *Did it move?*

It did move, he thought. The strange object seemed to expand for a moment.

Then he heard his father's voice again. *JENTORU.*

"Uh-oh!" came a singsong voice from the farthest cell.

Yamane spun around and stumbled toward the exit, nearly tripping over his own feet as he went. *Why am I running?* he thought, realizing that a part of him actually wanted to remain.

For a moment, the "woodshed" was flooded with light as the outer door swung open, but the sound of a bolt slamming home brought back the darkness, concealing the room and its secrets.

In a far corner, near the ceiling, there was a brief flutter and the black shape was gone.

On the floor of his cell, R. J. MacCready opened his eyes. He blinked several times, in a vain attempt to focus.

"Th-Th-Th-Th-That's all, folks!" came a voice from the farthest cell. It was followed by muffled laughter.

Mel Blanc? What the hell is he doing here? MacCready thought, just before he slipped back into unconsciousness.

Colonel Gerhardt Wolff did not know much about Dr. Kimura's bloodstained history, nor did he care. His only concerns were that Kimura's team had brought with it, first by supply submarine, then overland, the tools necessary for the refinement of biological weapons and (just as important) the components for bombs capable of dispersing these pathogens from Sänger's *Silverbirds.*

But Wolff, a trained microbiologist himself, knew from the start that there would be questions—*serious* questions.

Were the modified strains of anthrax and bubonic plague Kimura had brought with him anything more than psychological weapons? And if not, how many people would the bombs actually kill?

Then there were the rockets themselves and the strange sleds that would launch them along the monorail. *Would they even work? And now, thanks to the trigger-happy missile crew, would there be enough time to launch them?*

Wolff was still furious that his men had shot down an Allied reconnaissance plane that morning. The woman test pilot, Hanna Reitsch, had been present during the attack, and, initially at least, he suspected that she might have encouraged it. Apparently, though, the entire incident had been an accident—"a glitch in the technology."

"The missile launched the second we placed it on standby," the crew chief claimed. "Once the *Wasserfall* was airborne, we took down the target, rather than have the enemy pinpoint our position."

Although Wolff had to admit that it was a plausible explanation, he gave no hint of this as the chastened and grim-looking missile crew stood before him. *Accident or not, the entire mission had been jeopardized.*

"Your actions will of course trigger a larger Allied probe into the region," Wolff had told them—men he might have imprisoned or even executed had they been standing on German soil.

But they were far from Germany and killing his own men would only have deepened the dread that was already settling over *Nostromo* Base like a shroud. It was a dread that had little to do with their mission or an accidental missile firing. It was a dread that had everything to do with the mysterious deaths of several of his men, deaths now being referred to as "blood-drainings."

Something that struck Wolff as particularly odd was the reaction of the local Indians they'd bribed into helping them. He knew that some of his new employees spent their leisure time skinning captives from opposing tribes with their obsidian blades.

But the "hired help" had not killed his men and although they feigned indifference to the blood-draining deaths, Wolff could tell that these residents of Hell's Gate were not only terrible liars, they were frightened. Badly frightened.

They have seen this before, the Colonel concluded. *It's not just a ghost story to them. I can see it in their eyes.*

Wolff was reasonably confident that the rocket men could get the *Silverbirds* to fly, dropping multiple warheads from the unassailable "high ground" of space. The problem was getting the rockets away before their location was discovered, while assuring that their payloads were sufficiently deadly. Now, however, there was a new problem; the insufferably talkative Sänger had let it slip that his protégé might be losing his focus on the mission at hand.

The colonel headed off angrily to the large, climate-controlled hangar where Eugen Sänger and Maurice Voorhees were working on their rockets.

Colonel Wolff strode into the hangar followed, as always, by Sergeant Schrödinger, who closed the door, then stood in front of it. Wolff collected himself and approached the younger scientist.

"How long was it that you studied in New York?" he asked in his calmest voice.

"Two years," replied Voorhees, who was squatting next to an assemblage of steel and wiring.

Wolff moved to his own desk and began writing in his mission log. "And for the record," he looked up and asked, trying to project a calming smile, "while you were there, did you ever encounter Harold Urey?"

Now the young rocketeer straightened and turned toward the colonel. "I did. He was a visiting professor."

"And did he ever discuss with you his ideas for a uranium-powered spacecraft?"

"Yes, but it wasn't a discussion, it was a lecture. He said that it would be possible to travel all the way to Mars with a propulsion system of that type, if only he could find a way of refining enough uranium-235."

"A significant problem, yes?" Wolff asked, probing now. He noticed that Sänger, the older rocket man, was suddenly looking uneasy.

"A significant challenge, but it *is* possible, I think. And others thought so as well."

"Others?"

"I remember one student, Isaac—" Voorhees trailed off for a moment, then for another. "Asimov. One day he had this idea about giving Urey's fission rocket an added kick and he was so proud, presenting his ideas to an expert of that caliber. But for some reason Urey became agitated about the whole thing. He began shouting at us that it would never work—shouting at Asimov, mostly. After that, Urey did not mention uranium power again."

"But you . . . still believe it's possible?"

"Nuclear propulsion?"

Wolff nodded. "All the way to Mars?"

"It's possible, but what we're building these days is completely insufficient to the task. We'll need to consider rocket design in a whole new way, like converting the enormous heat that develops from a throttle-up into thrust. If we can do that just imagine how far you could go at sixty or even a hundred kilometers per second."

"You seem to have been imagining quite a lot," Wolff observed.

Only now did Voorhees appear to notice Sänger's pained expression.

"I see too much of von Braun in you," Wolff said. "Don't you agree, Dr. Sänger?"

The elder rocketeer said nothing. Looking slightly embarrassed, he merely shrugged.

Wolff went on, shifting from a disarmingly calm tone of voice to distain: "Thinking always about the moon and Mars and not enough about our targets." He continued writing in his log, speaking as he did so. "Well, I think I've come up with a way for you to do a bit less dreaming. You will begin serving sentry duty tonight."

"But I'm needed here," Voorhees protested, taking a step toward the colonel.

Sergeant Schrödinger, who was standing immobile, uttered a menacing grunt.

Every German on the base knew it was unwise to cross Schrödinger. His story was legendary—the first member of the SS to have been captured by the Americans, and then to have escaped from Italy back to Germany. The Aryan giant had been caught trying to blow up a floating supply bridge. He refused to answer any questions, or to provide his name—even after a frustrated American officer punched him full-force in his still-open bullet wound. According to the stories, Schrödinger neither blinked nor winced, but merely returned the officer a half smile that sent an everlasting shiver through every man present. After his escape, he had walked all the way across the Alps from Italy, with a bullet in him—before removing it himself by making the necessary cuts and stitches, with no anesthetic.

His story had spread to the Allies as well. Their radio chatter was alive with it. "Do you think Hitler has many more like him?"

◆　　◆　　◆

Maurice Voorhees knew there were more like him. Schrödinger and the test pilot Hanna Reitsch and more than two million others had been carefully "civilized," from earliest childhood and with assembly-line efficiency, on the doctrine of racial purity, and in the manifest destiny of the National Socialist Party and a new world order. The Hitler Youth had been spoon-fed, the many hundreds of thousands of them, on the furies of superior arrogance and unceasing anger, sweetened with the intoxicants of sheer sadistic pleasure, and spite for spite's sake. Schrödinger was the perfect end product of a meticulous program of indoctrination—a carefully manufactured instrument among millions of others within the Axis nations. He was but a single example of the most horrifying and widespread system of child abuse the world had yet seen.

"Oh, yes, there certainly were more like him," Voorhees could tell his American adversaries. Enough of them happened to be right here, at *Nostromo* Base. And if asked, Voorhees could not honestly say that he was not one of them himself. He liked to think that he was basically a good man, standing above the gutter in which Kimura and Wolff were planning their bioweapons research. But while growing up, and while wondering what he might become— while asking his parents whether it was a good thing or a bad thing that he should join the Nazi Party, whether it would make them proud—he could not avoid looking back now to what his mother had always warned: "Show me the company you keep, and I'll tell you what you are."

Presently Voorhees tried to ignore the giant's stare and to put away the thoughts and memories that refused to stop haunting him, until Wolff placed his logbook back into a desk drawer and locked it. The meeting or interrogation, or whatever it was, was definitely over. But instead of leaving, Colonel Wolff removed a carefully oiled and cared-for case from another compartment and from that case he withdrew a violin.

Dr. Sänger, who seemed to be working on a new record for keeping his mouth shut, chose that moment to make his escape from the hangar.

"Please close the door," Wolff said, his voice having returned to its typical level of calm.

"Yes, of course," Sänger called back, pulling the door quickly closed again. His escape aborted, he turned toward the towering SS sergeant. "The humidity. Of course the humidity is bad for his—"

Schrödinger began to growl, and for the second time in as many minutes, Eugen Sänger was at a loss for words.

As the rocketeers watched, Wolff began playing. In fewer than three minutes, Voorhees and all of the rocket men had stopped what they were doing and started listening instead. The music grew louder and swooped steadily higher and faster, then swooped down again, mournfully beautiful. Voorhees looked around the room. Everyone appeared to have tears in his eyes, except for the SS giant.

The music seemed to intensify Voorhees's ability to look beyond the *Silverbirds*, to the moon and the worlds that waited somewhere on the other side of this madness. "Better days are coming," he had once told his life's one true love. "We are, after all, the country of Brahms, Bach, and Beethoven."

Unfortunately, his subconscious cried out to him, *Brahms, Bach, and Beethoven are not running the Third Reich.*

The music never did reach MacCready—at least, not the violin music.

When he opened his eyes again, Mac was unsure whether he was actually awake, or merely drifting through a concussion-induced nightmare. In either case, he was locked up in a dark cell that smelled like the receiving end of an outhouse. His arms were still bound behind his back, and he had the Headache from Hell. Then there was the man in the other cell. The annoying Boston accent had immediately pegged him as an American but the fact was, this fellow was *definitely* in rough shape.

"All gone, now," the man moaned, sounding like someone who had just lost his entire family. "All except me . . . and the new guy."

"Hey, buddy," MacCready called out, keeping his voice as low as possible. His right temple felt as if it had been slammed by a bowling ball.

There was no reply so he tried again. "Name's MacCready, R. J. MacCready. What's your name?"

More silence . . . then a sniffle.

"I asked you, buddy, what's your name?"

"Scott," came a reply, barely a whisper. "Ned." Then the man mumbled his rank and serial number.

Silence, then more sobs. Soft. Heart-wrenching.

MacCready recognized the name. Lieutenant Scott was one of the Rangers Hendry had sent in.

MacCready tried to sit up and just before he fell back onto his side he was able to see in the dim light that except for Scott's cell, the other enclosures appeared to be empty.

What happened to the rest of the Rangers? Dead?

The scientist exhaled a long breath, collecting his thoughts. "It's gonna be all right, Scott. We're gettin' you out of this place."

Nothing.

"Did you hear me? I said we're gonna get out of here."

"Na-ah," came the singsong response. "You're just one of the new shipment of *Maruta*."

Where have I heard that word before? MacCready thought. "*Maruta*. And what's that mean, Lieutenant?"

The man ignored him, seeming to take a sudden interest in something outside his cell. "Uh-oh, no more doggie on the ceiling."

MacCready struggled into a sitting position. "Lieutenant, that word—*maruta*—what's it mean?"

The Ranger responded with a mirthless laugh. "Pally, it means you are *fucked*."

MacCready winced. *Yes, and that's really helpful.*

Then, as if to assure MacCready that, indeed, things *could* get worse, Lieutenant Ned Scott began to sing loudly:

"I'm *maruta*, you're *maruta*, he's *maruta*, too! We're logs, we're logs, we're laboratory frogs!"

"Come on, MacFeelie, you know the words," Scott called, cheerfully. Then he followed up with a high-pitched giggle. "If not . . . you'll know them soo-oon."

MacCready rolled back onto his side and closed his eyes— hoping for an unconsciousness that refused to come—the madman's song repeating over and over again.

CHAPTER 14

Children of Blood

And in many places there are bats of such bigness
[encountered by those who have followed Columbus to
the New World tropics—bats, like large birds]. These
bats have often times assaulted men in the night in their
sleep, and so bitten them with their venomous teeth,
that they have been thereby almost driven to madness,
in so much that they have been compelled to flee from
such places, as from ravenous Harpies.

—Pietro Martyr d'Anghiera, 1525 (transcribed by
Richard Eden)

Nostromo Base
January 27, 1944
Twenty minutes before dawn

Tough luck, eh?" the corporal said.

"How is that?" Maurice Voorhees replied, looking outward as he leaned against
the bulwark railing of the I-400 conning tower. The fog was even
thicker at dawn and glancing down, he could barely see the *Nostromo*'s deck.

"I mean the colonel, doubling up the sentries. And with you being a rocket scientist, the doubling up is how you got enlisted for this duty, right?"

Voorhees turned toward the lanky twenty-two-year-old. "Yes, Corporal Kessler, *that* is how I got enlisted."

"Can't see a thing in this soup," Kessler said, waving an arm through the mist. "I'm going down to check the stern."

"But we're supposed to stay—"

"We're *supposed* to be protecting the boat," the corporal said. "How can you protect what you can't see?"

Voorhees remained at the railing, watching as the man slung his MP-43 and began to lower himself down a set of slippery metal rungs.

Then the corporal paused. "Are you coming, Dr. Voorhees?" he said in a hushed voice, his body language running in opposition to the unexpected burst of bravado.

Voorhees hesitated for a moment, then nodded. He caught just a hint of relief on the corporal's face before it disappeared below the conning tower deck.

A minute later, they had almost made their way to the end of the submarine's deserted and silent afterdeck. Even the parrots that flew squawking into the valley early each morning seemed to be sleeping late today.

"This place is not what I thought it would be," Kessler whispered. "I was wishing for coconuts and topless women."

Voorhees said nothing, hoping the man would take the hint.

"Sorry if I offend you, Doctor. I think you must have a girl-friend back home?"

"Corporal Kessler, if *this* is your idea of small talk I'd rather not hear it."

"Apologies. I didn't mean—I mean, it's this place. It's starting to make stories we hear about the Russian Front look like—"

Kessler stopped short and his hand went up. His full attention had focused instantly on something up ahead, along the deck. He squinted, trying to get a better look through the fog that hid the tail and aftmost section of the boat.

Voorhees could see something, too, just barely: small cloaked figures, three of them.

"Hey there," Kessler called. "What are you doing?"

There was a flash of movement and the figures, which appeared to be hunched over, drew back into the fog. Their movement was accompanied by a faint clicking sound.

Voorhees was surprised by their speed and even more so by their agility. Rather than rising up before running, the figures stayed low and scrabbled away. *Like crabs on a beach.*

The two men exchanged looks. Then the corporal raised his machine gun and began to move forward. Voorhees followed close behind, drawing his sidearm.

"They must be children," Kessler whispered, sounding anything but convinced. "Village kids playing around on the boat . . . right?"

Voorhees said nothing. *Whatever these things are,* he told himself, *they are definitely not children.*

The corporal stepped deeper into the mist. The figures came into view again, briefly. Then they jumped back, leaving behind three swirls of motion-disturbed vapor.

They're moving on all fours, Voorhees thought. *And they're small—too small to be human, too—*

"Who goes there?" Kessler barked, and Voorhees gave a start. The corporal's voice had broken on the second syllable.

There was no reply, only some faint scratches and clicks.

Corporal Kessler advanced toward the sound. The scratching stopped.

A picture formed in Voorhees's mind. *Claws.* Then another thought. *They're luring us in.* He tried to speak but discovered that his mouth had quickly become too dry. "Wait . . . Corporal . . . they're not—"

Kessler disappeared into the mist.

A t the same moment Corporal Kessler was descending from the conning tower to patrol *Nostromo*'s aft deck, Mac-Cready awoke to the harsh staccato of Colonel Wolff's baton being dragged across the bars of his cell.

Rolling upright, he squinted at the switched-on overhead lights, then locked eyes with the SS colonel. MacCready even managed a sarcastic grin. "Herr Tonic, I thought I asked for a nine A.M. wake-up call. Can't be nine o'clock already?"

Wolff's expression was blank. "You are a very funny man," he said, as he stepped away from the cell. "A good friend of yours could have used some of your humor, when I spoke to him recently."

MacCready was puzzled for a moment but then he looked over into the far cell. Lieutenant Scott was gone. *If he'd ever been there.* "That must have required some real effort, Herr Loss, taking on a guy who was starved and half out of his mind."

Wolff shook his head, as if he were a teacher disappointed in a student (it was a look MacCready was *really* starting to hate). Then the German nodded toward the same SS goon who had apparently busted him up the day before. As the giant stepped forward, MacCready saw that he was holding something—a Russian submachine gun, PPSh. Even through the veneer of mud, he could see that this particular gun had been equipped with a camouflage sling more appropriate for the Arctic Circle than central Brazil. It was unmistakably the gun that Juliano had given him.

MacCready felt as if he had just taken a blow to the gut. *Bob . . . Yanni.*

Only now did the colonel smile, pausing to relish the moment. "No more jokes?" he asked, finally.

MacCready sagged against the wall of the cell, remaining silent.

"Well then, perhaps you will find my offer to you amusing," Wolff said.

Only if it involves me sticking that machine gun up your ass before I pull the trigger, Mac thought. *These fucking monsters killed them. Bob. Probably Yanni, too.*

The colonel continued. "If you cooperate, that is, if you tell us *everything* about your mission, and what your people know about us . . . I can personally guarantee that your death will be swift." Wolff held up his right hand, extending his index and middle fingers. "Scout's honor, as they say in your country."

MacCready managed a smirk and shook his head, allowing his gaze to settle on a cockroach that was making a mad dash across the floor outside his cell.

The colonel gestured toward the giant SS man. "My name is Wolff. You have already met Sergeant Schrödinger, I think. Well, surprisingly he has come up with a rather imaginative laboratory procedure for cremating . . . medical waste. It concerns one of the missiles it was your misfortune to observe yesterday. The engineers tell me that it needs a bit of fine-tuning, although it performed quite well yesterday. Don't you agree?"

MacCready continued to watch the insect, which was making a beeline for the sergeant's boot. *Bob and Yanni . . . dead.*

"Now, imagine your body secured beneath a missile's engine just before our next test."

MacCready glanced up at the Nazi colonel. *Are you even human?*

Watching MacCready's reaction carefully, Wolff leaned in closer. Then he whispered, as if to prevent Sergeant Schrödinger from overhearing. "I've got to tell you, just between us, the method he has designed is completely inappropriate for disposing of live subjects. I saw this same experiment, once before, at the Hermann Göring Institute. The rocket blew pieces of meat all over the launch basin." He smiled at the memory. "It looked like red sauerkraut."

MacCready shook his head, before gesturing for the colonel to come closer. The officer leaned in again, just a little; Mac whispered through the bars. "Does your mother know you're involved in shit like this?"

Colonel Wolff drew back and turned away, his smile gone.

"I didn't think so," Mac called after him. Then he decided to keep going. "And I'll bet you just can't wait to tell me how much easier it'll be if I *do* cooperate."

Wolff spun around suddenly, laughing. "*Do cooperate?* That *is* if you do cooperate. If not, you'll find that some of the locals are rather obsessed with determining how long it takes a man to die if his skin is peeled off a centimeter at a time."

The colonel seemed to get lost in his own thought experiment. "An interesting question, no? From what I've seen I would estimate somewhere around—"

The sound of pistol shots stopped Wolff in midsentence. Two seconds later, Mac heard automatic weapons fire; but by then the colonel and his hulking bodyguard were already bolting toward the door.

By the time Wolff and Schrödinger raced up the *Nostromo*'s wooden gangplank, a crowd had already gathered near the stern of the sub.

"—like deformed children but impossibly fast." One of the men was telling a sergeant by the name of Vogt, who was looking even more arrogant and angry than usual.

"You shot up the boat because of—" Vogt snapped to attention.

"What has happened here?" Wolff demanded.

The sergeant began to speak. "Sir, Corporal Kessler says—"

The colonel's hand came up. "I will hear from Corporal Kessler," he said, calmly. "Those of you not involved in the incident may leave. Sergeant Vogt, you will remain."

The others immediately dispersed, and Wolff nodded to the corporal.

Kessler took a few deep breaths before recounting how he and the other sentry had been patrolling the aft deck when they saw what they thought were children. The corporal's demeanor now turned suddenly grim. His body seemed to spasm for a moment, as if he'd received an electrical shock. Then he craned his neck, looking past the colonel to a point on the deck. "But they *weren't* children," Kessler insisted, and his eyes widened. "They were . . . they were . . ."

"They were creatures, sir," Maurice Voorhees interjected.

"Yes," Kessler agreed. "And they sang to me."

Wolff studied the men's faces, alternating between them. *Have their brains capsized?*

Clearly the corporal was badly shaken, but the annoying rocket scientist appeared to be holding together just fine; his eyes were not those of a panicky man.

Wolff turned toward the civilian. "What does the corporal mean, *singing?*"

"I'm not sure. But these . . . things . . . they made a kind of sound."

"I felt them . . . inside," Kessler said, to no one in particular. "Telling me that everything would be all right."

"And did they also tell you to fire your weapons, Corporal Kessler?" Vogt interjected.

"*I* fired at them first, sir," Voorhees said, addressing the colonel. "The corporal seemed to be . . . incapacitated for a moment."

"They were singing to me," Kessler whispered.

Wolff made a motion for Voorhees to continue.

"These creatures were moving . . . moving toward the corporal in a predatory way . . . so I fired my pistol. Then they took off . . . and the corporal seemed to snap out of it. He fired at them as well. I . . . I believe he struck one."

Wolff knew that the scientist was protecting the soldier, but none of that mattered.

"So you're saying that you *both* shot up the boat," Vogt said.

Colonel Wolff ignored the sergeant. They all did.

"And then what happened?" Wolff's voice was almost soothing now. "Where did they go—these creatures?"

Voorhees nodded toward a section of the deck surface that had obviously been hit by gunfire. "They ran off the side of the boat."

Wolff looked past the damaged deck and out to where the river ran deeper. "So they swam away?"

"No, Colonel," Voorhees said. "There was no splash—more like a flutter. I don't think they ever hit the water."

"No splash at all," Corporal Kessler intoned. He too was staring out into the mist. "No splash at all."

CHAPTER 15

Leila

But first, on Earth as vampire sent,
Thy corpse shall from its tomb be rent:
Then ghastly haunt thy native place,
And suck the blood of all thy race.
— LORD BYRON, *The Giaour,* 1813

Outside Nostromo Base
January 27, 1944
Five minutes before midnight

The insect scuttled across a bamboo ceiling beam, tasting the air through porthole-like spiracles that ran down both sides of its abdomen. It had entered the ramshackle hut only seconds earlier, but already chemoreceptors, stimulated by elevated levels of carbon dioxide in the room, had begun relaying signals to the creature's brain. The electrochemical messages were translated into a simple directive.

FOOD

The assassin bug began its descent.

On the dirt floor below, a young woman rose from the thin

hemp mat on which she had been sitting. Crossing the short distance to the far side of the hut, she bent over a small figure sleeping there. The child shifted uneasily on a pile of rags. An old woman's uneven breath escaped from another rag pile, heaped against a thatched reed wall.

As Leila checked for signs that the boy's fever was subsiding, she wondered yet again how it had all come down to this. Once she had belonged to the most revered family in her village. But within a single day, her whole life was reduced to despair, loneliness, and near starvation. And now, instead of a growing sense of pride and bright thoughts of the future, her days were spent scavenging for herself, for her mother, and for her sickly child.

Leila shook her head. *It wasn't the boy's fault. And Seren̄bura̅ couldn't be blamed, either.* Both she and her husband had prayed for a child, for more than three years. *It was the shrine that was to have saved their family's lineage. It was all because of the shrine.*

She still mourned the loss of Seren̄bura̅, and every night, Leila replayed in her mind the scenes that ended their life together—as if by reliving the events she might somehow change their outcome. But of course things had not changed, and these days she knew better than most that the worst death of all was the death of hope. And so Leila habitually relived the past inside her head. It always began with her childhood friendship with Seren̄bura̅, then their wedding. And though their marriage had been cut short, she smiled at the thought that they had known more love than many people knew in a lifetime. The only imperfection in the union between their two families was that, after three years, she had not yet produced a male heir—or any child at all.

The couple knew that women had begun to whisper behind Leila's back, and at first she and her husband did their best to ignore it. But when the men began to taunt Seren̄bura̅, he responded with violence. During a particularly brutal fight, one of his opponents had lost an eye.

Sensing their plight, and concerned that the conflict might generate more violence if they did not intervene, the tribe's spiritual leaders, including Leila's own father, summoned Serēburā to the smoke-filled hut of the cacique. That night the medicine men's magic sent Serēburā into the Place of Visions, and there he remained for two days.

Upon his return, Leila's husband revealed nothing about what had taken place, but each morning thereafter, he awoke from uneasy dreams, and soon he began speaking as if possessed.

"I saw . . . a dead city," Serēburā told her at last. Leila noticed that his voice had taken on an unfamiliar monotone. "And within the city, a shrine. We must go there."

She asked him why.

"If we do this, if we leave an offering, the forest and the river spirits will grant us our child."

Leila had never heard of this particular shrine, but like others in her tribe, she was familiar with stories that told of a Lost City, a city built deep within the stone cliffs that soared above their valley. But Leila recalled other stories as well, stories that explained why the city was *never* to be visited. There were demons inhabiting the lost world behind the cliffs and it was said that they would kill any intruder. These were the tales parents told their children at night, stories meant to keep them from wandering too far from their mothers or behaving badly. And like the other monsters of her childhood, the Night Demons too had faded to a dim memory by the time Leila reached adulthood. Leila was torn between knowing that the shrine might not exist and a belief that the most important truths were sometimes hidden in dreams. In the end, she decided to make the two-day journey with her husband, in spite of her forebodings.

Leila remembered Sereburã uncovering a steep trail that clung to the rock wall. The wall itself had irregularly shaped sections that frequently jutted out into the path. Some of the protrusions had been carved to resemble strange animals—a stone jaguar straining its petrified muscles as if about to hurl itself into the void . . . a half-formed caiman struggling to be born out of solid rock.

On several occasions, Leila was convinced that she saw movement out of the corner of an eye, a shifting of shadows among the moss-shrouded crags and crevices. But whenever she looked more closely, the shadows were still.

The couple made their way upward until at last they stood beside a vertical scar that seemed to have been torn into the side of the cliff face. It was twice the height of a man and nearly as wide as it was tall.

As Sereburã prepared the red-glow lantern he had been instructed to bring, Leila peered into the cave and gave an involuntary shudder. Although it was midday, the light barely penetrated into a darkness that knew no end. Even more unsettling was a wind coming from inside the earth. It moaned as it passed them, carrying with it a rich earthy scent.

Cautiously, they moved into a spacious antechamber and, crossing it, they came to a steadily narrowing passageway. Here the scent was stronger, much stronger.

Like mushrooms and black soil, Leila thought, but just as she identified the scent with something safe and commonplace, she noticed that the current of air bore something else as well— something heard—yet unheard.

Singing, Leila thought, as the couple descended into the throat of the plateau.

Sereburã tried to quicken their pace toward the sound, holding the lantern-torch in one hand and gripping Leila's hand in the other.

For a reason she could not explain, Leila stood her ground. In fact, she leaned forward, straining to hear the strange song below the cave wind.

I will conceive a child, she thought.

And it was then that she nearly followed Sereburā, nearly pushed her hand deeper into his. But something stopped her. Something about the-voice-that-was-not-a-voice sent a chill down her spine. And it was a chill that paralyzed her legs.

Neither of them said a word but Leila could feel her husband's fingers slipping through her own, his thumbnail sliding across her palm.

And then he was gone.

When at last Leila staggered back into the village, she could provide no explanation for the disappearance of Sereburā. Summoned to the cacique's hut that night, she told the elders about the wind coming from deep within the earth, and about the voices it carried. She finished her story with the very last thing she could remember, her hand slipping from Sereburā's hand.

"What did these voices sound like?" the cacique had asked, leaning toward her.

At first there was only silence in the medicine man's smoky hut, but then there came a sound. It started as a soft hiss of air, then rose in pitch until it had transformed into a series of short notes, a melody lasting several seconds.

Leila realized that the sounds were coming from her. She closed her eyes and drew another long breath.

She was standing inside the antechamber.

Sereburā was walking away from her.

The dim passageway.

The light from her husband's torch throwing wild shadows onto the rock walls.

The clicking of claws on stone.

A flash of movement up ahead.

Something crawling along the ceiling.

Moving toward Sereburã, horrifyingly fast.

More than one. There were—

Leila gasped, interrupting her own strange melody.

Her eyes shot open. The elders were sitting motionless; even the cacique appeared to have been paralyzed. *What have I done?*

The tribal leader spoke a single sentence.

"She belongs to the Demons."

These were the last words Leila was ever to hear from him, or from anyone else among her people.

After the exile, Leila and her mother struggled to build and maintain a tiny thatched dwelling. It clung precariously close to a terrace on a steep hill overlooking the Valley of Mists. But even before the hut was completed, Leila knew that she was pregnant.

As the days passed, she took on duties usually reserved for men, becoming adept with the blowgun and bringing down peccary and capybara with curare-tipped darts. Her mother gathered nuts, fruit, and edible roots. Against all odds, their lives began to find a rhythm.

When the time came for Leila to give birth, the older woman helped with the delivery. And although Leila took a measure of pride from the fact that Sereburã finally had his son, it soon became apparent that the child had not escaped his parents' curse. As an infant he barely cried, and four years later he had yet to utter a single word. Physically, the boy had always been undersized, but lately he had begun to lose weight, his eyes sinking deeper and deeper into his skull.

Leila's mother, too, seemed weaker. Her once-beautiful face was now drawn and creased like an old mango, and she looked much beyond her forty-five years.

We will die soon . . . all of us, Leila thought, and as if to drive the point home, one day the old woman returned from another backbreaking trip to fetch water with a fantastic tale.

"Many *warazu* have come," she said. "They climbed from the belly of a giant fish."

Leila reacted to her mother's words with fear, though the fear had not been brought on by the magical arrival of strangers. Leila had heard similar confused talk from some of the old people whom she had loved and respected as a child. Their minds seemed to have gone suddenly soft.

"The old ones have run out of wise words," Leila's mother had told her then, "and now they are becoming children again."

Could this be happening to *her* mother?

Leila knew that people from a strange and heavily armed tribe had been arriving and departing for more than a year now. They came on rafts, laden with what appeared to be long vines of metal, heavy sacks of gray earth, and the makings for stiff metal huts. She had no idea why they had come or what the material was for, but she *was* sure that these men did not emerge from a fish.

"These *warazu* are different," the old woman continued. "Some of them have golden hair. And they worship a crooked cross."

Even as she spoke the words, Leila's mother could see the disbelief in her daughter's eyes, so she took Leila by the wrist, half-dragging her to a vantage point along the river's edge.

With a mixture of relief and dread, Leila saw that her mother had not slipped back into childhood. There were *warazu,* many of them. And their giant fish was actually a great black canoe of some kind, the likes of which she had never seen. A portion of the canoe even extended upward like the fin of a great fish. It was this particular fin that bore a pole, and from this pole there hung a cloth painted with the strange crooked cross her mother had described.

For the first few days, Leila watched the strangers from the fringes, and the more she watched, the more puzzling their behavior became. She also noted that the *warazu* were divided into several castes—like ants. Some were of normal height with straight black hair. Like her people, these men were quiet as they went about their work. Some of the *warazu,* though, were giants and indeed her mother had been right: Several of them did have golden hair. They spoke loudly, and in a harsh-sounding language that reminded her of spitting. Leila also noticed that both groups wore clothes that seemed well made but far too heavy to be practical.

From the start, and even when viewing them only from the edges of their encampment, Leila could see that most of the *warazu* acted more like conquering gods than visitors. And surprisingly, her people treated them like gods, accepting them and even working with them side by side. And work they did, from dawn until dusk and beyond, putting groups of newly arrived captives to the task of cutting and clearing the forest. Others used a giant arm to transfer strange objects from their enormous canoe to the shore. Their constant movement was another way that the *warazu* reminded Leila more of ants than men. They even used flying machines to carry their goods and, though the contraptions resembled gigantic dragonflies, the horrible noise and wind they produced were *nothing* like the delicate air dance of real dragonflies.

Although she had been banned from setting foot in her own village, the cacique had not actually forbidden her from visiting the *warazu* camp, and so each night Leila crept in among them, easily slipping past the guards (who she thought must be half-blind). Their strange metallic huts were hidden in the forest, amid tall stacks of mysterious objects. She followed the scent of rotting meat and vegetables and came across a mound of strange containers, hollow metal gourds that had once held food. Soon Leila began stealing the unopened gourds from their stacks, and after returning to her hut she cut them open with one of their own metal knives (also stolen). As distasteful as the contents often were, it was sustenance, and Leila quickly came to realize that the *Warazu Who Worshipped a Crooked Cross* had become her salvation—and her family's. "Thank you for the Crooked Cross," she told the river and the stars.

"This food will make you stronger," Leila whispered each evening, ladling unrecognizable meat and fruit into her son's gaping mouth. He often reminded her more of a hungry baby bird than her own child. The boy almost never responded, but from his general appearance, Leila knew that his health was improving with each passing week.

And then the screaming began.

At first the cries had come from slaves, most of them locals captured by the *warazu*. Some of the tattoos these slaves bore were familiar to her; others were not. Leila estimated that there had been more than two hundred of these wretched men clearing trees and hauling away stumps and rubble. For reasons unknown to her, the *warazu* had set out to uncover one of the ancient causeways that crisscrossed the tribal land. Then, instead of using the road for travel, they built a long, low wall out of wood and stone down its middle. The screams of the imprisoned, and especially those who tried to escape, often lasted for hours. Recently, though, a new cry had risen from the forest beyond the valley. It came one night as she was returning from gathering fruit and lasted only a few moments. A shout had come in the language of the *warazu* followed by a sound that was unmistakable to anyone who heard it—the gurgle of life torn from the throat of a dying man.

On this starry night, Leila tried to put the screams from her mind, as she looked out across the fog lake and contemplated another foraging raid. She hesitated just inside the doorway of the hut. A downward glance confirmed that her son and mother were still asleep.

The warazu *are posting more guards now,* she thought, knowing that her nocturnal descents below the surface of the fog lake and into the *warazu* camp had become increasingly dangerous. But she also knew that her family needed food and that she would risk *anything* to obtain it.

Leila stepped outside and shivered, not knowing if it was the night breeze or Sereburā's breath, absent these five years, that chilled her body. *If only something so wonderful were possible.*

A strange and beautiful music came from one of the metal huts, lasting forty-five minutes and accompanying Leila's descent into and return from the encampment. She was clutching an armful of canned food as she reentered her thatched home. Damp, musky air filled the tiny room.

The scent of black earth and mushrooms . . . and flowers.

A whisper, unidentifiable but familiar, broke the silence.

There was an out-of-place silhouette on the floor and Leila released a deep breath that became a gasp. She also released her grip on several of the metal gourds, but as her eyes quickly adjusted to the dark, she relaxed ever so slightly. The shadowy figure on the floor was her son.

Were you listening to the music, too?

"You should be asleep," she whispered, some part of her brain wondering why her mother hadn't stirred at the sound of the gourds clattering to the floor.

As usual, the boy said nothing.

"Go on," she said, gesturing toward his sleeping pallet. "It's very late."

The boy replied with a wet gurgle and for an instant—only for an instant—six eyes, not two, reflected the moonlight that angled in through a solitary window. She neither felt nor heard the rest of the cans dropping to the ground around her feet.

A moan escaped Leila, and as she fumbled to light a candle her mind tried to comprehend what she was seeing—or thought she was seeing: two dark shapes backing away from behind where the boy sat, retreating from the sudden spark of light.

The candle's flame held steady, then shifted, first to the left then to the right as breezes passed her on either side, foul-smelling and throwing impossible shadows onto the walls.

The cave. The shadows moving toward Serebura.

No!

Then the room was still.

"NOOOOO!!!" Leila cried, rushing to embrace her son, who folded into her arms like a doll.

She pulled back.

The boy's eyes were vacant, unfocused. Then his head flopped over to one side, with a sudden crack.

Leila extended an unsteady arm and the candle threw sputtering light onto the woven pallet where her mother lay motionless in a widening puddle of—

An instant later, Leila heard the sound of someone screaming. At first, she was startled that a person could create such a bone-chilling cry. She was not quite aware, yet, that the screams were her own.

CHAPTER 16

Stolen Food, Stolen Dreams

A conflagration will come upon the earth . . . and
plagues . . . And their error: that they acted against
themselves, this human race.

—EGYPTIAN REVELATION OF SETH (APPROXIMATELY FIRST
CENTURY B.C.)

January 28, 1944

Six beams of light probed the edges of a steep trail leading away from *Nostromo* Base. Colonel Wolff had decided to investigate the screams coming from the hill for himself, and, while the horrible sounds had instantly put everyone in the camp on alert (and on edge), the colonel found that his overriding emotion was inquisitiveness. *What could cause someone to scream like that—and for so long?*

He also perceived that Sergeant Schrödinger and the four soldiers accompanying him were anything but inquisitive as they followed the shrieks to their source—a small hut.

How had my sentries not noticed this place before? he thought, as they approached the structure. His flashlight beam paused at a pile of empty cans. *And what else have they missed?*

The colonel gnashed his teeth. *Too many mistakes.*

Wolff noted that one of the men with him was the corporal who had been on the deck of the *Nostromo* that morning. Now this same man had been ordered out of the camp and into the dark forest where an unknown killer lurked, a killer he might actually have seen. Wolff allowed himself a small measure of satisfaction. *Corporal Kessler is having a difficult day.*

They stopped just outside the simple dwelling, the cries from within having now settled into a prolonged moan.

At Wolff's signal, three of the unnerved soldiers rushed in, flashlights secured to their MP-43s, which they each held at waist level. Wolff entered next, with Schrödinger backing in behind him, his flashlight scanning the borders of the tiny clearing that surrounded the hut.

For several moments the Germans played their lights around the interior of the circular room, each attempting to understand the scene before him. They had all seen their share of horrors, and to varying degrees they had become numb to all manner of human mistreatment. But none of them had ever seen anything quite like this: a young woman, hysterical and clutching a pale, catatonic child . . . an older woman seemingly asleep in a pool of her own blood, too much blood for her to possibly be alive. Then there was the smell, the horribly incongruent smell.

Wolff gestured toward the withered figure of the old woman. "This one will be autopsied."

Then he turned to the mother and her child, a boy of perhaps four. "And these two—" He moved in closer, squatting beside them. The woman shifted her position, shielding the loose-limbed figure from the glare of Wolff's flashlight, but not before he had glimpsed the boy's eyes—*alive but blank and unfocused.*

Without warning, the child began shaking uncontrollably, his small body stiffening in his mother's arms. At the sound of a wet cough, Wolff took a reflexive step backward just as the boy vomited a mouthful of blood across his mother's back and onto the floor. Another low moan escaped from the woman as the child completed its transformation into a bloody rag doll in her arms.

The colonel was fascinated. *This is exactly how my men died.*

"Don't disturb these specimens," he said, never taking his eyes off the dying child. "Corporal Kessler, bring some body bags from the lab. I want this boy bagged and on Dr. Kimura's examination table in fifteen minutes."

Corporal Kessler gave Wolff a puzzled look, "Sir, but he's still—"

"Now, Corporal!" the colonel shouted. It was the first time any of them had heard Wolff raise his voice.

Kessler bolted from the hut, careful to avoid tripping over the cans that lay scattered in the blood.

From their perch on the hillside, the twins tracked the chaotic comings and goings of the bipeds. Four of them were now half-stumbling down the steep incline, burdened by their weapons and by the weight of a prize the bats had earned.

FOOD, the female signaled with the ultrasonic equivalent of a human sigh. She could still taste it, though most of the liquid was currently soaking into the ground. And if they waited much longer—

The four bipeds struggled past the trees where the twins hung in silence. The siblings could smell it—even through the thick material that covered their prey. The smallest meal was still alive, and they could feel the lingering liquid heat and the turbulence as the food drained out of him and sloshed inside the membrane in which the intruders had wrapped him.

The female sensed a vibration that ran through her brother's body into the tree trunk from which they hung. She could feel his claws tearing deeply into the bark.

The male roared in ultrasonic silence.

MacCready awoke from a dream about cool mountain streams to the sound of the outer door being opened. He was expecting to see Wolff or the SS giant, back to finish what they'd started. But instead, he watched a pair of German soldiers carrying a hysterical and blood-covered woman toward one of the cells. *Scott's old cell,* he thought, suddenly remembering the lieutenant's mad song.

MacCready sat up. "She win a date with Sergeant Frankenstein?"

Both of the uniformed men seemed startled by the sound of another voice.

Relieved to see that it was only a prisoner, one of the soldiers shot his companion a puzzled expression. *"Was sagte er?"*

"Er scherzt darüber," the other replied.

Although MacCready's ear for German speech had grown a little rusty in recent years, he did notice that, unlike his earlier handlers, one of these guys was actually being quite gentle as he ushered the woman into a cell. He also noticed that the blood staining the woman's clothes was apparently not her own. Still, she slumped to the floor even before the soldier backed out of the tiny cell.

The man secured the cage door and turned wearily toward MacCready. "You think this is a joke?" he inquired, in heavily accented but very serviceable English.

MacCready said nothing, noting that the man's eyes were set

deeply within dark circles. Though only in his twenties, his features seemed stretched tightly over the bones of his skull, giving him a haunted appearance.

The soldier gestured toward the woman. "Her family was killed by the . . ." He struggled in vain to find the right word. *"Blut kinder."*

MacCready sat up straighter. *Blut kinder? Blood children.*

The man's partner looked on, his puzzlement turning to annoyance. *"Kessler, warum sprechen sie mit einem Gefangenen?"*

The corporal ignored him. "The *blut kinder* came down from the trees. They killed her mother und her son. Drained them . . . like pigs."

MacCready's body responded to a sudden release of adrenaline. His mind responded, too, becoming clear and instantly relieved to be focusing on something else besides horrible news, aches, pains, and his impending death. Thankfully, they had untied him.

The draculae. *He's talking about the* draculae*!*

The considerable portion of MacCready's brain that dedicated itself to self-preservation saw an opening—a tiny crevice of light—and he headed straight for it. "Blood children—now *there's* a load of native bullshit," MacCready said, finishing up with a dismissive wave.

One of the men turned to leave, but the haunted-looking man rushed to the bars, his eyes wide. "I saw them! *Es geschah an diesem Morgen!*" he cried. "They were like deformed . . . children. Crouching. Scrabbling."

"And her family was bled to death?"

The guard nodded. "Yessss." His voice could have been coming from a ghost.

For MacCready, it all seemed to make perfect sense. Vampire bat saliva contained chemicals that kept victims bleeding as the bats fed, and for hours afterward. Even normal-size vampire bats left behind particularly gory scenes, long after abandoning their unsuspecting prey. *Big fucking vampire bats equals big fucking bleed-out,* he reasoned. Thorne had been right. The Germans had either awakened the *draculae* or provoked them. And now, whatever Wolff's mission was (and evidently, it was a doozy), it had become bogged down in some deep and serious bat guano. Apparently though, and this was the important thing: *These guys have no idea what they're dealing with, at least not yet.*

Who killed my men? Wolff had asked again and again.

"Well, I'll tell you a secret, Kaiser," MacCready said, with as much nonchalance as he could muster. "I've seen them, too."

"You're lying!" Kessler shouted, kicking at the base of the bars. "You said yourself it was only native bullsh—"

"Yeah, I know what I said. But I have seen them." MacCready's voice was soothing now. "I've *heard* them, too."

Before the corporal could respond, MacCready decided to reel him in. "I was wondering . . . by any chance did you hear them singing to each other? Singing to you?"

"Singing," Kessler said, his voice a desperate whisper. He almost pressed his face against the bars, then thought better of bringing himself within bait-and-strike range of the prisoner, and stepped back.

"Well . . . I know what they are," MacCready whispered back.

The corporal straightened up. "That's imposs— How could you—?"

"I'm a zoologist," MacCready said. "And what do you think zoologists do?"

Kessler said nothing, but he seemed to have added "offended" to the haunted expression he'd worn previously.

"I just thought that maybe your Colonel Wolff would be interested in knowing what these *blut kinder* really are," MacCready said, gingerly lowering himself to the floor and turning his back to the wide-eyed corporal. "Maybe not, though. He does seem kinda busy."

MacCready closed his eyes and waited. Moments later he heard the outer door slam shut.

H e says he knows what these creatures are, sir. He says he's seen them."

Colonel Wolff shook his head. "Yes, Corporal Kessler. And did he also tell you how you might end the war and return home a hero?"

"Sir?"

"This American considers himself rather clever. But he is no different from anyone else. He knows he is going to die soon, and to buy himself some time, he will tell you anything you want to hear."

"But he knows things, sir. Things he could not—"

"That will be all, Corporal," Wolff said, with a dismissive wave of his own. "Please go to your bunk."

A t the far side of *Nostromo* Base stood the chemical prepa-rations shed. Voorhees had moved his operations there for the night, during what Wolff promised would now become forty-eight- and even seventy-two-hour shifts.

Voorhees knew that, having made Wolff's *scheisse* list, Schrödinger should have snapped him in two by now, if not for the fact that Sänger's *Silverbirds* needed at least one more stage of thrust beyond the sleds. Thus the old man was able to buy Voorhees at least a brief respite against death, by convincing Wolff that the young engineer was still necessary.

"You must have been mad to tell him about nuclear rockets going to other planets," Sänger had said, neglecting to mention that *he* had been the one who first mentioned it to the colonel. That, and a fear that Voorhees might be losing his focus on this mission. "Heisenberg's atom bomb program has failed and with that failure we have rockets but no payload. How much faith do you think our colonel has that Kimura's pathogens will prove to be an effective weapon? Personally, I have doubts. And then there you go, just like von Braun and the other dreamer, Heisenberg, talking about voyages to worlds other than our own.

"Madness!" Sänger cried, throwing his hands up in the air as he walked away. "How can I save you from your own madness?"

How, indeed, could anything be saved, anywhere, at this stage in the war? Voorhees knew that each *Silverbird* was an increasingly perfected marvel of scientific achievement, its full potential nearly indistinguishable from magic. *And what is the very first thing we human creatures think to do with it?* Voorhees thought. *We figure out new ways of blowing ourselves up!* Sänger himself had begun calling his *Silverbirds* "antipodal bombers."

And yet, here Voorhees stood, toiling on the weapon anyway. Increasingly, though, it was looking like a one-way flight, in which each of the space-planes would be thrown away, in much the same manner his new strap-on "bottle rocket" boosters would be discarded, once they were used up, and in much the same manner he himself had nearly been thrown away, for the mere utterance of a few wrong words. Everything and everyone was expendable.

As the clock touched 5 A.M., Voorhees's team was mixing and molding tube segments of aluminum powder and oxygen-rich resin for the strap-on boosters. They were just large enough and powerful enough to give each *Silverbird* an extra push toward space, kicking in after the monorail sled had served its purpose and before the main fuel tanks were employed.

Now, almost to a certainty, Voorhees could get each of Sänger's space-planes to skip like a pebble off the surface of a pond, down from space and across the upper atmosphere, at least as far as the other side of the world—all of this in approximately forty-five minutes.

In his wildest moments of abstract fantasy, Voorhees wished he could pilot one of the *Silverbirds* himself, perhaps landing it on an American salt flat, where it would be saved, hopefully pointing the way toward a better world to come, after the war. But this was not to be. He looked around, and he knew: "I am in Hell."

And always, at times like these, he asked himself, "Lisl, how did I ever get into something as horrible as this?"

CHAPTER 17

In the Shadow of Hydra

*We were told that our lives were not to be considered
in the destruction of this target.*
—Sergeant J. G. McLaughlan, 405th Squadron, RAF

*Christ almighty, boys! Just look at the fires—just look
at the fires!*
—Sergeant K. G. Forester, 90th Squadron, RAF

The European red deer had been in Peenemünde for roughly ten thousand years by the time the rocket men arrived. Both species were drawn in by the same features: calm waters, dense forests of ancient oaks and pines, warm summers, and solitude. During the twelfth century, the Germans used the natural deepwater harbor at Peenemünde to gain a foothold before driving out the Slavic tribes that had inhabited the region since the end of the Ice Age. Except for a seventy-year interval in the seventeenth century (when the Swedes had somehow taken over the peninsula), the harbor was used almost exclusively by German fishermen, and by ships supplying the village of Peenemünde. During the winter of 1936–37, fishermen, their families, and all the inhabitants of Peenemünde had received "requests" from the government "suggesting" that they should consider relocation. While some of the villagers understood immediately that a nod from *that* direction was as good as a shove, and decided to haul up stakes, others (fishermen, mostly) expressed a rather vocal defiance—at least among themselves. There had always been minor squabbles among these men, but they were united in their stance that *their* hard work put food on the plates of Germans, even those in Berlin. In an unprecedented show of solidarity, they voted a pair of their most articulate brethren to represent them on an appeal to the Chancellery: "We *must* be allowed to stay."

A week later, a team of marine engineers arrived at the deserted fishing village to begin construction of the extensive dock system that soon stretched like fingers into the dark, deep waters near the mouth of the River Peene.

Along the Baltic Coast

SUMMER OF 1943

The feeling of deceleration had awakened Maurice Voorhees from a fitful nap, just before his mind registered the sound of a train's whistle. He rubbed his eyes and yawned. When von Braun himself invited Voorhees to Peenemünde, he would never have believed his own mother if she had told him that the best day of his life and the worst day of his life could become the same day.

Looking out the window, he saw that the train was running on an elevated track. The hardwood forest he had been watching pass by when he dozed off was gone, replaced by marshland, partially obscured by a damp mist. The tang of salt in the air told him they were near the coast. There were buildings, scattered here and there, and the train slowed further as it passed a row of steep-roofed cottages. Voorhees read a weathered sign and the metallic squeal of brakes confirmed that "Zinnowitz" was a station stop. He yawned again but the sound of voices caused him to straighten up in his seat.

What on earth?

There were hundreds of people on the narrow station platform. Men *and* women. At first he had the absurd notion that it might be some kind of demonstration, but no, they were all jostling for position, waiting to board the train. Voorhees shifted to a window seat just before a crowd spilled into the passenger car. Within thirty seconds, they had filled every bench and staked claim to all of the available standing room. The riders seemed strangely subdued, speaking in hushed tones, if they spoke at all, but Voorhees was still able to identify half a dozen accents—northerners, Berliners. Someone was speaking Czech.

This is no ordinary commuter train, he thought, and almost immediately they were moving again.

A balding, middle-aged man had landed next to Voorhees with a grunt. He was clutching a lunch box, which he immediately opened. As the sharp scent of cheese rose from the box, the man unwrapped a hunk of sausage and bit off a sizable mouthful.

"Good morning," Voorhees said to his seatmate, bowing his head slightly.

"Mmmmmmm," he replied, rearranging the contents of the tin box.

"Zinnowitz is a beautiful village. Have you lived there long?"

The man looked at him for the first time. "You are new here," he said, with a heavy Bavarian accent. It was not a question.

"I'm Maurice Voorhees. Pleased to meet you."

The Bavarian stared at Voorhees's extended hand but did not take it. Then he turned his attention back to the contents of the lunch box.

Voorhees lowered his hand and turned back toward the window. The train had left the village behind and he caught a glimpse of the Baltic Sea before it disappeared behind a blur of pine trees and sand dunes.

Yes, I am new here, he thought, suddenly feeling very much alone in a train car full of people, every one a stranger. *I am new here.*

After several minutes, the train slowed again and Voorhees thought that they must be arriving in Peenemünde. *Finally.* He pressed his face to the glass, trying to get a look forward.

They *were* approaching something, moving progressively more slowly, and suddenly the apprentice rocket designer felt frozen in place, his excitement turning to confusion. The view was partly obstructed by a twenty-foot-tall fence topped with barbed wire. Within the seemingly endless, fenced-in enclosure stood row after row of squat, unpainted buildings, interspersed with guard towers.

This is Peenemünde? he wondered, feeling a churning deep in his abdomen.

Then, as the train's deceleration continued, Voorhees saw men in ragged gray clothes, standing in a sandy yard. *Or are they statues? But why would anyone put statues here? Why would—*

One of the statues locked eyes with him. *Save me!*

Voorhees flinched as if stung by a wasp, and a part of his mind cried out, *Turn away! Now!*

But even as the train continued to draw slowly away, the statue man's eyes did not let him turn away, and they held each other's gaze, until the last possible second.

"What is this place?" he said to the Bavarian, in a low whisper. The man gave no answer, and made no eye contact. He simply sat silently, looking down at his own folded hands. He had already given the only answer he could: *You are new here.*

By sundown of that first day, Voorhees was buried deeply enough in his work that he was able to forget that the statue man—and anything else outside his little world of rockets— really existed. *This is a good way to be, at this kind of time,* he decided. There had been no tour of the facility and no formal introduction to his colleagues, and this, too, was good. Within minutes of stepping off the train, he was brought to the Peene-münde Propulsion Development Laboratory, where he was al-lowed to bury all of his thoughts in the new rocket engines— which had begun to develop problems, *big* problems. The reports revealed that the engines were developing an alarming tendency to melt through during flight. A week earlier one of the V-2s had spun out of control, crashing into a Luftwaffe airfield, and although no one was killed, four planes were destroyed and the explosion had left a large hole in the ground. Even more unfor-tunate was the presence of *Reichsführer-SS* Heinrich Himmler, who had come to Peenemünde to watch the test. According to one of his new coworkers, after the explosion Himmler twisted his face into a smile and commented, "Now I can return to Berlin and order the production of close-combat weapons with an easy conscience."

Maurice Voorhees sat in a deserted corner of the mess hall contemplating the V-2 launch failure. To a passerby, it might have seemed that he was focused, to a strangely intense degree, on a thin crack that ran along the inner rim of his empty coffee cup.

But the rocket man's imagination was actually walking around in his own internal 3-D picture of the engine's combustion chamber, reenacting its destruction from within the engine itself.

It was a perplexing problem. Recent successes at increasing thrust and fuel efficiency were being mirrored by an as yet untamed increase in temperature—rising quickly above twenty-four times the boiling point of water, and above the melting point of the combustion chamber itself.

The obvious solution was to build the engine parts out of more resilient alloys, but with proper metals in short supply, the Peenemünders had been ordered to rely on steel. *How can we stop the steel from cracking, and eroding, and melting?* Voorhees wondered. *How can we—*

Voorhees ran his right index finger over a slice of buttered toast, then held the digit up in front of his face. As he watched, butter began to run down his finger—coating it. Using his other hand, Voorhees picked up the cracked coffee cup and ran his butter-coated finger along the inside. Peering into the cup, he could no longer see the contours of the tiny fissure. Voorhees smiled to himself and looked up, into the eyes of a beautiful, bespectacled face.

"May I join you, Dr. Voorhees?" she asked. The woman had already been sitting across the table, in front of him—for how long, he had no idea.

"Oh . . . ah . . . yes," he said, setting down the cup. Noticing his butter-coated finger, he rested his hand stiffly on the table.

"That's a unique way to take your coffee."

"Yes . . . I mean, no. I . . . I was working."

"I see," she said brightly. "I'm Lisl."

"The pleasure is mine," he said, automatically extending his hand to shake hers, before remembering his buttered finger.

She handed him a napkin.

"Thank you, Lisl," he said, wiping his hand. "But how did you know my name?"

"Why, *everyone* knows who you are," the woman said. "Don't they?"

Voorhees sat up a bit straighter. Hadn't he recently overheard a colleague at the university refer to him as "the next von Braun"?

"Well I—"

The girl started to laugh, and seeing this, Voorhees made an uneasy transition from boastful to puzzled.

"What?"

"It's written on your lab coat, you silly duck."

Voorhees looked down at the neatly stamped signature on his pocket protector, then hid his face in his hands.

"You're new here, aren't you?" Lisl asked. It was the second time that day he'd been reminded of this fact, but this time, he responded with a laugh.

Early the next morning, he took Lisl Mueller on their first date. It started out well enough. Lisl had clearly impressed Voorhees with her lifelong dream to become a physician, and she had further impressed him with her feat of having talked her way into her current job of medical assistant. Yes, it had all been going so clearly well, until he suggested that they take a walk through a nearby field. "I want you to see something special," he had said.

Unfortunately, though, among the adjectives Lisl might have used to describe sitting beside a hole in the ground, *special* was not on the list. The crater, Voorhees explained, had been formed by yet another failed rocket launch. Her feet dangled over the crater rim as she watched Voorhees crawling through clumps of dirt and twisted metal in the bottom of the pit.

"You sure know how to show a girl a good time," she said,

checking her watch, for what he would have noticed, had he been paying attention, was the tenth time. Finally, she picked up a pebble and bounced it off the back of his head.

"Ouch!" he cried, and stood up. Shielding his eyes from the sun, he squinted up toward where she was sitting. "Why did you do that?"

"Sorry. The ground's a bit shaky up here. I think this whole thing could let go at any second."

"That's impossible," he called back. "These crater walls aren't steep. I'd say the whole thing is completely stable."

"Well, maybe it's not the crater that's getting unstable."

"But look at this," he said, standing up excitedly. He held up a jagged piece of dark green–painted metal, about the size of a dessert dish.

"That's really nice, Maurice, but I think I just saw a wild dog."

"It's part of the V-2's thrust director assembly."

"The what?"

"Wait a moment, I'll bring it up."

"Please Maurice, don't—" Lisl stopped. Voorhees had already scrambled halfway up the wall of the crater and a few seconds later he'd hauled himself over the rim.

"—bother."

"It's no bother, really. Just look at this!" he said, presenting the metallic scrap to her as if it were a Fabergé egg. He was covered with dirt and smelled as if he had spent the whole morning rolling around in a campfire pit.

"That's . . . really interesting," she said, but he knew, all these months later, that she had probably thought of saying, *That's a jagged piece of shrapnel.*

"You can touch it if you want," he offered.

Lisl frowned at him.

"Go ahead. Please—touch it."

Afterward, her diary had recorded, "*Definitely* weird, but still cute."

She pressed an index finger to the cold metal, then forced a smile. "And getting more weird by the moment," she had written.

"You're touching something that was almost *out there*," he tried to explain.

Lisl sighed. "You're already *out there*, Maurice."

"No, wait. We take metal and silicon out of the earth and evolve it into something more than it was. We give it a part of our consciousness—the soul in the new machine, bound for the new wilderness. Do you understand what this means?"

"Try *making* me understand, Maurice."

"In a hundred years, we'll have known the moon and the planets and I'm sure we'll be reaching toward the stars and the unexplored deeps of space. Gazing back upon Earth from so far away, it will become all but invisible."

Lisl shook her head, very slowly. At first Voorhees merely believed she had reached a kind of saturation point on the subject. But there he had underestimated her. "Look around us," she said. "You, von Braun—you point your eyes at the moon and the stars, but that's not where your rockets will be aimed. Think about the cities these weapons will hit." She gazed into the pit forlornly. "Once you finish working out the kinks."

Voorhees had flinched at the word *weapons*. "Yes, well, the military will use the rockets at first, against *military* targets." Then he whispered, "But who knows how much longer this war can last? And after that—one day rockets will orbit the earth, landing on runways as far away as America and China."

She uttered a cry of frustration and stood, dusting herself off. "But we are at war with America and China. Have you forgotten that?"

Voorhees had no reply.

Lisl shook her head again and turned from him. "Your far frontiers," she said, walking away from the crater. "One day you'll go too far. If you haven't already."

Thinking back, Voorhees could not recall how many weeks had passed between his "first date" with Lisl and the afternoon that von Braun let out the words that confirmed Lisl's worry that he was already in deeper than he understood. He had arrived early to a staff meeting with Dr. von Braun and the members of the Propulsion Lab. As he turned a corner, there in the hallway was the leader of the rocket men, speaking to General Dornberger, the Wehrmacht officer who ran Peenemünde.

"We aim for the moon," von Braun had said, then giving a shrug, "but sometimes we'll hit London."

Voorhees pulled up short, wondering if perhaps he had misunderstood. The two men turned to him as he rounded the corner. Although they said nothing, their expressions told him that he had not misheard or misunderstood anything. Voorhees nodded at them as he passed, wishing he could rewind the last thirty seconds, wishing he could have been a minute late to the meeting rather than a minute early.

During the last night that he saw either von Braun or Lisl, Voorhees was called to a gathering for the famous test pilot Hanna Reitsch. One of Hitler's die-hard supporters, Reitsch had arrived at Peenemünde earlier that day "to help with the latest V-1 tests." Voorhees, having heard that Hitler's pet aviator once crash-landed a glider into a stadium full of crazed Brazilian soccer fans, expected that the meeting might be interesting. (Now, at *Nostromo* Base, he was sorry that those soccer fans had not torn her to pieces.) He remembered hesitating outside the officer's mess hall, watching as the moon climbed nearly ten degrees up the sky, before he stepped inside. Voorhees understood, perhaps even more clearly than von Braun, that their great machines were being aimed at the wrong planet.

Y ou know, I never planned to become a test pilot," Hanna Reitsch had said. Voorhees noted that the famed aviatrix was a shade over five feet tall, slightly built, with close-cropped blond hair. "When I entered medical school," she continued, "my dream was to become a flying missionary doctor in Africa."

Several of the men chuckled but others might have been reminded of how the Treaty of Versailles had clipped Germany's wings in 1919. With her country's air force dismantled by decree, missionary work and gliders were two of the only ways that a German could ever hope to fly. Now she flew experimental aircraft, including a new class they were calling "jets."

She had stood in the Hearth Room of the officers' mess, surrounded by a crowd of approximately twenty mesmerized admirers, engineers and officers mostly. A few, though, stood away from the crowd. They detested this woman, solely because of the heights to which she had risen (literally and figuratively). Heights that they could never hope to attain—even as men.

"Time has a way of rewriting our decided paths," Reitsch said, "of setting us upon destinies we'd never planned for, or even dreamed of."

Thank God Lisl hadn't come, Voorhees thought. He knew that when Adolf Hitler ascended to power, the vivacious pilot quickly became one of his favorites. Her fame peaked after she piloted the world's first helicopter, whereupon the *Führer* himself appointed her an honorary flight captain. She was the first woman to garner such rank. *Now here she was in Peenemünde—far removed from gliders or soccer stadiums.*

"Destinies we'd never dreamed of," she emphasized. "Unfortunately, these are challenging times, my friends. So no more talk about me. I'm here with an announcement and a proposal. Some of you already know why I'm here, but I'll now make it official. This week I plan to test-fly a piloted version of the V-1, the V-1e."

There were audible gasps from some of the crowd but a few of the men stood by silently. They had either worked on the prototype before coming to Peenemünde or had heard about it from coworkers. Others, like Voorhees, were completely taken by surprise.

The gasps died away and after a moment the room went so silent that the grandfather clock in the corner could be heard emitting its single chime—forty-five minutes past midnight, forty-five minutes into the new day.

"Where is the cockpit?" someone asked rather meekly.

"On the fuselage, directly in front of the pulse engine," the test pilot replied.

There was a momentary pause, then it seemed that everyone present had a question or a comment.

"What about landing?"

" . . . or bailing out?"

" . . . with a flight time of only thirty-two minutes . . ."

" . . . and a range of only three hundred kilometers . . ."

" . . . putting severe limits on any potential targets!"

"Gentlemen, gentlemen," Reitsch said, raising her hands to calm the crowd. "*Understand*—again—that these are challenging times. But the *Führer*'s call is our sacred order! And now he calls on us to meet these challenges and to overcome them. The design of this craft is the product of the Luftwaffe's greatest minds."

That's what I was afraid of, three of the scientists thought, simultaneously.

"As approved by our brilliant *Führer,* a pair of V-1e's will hang below the wings of our bombers like mistletoe hangs from its host plant. The bomber will draw close to the target . . . then release her mistletoe. The pilot will steer the V-1e, lock on to the target, and then bail out. Since the V-1e will have been destroyed along with its target there will be no landing. You'll be happy to learn that just last week the *Führer* himself told me—"

"Bail out at six hundred kilometers per hour?" Voorhees interrupted. "From directly in front of the engine intake? What happens to the canopy? What happens to the pilot?"

There were several more audible gasps and many of the faces in the crowd turned toward Reitsch, expectantly. But the test pilot said nothing, and her silence told them everything they needed to know about the potential for a successful bailout.

Voorhees turned to the man next to him and spoke loud enough for everyone to hear, "That thing is a death trap *and* a piece of shit." *What am I doing?* he thought. *And why now? Am I losing my mind?*

The grumbling had grown louder now. Nobody had ever heard Voorhees speak like this. The officers present made a point of stepping away from the scientists. And the stepped-away-from scientists now regarded Voorhees as one might regard a stranger who had barged into a wedding.

No, I'm not *losing my mind,* Voorhees thought. *It's von Braun's words, getting to me. It's the Statue Man. It's Lisl.*

Hanna Reitsch shot Voorhees an icy stare that lasted only a second, then she was smiling again, as if his last comments had never been uttered. "Of course, I was the first to sign on, and as of a week ago I was pleased to report to our *Führer* himself that we have over one thousand volunteers."

Looking around, Voorhees could see that the pride in her voice contrasted with the mood in the room. There were no more questions, and many of those present were trying to think of excuses for hasty but less than obvious exits; the late hour or paperwork that suddenly needed shuffling.

"A thousand heroes! *Heil Hitler!*" Reitsch shouted, but for several seconds, there was no response, until a pair of officers snapped to attention and returned Reitsch's Nazi salute. However, their voices served only to emphasize the dread that had settled on the men. A few of the scientists appeared to be in shock and even the officers looked uncomfortable, shifting in place as if their boots had suddenly shrunk two sizes. No one said a word.

Voorhees shook his head, realizing at long last that the Dream was dead. And it had been ridiculous all along, now that he thought about it. For what was the Dream? Nordic mythology sewn together with romantic notions from the nineteenth-century? Jules Verne, H. G. Wells, and the Chariot of Odin arching toward Mars. *It was ridiculous and now it is over.* "A thousand suicides," he muttered, and turned away.

"*Heroes,* not suicides!" Reitsch snarled at him, the soft features of her face suddenly pulled tight. "The Leonidas Squadron!"

Voorhees took a deep breath, then let it out. He felt exhausted but turned to face the test pilot. "With all due respect *Flugkapitän* Reitsch, wasn't it King Leonidas who led the three hundred Spartans to their deaths at Thermopylae in 480 B.C.?"

Reitsch seemed surprised for an instant, then she smiled at the engineer. Voorhees thought, *This must be what a captured bird feels, just before the cat's nervous system initiates a death-dealing bite.*

"I took you for a coward," Reitsch said calmly, "but I see now that you are more than that. You are a coward who knows his military history."

Then the room trembled slightly and, as dust sifted down from the ceiling, they heard the wail of sirens.

Operation Hydra was, this night, at this point in history, the largest single bombing sortie ever carried out by the RAF. Currently, Voorhees and his colleagues were in the bull's-eye of nearly six hundred Halifax, Sterling, and Lancaster bombers. They were trying to kill him and as many of the other rocket men as possible. But now the party for Hanna Reitsch had intervened, putting many of them only steps away from a bomb shelter.

Voorhees, however, wasn't thinking about the bomb shelter. He emerged from the officers' mess with only one thought. *Lisl. I must find Lisl.*

Someone grabbed him, forcefully, by the arm. "This way!"

"I must find Lisl!"

"No time for this," the soldier said, and smacked him with a gun butt. "Come to your senses and get in."

Voorhees went down the concrete steps, half-stumbling, half-pushed. He heard the blast door slam shut above him, and then the six hundred giants came stampeding, directly overhead.

After an hour, Voorhees heard only the faint crackle of burning wood from above—thousands of tons of burning wood. The last of the enemy bombers had moved on, and soon after, a siren sounded the "all clear." Someone gave an order, "Everyone outside to help!"

Voorhees emerged into pitch black—even though the moon was full this night. The world was eerily quiet, considering all that had happened. The smoke made it hard to see, and even harder to breathe, but the red glow, burning through from every direction, gave the impression that every building had been destroyed.

The engineer looked around. Nobody was paying attention to him now.

Maurice Voorhees disappeared into the smoke.

I t had ended for Voorhees and Lisl much as it began—in a crater. The second and final crater had once been Lisl's dormitory but that building had disappeared—utterly disappeared. In the bowl of the crater, Voorhees had located tattered pieces of garments belonging to at least a dozen people, and broken crockery that turned out to be chips of bone. Hope forever died the moment he found a familiar shoe. It was spotlessly clean and still warm.

When two of Sänger's men found Voorhees, the morning after the RAF's Operation Hydra had reduced much of Peenemünde to a smoking ruin, they did not know if the man they had been ordered to ferry to the newly arrived *Demeter* would ever be right enough in his mind to be of any use again. They had looked down from the crater rim upon a man whose expression gave the impression of a scientist working on a difficult mathematical problem. Although their memory of the event would blend undetectably with the chaos of the weeks to come, their initial impression was perfectly correct. Maurice Voorhees, who had an ability to "walk around" the intricacies of a rocket engine in his head, with every aspect of its three-dimensional geometry intact, did not know how to collect Lisl—or how to bury her.

CHAPTER 18

Lifeline

*Too much sanity may be madness and the maddest of
all, to see life as it is and not as it should be.*
— MIGUEL DE CERVANTES

January 28, 1944
5 A.M.

Science had always been MacCready's refuge, but tonight, in his cell, not even
the *draculae*—his wonderfully obscene
discovery—could save him from sliding down again into darkness.

Not very far ahead of first light, the distant, fog-muffled
screams had ceased. Those who came and went in the night, removing the blood-spattered native woman from her cage, had neglected to shut off a lightbulb near the ceiling. Mac saw his own
shadow stretched across the floor. He did not fully believe that his
new bid to stay alive was going to succeed, and he was reasonably
certain that in a day or two, the shadow on the floor would be
that of another.

Little snatches of sleep came and went despite the interruptions. Survival instinct and prior mission experiences had seen to this, for the scientist knew he would need every watt of alertness and verbal sparring power if he ever got another audience with Wolff.

At least there are no draculae *in here,* he thought.

Outside, they, and not Wolff's soldiers, were the real agents of the night. In retrospect, Mac's contact with the creatures had been like receiving a personal message from the dark. He could not shake the feeling that sentient beings had surrounded him and looked right into his brain, using senses like those of some alien race. A bite from any of them was clearly deadlier than cobra venom, and yet there seemed an even more frightening intellectual quality about these beasts.

Why the fuck didn't they kill me? he wondered. *And how long until Wolff puts an end to my reprieve?*

He had determined to force himself into an hour or two of uninterrupted sleep, but the shrieks in the night allowed the zoologist's imagination to flit too easily over thoughts of what Wolff must have done to Bob and Yanni. After becoming slowly accustomed to how the war had erased everyone he loved, his brief reunion with Bob Thorne was an unexpected lifeline back into a saner world—back to humanity. The line had been cut the moment Wolff showed off the Russian machine gun, with its unmistakable signature of arctic camouflage. Until that moment, Mac really did feel as if he were becoming human again.

Now there was hardly anything left to live for. Nothing except revenge and the mission.

CHAPTER 19

Carrier

*Some of those who rush into this madness do not realize
that they are foolish, but think they are wise. . . . Do
not think of them as human beings, but consider them
as animals. For as animals devour each other, so also
people like this [shall] devour each other . . . since they
love the delights of fire, they are slaves of death.*

—GOSPEL OF DIDYMOS JUDAS THOMAS (FIRST CENTURY
A.D.)

January 28, 1944

5 A.M.

It was not the tragic way the boy had died
that kept Wolff and Kimura awake through
the night; it was not the disturbing manner
in which vascular and muscular systems had failed in the end,
causing the child to vomit up portions of his own stomach. What
kept the pair manically alert was the realization that these mani-
festations resembled disease processes. Wolff and Kimura, driven
by motives that would remain unknown to historians and anthropologists of the future, loved the delights of fire, and pes-

tilence, and human suffering. Trapped either by the genes that rendered them "born rotten," or by their times—or trapped by some obscene combination of both—they had willingly (indeed, gleefully) become slaves of death.

Colonel Wolff wore a puzzled expression as he stared down into the boy's lifeless eyes. "How can a human body sustain such bleeding?" Wolff asked the corpse. He paused, as if waiting for a reply, then turned his attention yet again to a pair of odd-looking wounds—half a centimeter across and located midway between the child's right ankle and the back of his knee. *Bitten from behind,* he thought, noting that the wounds were *still* oozing blood, so many hours later. *Why hadn't they—?*

The sound of a scalpel hitting the floor drew the colonel's attention to an adjacent table and he peered over the top of his surgical mask. *Clumsy heathens,* he thought. Nearly five hours had passed since his men had brought the bodies down from the hill. But even now, two members of Dr. Kimura's medical team, their isolation-suited arms buried below their elbows in gore, continued to probe the flayed-open remains of the old woman. Wolff knew that any ill feelings he might have harbored toward the Japanese scientist and his men were meaningless. What *was* important was the fact that they were clearly well versed in the biology and chemistry of death.

Wolff leaned in closer, examining the strange wounds again, this time with a hand lens. *They're not puncture wounds,* he thought, noting instead that divots of flesh had been removed with apparent surgical precision.

What could have done this?

Kimura entered the room carrying a tray of microscope slides and blood samples. Immediately, everyone, including Wolff, looked up from his work.

The odd-looking man said something in Japanese to his colleagues, who exchanged glances but made no reply. Kimura turned toward the colonel.

"This is no typical anticoagulant," he said in fluent German. "Not a chemical, as delivered by the bite of a leech or mosquito. In this case the bleeding was definitely caused by a bacterium."

"Then we *are* looking at an infection," Wolff said.

"Yes, and no," Kimura answered. Handing the tray to an assistant, the physician nodded toward the body of the boy. "The microbes entered through those cutaneous wounds," he explained. "Once inside the circulatory system, they initiated massive hemorrhaging, all within minutes. This process is absolutely unique."

Wolff spoke through his mask. "But the animal experiments we performed last night—none of the lab rats bled out after being inoculated with the boy's blood."

"Nor did the last of the American Rangers exhibit any ill effect when I repeated the experiment on him," Kimura added. "Our vivisection proved that. The young woman who was with the boy also remains uninfected, and I've injected her three times already."

"But if it is a microbe, then tell me why it isn't transmittable," Wolff demanded.

"Because the bacteria were already dead by the time we sampled the blood. What puzzles me is how the organism can work so quickly and on such a systemic scale. After the bite, it must divide—remarkably fast, according to my slides. Minutes later, the newly divided and thin-walled cells simply rupture, releasing a flood of whatever this hemorrhagic toxin is that they've produced. By the time a victim bleeds out, all of the microbes have died. Basically, the pathogen neutralizes itself."

"And the toxin?"

Kimura shrugged. "Apparently it gets used up or is quickly denatured by the body."

"Which is why their blood was useless as an infective agent?"

"Quite correct."

Wolff nodded thoughtfully. "But how can this microbe survive if it dies along with its host and what is its biological purpose?"

Kimura smiled. "Your men, and these two savages," he said, gesturing toward the corpses of the old woman and the child, "they were never hosts." Then the disease-warrior paused, seeming to savor his secret for one final moment. "They were *prey*."

Kimura crossed over to an acrylic glass window—a portal looking out at what appeared to be an endless wall of fog and trees. "The host is out there somewhere," he said. "Although 'carrier' would be a far more accurate description."

"Carrier?"

"Yes, a snake or scorpion. Something that bites, something we haven't seen yet. A carrier that allows the bacterium to live in its mouth."

"You are describing an endosymbiont, correct?"

"Precisely," Kimura replied. "Just like our intestinal flora. These hemorrhagic microbes thrive and multiply within their carrier-animal, essentially getting a warm, safe place to live until—"

Wolff's eyes widened. "—until the host bites its prey, transmitting some of the bacteria to the wound."

Kimura smiled again. "Then the pathogen upholds its side of the bargain, causing the prey to bleed out, thus providing food for the carrier, which apparently feeds on the blood."

Both men took pause, simultaneously contemplating the same unspoken question.

It was Kimura who spoke first. "It seems, Colonel, as though our choice for a rocket launch site might be fortuitous for a completely unexpected reason. If we can culture fresh microbial spores, we may have a payload far more terrifying, far more efficient, and far more demoralizing in its effects than the anthrax and the bubonic plague we have been planning to employ."

"A big 'if,' Doctor, especially given our time constraints," Wolff added, but his mind was racing. "Can you recover *anything* from the blood of these two?"

Kimura shook his head. "Nothing but dead, ruptured bacteria. What we need is a fresh source of the active microbes. What we need is—"

"—one of the carriers."

"Yes, and we'll need it alive, whatever it is."

Wolff made no reply. His mind had already reviewed the previous morning's incident on the deck of the *Nostromo,* as well as his most recent conversation with the very same Corporal Kessler.

The colonel peeled off his surgical gloves, threw down his rubber apron and mask, then headed for the door at a brisk pace. "Come with me, Doctor," he called over his shoulder as he exited the lab. "You may find this interesting."

"Perhaps you have figured out a way to untangle our sister boat," Kimura responded in his native language, and under his breath. The doctor thought he heard one of his assistants give a short chuckle at the Nazi-directed sarcasm, but by the time he glanced over, they had all resumed their grisly work.

"Ten minutes ago I solved our most vexing problem!" Kimura shouted at them. "The Nazi had been as clueless as a newborn. I solved it!"

None of his men looked up.

"But now, here he is, issuing orders as though it had been his idea all along."

For a fleeting moment, the Japanese biologist pictured the pristine conditions of his laboratory in Manchuria—*the gleaming surgical instruments, the limitless supply of test subjects. A place where no one gave me orders.*

He allowed himself a brief sigh, and then struggled to catch up with the German officer, his wooden clogs tapping out a rhythm that increased in tempo as he sped up. The ungrateful Nazi was apparently heading toward the "woodshed," where they stored the *maruta.*

There had been no beating. Not even another threat of becoming part of the rocket's red glare. And when the colonel arrived, it wasn't the enormous SS sergeant who accompanied him, but a strangely clad Japanese civilian. *This is promising,* MacCready thought.

"Corporal Kessler tells me you know what has been killing my men," the officer said.

MacCready wondered just how many of Wolff's men had been killed. *And with this kind of high-level personal interest, evidently it was a bunch.*

"That's right," MacCready said. "I was studying them when one of your local thugs decided to plug me with a dart."

"Save your zoology story, Captain MacCready," Wolff said with a smirk. "We know why you were sent here."

MacCready managed a smirk of his own.

The German continued. "In any event, we are men of science and this is a situation that calls for . . . adaptation. As such, I am making you a new offer. Help us hunt down the creatures that killed my men. Help us find and destroy these *blut kinder.*"

"Or?"

"Or this morning, instead of accompanying us, Sergeant Schrödinger will turn you over to the very same locals who have already found you to be such an exceptional dart target."

This time MacCready feigned uneasiness (which was pretty damn easy to do). But in reality they both knew that Wolff's offer was a no-brainer. And in fact it was *exactly* what he had been hoping for. It was his only chance. *Even if I can't make a clean escape after leading them to the* draculae, *maybe I can somehow get the word out to Hendry before I die.*

Wolff let out a short laugh that MacCready found unnerving, considering its source. "I know exactly what you are thinking," the colonel said. "So, yes, help us to track down and eliminate these pests and, who knows . . . perhaps you will escape."

Perhaps I will, asshole, MacCready thought, but he allowed Wolff the last word.

"Then we will hunt *you*."

E ven though the temperature inside the dead tree was a perfect 104 degrees Fahrenheit (with a humidity of nearly 100 percent), the mother found it impossible to sleep. Her movements eventually woke the child, who scrambled over to hang by her side. She responded by regurgitating a small measure of biped blood from the pouchlike portion of her stomach, where it had remained undigested—an emergency reserve system that characterized all vampire bat species. The child instinctively leaned in. Vibrating with anticipation, he drew nearer, face-to-face, and fed from the pool in her mouth. When the child had finished, he pulled away and hung silently, drifting back toward sleep. Not a single drop had fallen into the dark cavity that stretched below them.

The mother knew that the bipeds had become more difficult to hunt and their strange behavior was a clear indicator that they were now aware of her family's presence. The bipeds no longer walked the forest at night. But more alarming than this was the scent of fear that spread from their strange nests into the surrounding trees.

There was another problem that kept the mother awake long into the pre-dawn hours. She was losing control of the twins. While this was a normal part of their maturation process, the unexpected presence of the intruders in such alarming numbers was making the twins' newly acquired independence even more difficult to direct. Their latest encounter with the bipeds on the hillside above the river had been the turning point, and now her maternal instincts had led her to a decision.

She emitted a series of clicks that instantly aroused the twins as well as the blood-groggy child.

NO FOOD DANGEROUS BIPEDS

The child shivered and moved in closer, while the female twin remained motionless. The male twin, however, responded by unfurling and stretching his wings in succession. As his sibling watched, the bat took a sudden interest in a kink of wing membrane and deftly smoothed it out with his teeth.

Undeterred by this show of defiance, the mother released a directional pheromone from a pair of glands near the base of her wings, signaling a return to the Stone Cave, their ancestral roost.

This time however, the male abandoned his feigned lack of interest, hissing an angry response.

There was a flash of movement and the mother shifted position, sensing the male's rapid approach from below. Instinctively, she spun toward him, mouth open, teeth glistening.

But instead of attacking, the male brushed past her, using his elongated thumbs to hoist himself toward the rim of the tree cavity. He was nearly full-size now, and she did a quick sidestep to avoid contact with his muscular body.

She felt a brief downdraft of air . . . then listened to a stream of navigation calls, moving away rapidly . . . fading . . . gone.

A moment later, the female twin scrabbled up the steep cork wall on the opposite side of the cavity. Just before reaching the opening, she turned and let out a single hiss. There was a flutter of movement from above and a brief rain of dislodged bark. The other twin had decided to join its sibling.

The child sidled in closer, seeking the comfort of the mother's body. But without thinking, she bit him on the ear, harder than she had ever bitten him before. He responded with a cry of pain, and the release of fear pheromone.

The mother scrambled up through the top of the trunk, intent to begin a search for the twins, but the search was thwarted even before it began. The air directly overhead had become a confused and crowded maelstrom of insects in flight. Moths of all sizes were descending from the treetops, whirling past each other and warping the mother's echolocation calls with close-up reflections from every direction. Adding to the confusion was the sudden arousal of miniature, insect-eating bats, scores of them; their echolocation calls were making it harder to interpret the information returning from her own sonar pings. The mother had experienced such swarms many times before and knew that communication would be difficult. This time, though, she decided that she could not wait.

FOLLOW, the mother signaled to her child, then scrambled upward.

The child emerged through the top of the dead tree and launched himself into the disorienting cloud of insects and their noisy hunters. His ear still stung from her bite; and now anger and pain were spilling over into a new emotion—defiance. Probing ahead with calls of his own, he could sense his mother's panic as she stiffened her wings and glided below the maelstrom, searching in vain for the twins. There was nothing to be seen below the reflective moth layer.

The child had also come down below the swarm, but suddenly his signals, radiating from behind her, ceased abruptly. The mother executed a tight roll and flew back into her own slipstream but the child was no longer following her. Without any warning or cry, without any signal at all, he simply disappeared.

CHAPTER 20

The Hungry Earth

Whence do you come, slayer of men; or where are you going, conqueror of space?
　　—GOSPEL OF MARY (APPROXIMATELY FIRST CENTURY A.D.)

Nostromo Base
January 28, 1944
8 A.M.

The seven soldiers, standing in a rough cluster, snapped to attention as Colonel Wolff approached. He acknowledged them with a nod, then ordered them to stand at ease.

Beside each man sat a heavy field pack and Wolff knew that in addition to their normal supplies, his team would have tucked away some rather specialized equipment—lamps designed by the local Indians and enough Nazi firepower to slaughter every living creature larger than a squirrel within a two-hundred-meter radius.

"According to our indigenous friends," Wolff announced, "our men were attacked by demons that townspeople refer to as *chupacabra*. These 'monsters' are said to inhabit a cave deep within the plateau. It seems that they have taken exception to our presence here."

The colonel paused, scanning the group, looking into each man's eyes. He took satisfaction from the fact that, as absurd as his statement might have sounded, none of them had so much as flinched, nor did they raise a single question. *Schrödinger . . . Vogt . . . these are not men who would question anything I have deemed important enough to tell them.*

Wolff gave another nod, barely perceptible this time, before continuing. "According to our terminally obnoxious American guest, the locals are mistaken. The creatures that killed our countrymen are *not* demons; they are blood-feeding animals the size of large cats. Animals possessing no more supernatural abilities than those of a leech or a tick."

Wolff continued. "As much as it pains me, I find that I must agree with the American, a zoologist as it turns out. In truth, he seems to know something about these creatures." Then he turned toward the increasingly haunted Kessler. "And like you, Corporal, he has apparently seen them."

Haunted or not, the colonel never considered leaving Kessler behind. In addition to the man's firsthand "experience" with the creatures, he also spoke fluent English. This would come in handy, since the American would be accompanying them and, together, Wolff and Kessler could play the old American trick, called "good cop, bad cop," all the way to the *chupacabra* lair. *On a one-way trip,* Wolff thought, having already spoken to Sergeant Schrödinger about that particular arrangement, once MacCready successfully led them to the creatures.

"Our mission is a simple one," the colonel went on. "With the aid of two local guides, we will find this cave, collect one of these animals, several if possible, and return them here, alive."

Wolff watched Kessler shift his weight uncomfortably, and once again he addressed the man directly. "Since the success of the entire mission may depend on our ability to procure these specimens, we cannot fail."

They exchanged "Heil Hitlers," but Wolff did not dismiss his men. "There *is* one more thing," he continued. "Something of equal importance. As far as our prisoner knows, this is a mission of extermination, not capture. And it must remain as such, in his mind."

Then the colonel locked eyes with his longtime underling. "Sergeant Schrödinger."

The giant came to attention.

"Retrieve the prisoner. We leave for the plateau in fifteen minutes."

As the sun climbed within an hour of high noon, R. J. Mac-Cready emerged from the dense forest into a clearing. He took the opportunity to sneak another backward glance, but as before, the SS sergeant was still there, machine gun trained at the center of his back. Since their departure, Mac had been trying hard not to think about the consequences of the Big Guy tripping over a root or getting bitten by a wasp. Instead, he concentrated on the visual inventory he had made before leaving the German camp: heavy equipment, piles of supplies, and a shitload of construction going on, all of it well hidden by the forest and the damnable fog that shrouded the valley. Then there was the fuel, stored in huge pressurized tanks. His overall impression was that the site's high secrecy quotient had *something* to do with the strange missile they'd fired at the recon plane. *But why set up a base here?* he wondered. *Whatever they're up to, they're building something big.*

MacCready now feared that weapons similar to the guided interceptor that had taken down the recon plane were being prepared to reach out from Brazil. And whatever the specifics of their plan might be, he knew that he had to escape, or at least get this information back to Hendry. *Especially now that Bob and Yanni are gone,* he thought.

Although it could never make up for the murder of his friends, he took some satisfaction in the knowledge that the Germans had suffered their own casualties at the hands of the *draculae.* Just as important, he knew that these deaths had made Wolff and his pals extremely eager to learn the real identity of the creatures, a fact that was currently keeping him alive.

At this point, what harm would come of identifying the phantoms to his enemies? It was the sort of information that he could barter safely in the hope of completing his mission, in time to prevent them from completing theirs—*whatever that is.* In a horrible run of misfortune and tragedy, this had indeed become a bit of good fortune.

Up ahead, the front half of Wolff's group had stopped beside a river. It was about forty feet wide and although the water appeared to be no more than waist-deep, the current was moving at a fairly dangerous clip.

He could see that the two local guides, who had gone ahead of the group several minutes earlier, were already standing on the far bank. One of them was using his bow to point out a presumably safe path for Wolff and the others to follow across the boulder-strewn waterway.

One by one, the members of Wolff's hunting party hoisted their packs higher and waded in at the indicated spot, soon leaving only MacCready and his hulking escort to bring up the rear.

MacCready scanned the far bank. He found it odd that the second guide had moved to a position slightly upstream from his friend and the continuation of the trail.

What's this guy up to?

The Indian stood on the rocks and waited until the Germans were distracted by the precarious crossing, then he let loose a stream of his own.

Nice move, MacCready thought, his gaze tracking from the arc of urine to the place where Wolff's men were making their way across the stream. He slowed down just enough to avoid a shove into the current from the hulk, allowing time enough for the end results of the guide's "private salute" to pass downstream.

MacCready had waded about halfway across when unexpectedly one of the soldiers approaching the far bank began screaming and thrashing about violently. Everyone else froze for a moment, but just as quickly weapons were drawn and each man scanned a section of tree line for signs of an ambush.

Meanwhile, the weight of the stricken soldier's pack had flipped him onto his back like a turtle, allowing MacCready and the others to see that he was clutching at the front of his pants. The man began to float downriver.

Before the soldier could drift very far, though, Colonel Wolff shouted something and two men splashed over and intercepted their frantic comrade. Grabbing him under the arms, the pair staggered the last ten feet to the shore. There the screaming man immediately fell to the ground and began tearing at the buttons of his field pants.

Instinctively, MacCready checked to see if the sudden commotion might have sidetracked the SS sergeant. As expected, the giant had maintained not only his distance but also his concentration.

The American gave Schrödinger his best "who, me?" and continued across the river. When Mac emerged from the water, a small crowd had gathered around the agonized soldier.

As MacCready watched, two Germans forcibly held the man down while one of the guides drew an obsidian blade from a leather scabbard. Not surprisingly, the screaming man became even more terrified as the knife-wielding Indian moved toward him with a menacing grimace. Then, in one swift motion, the guide slit open the soldier's pants, but not the soldier himself. There followed another blur of movement and this time the man's underpants were sliced open. Immediately the group seemed to take a collective step backward, but their retreat had nothing to do with modesty or embarrassment. To everyone present it appeared as if the screaming man was wrestling with his own penis.

"*Es ist in meinem penis!*" the man screamed, and a moment later those standing close enough (too close, actually) got a look at exactly *what* the man was wrestling with.

Even MacCready got a glimpse—just long enough for him to see that the tail section of a tiny fish was protruding from the soldier's besieged beanpole.

"*Es ist in meinem penis!*" he screamed again, his eyes wide, imploring someone to help—at which point, one of the man's friends did step forward; but as he did so, the fish gave a violent wiggle. As the would-be rescuer watched, the visible portion of the creature seemed to shorten considerably and it worked its way another inch further *upstream*. Now only the wriggling tail fin was exposed.

Colonel Wolff stepped away from the chaotic scene and addressed the guides in Portuguese: "*Qual é aquela coisa?*"

"*Ele é um candiru,*" one of them replied.

"Oh shit," MacCready muttered, though apparently not quietly enough.

The colonel spun toward him. "What?"

"I'm pretty sure he said it's a candiru."

"And what is this . . . candiru?"

"A parasitic catfish, *Vandellia cirrhossa*."

"A catfish?"

"Yeah, they usually attack larger fish, latch on to their gills, then feed on the blood pumping through them. Very messy eaters."

"But what is this fish doing *inside* him?"

"Candiru get excited at the scent of urine," MacCready said. "Probably because it's full of the same nitrogen compounds their prey excrete from their gills. Fish don't urinate."

As Wolff turned back toward his men, MacCready glanced over at the guides. "Walks with Empty Bladder" was now casually scanning the sky, as if searching for rain clouds or maybe butterflies. MacCready had to suppress a chuckle. "Your man must have relieved himself while he was wading across the stream," he announced. "His new pal evidently took a wrong turn at Willy's willy."

"And how do we get this . . . *parasite* out of him?" Wolff asked.

Mac shook his head. "From what I hear, there's only one way to remove a candiru."

"And what is that?"

The American responded by making a scissoring motion with his index and middle fingers.

Now it was one of the guides who turned away, feigning disgust but in reality hiding a grin.

Less than five minutes later, the expedition resumed its trek toward the plateau—minus the traumatized soldier. Private Schoeppe had been sent back to *Nostromo* Base, limping, whimpering, and desperately clutching one end of a string that had been fastened around the base of the candiru's tail fin. He had also been given instructions for the "necessary surgery."

"Now, that guy's going to have a serious story to tell if he ever gets home from the war," MacCready said to no one in particular.

Just up ahead, Corporal Kessler turned back for a moment, "You are right, MacCready, but I think it will be a *short* story."

The American smiled, suppressing the urge to keep the exchange going for fear of getting coldcocked again by his outsize SS buddy.

T he Indian guides also watched as the sad-looking *warazu* stumbled past them. They had neglected to tell the strangers that there was indeed another remedy for a candiru attack. This one involved inserting a potion made from the unripe fruit of the *jagua* plant into the stricken orifice. The extract killed the candiru and dissolved its body, allowing the remains to be urinated out within a day or two.

"Such a common plant," one of the men said, shaking his head and grinning.

"I have seen many of them this day," said the other. Then he turned and slashed at something growing across the trail.

S ix hours earlier, in his lab, Maurice Voorhees had his second encounter with the *blut kinder*—then decided not to tell anyone about it. Finding Kessler gone, and with no one giving him even the vaguest reason why Wolff had taken the soldier away into the forest, it seemed to Voorhees that the better part of valor would be to keep his mouth shut. Speaking about what he knew of future propulsion systems had already gotten him into trouble.

Talking about *known unknowns* might be even worse. What he did know was that Kessler's unknown phantoms were not only efficient killers but skilled infiltrators as well.

Independently Wolff had come to suspect the same thing. Before he left, he issued a command that the perimeter patrols were to be pulled inward to the vital nerve centers of *Nostromo* Base. The most efficient use of manpower, logic dictated, was to reduce the overall surface area of the defensive lines, primarily to the three buildings where the final stages of chemical manufacture, sled and rocket testing, and—soon—payload development were racing toward completion.

As an extra precaution against intrusions by the phantoms, there were now four armed observers on the roof of each shed, keeping watch by aid of the latest copies of MI-5's infrared binoculars. If these creatures were warm-blooded, as Kimura seemed to be convinced, any possibility of them scrabbling unseen, onto or into the buildings, could be eliminated or at least greatly diminished. The premise seemed to be that the apparent cunning and stealth of the night visitors could be counterbalanced by excessive vigilance. Wolff was evidently betting on the superiority of the human mind.

This should have been a good bet. But on the same morning Schrödinger woke the American prisoner for a trek to the night stalkers' lair, Voorhees missed the first breakfast call, having worked through the night and even through his shift break. Then, while his machinists were released for breakfast, and as the predawn fog crept in toward high tide, something else came into the *warazu* compound—undetected.

For several days, virtually all of Voorhees's thoughts had been concentrated on increasing the range of the *Silverbirds*. Sänger's original designs fell short of the efficiencies necessary to overfly their targets, and the new "bottle rocket" boosters, for all their power, were not quite enough to make up the difference. Now Voorhees had the machinists stripping and scraping away every sacrificeable gram of mass from the two space-planes. By doing so he hoped to further extend their range, thus giving their pilots at least some small chance of not having to eject from their ships or letting them crash unguided into mountains, enemy territory, or even the sea.

Reducing mass meant that the pilots would carry neither food nor water; no life rafts, no survival kits—nothing weightier than whatever could be fit into the cushion at the pilot's back and neck (which would serve double duty as a life vest). Even the backup parachutes had been eliminated, all in the hope of extending flight range, all in the hope that a skid-crash on a friendly runway, with empty fuel tanks, might save the ships. "The Leonidas Maneuver," he would call it. *Reitsch would love that one.* Voorhees removed metric tons by stripping out the landing gear, along with its associated bracing and hydraulics. Still . . . each rocket would have fallen short of its safe haven by at least a thousand kilometers. Adding to the difficulties, they were now completely out of materials with which they could manufacture another batch of solid, aluminum-based propellants. Voorhees, however, discovered that he could make up for the shortfall with a newer and very carefully mixed set of chemicals, set into a cowl of tanks, or pods, paired near the tail of each bird. These hypergolic propellant pods were fueled by two substances that so hated the presence of each other that, when combined, their simultaneous combustion provided almost as much thrust as the bottle rocket boosters.

The real problems lay in the extreme toxicity of the two propellants, and in keeping the pilot from being anywhere near them. The fuel had a power to scorch human flesh with a ferocity that reminded him of mustard gas. And that was the *milder* half of the formula. The fuel oxidizer, if splashed onto a block of ice, would set the ice itself afire.

Nonetheless, Voorhees and Sänger were confident that both components could be safely contained and pumped into the appropriate thrust chambers by a simple throttle control. And so as Colonel Wolff began mapping a secret expedition to the plateau, and as the mother *draculae* lost her child in a cloud bank of moths, Maurice Voorhees finished testing the leakproof construction of the final propellant tank. Now Sänger's rocket bombers would reach their destinations.

Such simplicity, he thought, with a distinctly prideful feeling. *I could fly this craft my—*

Voorhees realized that he was no longer alone.

At first, there had been an inexplicable sense of calm, but immediately, a part of his mind screamed out to him, that the sudden intensity of a deep, penetrating peace was thoroughly unnatural in a place like this.

GENTLE

His gloved hand relaxed, and slipped down a notch against a helium nozzle that supplied pressure to the test equipment.

Voorhees turned his head; despite what his other senses were detecting, among them the out-of-place scent of gardenias, his eyes were showing him that he still appeared to be alone.

"Is that you again?" he asked, already knowing the answer. "Where are you?"

In that instant, a sonic search beam probed Voorhees to depths he failed to understand. He felt naked, and alone, and revealed. The unnatural sense of peace was suddenly in conflict with the new vibrations that were reaching through him, as if both sensations were born of a subtle clumsiness—and which in one awkward moment produced a sense of alarm. His eyes ticked back and forth, up and down, looking from walls to ceiling and down to the floor. No one and nothing was there.

The refreshing feeling of a soft, inner touch washed over him again, as if in sudden response to the aberrant wave of uneasiness.

GENTLE

Voorhees could not resist. Though he heard voices he knew could not exist, the overmastering calm refused to leave him. And finally, it became the voice of his mother, creeping into his skull.

He was suddenly more tired than he thought possible, and more nauseous than he had been since his dressing down from Wolff two days earlier. He put a gloved hand to his stomach, and started to relent.

The voice in his head was changing, now—not his mother any longer, but Lisl.

GENTLE

"Dear God," he whispered. The beast tried to push deeper, tried to keep him under control, but all Voorhees could visualize now was Lisl as he had last seen her: naked white ribs and scraps of spine that were never meant to be seen by a loved one.

"No!" he shouted, and moved his hand toward the helium pressure valve. He glanced down. The . . . *thing* had been barely more than a meter away the whole time. Four slender limbs, two of them bound in black membranes, anchored the creature to the underside of Voorhees's workbench.

Then he looked into the *blut kinder*'s eyes. They were not expressionless, like the eyes of a snake, or a shark. Quite the opposite: This was the face of a sentient being, one who was simultaneously gazing into him with curiosity, as if asking questions of its own. It craned its little head upward and nearer.

You're smaller than I thought you would be, Voorhees told himself, and he began to believe it looked far too thin and tame to be dangerous.

Fool me once, shame on you. Fool me twice—

His hand hit the valve, jetting a microburst of helium laced with a red misting of propellant across his glove and across the table, and near the creature's face. It managed to shield itself with a wing before the burst could brush over its eyes.

Initially, Voorhees had cursed his carelessness for somehow letting the beast creep literally under his nose without notice. But now he could understand how he had failed to detect its approach. It was impossibly fast, and just as impossibly silent. Only during a panicked pivot and a dash to the far side of the shed did its claws make any scratching sounds at all.

Voorhees coughed and bolted toward the front door, which he kicked open.

The creature managed to cover the same distance at least three times faster than the scientist and flitted through the same door. The beast ran with such astonishing fluidity that Voorhees's eyes and mind were unable to truly follow it.

The guards outside, unfortunately, had the same problem. In that moment, they could never have aimed and fired at the intruder with any hope of clipping it. In the end, the men never saw the creature, taking aim at Voorhees instead. And it would have ended there for him, as he burst through the door into open air, if one of the more observant and agile sentries had not slapped his partner's gun away from the engineer's direction, causing it to fire harmlessly into the sky.

Only moth dust fluttered down. Silent.

CHAPTER 21

And You Shall Fight Legends

No use wasting your bullets, Martin. They cannot harm that bat.

—*Dracula* (THE MOTION PICTURE), 1931

R. J. MacCready had long suspected that the Europeans' first encounters with vampire bats in the New World must have contributed to vampire lore in general, and to the vampire's mythical association with bats in particular.

Although stories about bloodsucking bats began to circulate in Europe soon after Columbus's third voyage, in 1498, it was Hernán Cortés and his Conquistadores who were likely the first Europeans to come into direct contact with them. The creature known to MacCready as *Desmodus rotundus,* the common vampire bat, was not much larger than a hamster, but Portuguese Jesuits, returning to Europe from the New World tropics, spoke of them as if they were as large and fierce as spawn of the devil. Historians dismissed the accounts. Now, with *Desmodus draculae,* the common vampire's outsize cousin, evidently still very much alive, Mac wondered if the legends of shapeshifting, man-bat vampires—which had spread through Europe by 1725—might actually have been helped along by sightings of a South American version, the *chupacabra.* By the end of the nineteenth century, a London theater manager by the name of Abraham Stoker had taken the swift and cunning titular creature from John Polidori's tale "The Vampyre" and transformed it into his masterpiece: *Dracula*.

And so, as MacCready saw it, a story begun by frightened sailors and priests had spread to Europe and come back to the New World in the early twentieth century, ably aided by Bela Lugosi on the silver screen. It seemed only natural to Mac, if also delightfully ironic, that when bone fragments from an Ice Age cave in nearby Venezuela were identified as belonging to an unusually large vampire bat of the genus *Desmodus,* science would come full circle—christening the species *draculae.*

Lost City of the Mato Grosso

JANUARY 29, 1944

On the second day of their trek, by the time the sun began climbing down the sky, Wolff's party was already following the narrow, weathered trail that led up the cliff face. During their infrequent rest periods, MacCready tried to admire the view, especially the strange stone carvings. They were everywhere, but with his hands still bound, and a gun muzzle pressed against his back, he figured that this particular trek was no place for sightseeing. In fact, he found that climbing the steep trail was an even bigger pain in the ass than stream crossings had been.

The two Indian guides led them halfway up the plateau, finally stopping outside a vertical slash in the stone. MacCready noticed that nobody, least of all the guides, seemed very excited at the prospect of entering. And to judge by the reaction of these local "pranksters," this was the entryway they had been searching for—a portal into the lair of the *draculae*.

One of the soldiers opened the backpack he had been carrying and produced a trio of odd-looking lanterns. To MacCready, they resembled a homemade version of something one might find at a campsite, except that these candle-based lamps cast their beams through translucent shells that had been dyed red.

MacCready nodded in recognition. It was similar to a lighting method used by researchers to study nocturnal mammals. They were wisely counting on the *draculae*'s visual system being similar to other creatures of the night—insensitive to red light. Heat was another issue altogether, and the locals who had advised the soldiers in their choice of supplies must have learned this, long ago. The interior of each lantern was cleverly insulated, in such manner that the candle's heat was blocked from warming the lantern's outer surfaces, letting out only the red light, and a narrow streamer of warm air that could be detected only directly overhead.

We'll see the bats but they won't see us. Hopefully.

He glanced over at the guides who were currently in discussion with Wolff, evidently assuring him that the lantern lights could not be seen by the *blut kinder*.

Now, how the hell did these guys know that?

MacCready also noticed that the powwow had gotten rather animated, and that whatever Wolff was selling, the pair apparently wanted no part of it.

He watched the German stalk away from the guides, who had definitely held their ground. *Even if they do wear their hair like Moe Howard,* Mac told himself, *they are fucking far from stooges.* In fact, they seemed to be the only ones who knew exactly what they were all up against.

The colonel spent several minutes quietly briefing his men, and in response, most of them whipped off their packs and began to hunker down along a ten-foot-wide lip of stone, cut into the cliff—an entranceway into the plateau. Although he could not see very far inside, MacCready could tell that the portal had been modified, centuries ago, into a wide antechamber that narrowed dramatically, beyond which the far walls transitioned from shadow to impenetrable black.

He sidled awkwardly up to Corporal Kessler, who was sitting with his back against the cliff. "What's going on here?"

"The guides will go no farther," Kessler replied. "They said that the people of the Forbidden City were exterminated by the gods; but that if we enter this place there would be no gods—only demons. Only *chupacabra*."

"And?"

"And so most of us will remain outside for now."

Now that's a relief, MacCready thought. As dangerous as the *draculae* were, they were also a fascinating zoological phenomenon; as such, he did not exactly relish the idea of watching as Wolff firebombed or machine-gunned the bat roost into oblivion, before he, himself, was put to death.

Another of Wolff's men barked out an order in their direction and Corporal Kessler responded with a halfhearted salute.

"Seems as if you, MacCready, will get to see the *blut kinder* again."

"How's that?" the American asked, and for the first time, he saw something that passed for satisfaction on Kessler's face.

The corporal drew a knife and motioned for MacCready to turn around, then he cut the leather band that had bound his hands together. "Because you are going in there with Colonel Wolff." He lowered his voice. "And your friend, Sergeant Frankenstein."

◆ ◆ ◆

Horizontal line His hands now free, MacCready led the way, carrying one of
the three Indian lanterns. He was followed by his SS shadow,
while the colonel brought up the rear.

Twenty yards into the cave's spacious antechamber the natural
rock walls funneled into a narrow corridor of hand-hewn stone.
MacCready paused, but an immediate increase in pressure from
the sergeant's gun muzzle was all the prompting he needed to keep
going.

At four feet wide and extending not much higher than the
top of his head, the claustrophobic passageway was covered with
eroded pictographs and paintings—the remnants of a lost plateau
culture. Although unable to examine the walls except in passing,
MacCready was still fascinated by the strange markings, animated
as they were by a flickering, crimson-tinted light that would have
made Dante feel right at home. He wondered if Fawcett, the lost
English explorer, had made it this far—or perhaps had died here.

Deeper into the corridor, a grunt from behind caused the American to smile briefly. "Watch your head, Sergeant," he whispered,
before a "shhhh" from Colonel Wolff silenced him.

Besides the inscriptions, MacCready found something else
about the cave that seemed odd. A flow of air blew past them as
they moved, sometimes barely perceptible, at other times a humid
breeze that carried the scent of something distinctly organic.

It's as if the plateau itself were breathing, MacCready thought.

Several minutes later, the unlikely trio located the source of the
"breath." The hot air was wafting up through a circular, manhole-
size opening in the rock floor, rimmed by carefully cut-and-placed
stones. The smell was strongest here as well—acrid and almost
painful to inhale, and now MacCready knew *exactly* what it was.

He knelt down to peer over the rim and felt Wolff move in beside him. It might have been a perfect time to flip the Nazi into the abyss if not for that fact that Sergeant Schrödinger had remained standing, with his back pressed firmly against the far wall, and with his machine gun barrel aimed directly at MacCready's head.

"What is that smell?" Wolff whispered.

"Guano," MacCready whispered back. "Bat shit, with a chaser of bat piss. That's the ammonia."

"The creatures, the ones who killed my people, they are down there?"

MacCready shrugged his shoulders. "Not sure yet," he replied, hoping that his acting ability was holding up. "I need you to hold on to my legs," he said, very quietly. Then, as carefully and stealthily as possible, he slid down on his belly and extended a lantern into the chasm.

As the American stretched his upper body deeper into the hole, he felt Wolff's iron grip around his ankles. What he could not see was the look exchanged between the colonel and Sergeant Schrödinger.

F ive wingspans from the point at which MacCready's lantern sent forth a rusty red circle of light, the mother slept. The child was also asleep, though fitfully so. His position, well away from his mother and the others, was a new and serious development. There was a raspy sound coming from deep inside his chest, and a sick smell from one of his wings. He was beginning to suffer from the blast of gas directed at him in the biped nest.

The child would either heal or he would die, but until then he would be isolated from the others in the roost.

Nearby, the lead male awoke with a cramp in his right shoulder. He had been dreaming about the bipeds.

The strange sounds they made before they died.
The taste of their blood.

The thought made him shiver with something like anticipation, and he began to unfold his wings.

T he entire top half of MacCready's body was now hanging into the subchamber, and with the lantern extended downward, he squinted to see beyond the blood-red glow. For a moment, there was nothing but glare, but then his eyes became acclimated. He saw a ledge along one side of the hole, perhaps five feet wide, but then it fell away, dropping thirty feet to the floor of the cave, a floor that was littered with ancient bones.

It's a tomb . . . or a sacrificial chamber, his darker side added, even as the shadows began to play tricks on his mind. *It had to be the shadows,* he thought, because for a moment it almost seemed as if the bones were—

MacCready nearly dropped the lantern.

—*moving.*

And in the next moment he *knew* that it was not his imagination.

The floor of the subchamber was slowly roiling like warm, convecting tar. Disarticulated skeletons, darkly stained, writhed in a sea of semisolid matter that seemed to be alive itself. Even worse, there were the sounds: the bones clicking and scraping against each other as the mass tumbled slowly over itself. A skull surfaced like the head of a drowning man in a bottomless pool. But what poured out of the eye sockets wasn't water. *It was*—

Something registered in MacCready's brain. Something familiar.

The smell above; the movement below.

He remembered a similar scene, minus the telltale evidence of a lost civilization, deep inside a cave in upstate New York.

MacCready let out the breath he forgot he'd been holding, realizing that ancient human remains were being animated by millions upon millions of insect larvae, larvae that were thriving in a dark layer of organic tar and bodily fluids that was constantly being renewed from—

—*above.*

But that means . . .

MacCready swung the beam slowly higher, and peered across the ceiling of the tomb. Hanging in utter silence was the source of the beetles' feast: a hundred dark silhouettes.

Like giant Christmas tree ornaments.

In the dim red light, one of the fusiform shapes unfurled, revealing wings ten feet across.

Catching a glimpse of the creature's head in profile, Mac-Cready was reminded of something the half-mad Lieutenant Scott had said: "No more doggie on the ceiling." But only now did the real meaning of that statement become clear.

A hell of a time to figure this out, he thought, his mind quickly transitioning to more immediate concerns. MacCready slowly moved his free arm up through the opening, waving his hand in a circular motion that he hoped would translate to "Pull me the hell up—*now!*"

It did.

"Time to get out of here," he whispered to Wolff, keeping his eyes on the opening in the floor even as he crab-walked away from it. "*Very quietly* out," he added.

"What did you see? What are they?" Wolff whispered back, but he did not move.

"They're bats, Colonel. Big, fucking vampire bats."

"Fascinating. They are mating?"

"No. Surviving," MacCready replied. "And doing a better job of it than we're gonna do, if they figure out we're up here."

"And this is what killed my men?"

MacCready nodded and planned his bid for more time. "You got it. But there's too many of them and too few of us. Unless you want all of your men killed, there is no way to exterminate them right now."

"Can we capture one?" Wolff asked, unable to mask his excitement—and at that very moment MacCready realized that he'd been had.

This little expedition has nothing to do with dead Germans and eliminating their stalkers. But why do they—

Before he could finish the thought, a loud grunt echoed off the stone corridor. Both men flinched at the sound and turned toward Sergeant Schrödinger. The giant was leaning against a wall and staring at the eight-inch cave centipede that hung from his right hand.

MacCready threw a glance at the hole in the floor, then brought his forefinger reflexively to his lips, as if to shush the stricken man. If the bats heard them, this play's final act would come quickly, Lady Macbeth style. The sergeant, however, was definitely preoccupied. The arthropod's pincers were powerful enough to pierce boot leather, and now they were efficiently slicing beyond the fleshy pad below Schrödinger's thumb, digging into bone and locking like the jaws of a poisonous, hydraulically driven vise.

The sergeant held out his hand to Colonel Wolff, his eyes trying to conceal pain as the centipede threw its body into a series of exaggerated S shapes. Schrödinger flailed his arm out, slamming the back of his hand into the wall with bone-cracking force. He let out a slight grunt, turned, and disappeared into the darkness.

They could hear him crashing blindly down the stone corridor, trying to make his way back again toward the imagined safety of the cave entrance.

For a moment, the American captain and the German colonel exchanged equally surprised looks, but just as quickly they both turned toward the opening in the floor. There were new sounds rising through the hole in the tomb, stirred by Schrödinger's commotion.

click, click, click, click, click, click, CLICK, CLICK

"Flatten yourself against the wall," MacCready whispered, hoping that Wolff was not about to follow the sergeant's noisy lead—and knowing that if the colonel did run, all three of them would be slashed open and pumped full of anticoagulant saliva. MacCready also knew that, like the goat under the Brazil nut tree, he would still be alive while the *draculae* drank him.

I n the lair of the vampire bats, the colony was awake.
The reaction to the sounds from above was immediate and synchronized.

BIPEDS, the *draculae* signaled to each other.

Then, with the relentless precision of wasps sent to protect their endangered hive, four dark shapes scuttled across the ceiling toward the circular opening. The bats skillfully maneuvered an obstacle course of stalactites, moving as easily through the rooftop forest of columns as if it made no difference to them that their world was suspended upside down.

M acCready placed his lantern on the floor and in one rapid motion pressed his body into a depression in the cave wall.

Colonel Wolff quickly mimicked him. As much as he wanted to flee, now that he was free of the gun that had been continuously trained on him, MacCready's life depended on remaining still— *absolutely* still.

Four large shadows erupted through the hole in the floor. At first they were formless and abstract—wild shapes pouring out of the ground—gliding effortlessly up the walls. But shadows did not make sounds, and these hissed at each other, filling the chamber with a musky aerosol that reminded MacCready of skunk oil.

One of the creatures scrabbled past MacCready's face, claws clicking against the ceiling. And in the glow of the Indian lanterns, he finally got a clear picture of the vampires. *Like animated gargoyles,* he thought, and the part of his brain that could never turn off zoologist mode noted that they moved as gracefully on vertical walls, or even across the ceiling, as jaguars moved across the ground. He was familiar with similar gravity-defying moves in smaller creatures like roaches and chameleons, but *never* had he seen the like in an animal of this size.

And then, without warning, all four of the gargoyles disappeared down the corridor, toward the prey that was currently making the most noise.

If Schrödinger hates centipedes, wait till he sees what's coming.

MacCready eyed the colonel, who was still pressed into the depression.

Just as he began to ease away from the wall, MacCready noticed something that caused him to freeze. There was a flutter of movement, and another dark shape emerged from the subchamber. This one was smaller than the others, and it hauled itself out of the hole with considerable effort. Then the creature stood on the floor, breathing hard, *listening.*

MacCready fought the urge to close his eyes. *It's a young one.*

The bat sniffed at the air and then did something completely unexpected: It sneezed.

MacCready held his breath and the little vampire drew nearer, its face moving into a lantern beam and casting its features in deep red, horror-movie shadows. Mac could not escape the feeling that the bat smelled something familiar, not just a human scent, but *his* scent. And his subconscious sent up an image. *The tree . . . the staked-out goat.*

In the distance, Schrödinger was now making thrashing sounds against the corridor walls.

The littlest vampire pivoted toward the sound. The creature appeared to hesitate for an instant. Swiveling its head slowly from side to side, it cast out high-frequency bursts, barely discernible to the humans.

As MacCready watched, the young *draculae* pressed its chest to the ground, as if it were a human about to perform a push-up. Then, all in one small part of a second, the bat's oversize pectoral muscles catapulted it into a hop that carried it down the darkened corridor in a blur of motion.

The men remained motionless, their bodies still pressed as deeply into the cave wall as physics would allow. Only their eyes moved, and then only for an instant, as each man's gaze was drawn back to the hole in the floor.

Are there more of them coming? MacCready wondered. *Should I—*

A strobe of automatic gunfire came from Schrödinger's direction. The staccato roar was painful in the enclosed space and MacCready resisted the impulse to fling up his hands to cover his ears. Particles from the cave ceiling shook free and fell around him. There was another burst of machine-gun fire, shorter this time. They turned reflexively toward the source and the last few flashes revealed the giant sliding down onto his knees, firing his weapon. He let out a series of increasingly unintelligible curses, which deteriorated into a new and surprising sound. This was the end of SS Sergeant Schrödinger. The legend, who once grinned at his captors when punched in a freshly bored bullet wound, was crawling on all fours toward the cave entrance, bat-bitten and whimpering like a little girl.

MacCready glanced at Wolff, whose attention had been drawn to the disquieting whimper. *His next move will be to execute me.*

As if reading his mind, the German slowly turned to face his prisoner. Wolff's movements were deliberate and unhurried. His face bore no emotion. And as the colonel's right arm began to rise, MacCready knew that there would be a Luger attached to the end of it.

This is it!

MacCready gestured in the direction that Schrödinger and the bats had gone, and for a split second he saw puzzlement in the German's expression. As the colonel's gaze broke away, MacCready hurled himself off the wall, going completely and perplexingly airborne in the confined space. Wolff turned back just in time to see him execute a perfect dive—directly into the hole in the floor.

T he dive left the colonel momentarily stunned. He had fully anticipated a feeble attempt to run deeper into the corridor. *But this? This?*

Wolff remained motionless. His gun arm had been late in tracking the movement of the American but he left the pistol pointed toward the opening in the floor.

Will there be more of these creatures emerging? he wondered. *How many of them can there be? Five? Five hundred?*

The colonel decided to wait another minute and, while acknowledging that there was little time to ponder the prisoner's
suicide leap, he had to admit that it had been completely unexpected, and in its own way, admirably spectacular.

*Evidently the man preferred dashing his brains out at the bottom
of a filthy cave to the efficiency of a single, finely crafted bullet.*

On second thought, though, Wolff knew that a head shot
wasn't *exactly* what he had planned for the smart-assed American.
*It would have been more like a bullet in each knee. All the better to
keep any more of his little bat friends occupied if—*

The colonel anchored his mind to more immediate matters . . .
survival . . . *and the mission.*

Yes, above all else—the mission.

Wolff moved away from the wall, bending to retrieve a lantern, all the while keeping his pistol trained on the hole from
which the bats had emerged. He approached the opening tenta-
tively, holding the lantern out. A breeze rose up out of the dark,
setting the red and yellow flame into motion. The German officer
went down on one knee.

There was a stone ledge just below the rim but his eyes moved
quickly past it, drawn to the floor of the chamber. *Something moving.* The colonel shifted the light, struggling to obtain a clearer
view, *hoping* it was only the American twitching and dying on the
floor, before realizing that the floor itself was moving.

Rice, Wolff thought, incongruously. But rice was indeed exactly what it looked like—a deep pool of live, unusually fat rice
grains, set in motion around once-towering stalagmites, now
half-sunk in a lake of black matter.

There were bones in the rice. But no body. And no more bats.

The officer lay down on his belly. "Where are you?" he whispered, as much to himself as to MacCready. Now he could see the

entire floor of the subchamber clearly, but there was *still* no sign of the American.

Could he be—

The colonel's brain registered a new source of movement, this time out of the corner of one eye. Now he swung the lantern back to the level of his head, illuminating the roof of the subchamber. Without the hulking sergeant anchoring his feet, Wolff was unable to attain MacCready's panoramic view, but what he saw was clear enough. Something resembling a wave was rippling across the ceiling—a wave of teeth and reflecting eyes, advancing toward him.

Wolff jumped to his feet but even as he backed away, his eyes remained focused on the hole.

click, click, CLICK, CLICK

The Nazi officer turned and sprinted down the corridor, lantern in one hand, Luger in the other.

Behind him, the clicking grew louder.

The past ninety seconds had seemed longer than any hour to MacCready. He was lying facedown, trying to catch the breath he had lost diving onto the stone ledge. The landing was as soft as he had hoped for, which was a good thing *and* a bad thing. The good thing: His neck wasn't broken. The bad thing: His dive had been cushioned by two feet of living bat guano, and now the plethora of cave-dwelling species—spiders, roaches, maggots— who called the place "home" were eagerly probing their unexpected but welcome new food source.

One of the troglodytes had already scurried through a tear in the leg of his field pants, but before the intruder could head too far north, MacCready swatted at his thigh. He experienced a small measure of relief at the crunch of a chitinous arthropod body.

Golden cave roach, he told himself. *That's gonna leave a stain.*

He felt a pinch on his uncovered wrist and another on his cheek. *Pseudoscorpion?* A sudden frenzy of tiny jointed legs spread across his back, and something the size of a walnut muscled its way past the ineffectual barrier of his shirt collar. *Cave crab, definitely,* he confirmed. MacCready had decided that the only way to keep a grip on his composure was to take a mental inventory of the creatures that were now beginning to eat him alive. Nevertheless, he hoped that the living membrane of "cave bugs" would blanket him completely enough, and fast enough.

MacCready also concentrated on keeping his mouth and eyes closed, as a tide of grateful hunters swarmed over his shoulders, neck, and head, staking thousands of tiny claims.

He could not see the glow of Wolff's lantern from above, but he could hear a muffled voice.

Can he see me? MacCready wondered, trying to concentrate on something else and coming up with a question. *What could be worse than this?*

It took a second or two of thought but the best he could come up with was rabies. *Foaming at the mouth, dementia, and the destruction of my central nervous system.*

Yeah, rabies would be bad. Even worse than this, he thought, until it occurred to him that simply breathing the air in an infected bat cave could transmit the very same virus he'd just conjured up as an *"even worse-case* scenario."

Keep it together. Think of something else, he told himself. And so he did—sort of.

I wonder if there have been any studies on rabies transmission through inhalation?

Probably not, he concluded, and he pictured himself assigning that particular project to Major Hendry. But then, as insect claws tried to pry open one of his eyelids, he realized that it was too late—the study was going on right now, and he was the lab rat.

MacCready's mind had just shifted focus again—*how long would it take these things to reduce me to a skeleton?*—when something large landed on his back.

The creature hissed and shook itself violently, and he could feel sharp claws, even through the layer of arthropods that had gathered there to dine.

Then the pissed-off *what-ever-the-fuck-it-was* hopped off.

Yes, rabies is starting to look like a plan, MacCready thought.

Colonel Wolff rounded a bend and slid to a halt near the end of the stone corridor. Sergeant Schrödinger had nearly made it to the cave entrance but now his body lay thrashing a few meters inside the antechamber.

Wolff bolted toward him and got off two shots from his pistol, but not before the creatures gathered around the sergeant had scrabbled away, disappearing into cracks and crevices like shadows before the sun.

They were feeding on him, he thought, vaulting over the dying man's head.

There was a flash of movement to his right and Wolff fired again. This time he heard the unmistakable impact of a bullet on flesh. There was a screech, and he glimpsed one of the beasts spinning wildly on the ground.

Wolff ran on, inhaling the scent of gasoline. He could see the cave entrance now, fifteen meters ahead. His men were spread across the opening.

A vibration ran through his body—*strange but not unpleasant,* he thought briefly.

"Don't shoot!" he shouted.

Ten meters to go.

There's no need to run, an inner voice told him. And he had to admit that the pinging sensation was actually quite pleasant.

He both felt and heard a leathery flutter from above and behind.

Three meters.

Slow down, son, the inner voice urged.

Just ahead, he could see Corporal Kessler bending down—a mime lifting an invisible curtain, in reality the lower edge of a thin net that had been strung across the cave entrance.

STOP!

Wolff ignored the inner voice and dove past the corporal's feet. As he did so, there came a rush of air from the place where his head had been only a split second before.

Simultaneously, the pleasant vibration running through his body transitioned into an earsplitting shriek of anger, fear, and frustration.

The colonel rose to his feet—others were at his side now, relieved and familiar faces. The obsequious Sergeant Vogt was even trying to dust him off but the officer waved the man away and turned back toward the cave.

The screeching sounds were coming from a dense tangle of hair-thin mesh—*a mist net, the Japanese had called it.* The Asians had used these nets to capture birds for the soup pot but now theirs had ensnared something far more dangerous, and far more important.

As if to remind Wolff of that first point, the bat's head came into full view as it struggled to free itself from the hopeless tangle.

It flashed a snub-nosed muzzle full of teeth, which quickly began to slice through the woven web. Up close, the creature appeared smaller than the four he'd seen feeding on Sergeant Schrödinger, but right now the size of the specimen was the very least of his concerns.

The colonel nodded to two men standing on either side of the cave entrance and their response was synchronous. Each pulled back the netting just far enough to allow the lighting of the fast-burning demolition fuses they had set previously. Twin flames raced each other ten meters into the antechamber and there was a whoosh of expanding air as a wall of flame all but sealed the entrance to the plateau from the outside world.

The Germans watched carefully, training their automatic weapons at the smoky wall and whatever might have survived behind it. But nothing came through the flames. Except for the high-pitched clicks produced by the writhing nightmare in the mist net, the only sound was the crackle of burning brush.

Wolff pointed at the struggling *draculae*. "Get this animal into a bag before it harms itself."

A minute later, two privates clad in heavy leather gloves stepped forward and approached the net, cautiously.

"I'll attract his attention," a private named Auerbach told his partner. "You sneak around from behind with the bag."

Private Horst, an ashen-faced eighteen-year-old, nodded but seemed far too nervous with his assigned task.

Auerbach nodded to the other man, then started waving his hands around. "Hey, ugly boy!" he called. With a sense of relief he saw the bat's head turn toward his diversion, but any relief evaporated immediately as the creature's black marble eyes locked on to his own.

As planned, Private Horst moved in behind the bat, which

was no longer screeching and struggling. Silently, the teenager held open a large canvas bag and took a step closer to the tangled net.

Private Auerbach had intended to continue drawing the animal's attention but now he stood paralyzed by the creature's stare—by its *probe*. Without thinking, he tried to whistle but found that his mouth had gone dry. As Auerbach blew a soundless puff of air, he never saw his partner, rushing forward and throwing the open mouth of the bag over the lower half of the entangled animal.

"Hah," Horst cried in triumph, fumbling to pull the bag upward over the animal's flailing wings.

The commotion pulled Auerbach away from the *draculae*'s stare just in time to glimpse the creature's head rotating nearly 180 degrees. That quickly, jaws sunk into Private Horst's left glove. Horst's eyes registered shock, and he pulled back reflexively. *"Shiest!"*

The bat let out something like a growl and bit down harder.

"Let go of me!" the private screamed, pulling backward but unable to free his hand from the glove. Now the bat's neck was stretching through a tight opening in the tangled net—and still, the beast would not let go, even as the nylon mesh tightened around its throat.

"Shoot it! Shoot it!" someone yelled, and Corporal Kessler moved closer, pistol drawn, angling for a clear shot.

"Stand back, Corporal," Colonel Wolff said, pushing the barrel of the corporal's gun aside and moving quickly into position.

Kessler felt a surge of relief. *At least I won't be the one killing the colonel's prized specimen.*

A single shot immediately followed, and Kessler jerked backward as a shard of flying bone bit into his cheek. Private Horst slumped to the ground, his now-empty glove still hanging from the creature's mouth. The exit wound in the private's skull had been aimed precisely, to assure that no speed-slung scraps of skull struck the bat.

Wolff pulled back on the Luger's hinged toggle lock then released it, extracting the spent shell and setting another cartridge into the firing chamber. He turned to Sergeant Vogt. "Please assist Private Auerbach with the specimen, Sergeant. Then assemble the men. We are leaving."

T he mother heard the screams of the child through the blinding wall of heat and light blocking the cave exit. There was nothing she could do for him now, just as there was nothing she could do for the lead male who lay crumpled and burning in the antechamber.

The child's calls had become muffled and difficult to distinguish and the mother turned away from the painful glare and scrabbled back into the relatively smoke-free corridor. The others were coming. She could smell their confusion and their anger. She waited for her roost-mates to arrive, waited until their bodies covered the walls and ceiling of the stone passageway, a rippling mass of energized fur and flashing teeth. They bristled and seethed and hissed, but she waited for them to go silent.

Then she communicated to them what they must do.

D eep within the cave's subchamber, the tiny creatures that were still feeding on their unexpected food source responded with something resembling startled surprise, when their meal rose up and began to shake violently. Most of the arthropods simply fell back into the warm comfort of their guano world. But others, especially those who would not (or could not) stop eating, were killed, their smashed and broken bodies eagerly received by the hungry masses waiting below. Then, before the cave creatures could reclaim the gigantic mountain of flesh, it was gone.

CHAPTER 22

Descent

We humans have written our history in the perversion of nature.
　　—Botanist Robert Thorne, as quoted by R. J. MacCready

C olonel Wolff had broken radio silence, and even though the message was coded in an obscure native dialect, he still felt uneasy. *Any radio signal out here will serve as a beacon.* But now time had become the overriding factor and the colonel was beginning to doubt that they would have enough of it. Timing and logistics were everything, which made the fate of the American even more relevant.

He is definitely a survivor type—and that is bad.

Wolff hated the thought of leaving the plateau without proof that the man was dead, yet there was no alternative.

Standing before his men, the colonel noted that the group had grown smaller by three since their last briefing. They were gathered near the cave entrance just outside a newly hung mist net, which he hoped would prevent the surviving bats from getting out. The shredded, scorched, and bloody remains of the first two nets had been cut down and tossed off the cliff. According to plan, they had set additional charges along a fissure that ran along the antechamber threshold and elsewhere. Wolff was taking no chances; the floor was rigged with trip wires.

If MacCready emerges from this entrance he'll get quite a surprise.

The colonel spoke, keeping his voice low, as if afraid of being overheard. "While it *appears* that our American prisoner is dead, for the sake of our mission, we *must* be certain. For that reason, Private Auerbach and Private Schmidt will remain here, halfway down the trail."

Wolff moved in closer, his gaze alternating between the two men. "Our little camp here will be abandoned soon; at least it will appear that way. You two will keep yourselves hidden and kill anyone or *anything* that comes down that trail. When you are quite certain that the American's body is beyond all possibility of resurrection, you will proceed to the base of the trail and wait there, where our indigenous friends will find you."

The colonel paused while they saluted, then he continued. "Sergeant Vogt and Corporal Kessler, you will descend the trail with our guides. Scour the forest for any sign of the American. If by some chance he has escaped, the Indians will pick up his trail. Should they capture Captain MacCready, please give him my personal regards, then allow our local colleagues to satisfy any curiosity they may have about him. Once they have separated the American from his burdensome life, rendezvous with Auerbach and Schmidt and return to base."

Sergeant Vogt raised his hand, looking like a schoolboy asking his teacher for permission to pee.

Wolff acknowledged him with a nod.

"Excuse me, Colonel, but what about you? What about the . . . specimen?"

As if to answer the sergeant, there came a sound from below and across the valley, a rhythmic beat that sliced through the late afternoon air, growing steadily louder.

The colonel said nothing but turned instead, focusing his gaze at the double-bladed flying machine that had risen from distant *Nostromo*'s sea of fog.

Now the men outside the cave entrance could see that there were long black threads extending from the bottom of *Dragon I.* And as the cargo helicopter gained altitude and moved nearer, they saw that the threads were cables attached to a large steel basket. They all recognized the pilot, identifiable by her unmistakable blond hair.

The Führer's gifted pet, Wolff thought. *Flugkapitän* Hanna Reitsch gave a single wave, and through a swirling cloud of dust Colonel Wolff returned it. His men struggled to secure the front half of the metal cage—which Reitsch deftly placed on the narrow ledge. Kessler and Vogt ran forward carrying the canvas-and-net bag. Animated from within, the bag hung by leather cords beneath a pair of bamboo mist net poles.

"Don't lay it down!" Wolff shouted, pointing into the enclosure. "Suspend the ends of the poles onto the crossbeams."

The men did as they were told, but their minds were busy with other issues: dead comrades; the horrible creature struggling within the bag; the very real possibility that more of the monsters would soon come pouring out of the cave entrance; and the certainty that when the giant vampire bats did emerge, there would be hell to pay.

Corporal Kessler tried hard to stow away these thoughts, especially since a more immediate threat to his survival was to secure the pole suspending Colonel Wolff's specimen to the back half of a cage, which dangled and pitched high above the valley floor. The arrangement presented him with numerous ways to die, none of which involved "a bed, a bottle, and advanced old age."

• • •

R. J. MacCready ran a hand down his right forearm, noting that it had already swollen to one and a half times its normal size. He tried to think positively. *If my arms were still tied, this one would've burst like an overstuffed sausage.*

No, that visual didn't help.

After hoisting himself to the top of the labyrinth's subchamber just long enough to snatch one of the lamps, MacCready had ducked down again onto the ledge of guano and little "biters" and followed the first corridor he could find that led away from the smoke-disoriented mass of bats on the antechamber level above. With any luck at all, the scientist hoped, many of them were preoccupied up there, with Sergeant Frankenstein and his friends.

The plateau seemed to be literally honeycombed with damp underground passages. The one he chose led deeper into the weathered rock and, initially, uphill into thicker, choking smoke. He knew that fresher, smoke-free air was blowing upward through a passage beneath the roost chamber. He also knew that the fresh-air "low roads" were the paths the bats would most likely choose, and which he therefore needed to avoid. Using his filthy shirt as a smoke filter, Mac decided to follow the fumes along the higher corridor, far uphill and far beyond the "manhole" through which he had entered—away from Wolff's Nazis and away from the determined procession of *draculae* he hoped would have killed them all by now.

"Somehow, I doubt it," he mumbled, finding a sharp downward bend in the "high road" that allowed him to crawl along a narrow passageway into more breathable air. He descended another two hundred yards deeper into the plateau before encountering a fork in the passageway. Mac decided to take the wider of his two choices, until a steady gust from a crack in the ceiling nearly extinguished the lantern, forcing him to consider doubling back. Coaxing the flame slowly and more fully to life, and shambling forward in the dark, he was lulled into a false sense of security. He had, after all, entered a region in which the ground was level and he could stand easily. When at last the lantern completely illuminated the path ahead he was reminded of his last discussion with Major Hendry: *This is no time for complacency.*

The drop-off was only about twelve feet, but the floor of the dead-end chamber was covered with stalagmites—pointing up at him like a field of swords.

MacCready shook his head. *Why worry about Wolff and the* draculae *when your own stupidity can kill you?*

Some thirty minutes after doubling back to the fork, Mac-Cready extruded himself through a rib-compressing crevice and into late afternoon daylight. He took a small measure of satisfaction from the fact that this exit had deposited him far beyond the sight of the cave entrance he and his captors had used earlier.

The respite and the fresh air also gave him a chance to think. MacCready initially believed that, like their well-known counterparts, the *draculae*'s salivary glands produced an array of anticoagulant chemicals that would be applied to a wound immediately after the prey was bitten, thus preventing the victim's blood from clotting. The fact that the *draculae* bite caused a far more spectacular flow of blood had forced him to consider an alternate hypothesis. Maybe these creatures had a different bite physiology—based not on chemical anticoagulants but on something else. But what?

He knew that certain monitor lizards transmitted whole consortia of bacteria through their bites, then tracked down their fever-weakened prey at their own leisure.

What if the draculae *had evolved something similar? And what*

if Wolff's team was seeking just such a hemorrhagic pathogen, some-
thing that could be used as a weapon?

The choice the German had given him—the choice of ways to
die—had telegraphed as much. It should have been easy, from the
start, to peg Wolff as a biologist, possibly even a microbiologist.
He had threatened death under a cluster of rocket engines, and let
out that this had originally been proposed as a means of *sterilizing*
specimens. Of this much, Mac was reasonably certain: One did
not go to the trouble and expense of assembling a missile base in
the middle of the Brazilian wilderness merely to hurl one- and
two-ton payloads of dynamite or poison gas at the enemy. Wolff
was a man on a rather larger mission.

And now he just might have stumbled upon a new payload, some-
thing far more deadly than anything they'd brought with them.

MacCready's plan hadn't changed, it had only been interrupted. But now his mission was more urgent than ever. Get back
to Cuiabá. Contact Hendry. Let him know of the coordinates of
the base and the enemy's mission. It was worse than he could have
imagined initially. This was biological warfare. *And if I know*
Wolff, he's already snagged a couple of these bats by now.

After carefully scanning the surrounding cliff for signs of anything that might possibly shoot darts or fire a rifle, MacCready
focused on the rock-strewn but serviceable remains of what appeared to be an alternative trail leading off the plateau.

This is too easy, he thought, while another part of his mind
wondered where this "negative-attitude thing" had suddenly
come from.

If Wolff's alive, he's looking for me. And if his guides know about
this trail, they could be on it already—waiting.

MacCready surveyed the open expanse of the valley below,
took a deep breath of fresh air, and squeezed back into the narrow

crevice. *I'm not going anywhere in broad daylight,* he thought as he shimmied down deeper into the dark.

He was actually looking forward to meeting Wolff again. *When we do meet, it'll be on my terms.*

Waiting until dusk, MacCready poked his head out of the fissure, took a last look around, and then began his descent. He found himself pausing frequently (*too frequently*) as he fought off waves of nausea and dizziness, waves that seemed to be coming at shorter and shorter intervals. *If I pass out now, I'm dead,* he thought, trying to focus on feeling his way down toward the forest without glancing at the darkening abyss that stretched out beyond it. After two hours, he reached the base of the plateau, intact and with no sign of pursuers, human or otherwise.

He focused on everything he could remember about Major Hendry's map of the region. Now MacCready wished he'd paid just a bit more attention to it as he dredged up what few useful details the map might have offered.

What I need is some high, dry ground, he decided. *Something I can move across quickly.*

Then it came to him. "Got it."

He hoped.

CHAPTER 23

The Gift

From the moment I saw the Mato Grosso Plateau,
and the strange world that surrounded it, I knew I had
found the setting for my story.
  —Sir Arthur Conan Doyle (on the inspiration for
  his novel *The Lost World*)

January 30, 1944
5:15 A.M.

Shortly before dawn, R. J. MacCready stood before a vast primordial swamp. Dead tree trunks protruded from mist and black water. The air, which had a delicate rotten-egg bouquet, was also thick with mosquitoes. To top things off, he was feeling feverish and unsteady.

"High and dry," he mumbled, waving ineffectually at a cloud of flying bloodsuckers that seemed to be celebrating his arrival. *Great, I need more insect bites.* And the thought reminded him of something. He swore at himself for not remembering it sooner.

With a shaky hand, he reached into his shirt. Groping around with swollen fingers, he was surprised to find the leather cord still in place—and, even more important, Yanni's delicate-looking little vial, intact—having survived his encounters with Team Wolff and the troglodytes. *Great name for a Greenwich Village bebop group,* he thought.

"If you go into the swamps, rub this on," he remembered. *"It'll keep ya from gettin' bitten."* Yanni's serene, caring face flashed in his mind. MacCready felt suddenly even sicker at the thought of her and Bob Thorne, dead.

MacCready used his fingernail to pry open the tiny bottle and immediately turned his head away, grimacing. "Creeping Mother of Shit . . . what is this, *eau de squid*?"

Still, smell or no smell, MacCready dabbed a blob of the oily stuff onto his palms and spread it over his bug-ravaged neck and arms. The bottle remained nearly full, so he recapped it, took a last look around, and waded into the algae and scum-covered bog.

By the time he'd slogged twenty yards, the swamp water had nearly reached his chest but the feeling was surprisingly soothing. At least the murky water would help wash away the dried bat guano and crushed bug glaze that covered him from head to foot like a fecal exoskeleton.

What was more important, though, was that he had not seen a soul since his dry dive back in the cave; hadn't heard any gunfire, either. Might he just have succeeded in eluding his pursuers? Still, he knew better than to take chances, and continued moving as stealthily as possible from one muddy island to the next.

He was approximately a hundred yards into the swamp when, as Bob Thorne might have phrased it, "the shit-hammer fell." It began with the sound of a careless stumble and splash, and was followed by an exclamation in German. He was being tracked.

The Nazis' presence now revealed, his pursuers immediately picked up their pace, splashing through the water with no regard for stealth. He could hear the suck and drag of deep mud against their boots.

"MacCready . . . we hear you," someone called, and he recognized Corporal Kessler's voice. "It's no use. Give yourself up."

There was a pause, and he could hear a short exchange in German.

"We don't want to kill you." It was Kessler again. "We are just looking for our guides. Have you seen them?"

MacCready winced, reining in the part of his brain that already had three snappy answers to the stupid ruse locked and loaded, and which was *begging* to respond with one of them. Instead he ducked behind a long-dead tree trunk and quickly scanned the swamp ahead of him.

"Damn it," he mumbled. The tree line that marked the beginning of the forest was more than a thousand yards away.

Nowhere to hide, he thought, hunkering down with his back against an all-too skinny section of dead tree. Now he could hear the labored movements of the Germans as they waded into deeper water.

They're close now. Real close.

MacCready's mind raced, desperately searching for a way out.

He thought about submerging himself and swimming as far as he could underwater, but just as he prepared to fill his lungs for the underwater dash, a bullet clipped the tree trunk and he was spattered by blood.

Before he could even wonder where he had been hit, he heard a loud splash.

I don't think *I'm shot,* he told himself, *so what's with all the blood?*

Patting himself down as he searched for a bullet wound, Mac-Cready turned reflexively toward the splashing noises and caught a flash of cyclopean movement.

The two Germans had been wading less than ninety feet away, between a pair of ancient and rotting tree trunks—but the dead wood had somehow come to life.

The tree trunks are moving, MacCready's brain registered. *And they've got eyes!*

Corporal Kessler, who had apparently been using one of the "trees" to pull himself along, was now giving MacCready a puzzled, pleading expression; even in his fevered condition, the American knew that the expression had something to do with the fact that the corporal's right arm had been removed at the shoulder. Arterial blood pumped in a pulsating flow that mimicked Kessler's racing heart.

MacCready required several more seconds to wrap his mind around the fact that these tree trunks weren't tree trunks at all. They were the superbly camouflaged heads and necks of a pair of turtles—enormous turtles. And although their shells remained hidden below the water, he calculated that they must be ten feet across.

An instant later, Kessler's body jerked downward and disappeared under the black-green surface of the swamp. Except for a swirl of red foam, it was as if he had never existed.

The other man shared none of Kessler's luck. His "tree trunk" had struck him in the abdomen, and he screamed and flailed against the knotty armor with his fists.

The astonishingly bizarre turtle seemed to draw back from the blows and as it did, something pink and wet trailed away from the screaming man. The German tried desperately to reclaim his intestines—to put them back inside.

A third tree trunk mimic, this one an arm's length away from where MacCready stood, opened its golden eyes and began to move. Its watermelon-size head turned toward him and a pair of nostrils, as wide as silver dollars, flared and sniffed. Then, inexplicably, the bullet-wounded turtle turned and glided away, leaving little noticeable wake but a trail of its own blood as it steered directly toward the stricken German. Veering away from the food at the last moment, the newcomer rammed its body against the man's attacker.

The turtles sideswiped each other with their necks. *Like sparring male giraffes,* Mac thought. And as the creatures vied for possession of the soldier, they hissed and snapped at each other. MacCready suddenly recalled the strange battle cries of the *Tyrannosaurus rex* in *King Kong.*

As Mac watched the distracted giants, the dying man took the opportunity to reel in another length of his intestines. For a moment, just for a moment, it appeared as if he *might* win the struggle to reviscerate himself. But as the soldier staggered away from the behemoths, the sparring session ended abruptly and the creatures turned their full attention toward him.

In the end, the turtles divided and shared their meal. And when they had finished, they drifted slowly apart—then froze. In little more than an instant, they transformed themselves back into tree trunks again.

MacCready, who hadn't moved since the attack began, stared at the swamp ahead. He could see scores of dead trunks, maybe *hundreds.* Without thinking, he reached into his shirt and withdrew Yanni's bottle. This time with no grimacing, and with little wasted motion, he spread the oil over his arms, head, and torso—much more liberally, now.

"'It'll keep ya from getting bitten,' she says. Fuckin' A!"

●   ●   ●

MacCready sniffed at the empty bottle and tossed it into the brush.

Too bad this shit doesn't repel insects like it does giant turtles.

As his first hours out of the swamp became a day and then two days, the constant assault by flies and biting midges of unlimited variety rendered him more and more feverish.

By the third day, his body was losing water faster than he could replenish it by chewing on moisture-filled stems and roots. As for the bites, medicinal tree bark helped to stabilize his fever but failed to bring it down.

On the fourth day, paranoia had begun to set in. Someone was following him.

But even paranoids are sometimes right, he told himself. Through fever and self-doubt, he knew this was one of those times.

Years of field experience had taught him to pay attention to sub-conscious warning signals—a few molecules of smoke or a minute change in the pattern of birdcalls, never sensed consciously. There was no ignoring the warning bell from within, so he zigged and zagged his route, traveling by night and navigating by stars when-ever breaks in the clouds allowed it.

By the fifth day, he needed protein, and he needed it badly.

A termite nest would have been helpful. A single queen would keep me going.

Ultimately, though, he settled for a snake—*species unknown*—too slow either to strike or avoid getting clobbered. MacCready knew that beneath the skin and scales, the long ribbon of muscle was a cold and bloody petri dish if eaten uncooked, sure to make him even sicker in a day or two. But he dared not start even the smallest campfire. His subconscious seemed to be crying out that he did not *have* a day or two. The zigzag wasn't working. Someone out there—the Nazi Wolff pack, no doubt—was gaining on him and so he carried the remains of the snake with him, trying his best to leave no trail. *Salmonella never tasted so good,* he thought, chewing on the last of the meat.

On the sixth day, Mac knew that his pursuers were closing the gap. He had to appreciate the fact that these guys never yelped from a sting or bite, or any of the other occupational hazards of a tropical wilderness pursuit. *Damn, these bastards are good,* he told himself, with a reluctant sense of admiration.

Seven days after his encounter with the turtles, the snake meat began to bite back. With his energy all but completely sapped, he hunkered down behind a tree fall, clutching a bundle of sharpened sticks and a makeshift *atlatl* to propel them. *My sorry-assed arsenal.*

"Remember the Alamo," he muttered, knowing that the only thing to be decided was which of his two enemies, his pursuers or the forest, would take him down first.

W hen the trackers found Mac several hours later, he was mumbling to himself about giant turtles firing off Nazi missiles.

Now I'm definitely seeing things, he thought, watching as a man and a woman dropped their backpacks and rushed toward him. *These guys look like Bob and Yanni.*

"Mac?"

Jeez, it even sounds like Bob, he thought, and that convinced him to play along. "Sorry, Bob, no rolling papers."

"Don't worry, Mac. I got it covered."

MacCready turned to the other apparition. "Hey, Yanni."

"What's buzzin', cousin?" came the reply.

"Nuttin'," MacCready said, then he dismissed the apparition with a wave of his hand, "'specially since you're both dead."

"How do you figure, Mac?"

"Fuckin' Nazi showed me that Russian grease gun."

The hallucinations exchanged brief confused looks before apparently deciphering their friend's last comment.

The Bob mirage smiled sheepishly. "Yes, well . . . about the so-called grease gun . . ."

"Spill it," the female ghost added, sounding disappointed.

"Hey, who has time to pack the gat when some Nazi asshole and his button men are bustin' down the door?" the Bob mirage chimed in, defensively.

Mac stood up on wobbly legs, now acutely aware—mission-aware. These were not mirages. Bob and Yanni were alive. There was no time to waste, sick as he was. "Did you get to Queequeg-bah? Get a message out to Hendry?"

Yanni threw her husband a puzzled expression.

"He means Cuiabá," Thorne explained, then turned to his friend. "No dice, Mac—as we found ourselves immediately on the lam from the Krauts. But since we also thought they'd iced *you,* it is no little relief that Yanni picked up your trail three days ago."

Yanni held the empty bottle of turtle repellant up to Mac's face.

MacCready struggled to keep his eyes focused. It was *still* their voices but now they were fading echoes. "Yeah, works fine on turtles," he said. "You got something for vampire bats and Nazis?"

And with that he collapsed into Bob's arms.

Yanni moved in quickly and together the couple gently lowered Mac's body to the ground.

"Ingrate," Yanni muttered.

CHAPTER 24

Marching to Valhalla

*I hope these new mechanical meteors will prove only
playthings for the learned and the idle, and will not be
converted into new engines of destruction to the human
race, as is so often the case of refinements or discoveries
in science. The wicked wit of man always studies to
apply the result of talents to enslaving, destroying, or
cheating his fellow creatures.*
    —HORACE WALPOLE, 1785

Nostromo Base
February 8, 1944

By late morning, the two spacecraft lay gleaming in their wooden cradles, ready to be sled-mounted, ready for their tanks to be pumped with fuel and oxidizer, ready to roll out onto the tracks, one after another, toward their shared, central launch rail.

Colonel Wolff was looking for any excuse to get away from the rocket scientist, Sänger, who had once again fallen under the spell of his own voice while briefing the science teams and *Silverbird* pilots. Trimmed of excess verbiage, Sänger's message was that "everything was proceeding as planned," but the man had dragged out every possible speck of rocket-related minutiae until even Voorhees looked bored.

" . . . so the same vectored explosives I designed to dig diamond mines in Africa are now *redesigned* to propel my *Silverbirds*."

It was about the point at which Voorhees looked like he was actually about to nap, that Colonel Wolff was approached by one of Dr. Kimura's assistants, who gestured toward the door, emphatically. Wolff exited the meeting swiftly, without a word, and without acknowledging Sänger.

As the colonel walked the muddy path between buildings, his thoughts drifted back to the recent expedition to the cave. Ultimately, the mission had been a success—if only because he had managed to return with a live specimen. More important, his people were managing to keep the creature alive, although he had been infuriated to learn that that Kimura was using local "volunteers" to study how the bat attacked and fed, something the doctor had done without asking Wolff's permission.

"All of my *maruta* have been burned up," Kimura had responded matter-of-factly when confronted. The volunteers were evidently women living above the fog line. "Alone in huts," he explained, "just like the two witches and the boy." According to Kimura, they were easy pickings for his men. "Outcasts. No one will miss them."

Wolff was not so sure. He knew that up until now, their reluctant Indian allies had been placated by generous gifts that included crates of canned meat and fruit, and finely honed German steel. But now the locals were dying at the hands of his own people. And that was definitely *not* a recipe for appeasement.

To make matters worse, there was the realization that securing the specimen had come at a steep cost, seven men, valuable men, including Schrödinger, and quite possibly Vogt and Kessler. The two guides were never seen again. Then there was the unfortunate Private Schoeppe, catheterized by an even more unfortunate catfish. Neither of *those* two specimens had made it back to the base, which was doubly disappointing. He had looked forward to seeing a candiru up close.

What an interesting interrogation aid, Wolff thought, just before stepping into Kimura's Bio Lab.

"The bacterium has proven to be surprisingly cooperative," the Japanese scientist announced as the colonel entered. "Especially for an organism that was completely unknown to man until only a week ago."

"Cooperative?" Wolff asked, picking up a surgical mask.

"Well, once we learned how to control and muzzle your little horror, obtaining saliva from it was not much of a problem." Kimura understood, already, that what he really needed was another half century of technological development to truly comprehend how the *draculae* microbe worked. No one knew what a genetic code really looked like, and yet the secret of how the *draculae* symbionts caused rapid bleeding was down there somewhere, in the bacterial genes, the secret code of life. The microbiologist discovered, however, that he did not have to know very much about bacterial genetics to isolate a biological weapon from the beast's saliva. Ignorance had turned out to be no obstacle to application.

"The challenges became interesting but never serious," he explained to Wolff. "I'm guessing that this bacterium normally resides in the bat's salivary glands. Nothing too interesting there. Initially, I was puzzled by the microbe's strange reproductive cycle. But as is usually the case, getting this one to multiply was not at all difficult. In fact, once I infused the agar growth media with fresh plasma, the bacterial cultures experienced exponential growth. Just as suddenly, though, they died."

Wolff interrupted. "Yes, yes. I was there. Remember? But isn't that the problem? How can you culture the pathogen and prevent it from entering the self-destructive phase of its life cycle before it can be packaged and launched?"

"Ah, the unique microbial suicide that follows soon after the bite of your winged nightmare."

"The same," Wolff said, beginning to lose patience.

Kimura puffed himself up slightly, and with a wave of a chubby hand he dismissed a challenge that had, in reality, taken his team several days of nonstop work to overcome.

"We know that when the bat bites, the bacteria enter the victim's blood—"

"Yes, yes," Wolff interrupted again, making a cutting motion with his hand. "Would it be too much to ask for something I don't already know?"

Kimura bowed slightly. "Of course; my apologies. It appears that there are factors in the blood of an adult victim, and even in juvenile blood, that initiate the autolytic phase of the bacteria's life cycle. As the bacteria disintegrate, something they release causes the prey to bleed out. Now, by using fetal plasma, even umbilical extract works nicely, we have successfully bypassed the bacteria's exposure to ASF."

"ASF?"

"I call it Autolysis Stimulating Factor."

"And where did you get this fetal tissue?"

Kimura smiled. "More volunteers," he said cheerfully, gesturing to an examination table where a gore-stained sheet lay crumpled into a ball. "Savages."

He's using our useful allies as lab rats as well as bat food. Wolff put the thought away, nodded, and simply said, "Proceed."

"I was able to determine that bacteria cultured in ASF-free growth media multiply explosively but then enter a dormant phase. I would expect to find a similar dormancy taking place somewhere in your pet."

"Like a seed," Wolff said, as much to himself as to Kimura. But there was no mistaking the rising excitement in his voice.

Kimura smiled again. "Very much like a seed . . . an apt analogy. A seed waiting to be planted . . . waiting to hatch out once it enters a victim's body."

"But a seed that will never grow into a tree," Wolff added.

"True. Once the seed is watered, it dies and spreads its poison. The original culture carries on in the host."

"So there's absolutely no chance that this seed will multiply and show up at our front door once the enemy has been destroyed?"

"Correct, again."

After savoring his moment of one-upmanship, the Japanese biologist gestured toward two rows of small, pod-shaped structures—mission-ready components from his lab in Manchuria that he had brought aboard the *Demeter*. Now, pulsing with life's surge, they had been mounted under a climate-controlled isolation hood.

Wolff was about to ask how he planned to infect entire populations with the bacterium when Kimura brought an index finger up to his lips.

"Shhhhhh," he whispered. "The children are sleeping."

By the morning of February 8, two days after his rescue, R. J. MacCready was up and about, no longer needing reassurance that his friends were not ghosts.

"Gotta stop Wolff," MacCready said. "Gotta blow that place."

"Of course, Redundzel," Thorne said. "Just like you've been ranting for the last two days. Although walking ten feet without falling on your face is usually a requirement for attacking a missile base."

"You need to walk at least *twenty* feet, Mac," Yanni added.

The trio had kept a low profile since their reunion. Yanni had built a well-camouflaged lean-to and nursed MacCready back to health with a combination of leaves, tree sap, and smashed seeds. Thorne was assigned sentry duty and did what little cooking they dared over a small campfire lit for the briefest periods each day.

"With you in broken-record mode, once we deciphered this *crying Wolff* thing, we took the liberty of procuring you some very interesting supplies."

MacCready glanced over at Yanni, who gestured toward a backpack set a conspicuous distance from their tiny camp. "Tick tick boom," she said with a smile.

"You guys got me explosives? How the—"

"Seems this gold miner we ran into was more than a little intrigued by my recent trade proposal," Thorne said. "A sack of mushrooms I collected for a sack of TNT."

MacCready shot his friend a puzzled look. "Mushrooms?"

"Funny mushrooms," Yanni added. "Got it?"

MacCready nodded.

"So what's your plan, Stan?" Yanni said. She was carving a long, skinny piece of wood.

"We need to get a message out to Major Hendry. Enlist his help."

Bob and Yanni began laughing, simultaneously. "Look around you, Mac. Mushrooms and TNT we got, but shortwave radios? They are not in season. So *now* what is your plan?"

"The plan is I'm goin' back to that Nazi base . . . real sneaky-like. Then I'm gonna blow that fucking place up."

Thorne shook his head. "You really don't want to do this, do you?"

"What's your alternative?"

"Head to Cuiabá, radio your pal, Hendry."

"That'll take days. And we don't have that kind of time. With me missing, he's probably sent in another team. Maybe they're closer than Cuiabá, but who knows what direction they'd be coming from?"

"Yanni can help us solve that problem."

"That's fine, but even if we find them today, it'll be days before they can send in the proper ass-kicking gear." Mac slammed his fist down on the dirt with determination. "And *that's* why I have to go in there."

"Okay, Mac," Yanni said. "One thing, though."

"What's that?"

"We are goin' wit you."

MacCready started to object but Thorne held up a hand. "Do not bother yourself. We will not budge on this topic."

"Nope." Yanni put down her carving and began stirring the cooling contents of a wooden soup bowl.

"That smells delicious," MacCready said, hopefully. "What-cha cookin', Yanni?"

"Mac, you do not want *this* soup."

Thorne finished for her. "Poison arrow frogs."

CHAPTER 25

Preparations

*The importance of information is directly proportional
to its improbability.*

—A FUNDAMENTAL THEOREM OF INFORMATION THEORY

February 11, 1944

At daybreak, the engineer Maurice Voorhees stood beside his monorail track as
Dr. Eugen Sänger ducked beneath the
undercarriage of the rocket sled. It was covered by moisture-
protective tarps.

"Very nice, Maurice," the older man called out. "The groove
you designed into the track's upper surface was a brilliant idea."

"Thank you," Voorhees responded, sounding distracted. He
had been scanning the tree line that ran along both sides of the
track. The jungle plants were already sending out runners and
tendrils, thin green arms reaching out for the rebar and wood
rail. *Only a few months from now, they'll have it completely covered.*

"In fact I have no idea why I did not think of it myself," Sänger
said, as he emerged from under the tarps. "Maurice—" The older
man stopped momentarily, noting that his audience had wandered away from the track.

Voorhees was staring at a spot deep within the tangled foliage.

"There is no noticeable sag in the track, either," Sänger said, then he kicked at the ground with his heel. "It is clear that using this ancient stone road for a base was a brilliant decision as well. The last thing we need is for the *Silverbirds* to sink with their launch track into this miserably thin tropical—"

Maurice Voorhees heard none of it. He was imagining a *Silverbird* tearing along the rail atop the rocket sled he had designed.

Something slapped Voorhees hard on the back and he spun around with a start, relieved to see that it was only Sänger.

The older rocket man shot him an odd expression, then continued. "But the real test will come tomorrow. Won't it? That is when your friend Hanna Reitsch uses the *Dragon* and my pulley system to seat the *Silverbirds* onto your sleds."

"She is not a friend," Voorhees snapped.

"Yes, but she is an extremely gifted pilot," Sänger countered. "To have landed one of those shit-propelled V-1s in one piece? The *skill* involved?"

"Yes, and she also proposed a squadron of suicide aircraft," Voorhees said, dismissively. "How very heroic of her."

The younger engineer said nothing more, trailing off into thought again. He had been a very young man when the bombs fell on Peenemünde, but the past few months had aged him many years. The work appeared to have the opposite effect on Sänger, who seemed to be getting stronger. The man would have been perfectly happy to carry the war from central Brazil through Europe down to the Nile and Jordan rivers, until the end of civilization itself, if requisite, until finally it was fought with sickles and knives, and sharpened sticks.

Unmoved by Voorhees's condemnation of the female test pilot, Sänger simply continued his monologue: "Once that's done,
I estimate that fueling the rockets and their sleds will take the
better part of two—at most, three days. After that, our work here
will be nearly completed. And then it will all be up to the pilots.
Of course, all of this depends upon the completion of the weapon
by that fat little Jap . . . I can never remember . . . what *is* his
name, Maurice?"

But Voorhees never replied. *My sleds, the beautiful control systems I designed, the guidance systems, all of it will soon be destroyed.*

"Maurice . . . are you listening to me?" Sänger said.

Wasted.

Despite all of it, there had to be a better day coming, he tried
to convince himself. He just did not know how to get there yet.

But, he told himself, *I'll think of something.*

In the Bio Lab, Dr. Akira Kimura had just put the finishing
touches on the six pathogenic reentry vehicles, or "cluster
bombs." *Three for each of what's-his-name's Silverfish.*

The bacteria within each bomb now rested (*comfortably,*
Kimura imagined) in beds of ultrafine sand, sand that would be
dispersed for miles in every direction once a whole series of cylin-
drical "bomblets" popped apart, high over their targets.

Until then, his "children" could sleep peacefully, safely isolated from exposure to the damp tropical air. Their nurturing and
safety had been his primary concern for the past week.

*Who knows what disgusting thing might try to contaminate them
as they sleep?*

To minimize the risk, the little incubation chambers themselves had been outfitted with parachutes, thus *becoming* the

bomblets, dozens of which would be parceled into the six cluster bombs, each designed to "blossom" at a predetermined altitude. Like the *Silverbirds,* Kimura's bomblet system had almost been launch-ready on the day the *Nostromo* arrived at Hell's Gate, with the only modification being substitution of vampire bat pathogens for his Unit 731 anthrax strain.

What will the Americans think when they see the parachutes? Kimura wondered. *And the insignia we've designed.*

He hoped they would be frightened—*although not to death. That would be too soon, and it would spoil the fun.*

Kimura was satisfied that all the difficulties of testing and preparing the bomblets were conquered. The other bit of good news concerned the *draculae,* who had doubtless taken care of the MacCready problem. The disease warrior imagined that the plateau at sunset must have been like a violently shaken hornet's nest, after Wolff and Reitsch helicoptered out with their specimen.

"We yanked the dragon's tail," Wolff had told Kimura, "then left the American to burn."

Nightfall, in the forest two miles outside Nostromo Base

FEBRUARY 15, 1944

MacCready had told Yanni he would do better than walking twenty feet without collapsing. He was determined to cover twenty miles. And by now he had done just that.

"So what is he *really* doing in there, Mac? This so-called Wolff and his pals?"

"I have no doubt at this point that they're trying to multiply whatever the bats are carrying in their mouths—some form of hemorrhagic shit—quite possibly a bacterium."

"And what makes you think this, again?" Thorne had heard his friend's explanation several times already but he was apparently *still* trying to convince himself that Mac was no longer delirious.

"Look, the wrecked submarine they found downriver was a Jap design—and there were Japs in that camp. It isn't a coincidence that Japan is running the world's largest biological weapons program."

"And what, they are in cahoots with the Krauts to develop germs?"

"Bioweapons, disease bombs. Same shit they've been experimenting with somewhere in Manchuria. We've had reports of unnatural plagues breaking out in occupied regions of China."

"This is low of them," Thorne replied.

"These guys probably have a new delivery system going as well. There was fuel all over that base. From the smell of it, I think they were farming methane."

"So, you are thinking that any day now, this Wolff flings a missile at London or New York, full of something he grows out of your bats?"

"Something like that."

"Mac, not to be a pain in the neck but did you also consider that this might be worse than disease-bombing a city?"

MacCready gave a funeral laugh. "I'm trying not to think that far ahead. But go on."

The botanist continued. "Once these bacteria are out in a new environment or under the microscope of some other lab jockey, *that* is where the real trouble starts. Shit mutates, Mac. This is a basic law of living things."

"What are you getting at?"

"Let's speculate that there's maybe a thimbleful of this bacterium in nature, in all the bats that are alive. It's no stretch that Wolff and his goons are already able to isolate this thing. If so, they could be multiplying it by the pound. Now, what if they tamper with it—progress it beyond its natural host?"

"That would be bad."

"*Real* bad. And if this stuff doesn't bite him in the ass, if someone carries any of it to labs outside Brazil . . ."

MacCready finished the thought. "Then we could be looking at the biggest shit-stomping of all time."

"Okay," Yanni said. "Like you need one more reason to blow it all up."

"But how?" her husband asked.

"I keep thinking back to those fuel reserves I saw back at the base," MacCready said.

"Fuel blows up," Yanni added.

"Well, this is a good start," Thorne said with a clearly forced grin. "I suppose we'll just keep making up this famous plan as we go along."

"You got a better idea, Leaf Boy?"

The botanist did not answer, instead allowing his gaze to fall on the pristine forest just beyond their tiny shelter. "What civilized person builds a disease weapon from something they pluck out of a place like this?"

MacCready remained silent.

"Civilization," Thorne said. "Interesting concept, piss-poor execution."

MacCready appreciated the sickening irony of Thorne's statement. He had long ago accepted the fact that his old friend was one of the world's most powerful shit magnets. So, naturally, once

Bob Thorne decided to get away from civilization, civilization in its worst incarnation would plot to set up camp in his backyard. The odds of it happening that way were probably one in millions. And that seemed just about right to Mac.

It had seemed impossible.

Therefore, quite naturally, it occurred.

CHAPTER 26

I See You

We are of nature, not above it.
—Stephen Jay Gould

Nostromo Base
February 16, 1944

Deep within the hull of *Nostromo*, where the captive *draculae* was held, Wolff's feelings of claustrophobia, of the jungle closing in from the fog, of his entire operation now falling apart, grew stronger each passing day. He found it odd that a three-night hiatus in *draculae* attacks, rather than easing his worries, had intensified them. On several occasions he found himself standing before the captive in his lab, and his observations had brought him, independently, to MacCready's belief that the animals possessed intelligence at the level of a higher primate—a rhesus monkey or even a chimp.

Like the Allied forces, the bats are up to something, Wolff supposed, straining to keep his paranoia below the surface. *Like the Allies, they are probably thinking it through, observing, and waiting.*

His only hope was that somehow he would get the two spaceplanes and their payloads away *before* the attacks came and the jungle swallowed them all. After the *Silverbirds* were launched, and safely away, nothing else would matter. Wolff had no illusions about his fate. Once Hanna Reitsch was up there, winging her *Silverbird* across the Atlantic, and once his other pilot, Lothar, was out of the atmosphere and targeting Washington, Pittsburgh, and New York with his reentry pods, *Nostromo* Base and all of its inhabitants would be expendable.

The mother hung from a dead branch, flanked by the twins. There were two bipeds standing on the riverbank. They seemed to be concentrating on two small, glowing objects. She could "see" them quite clearly through the reeking smoke they were producing, could hear the food pulsing faster and faster within them, though the bipeds were standing still. They stood just downriver from the biped nest where the child had been brought so many nights earlier, the last time the mother had heard him or even sensed his presence at all.

The twins had already moved into position, their thumbs and feet locked on to the bark of the tree, bodies suspended head-downward, twenty feet above the ground.

GENTLE

Private Richardt Woessner suddenly felt better then he had since his arrival at *Nostromo* Base. Standing guard near the submarine was dull work, but he felt a flash of contentment. "Is there something new in these cigarettes, Hans?"

"Hans?"

Woessner turned and saw his friend lying on the ground. "What—"

Something bit him in the shoulder. Something else bit him in the neck.

Yanni lowered the dart gun as the Indian canoe they'd "borrowed" pulled stealthily up to the bank next to the collapsed men.

"Nice shootin', Tex," MacCready whispered. "Get the guns, float the stiffs."

After sending the bodies of Private Woessner and his friend Hans adrift, MacCready and the Thornes began a canoe-based recon using the fog as cover, careful not to raise an alarm or accidentally ignite their supply of tree-sap-smeared TNT sticks. "Sticky bombs," Mac had called them. "We'll slap 'em onto anything that looks like it needs blowin' up."

Near the center of the lagoon, not far from where the submarine was moored, the trio paddled up to a series of strange pipes and support struts. Each pipe began at an openmouthed cone near the water's surface, then converged toward a single point on the shore.

"Just like I thought," MacCready whispered, his index finger tracking the array of cones from the lagoon to what he expected, if he could see that far, would be a series of pressurized tanks on shore. "They're collecting natural gas, bubbling up from the river bottom."

"What for?" Thorne whispered back.

"That missile I told you about, the one that took down the recon plane. I think they've got something bigger in this sub—something big enough to carry their bioweapons."

"Hit the sub then?" Yanni offered.

"Not directly," Mac replied.

"Then what are we goin' after?"

MacCready smiled. "Fuel blows up. Remember, Yanni?"

Yanni smiled back at him.

Mac acknowledged her with a nod. "If those fuel storage tanks are as full as I think they are, if we blow them they'll take out the sub and maybe the whole base."

F rom the far side of *Nostromo* Base, the rocket team heard the lagoon erupting into chaos—explosions and gunfire, a tremendous amount of gunfire.

Maurice Voorhees knew immediately that it was an enemy attack. *An amphibious assault! How many have they sent?* he wondered. *A hundred? Three hundred?*

At the moment the first bombs went off, Voorhees and an assistant had been making a final check along the sled rail—ninety meters downrange of the rocket sheds. With the two *Silverbirds* now fully fueled, and finally prepped for takeoff, the timing of the raid seemed perfectly consistent with everything else about the engineer's life: *So close, and yet so far away.*

Now, he supposed, the door to space was about to be destroyed, and he along with it.

So far, though, his luck seemed to be holding out. The explosions were coming from the direction of the *Nostromo*—and the fuel depot. The first near miss occurred when a piece of generator, trailing an arch of flame, pounded a crater into the ancient roadbed, two meters from the rail.

No damage.

Simultaneously, a leather glove with a hand still in it struck his face. The slap sent Voorhees and his assistant running, as more pieces of blast debris fell—lighter material now—sheets of tin roofing and glowing red embers of paper.

By the time Voorhees reached the *Silverbirds*, Hanna Reitsch was already seated in the cockpit of the first ship, impatiently waiting as Dr. Sänger recited the prelaunch checklist. The two rocket-bombers sat on adjoining forks of a Y-shaped section of track that converged onto the monorail.

"Scrap the goddamned list!" she cried abruptly, pulling the canopy shut so fast that it nearly clipped off the rocket designer's fingers. Without hesitation, she began locking it down.

"Get off!" she screamed at Sänger, who made no reply as he leaped down, then ran toward his young protégé.

Voorhees noticed that the cockpit of the second ship was open and empty.

"Where's Lothar?" Voorhees demanded over the sound of machine-gun fire, but Sänger did not hear him. He seemed to be thinking about something else.

Voorhees brushed past the rocket man and climbed up onto Reitsch's *Silverbird I*.

Avoiding eye contact with Reitsch, he performed a last double check of the canopy's seals. He felt a sudden bump, then a rush of relief as he saw that the movement had been caused by a min-iature locomotive that was struggling to slide the *Silverbird I* and its sled into its final launch position.

Voorhees jumped down to the ground and shot a glance at the second rocket. It was still empty. "Where is Lothar?" he shouted at Sänger.

But once again, the rocket man never heard him. As the words left Voorhees's mouth, another wave of explosions occurred, much nearer this time, but luckily still too far away to have an effect on the monorail.

This won't last, he thought, and almost immediately, more gunfire erupted nearby.

Even before the *Silverbird I* hit its mark on the straightaway, Reitsch fired the sled engines—which thundered to life, blast-furnacing the locomotive and its driver before the man could back his vehicle out of the way. Several technicians working nearby dove for cover as hot gases and locomotive fragments blew past them, instantly setting the *Silverbird I*'s vehicle assembly building aflame.

Incredibly, given his lifelong love for rockets, it never occurred to Voorhees to watch, or even to realize, that he was in the very midst of nothing less than the launch of the first "manned" space-craft.

But now was not a time for watching. There was no time left for anything except the *Silverbird II*.

MacCready's plan had begun to go south the very instant that his first sticky bombs detonated next to the fuel tanks. Some never exploded at all, while those that did failed to penetrate the tanks, which were more like Thermos bottles, well protected by layers of insulation. What the bombs *did* accomplish was to alert the entire base.

After the blast, the trio tried to take refuge in the forest, a safe distance from what they hoped would be a base-ravaging ball of flames. But there had been no fireball. Instead it was as if they'd stepped on a hive, and the base defenders were swarming like wasps, firing their weapons in a hundred different directions, shredding trees up to a quarter mile away but finding no targets.

"What are they shooting at?" Thorne wondered out loud.

"Us," Yanni replied.

Now came a new sound, the velocity-driven buzz of enormous blades cutting through the air at high speed.

"What the hell is that?" Thorne cried, pointing to something that looked like a giant dragonfly rising above the tree line. The machine's rotors were so powerful they tore holes in the fog, drawing down clear air from above.

"They've spotted us!" MacCready shouted, as a round buried itself into a tree nearby. He could see the aerial marksman, as unlikely a candidate as any for an assassin. The man was fat and clad in what appeared to be a kimono and the sheer incongruence of it held him spellbound until—

In a flash of recognition, R. J. MacCready saw the perfect geometric alignment.

Raising Private Woessner's MP-43 skyward, he sent a stream of lead toward the helicopter's port-side blade. The whole machine shuddered and whined, then tipped suddenly to port.

"Watch this, kids!" Mac called out.

Slowly, almost gracefully, the helicopter angled into the steel girders of a dockside crane, which in its own turn fell with the wounded *Dragon I* toward the methane tanks, squashing them like eggs. MacCready braced himself for "the big one" but remarkably neither the helicopter nor the methane exploded. The German pilot jumped out, and to judge from the speed at which he sprinted away, had escaped with no injuries at all. Without an ignition source, the supercooled liquid flowed across the ground like water.

"Time to go," MacCready announced. And as Mac glanced back over his shoulder, the kimono-clad man crawled out of the tangled helicopter wreckage and blundered directly into the chemical stream.

Even from this distance, and while they fled from the spreading death tide, MacCready and his friends could hear the man screaming in startled surprise, as his feet snapped off at the ankles, frozen to the ground in a pair of wooden clogs.

Finally, the rivers of methane found an ignition source, cracking open two leftover canisters of Voorhees's hypergolics. The blast wave rocked the *Nostromo* over to one side, piercing the hull with speed-slung machinery.

MacCready felt the heat of the fireball on his neck—the weight of his still bomb-laden backpack driving him forward and onto all fours. He and the Thornes were scattered like bowling pins. Quickly regaining his footing, Mac turned and saw the fog glowing ruby red under the fireball. Smaller, secondary explosions were igniting all along the shoreline.

We did it! We did it! He almost allowed himself an indulgent grin but realized there were still plenty of well-armed bad guys around. Fortunately, most of them seemed to be on fire.

And then came another rumble—this one from directly in front of him. Another rumble and another glow. His heart gave off what was becoming, these days, an all-too-familiar sinking feeling. MacCready knew this sound. He'd heard it at Chapada and again when Wolff's team took down the recon plane. It was the sound of a rocket engine, an entire cluster of them.

"Motherfucker!" he yelled, and began running in the direction of the sound. He slid the backpack down onto one forearm, concerned now that it felt too light for the job that lay ahead.

If it's not already too late.

L ess than ten seconds after Reitsch ignited the sled, Voorhees finally saw, in the receding glare, the second pilot, Lothar, staggering toward him, his back spewing smoke. His right hand was missing; the other, still clad in a glove, was pressed against his abdomen.

"Looking for something?" Voorhees asked, wiggling the fingers of his right hand. Lothar and Hannah Reitsch were thick as thieves, cut from the same abominable block. He'd heard a too vivid description of what Lothar had done to the prisoners before Akira's dissections began, including the woman with the bled-out child.

Voorhees pointed to a hand on the ground. "Is that yours?"

Lothar gave no response. He simply fell on his back with something ropey and pink flowing over his remaining hand. The air suddenly smelled like the bottom of a cesspool. In his last conscious moment, as the glow from Reitsch's rocket disappeared, the pilot's eyes met Voorhees's pleadingly, and the dying man opened his mouth. Voorhees watched in shock-state fascination as a red bubble formed, grew large, then burst.

He continued to stare at the dead man until Colonel Wolff appeared at his side, standing calm in the turmoil. "It seems as if Reitsch's protégé has been disemboweled," he observed, tapping Lothar's torso with his boot.

Voorhees wiped something thick and wet from his cheek. "No shit," he said.

Still calm, the colonel gestured toward the *Silverbird II*. "So, rocketeer, do you think you can fly this thing?"

"Without a doubt, Colonel," Voorhees said, watching as Wolff's face widened into a grin.

The trio of *draculae* overflew the battered biped nest several times but there was still no sign of the child. Everywhere, even through the thick confusion of burnt-forest smells, the scent of wasted food was noticeable—to the twins, tantalizingly so.

With no thought of food, the mother dipped her right shoulder, while simultaneously flexing the elongated digits of her wing-hand. The bat's body instantly responded by wheeling hard to the right, its wings carrying her beyond the shattered forest and out over water.

The twins followed closely behind, deftly mimicking their mother's movements, and they remained silent as she emitted a series of calls that probed the area just offshore. Instantaneously, the altered high-frequency signals returned, painting, in her brain, a three-dimensional picture of the enormous log that had brought the bipeds into their territory. But something about the structure had changed since their last, aborted hunt there. Now there were no bipeds, and the flattened surface where they had waited in ambush days earlier was tilted oddly to one side.

After overflying the structure, the mother angled away, gaining altitude with a flick of her thumbs that changed the flow of air over her wings. The child was gone and now they would return to the stone roost, before any more of her children disappeared.

The mother began casting long-range signals toward the faraway cliffs, when suddenly the female twin screeched an alarm call behind her and fell out of formation.

NO! the mother called; but by then the twins had already completed a tight loop and were speeding back in the opposite direction.

Furious, she followed them, but even before completing her own loop, she heard it.

The calls were coming from inside the giant, floating log.

The mother caught up with the twins just before they peeled out of their side-by-side formation and sped past a jagged hole in the log. She flew straight over the gaping tear, simultaneously gathering information and sending the child a message of her own.

The *draculae* wheeled around again, as if preparing for another reconnaissance pass, but this time they drew the leading edges of their wings upward. The braking maneuver caused them to lose both altitude and speed, and the finely controlled stall brought the trio to a synchronous and silent landing on the *Nostromo*'s broken deck. Seconds later they disappeared down an open hatch.

B elow and behind Hanna Reitsch, the world was in shadow. Directly ahead, the stars were dust, and the same blackness seemed to go on forever . . . until the line of daylight began advancing toward her, at hitherto unattainable velocity. Dawn was striking across the western Atlantic, just now about to touch parts of Brazil and the easternmost tip of North America.

As predicted, Reitsch was following the curve of the earth in free fall. She resisted an urge to enjoy the sensation, instead concentrating on a problem. Down there on Earth, gravity normally kept the contents of a vehicle's gas tank sloshing on the bottom, close to its uptake line. Because the *Silverbird* had neither gravity nor a bottom, the fuel and fuel oxidizer existed as globules—most of them floating far from where the fuel uptakes were located.

But now I will take care of that, she thought.

And as she sped toward daylight, it came time to test Sänger's maneuvering systems. In accordance with the instructions of the rocket men, she vented a small amount of air from the tanks into the vacuum of space. As they had predicted, the effect was like a child's balloon, released and allowed to fly free: The rocket was jetted forward, ever so slightly and, she hoped, just enough to force the remainder of the liquid fuel "downward," into the throats of the engine uptakes.

Now Reitsch knew for certain that she could make brief ignitions and course corrections at will.

She began to orient her spacecraft for reentry.

So, she told herself, *it seems that the insufferable asshole and his disciple were good for something after all.*

Morning and noon came at her with astonishing rapidity, flooding the cockpit with light. But it was late afternoon that interested her most. Late afternoon in the Ukraine, which was sweeping up ahead, silently, moving toward her like the unstoppable minute hand of a giant clock.

Down there on Earth, in the Cherkassy Pocket, 65,000 German soldiers were surrounded by as many as a half-million Russians. If the *Silverbird* came in on target, and if her payload did its work, more than half of the Russians would soon be dead, and by dusk the Germans would break free. In preparation for Hanna Reitsch and the dawn of disease warfare, the 24th Panzer Unit, which had slogged north through mud and melting snow to relieve the trapped German forces, suddenly halted its advance and turned back. The order had come directly from Berlin, the moment *Nostromo* Base broke radio silence and announced, "The first bird is away."

Even from the other side of the sky, Hanna could see faint signatures of an early thaw across the Ukraine.

An early thaw.

That is how it began.

CHAPTER 27

Daedalus Wept

The heavens call to you, and circle around you,
displaying to you their eternal splendors, and your eye
gazes only to Earth.
　　—DANTE ALIGHIERI

During the minute leading up to Maurice
Voorhees's launch of the *Silverbird II,*
explosions lit up the mist on every side.
Amid the mental checklists and prelaunch preparation, he mar-
veled at the bravery of a technician who calmly drove the *Silverbird II*'s miniature locomotive to set the craft into its proper
launch position, then gave the "Go!" signal before scrambling
away from his steam engine.

They're going to blow the track, Voorhees told himself, knowing
that the margin of error between successful launch and total destruction would probably be measured in tenths of seconds.

As Voorhees prepared to "light the candle," he watched Wolff
sprint past the starboard side. He gave a passing thought to the
possibility that the colonel, his mission now complete, was simply
getting out of the sled's blast range; but a sudden commotion
on the port side told him otherwise. Someone dressed in a filthy
Allied uniform dropped an empty backpack and was running
away from the track. He fired at Wolff and anything else that

moved. Something about the running man's movements—*was it confidence?*—made him suspect that this guy had just jammed the contents of his backpack very close to where he currently sat, strapped in and helpless.

"Go! Go! GO!" Voorhees screamed to himself, punching the red ignition button. And as the sled engines flared to life with a deafening roar, his head was yanked backward against the protective cushion.

Once again his eyes were drawn to the port-side window, where he caught a glimpse of the running man, who had changed course and was now aiming a pistol at his rocket. The filth-covered shooter looked more like a *wanderarbeiter*—a hobo than a soldier. He imagined the hobo emptying his pistol at the *Silverbird* but then the ship had disappeared into a wall of smoke and flame.

As the sled-propelled space-plane raced down the track, Voorhees's own body mass all but paralyzed him. That quickly, the g-forces had turned the front of the rocket—though the ship was still traveling horizontally along the rail—into what he perceived as "up." Those same forces were now pressing his back into the "floor" with an apparent weight gain of a quarter ton or more.

Voorhees was terrified, but it had nothing to do with the stresses the launch had placed upon his body. He feared that, at any given second, a bomb attached to the rail or to the sled itself would detonate, sending the ship careening broadside and at bullet velocity into the trees. The image and its meaning—*instantaneous nonexistence*—reawakened memories of standing in a bomb crater, clutching a single warm shoe.

In bullet-time, close calls came and went without realization as his space-plane and its rocket sled accelerated down the monorail with reptilian indifference. The shock wave of the first bomb had been no obstacle to the *Silverbird,* for it detonated more than half a second after the ship passed over it, along the rail. Another blast was far enough behind that vibrations from the shattering rebar and wood never reached the pilot at all. The third device blew a hole in the rail a full two seconds after the sled had climbed the ramp and become airborne.

Lastly, the bomb that had been planted onto the sled itself by the camouflage-clad man detonated, turning the core of the sled's engine cluster into flaming shrapnel that shredded its nose cone; but by then the sled had been used up and jettisoned, and was already following its own trajectory, groundward and into the forest.

The *Silverbird II* was safely away, still accelerating and climbing higher.

Roughly two minutes after Voorhees had punched the ignition button, his "bottle rockets" peeled away and spun earthward, followed by the empty hypergolic fuel pods. With the ship accelerating toward the ionosphere, powered now only by its internal fuel tanks, the atoms through which the hull passed vibrated redder and brighter with each notch upward on the vehicle's speedometer. Inside the cockpit, the engineer shielded his eyes against the glare, but as the atmospheric gases rarefied to near extinction, the glow grew weaker and then went out.

Voorhees checked his stopwatch, counting down until he had arrived at the appointed moment. Then he reached down and eased back on the throttle. Immediately he felt a wonderful sensation of buoyancy—the first manifestation of free fall.

The freshly minted astronaut allowed himself the hint of a smile. "I've made it," he said, his voice breaking with emotion. "I've made it." The violence on the ground had been left far behind.

Directly ahead, the stars blazed forth so brightly that, even through tears, he could resolve Mars and Jupiter as actual disks, and not just points in the sky. Far to the port side, the lights of Caracas shimmered faintly, like a delicate, phosphorescent cobweb draped over the land. To starboard, the Atlantic spread before him, revealed in its immensity by the first predawn rays of the sun. Then, within seconds, the new day illuminated land and ocean alike, as if someone had switched on a floodlamp.

The wonder of it all held him spellbound for another minute, until the fiery glow of hydrogen and ozone returned, and the space-plane's nose began to swing earthward.

Below *Silverbird II,* in the shadows, Voorhees saw dawn's earliest light creeping toward Florida. But none of that was important anymore. He checked his stopwatch again, calculating a course correction that would have stunned Dr. Eugen Sänger, had he been there to observe it.

The mission had called for attacks on the American capital as well as the city of Pittsburgh, the center of the Allied steel industry. After that, the rocket would turn hard to the east, with the last bomb released on a trajectory toward New York City. Sänger had chosen the Empire State Building as a hypothetical ground zero, but all any of the rocket men could really say about the *Silverbird*'s targeting capability was that "it made sense—in theory."

Finally, if everything went as planned, the pilot would have a choice of either bailing out or trying to land the rocket, something like a seaplane, minus a seaworthy keel, off the southern coast of Long Island, where a submarine would be waiting to pluck the rocketeer from the Atlantic.

"Or at least, some of his body parts," Voorhees had joked, upon hearing Sänger's U-boat rescue plan for the first time. For some reason, his little joke didn't seem quite so funny anymore. Voorhees knew that if the North Atlantic presented so much as a one-foot swell (*and when didn't it?*), the underbelly and the wings would rip the multiton rocket into a thousand pieces. If he survived, the standard U-boat was not equipped to save the plane even if it floated perfectly intact. Either way, land it on water or bail out, his beautiful space-plane would die alone and pilotless, on the bed of the Atlantic Ocean.

But those plans had been drawn up long before Voorhees found himself the only man still alive who could fly the rocket. And not long after that, Maurice Voorhees had devised his own plan.

With limited time to work out the details, Voorhees decided to keep it simple: Kimura's bombs would be ditched over the Atlantic, where they could harm no one. He would then steer the ship's nose toward land, Virginia or Washington, D.C., itself, where he hoped to find an airstrip, or at least somewhere flat to set down for a long, long belly-scrape of a landing.

The engineer shook his head. *Yes, that's going to be a bit of a poser. But I would rather ski across flat concrete or through a field of corn than rough water.*

If he vented all of his fuel ahead of time, he might survive the landing. The ship's insides were, after all, mostly insulated, balloon-like tanks, filled with the liquid natural gas they'd collected from the river itself. With the tanks empty, the ship would be as light as a feather, more or less. Voorhees was confident that he could land the *Silverbird* intact and that, maybe, just maybe, the spacecraft could be saved, or at least replicated from its wreckage. Certainly, the Americans would see, in this ship, the world to come. *And hopefully, they would find something better to do with it.*

Now, less than a hundred kilometers below, Voorhees could make out roads and towns in the dim, pre-sunrise light, and he could distinguish clouds marching before the winds.

As the rocket-plane continued on its course, a hammerhead of air strengthened around the hull, bringing a sensation of weight back to Voorhees's feet and snapping him out of sightseeing mode. Voorhees made another course correction, just before the *Silverbird II* made a perfectly timed skip off the outer atmosphere, like a stone skipping along the surface of a pond.

High above coastal South Carolina, the horizon receded from the pilot—again, and the sky above became blacker as he regained altitude; but alarmingly, the glow outside the ship did not diminish as much as he had anticipated.

There's more gas outside than there ought to be, he thought, craning his neck to get a better view of the port side of the fuselage. What he saw plunged him into instant despair.

To anyone standing directly below, the fleck of light over North Carolina would have resembled a comet rising against the morning stars: a wisp of vapor nearly a third of a mile across, with a tail streaming tens of miles to the south.

But the apparition over the United States was not a comet—at least not a normal one.

Voorhees settled back into his seat, letting out a deep breath.

"One of the gunshots punctured a fuel tank," he said to himself, his mind flashing back to the takeoff and the determined hobo, firing his pistol as he ran.

Probably started out as a flesh wound, he reasoned. *Until the first "stone-skip."*

At that point, the "blowtorch" effect, as the ship bounced off the atmosphere, would have widened even a small hole into a full-fledged puncture. And now the unwelcome glow was a result of vented gases, excited by solar radiation.

The rocketeer glanced back, hoping that the flare of escaping gas might have ceased or at least gotten smaller.

It hadn't. The dial from one of the main propellant tanks continued to notch downward.

"Shit!" he said, gauging his position as the northeastern border of North Carolina rose on the port side.

"I can make it to Washington, D.C.," he told himself. "I *will* make it."

The second "stone-skip" was, as predicted, weaker than the first, and it gave Voorhees a small measure of hope that the wound in the hull would not worsen.

Thankfully, gravity was beginning to exert itself again and Voorhees was able to move his limbs more normally. He had found the disorientation of high-g and even zero-g interesting, but not entirely pleasant.

The engineer checked his watch and prepared for the next course correction. Soon, if the fuel tank lasted just a little longer, he would be able to make one final course change, jettison the bombs on a path toward the mid-Atlantic, vent off any remaining propellant, and set a glide path toward Washington.

"All right, time to—"

tap, tap, tap

"What the—?"

The sound, barely audible, had come from somewhere behind him. Voorhees craned his neck but it was impossible to see the bulkhead.

tap, Tap, TAP

It's definitely coming from inside the cabin.

Something has come loose, he assured himself, even as he felt a flutter in his belly.

Voorhees quickly ran through a mental checklist. There were pipes and ductwork back there but not much more. *What could be—*

TAP, TAP, TAP

It was coming from under his seat.

The flutter in his guts transformed itself into a worm.

Voorhees leaned forward, straining against the canvas harness, but he could see no farther back than the tips of his boots.

For a moment, he felt an odd vibration run through the seat frame, accompanied by a faint clicking sound. And then silence.

Kommen sie nicht herein.

But Voorhees knew that something *had* come in.

"It's all right," he said, trying to calm himself.

Then, without warning, he kicked back violently and felt the back of his boot impact against something soft.

Voorhees heard a snap, and a mass of flesh skittered backward.

He flinched as his uninvited passenger scrabbled against the aft bulkhead.

The scrabbling and skittering stopped. And then . . .

Nothing.

With both rockets now away and Eugen Sänger having set off on a final mission, Colonel Gerhardt Wolff gave the order to abandon the base. A minute later, a frightened-looking soldier handed him the backpack he had been ordered to retrieve from the *Nostromo*. Little more than a boy, the private helped Wolff slip the pack on, but before he could muster the courage to ask the colonel where he should go or what he should do, the officer slipped into the mist and disappeared.

After abandoning his bewildered underling, Wolff met up with an Indian guide at a prearranged point along a narrow trail leading out of the compound. The man was nearly nude, his body painted red and black. Without a word or an acknowledgment, the local turned and set off down the trail at a fast jog.

Wolff was unconcerned with his guide's appearance. The only thing that mattered was that the man was clearly knowledgeable about the escape route they were taking; as they zigged and zagged through impenetrable haze, the sounds of occasional gunfire and explosions began to fade behind them.

The rockets have been launched successfully, Wolff thought, breathing hard now as he chased the younger man. *And maybe . . . just maybe . . . I too will get out of here.*

Several minutes later, the colonel slowed as the guide came to an abrupt halt. Catching up to the painted man, Wolff could see that the trail ended at a small clearing, perhaps five meters across. In the center of the clearing, someone had lit and was maintaining a small fire.

"What is this?" he said, gesturing toward the forest beyond the fire. "We must keep moving."

But the painted man said nothing, and before Wolff could respond, a dozen Xavante tribesmen materialized out of the mist.

It was immediately clear to the colonel that his guide knew these men, each of whom was similarly unclothed and garishly painted.

The officer could sense someone coming up behind him as well. *I will not turn around,* he vowed. For a moment he actually thought about bolting into the forest. But there was something about the way the tribesmen were watching him that made him decide against it.

They want me to run, he thought. *They have even left a gap for me to—*

Almost gently, Colonel Wolff felt the weight of the backpack being lifted from his shoulders. Simultaneously, someone removed the Luger from its holster and, a moment after that, he could hear one of them rummaging around in his pack.

They'd love me to run. They—

Click. Click.

The sound had come from behind Wolff and he identified it instantly.

"No!" he said, and turning, he saw his former guide removing the Stradivarius from its case.

Wolff's eyes widened as the man clumsily stripped off the violin's protective wrapping and casually tossed the pads of desiccant to the ground. Then he did something that chilled the Nazi even more than the mishandling of his precious instrument. The Xavante tribesman looked up and smiled. There was something about his smile that brought with it an instantaneous sense of recognition.

I have seen it—practiced it in the mirror, Wolff thought, even as the Xavante extended his arm—holding out the violin as if bestowing a gift.

It is my smile.

Without thinking, Wolff took a step toward the violin, and immediately winced as the men who had been standing behind him each grabbed him roughly by an arm.

Still, he tried to pull free. "The humidity," he cried. Then he turned his head from side to side as if to convince his captors. "The moisture will damage the violin!"

But the Xavante showed little interest in the strange musical instrument, or the even stranger, misplaced pleas of their captive. They were far more interested in one of their own brethren, a man kneeling on the opposite side of the fire.

And so Colonel Wolff watched as well.

He watched through the low flames and shimmering air as the man unwrapped something from a bound leather pouch.

He watched as the Xavante began to pass around pieces of obsidian.

He watched as his former guide tossed the Stradivarius into the flames.

He watched it burn.

CHAPTER 28

Watch the Skies

The bay trees in our country are all wither'd.
And meteors fright the fixed stars of heaven.
The pale-faced moon looks bloody on the earth—
And lean-looked prophets whisper fearful change.
—WILLIAM SHAKESPEARE, *Richard II*

N*ostromo* Base was a smoking ruin, with bodies and parts of bodies strewn about, on the ground and in the trees.

MacCready and Thorne made sure to keep Yanni between them as they picked their way through the rubble. Both men carried their weapons at the ready.

Thorne spoke up: "Mac, do you hear that?"

"Hear what?"

"Nothin'. This party's over."

The gunfire and the explosions had stopped but they still moved cautiously through the wreckage of the compound—perhaps even more cautiously.

"Yeah, could be," MacCready replied. *Maybe this* is *over,* he thought. *Wolff's men have scattered. And why not? They've accomplished their mission.*

Mac brought them to a halt at the remains of what had clearly been a laboratory. The roof was torn away and one of the walls was blown out, allowing them a clear view of the building's interior. The signs of medical experimentation were immediately and horribly apparent.

"Look, we messed up back there—big time," MacCready whispered to Thorne and Yanni. "But we can still come out of this shit pile with something important."

"And what might that be, Mac?" asked Bob.

"We've gotta find the bats they've captured."

"And please remind me again. What is so important about these bats?"

"One word," MacCready replied. "Antidote."

"Check."

"Yanni, why don't you wait outside," MacCready said, eyeing a stainless steel table outfitted with leather restraints.

"Fat chance," Yanni replied, shooting him a dirty look.

"I will stay and cover your backs," Thorne said.

MacCready actually managed a smile. "Now that's one I never thought I'd hear from you, Bob."

While Thorne remained outside, MacCready and Yanni explored the ripped-up, blown-apart, and strewn-about medical equipment.

"Shit, no cages," MacCready said.

"Mac," Yanni called. "Take a gander at this." Behind a row of overturned lab benches, a canvas document pouch had spilled its contents. Leafing through a leather-bound notebook filled with drawings and foreign script, Yanni asked, "You savvy Jap?"

"No, can't read it. But let me see that," he said, taking the book from her. Several photographs fell onto the floor.

Yanni picked one up and examined it. "What's this, Mac?"

He squinted at the fuzzy black-and-white photo. "I don't

know, looks like pictures from space. Imagine that," he said. Letting the photo drop to the ground, he turned to more important concerns.

After flipping through the first hundred pages of Kimura's notebook, MacCready stopped suddenly, his eyes widening. He held the book open. "Look, Yanni, friends of yours."

The pages showed a succession of beautifully rendered sketches, each displaying a different live pose and a different anatomical feature of a *Desmodus draculae* specimen. One series of drawings in particular sent a chill through him. The artist had expressed an inordinate interest in an oversize set of oral glands. Even more chilling, because at first it seemed so out of place, was the final sketch—a gardenia.

MacCready tucked the notebook into the canvas pack, along with the photographs. "Come on." He pulled Yanni by the hand, leading her back outside.

Moving at a more determined pace, the trio quickly discovered the *Nostromo,* huge and incongruous in the shallow water. The deck and lower portion of the conning tower were partially obscured by mist but the boat seemed to be deserted. Mac thought this might have something to do with the fact that the sub appeared to be listing significantly to port.

MacCready nodded toward the wounded submarine. "All aboard."

With Yanni beside him, MacCready pulled up at the base of the gangplank.

"Yanni, you think Bob is square with you coming along?" he asked.

Yanni shot her approaching husband a quick glance. She shook her head. "Fuck no." Then they began to mount the wooden incline.

• • •

I n the *Silverbird II,* as another skip off the atmosphere ended, Maurice Voorhees let out a deep sigh. He had heard nothing more from his stowaway, but even the incredible sense of exhilaration he felt from the flight was tempered by the unsettling fact that *something* had gotten into the cockpit with him.

Maybe it's just a rat, he thought. Then just as quickly, he shook his head. "Who are you kidding, Maurice?"

Filled with a renewed sense of dread, the engineer strained against the harness once more, twisting around in his seat. But it was impossible to see the floor along the rear bulkhead, and after a moment he let his body uncoil with a grunt.

They left the canopy open. That's how it . . . Maybe it was frightened. Maybe it was looking for a safe place to hide. And for a moment, the thought made him feel badly about what he'd done. But as unfortunate as the encounter might have been for the creature, Voorhees still prayed that the thing was either dead or too injured to be a threat.

"All right, next crisis," he said, checking his watch and his trajectory again. *No more time to waste,* he thought, reflexively reaching down for the throttle with a gloved hand.

Then, without tapping or clicking, and with no warning at all, something sharp pricked his right index finger through the leather glove.

The engineer-turned-pilot yanked his hand away.

"Shit!" he cried, fumbling to remove the glove.

He stared at his finger.

No pain—maybe the skin's not broken, he thought. But just as quickly, he noticed a centimeter-long divot of missing flesh. And as he watched, the wound filled with blood, overflowed, and the overflow began to drift into the air.

"No! NO!" Voorhees cried, willing the blood to stop—but it didn't. He pulled the glove back on. His hand looked normal now but almost immediately, he could feel the glove filling with something slippery and warm.

Maurice Voorhees began to hyperventilate.

As the seconds passed, another "stone-skip" began; the *Silverbird* and its wounded passengers were hurled toward the top of another parabola.

Had he been watching, Voorhees would have seen the Virginia coastline coming into view—but from the port-side window, rather than the starboard. His encounter with the stowaway had thrown off his timing and he had neglected to release the bio-bombs on their "useless" mid-Atlantic trajectory. Nor had he made a required course correction toward the west. Instead the pilot was fixated on his own hand. The glove had swollen rapidly and now began to deflate, as spherules of bright red—some pea-size, others breaking up into a scarlet mist—poured from the slice in the leather. Through the horror, he was reminded of a magician's wand, but it was not magic dust that his index finger was spewing into the cockpit.

"Jesus," he said, moments before experiencing a sudden and painful buildup of pressure in his guts. This was followed by the equally unexpected relief of something letting go, and his pants were suddenly streaming blood as the g-force returned.

The course correction, he thought, finally and too late. But instead of checking the gauges arrayed before him, something made him look down again. There, beside him, was the injured bat. His scientist's brain worked frantically as if recording its last notes: *Much larger than the one I dosed with rocket fuel.*

As he stared in fascination and horror, the creature looked up at him, teeth glistening red. Then it turned back to feed at the pool that was forming around his feet.

The *Silverbird II* stone-skipped into yet another arc, and this time the air in the cockpit became so filled with blood that Maurice Voorhees could no longer see through the windows.

He struggled to maintain his concentration. *No landing now.* He was beginning to lose consciousness but just as quickly his thoughts became clear—one last time. *The bombs. The bombs.*

"LLLSSSLLL," he called, through lips that were losing all sensation. "*Lisl.*"

And as he began weeping tears of blood, he realized that he was losing control of his hands.

"I will do this!" he screamed (or perhaps the words were just in his mind).

With the g-forces beginning to build again, he flailed at the controls, deliberately swinging the *Silverbird* broadside into what he knew would be a hypersonic, superheated wind.

On a beach far below, a ten-year-old boy who had awakened early to chase sandpipers stopped to watch a comet blaze suddenly to life, cleaving before his eyes into a cluster of five dazzling diamonds. As they flew northeast toward the deep Atlantic, the diamonds—embers from Hell's Gate—broke apart, trailing smoke and sparks until they extinguished themselves in a sterilizing glare.

Three figures entered the *Nostromo* through a forward hatch, not far from the spot where something huge had torn a hole in the submarine's foredeck and hull. The boat was sitting dead in the water, having settled to the river bottom with a ten-degree list to port.

At the bottom of a steep metal ladder, cramped passageways extended away from a small circle of light like the arms of a spider.

Somehow Yanni had managed to scrounge up a trio of flashlights.

MacCready tried to dredge up anything he could remember about the deck plan of the *Demeter*, *Nostromo*'s grounded sister ship. "This way," he whispered, gesturing down one of the dark corridors. *I think.*

They moved slowly, supporting themselves against the walls to compensate for the odd angle of the floor, before pausing beside an open hatch in the "B" deck. MacCready aimed his flashlight beam down into "C" deck, revealing yet another open hatch in the deck below. *"D" deck? Shit. How far down does this thing go?*

He shook his head. "I think it's this way," he whispered. "I'll go first."

Nobody argued with him.

MacCready was halfway down the second set of ladders when a loud metallic groan filled the passageway. The sound was accompanied by a coarse, rattling vibration, as if a giant had decided to sandpaper the *Nostromo*'s hull. Just to show its gratitude, the sub shifted another five degrees to port.

Great, MacCready thought, *this thing's going to capsi—*

A sudden jolt caused him to lose his footing and he slid down the final four steps shins-first before landing on his rump with a splash. Completing his descent, MacCready was hit by a sloshing wave of water and fuel, as the knee-high surge on "D" deck made the adjustments required by physics.

Mac sat in complete darkness, groping in vain for his now-extinguished flashlight, when a spotlight illuminated him from above.

"Well, this descent of yours is somewhat less than smooth," Thorne whispered from behind the light.

After the Thornes took a more deliberate, and certainly less spectacular, climb down the ladder, they stood in a central companionway. It ran fore and aft, into the dark, and through eighteen inches of debris-cluttered water.

"Which way?" Thorne asked, trying hard to mask his nervousness.

MacCready took a flashlight from his friend, shrugged, then set off in the same direction he had been heading before.

"I have a question," Thorne whispered. They were wading single file through a claustrophobic passageway lined with gauges, pipes, and a maze of wires.

"Ask away," MacCready whispered back.

"What do you propose we do should we find these dra-coo-lay?"

"That's a good one, Bob; I'm not quite sure."

The botanist let out a deep breath. "This plan is sounding more than somewhat familiar. May I suggest we head topside and talk this out?"

"Over a smoke, of course?"

"Now there you go. And I have got some—"

MacCready's signal for silence halted his friend's quest for herbage.

The companionway led to an abrupt end. They now stood in ankle-deep water, outside a door-shaped hatch that was several inches ajar. A skull and crossbones had been stenciled on either side of the portal, and someone had scrawled something in German on the hatch itself.

The botanist gestured toward the sign. "I don't suppose this says 'Welcome'?"

"*Eintritt Verboten*," Mac replied. "It means stay the hell out."

"I agree, Mac. Especially since what makes you think your bats are down here, anyway?"

"We found the Bio Lab back there. And there were no bats. Where else could they be?"

"The plateau," Yanni replied.

"Nailed it, wifey," Thorne added, with no little measure of pride.

"Could be," Mac responded with a nod. "Do you two want to head back up there with me?"

The couple shook their heads simultaneously.

Mac smiled. "So?"

"Onward," Thorne whispered.

MacCready moved forward, directing a flashlight through the narrow opening. The shaft of light revealed a lab that appeared quite spacious—for a sub. Fallen boxes and toppled equipment blocked most of his view, but not the unmistakable scent of guano and urine.

MacCready turned to his friends. "It's definitely in there," he whispered. "Or was."

Yanni nodded in agreement, even as Thorne took a step backward.

"All right, let's go," Mac said, pushing the hatch open another six inches.

They entered the lab cautiously, stepping over the high lip of the hatchway. MacCready noticed that the threshold acted like a dam, holding back the water from the adjoining companionway.

At least our feet'll be dry, he thought.

Two cones of light scanned the room, one of the beams pausing momentarily at a steel table bolted to the floor. The scientific equipment it had held now lay strewn about broken. Finally, both beams converged on a row of metal cages mounted against the far wall. There were five of them, each large enough to house a medium-size dog. Four of the cages were open, their metal-barred doors thrown back revealing empty interiors.

MacCready focused his light on the only cage that remained closed. As he inched closer, he saw a flash of movement inside—a dark form, scuttling into the shadows. Mac took another step forward, his flashlight illuminating a bit more of the cage interior. He could make out a furry shape, huddled and shivering in the farthest corner.

He began to speak softly, "Hey there, little—"

Something smashed against the bars, and as Mac took an involuntary step backward, his beam illuminated glistening teeth and wild red eyes. The thing inside the cage was screaming now, high-pitched and shrill; and as the creature slammed itself back and forth against the inside of the metal enclosure, the horrible sounds were amplified by the tight confines of the lab.

"Yanni, get back!" Thorne screamed, but his wife stood her ground.

"Pipe down, Bob," she replied, calmly.

"It's a lab monkey," MacCready assured him.

"Oh, I thought—"

"Mac," Yanni said, from across the room, "come have a look."

She was staring down at something on the floor, and as Mac-Cready approached he could see that it was another monkey. This one was clearly dead, pasted to a thick puddle of its own blood.

Mac crouched down beside the animal, playing his own light across its body. His mind already flashed back to the stall in Chapada. "This happened recently," he whispered.

The botanist moved in to take a look. "Like . . . when, Mac?"

"Within the past few hours, probably less."

"But that means—"

MacCready held up his hand, silencing his friend again. Then he moved back to one of the open cages. The floor of this particular cage was thick with a coating of rust-colored matter. *Guano,* he thought. *Must be a week's accumulation.*

"This cage held our bat," he whispered.

Thorne motioned toward the cage door. "But this cage is opened from the outside. All of them are, except the one with Cheetah over there. So maybe Wolff's people decided to take these so-called dra-coo-lay with them?"

"Sure, Bob, to keep as pets," Yanni suggested, sounding remarkably earnest.

Thorne started to reply, and MacCready got ready to perform banter *interruptus,* when *something* stopped him—something that drew his attention to the darkest corner of the laboratory. But instead of aiming his flashlight there, he pointed it upward, so that the beam illuminated his own face.

"Huh?" Bob whispered, with surprise.

"It's all right," MacCready said softly, but not to his friend.

And with that, the face of a demon emerged slowly from the shadows, a face that held the scientist spellbound.

Holy shit, MacCready thought. *It's the—*

"Mac, what are you doing?" Thorne whispered.

Mac never acknowledged his friend's question. Instead, he decided to try an experiment he had actually been planning for some time. He began to whistle. At first he struggled to remember the simple melody, the one Yanni had used to serenade the forest behind her home.

But something about it wasn't right, and the cat-size creature reacted by stepping backward, its face disappearing into the shadows.

Damn, Mac thought. But then, before he could wonder what had gone wrong, Yanni was standing beside him. And so he tried again. Several notes in, she joined him, correcting him, even whistling a harmony to his melody, then taking the lead.

Song of the draculae, he thought, and as they whistled, a pair of bats—each much larger than the first one—crawled down from the shadows. A fourth bat, the largest, walked down the wall of cages, quiet as a ninja. The creatures crouched with their chests close to the ground, and MacCready noticed that their bodies were tensed, *like coiled springs.*

The juvenile bat had been "elbowed" backward by what seemed to be an Alpha male who behaved like an older sibling, but instead of retreating into the shadows, the little one skittered between its larger companions as if looking for a way to move forward.

There's something very different about that one, MacCready told himself, noting that its stance conveyed none of the barely contained violence displayed by its larger companions.

It shows no fear—only something like . . . curiosity.

Then, keeping the same quizzical look on its nightmare face, the *draculae* child cocked its head for a moment, issuing a series of high-pitched chirps, at once familiar but at the same time utterly alien.

Jesus, MacCready told himself. *It's trying to communicate with us.*

Yanni repeated the song again, and in Mac's mind, at that moment, nothing else existed. He felt Yanni's hand on his shoulder, motioning him to step aside with her, leaving a clear pathway to the door.

Without turning away from the bats, MacCready whispered, "Yanni, why—"

"There is no other way, Mac. If we want to live."

MacCready nodded. *I'm not crazy. It's not just senseless animal song: It's an understanding.*

A moment later, there was a flutter of movement and a whisper of parchment, then the clatter of claws receded down the steel-walled companionway.

One bat remained.

The mother crouched in a forward launch position, sono-scanning the three humans.

Go!

Then, like the other *draculae*, it was gone, vanishing down the companionway like a specter, and leaving in her wake the unmistakable scent of gardenias.

CHAPTER 29

Profiles of the Future

The survival value of human intelligence has never been proved, and may in fact be more a liability than an asset. Once a species reaches a certain level of intelligence, it has a survival advantage until such point that it develops sufficient power to destroy itself and everything around it. And it may be, then, that it always does. The universe may be full of planets on which high intelligence at the high-technology level has not yet developed, and also full of planets bearing the ruins of high-technology civilizations that no longer exist.

—ISAAC ASIMOV, 1986

Nostromo Base
February 17, 1944

By the time Major Patrick Hendry arrived by seaplane the next morning, with a serious contingent of special ops boys, MacCready and his two friends were waiting to guide them in. The monorail and most of the compound's buildings (what remained of them) were still gushing plumes of black smoke that mingled with the mists and rose above them.

As Hendry's men spread across the base, the major pulled a bottle of Jack Daniel's out of his pack. He followed up by producing a pair of shot glasses.

"How'd you get in here so fast?" Mac asked.

Hendry smiled. "Air recon, reported that half of Brazil seemed to be on fire. I figured it was you."

"Yeah, well, breaking things and killing people, setting shit on fire. That's what we scientists are up to these days. Isn't it?"

Hendry replied with a humorless laugh. "Mac, you don't know the half of it," he said, pouring a pair of stiff shots. "And speaking of which, we just heard from our boys back north. There were numerous sightings of an unnaturally bright meteor off the Virginia coast. It was heading south to north when it tore apart."

"Let me guess, it was heading directly away from our position."

"Quite a coincidence there, huh? Unofficially, they're calling it a Foo Fighter."

"And officially?" MacCready asked.

"A meteor."

"What about casualties on the ground? Any word on whether this meteor dropped any bombs along its path?"

"None whatsoever," Hendry responded, noting his friend's unease. "An eyewitness said, 'It simply flamed apart into a bouquet of bright sparks and disappeared over the ocean.'"

"A bouquet, huh? And what about the second rocket? Any more bouquets?"

"No . . . no word on that one. Intelligence thinks it was probably lost over the Atlantic as well."

Mac shook his head. "That's a stretch."

"So maybe we got lucky this time."

Hendry raised his shot glass.

MacCready hesitated, then lightly touched it with his own. "*This* time," he said. "But judging from a Japanese sketchbook and the type of lab equipment they left behind, it's pretty clear these guys figured out how to use pathogens in the *draculae* saliva to make a bioweapon."

Hendry nodded. "Makes sense. And you know what I always say about wounded animals, right?"

Mac waved off the rather obvious dig. "Smartest thing I've ever heard you say."

As if on cue, Thorne approached the men, seeming either troubled or looking for trouble.

"Ah, the World-Famous Botanist, I presume," Hendry said. "Would you care to join us in a toast to a job well done?"

Thorne flashed MacCready his best who-the-fuck-is-this-guy look then addressed the major: "Excuse me, bub, but last I heard, those rockets were heading down that track in one piece."

"One of them went down off the coast of Virginia," Hendry said quietly. "And that's classified information, Mr. Thorne."

"And the second one?"

Hendry paused. "Presumed lost."

"In any event, I will hold off on the celebrating, thank you." Thorne turned to his friend. "Mac, have you seen Yanni?"

Yet before Mac could scan the grounds, Yanni emerged out of the shifting mists—shadowy, as if she were a ghost.

"Hey, Yanni," Mac called, "I wanna introduce you to our brand-new fr—"

Something in her expression stopped him.

"You . . . must come," was all she said. Then she turned and headed back into the fog.

MacCready and Thorne exchanged puzzled looks, before jogging off after Yanni.

They quickly caught up with her and she led them through the smog and dripping foliage until they came to a clearing in the woods. The remains of a small campfire were still smoldering.

MacCready stepped into the circle, realizing at once that there were two bodies near the center of the clearing. One was lying on the ground at the foot of the other—which had been lashed upright to a wooden post.

MacCready crept nearer. *Something's wrong.*

"What is going—?" Bob Thorne froze.

Both of the "bodies" were Colonel Wolff. MacCready could see that, a centimeter at a time, the Xavante had put the Nazi to the same fate he once condemned him to by "choice."

Somehow, they had removed his skin in a single piece. Mac estimated that it must have taken many hours to complete the task. He was also fairly certain that Wolff had survived their artwork and been left to die.

Morbid curiosity led him to take a step closer, and a cloud of flies rose noisily into the air, angry at having been interrupted in their meal and their egg-laying on the staked-out man and his twin. The colonel appeared to have died staring down at the wet pile, which was already black with ants.

Scarcely breathing, MacCready began to examine the upright corpse. He placed a hand under its chin and lifted the head up. *The musculature is still quite warm,* he thought, looking at his watch. "Six hours," he said.

"Six *what?*" said Thorne, his voice subdued by shock. "I don't understand."

"After they've finished the job, it takes at least six hours for a man to die like that."

An instant later, Wolff rolled his lidless eyes and spat at him.

"Jesus Christ!" Thorne cried.

Incredibly, Wolff began to chuckle and his head stayed up, straining against visible tendons, as MacCready backed away, nearly toppling over Wolff's "*other* body."

"*Jesusss?* Where is *heee*?" The German looked at MacCready through air-dried and bug-bitten corneas, his voice damp air escaping from a tomb. "*Youuu* . . . I knew you weren't *deadddd*."

Uncharacteristically, MacCready could not think of a reply.

Sensing this, Wolff attempted what might have been a smile, several cordlike facial muscles drawing upward but with no lips to complete the expression. A moment later, the muscles relaxed and the Nazi concentrated on what he knew would be his final words: "The *Silverbirds* . . . I did *thisss* . . . Kimura's bomb . . . *You did thissssss*."

And with those words, Wolff's head slumped forward.

Thorne approached cautiously, half-afraid the Nazi would reanimate himself a second time. He was also unnerved by the strange expression MacCready wore.

"What does he mean by this, Mac?"

"I'm not sure, Bob," MacCready lied, looking rather unsteady and knowing that Wolff had called it correctly. He *had* done this. Looking back now, at each fork in the road, every decision seemed like the right one. Yet still, in the end, he wound up leading his enemies directly to the biological weapons they craved. *How*, he wondered, *might events have unfurled had his plane's collision with a scarlet ibis killed him at Waller Field? How much better would things have turned out?*

"I'm not sure," Mac repeated. He went silent, not knowing whose question he had just answered.

Yanni's voice broke the silence. "Mac, you need to see this."

She was holding open a notebook that she'd pulled from a small pile of Wolff's belongings. Mac took the book from her without losing the page she'd been staring at.

Colonel Wolff's lab notes were written in a clear and easily readable German script, but what immediately caught Mac's attention were his drawings of the plateau. They showed the cave entrance, the passageway leading to the *draculae* roost, and the subchamber itself. But it was a drawing of the cave's antechamber that caused MacCready's eyes to widen. Four small squares spread across the floor, each with a line stretching to a point several feet away. *They booby-trapped that cave,* he thought, recognizing what, to his mind, could only be trip wires.

MacCready scanned additional figures on the adjacent pages. One of them showed similar boxes arranged across the top of the plateau.

And what are these? he wondered, noting that the squares were arrayed along what seemed to be a series of fissures in the earth. Mac remembered the strong breeze that nearly blew out his lantern—*a breeze that could only have come down through one of these faults. While two of Wolff's men were being slaughtered by turtles, he must have been sending others back to survey weaknesses in the plateau roof.*

"Jesus," MacCready said, "they're going to blow that cave."

Absolutely not, Mac," Major Hendry barked, dismissing the request with a wave of his hand. The two men were standing outside the ruins of Wolff's and Kimura's lab.

"But Pat—"

"And that's an order. I'm sending you back with the first convoy to Cuiabá," Hendry announced. "You need a break."

"Pat, you don't understand. I've *got* to go up there."

"No, *you* don't understand. If any of these assholes survived, and if they've gotten back to that cave—let 'em blow it and God bless 'em. You are *not* going up there alone."

"But what about an antidote, and what if they're trying to capture another one?"

Hendry held up his hand. "Hold the bullshit, Mac. I can read German just as well as you. Wolff's entire plan was to get those rockets away and to make sure nobody on this side of the Pond ever got access to those microbes again. Ever!"

MacCready knew his friend's argument made perfect sense, and yet he had to go back.

Everything was turning upside down in MacCready's head. It seemed that the voices of his mother and little sister had already decided his course. Last time, he hadn't been around to prevent the deaths of an innocent mother and child. There was no choice in the matter. This time, without taking pause to question the sanity of his decision, Mac would do everything in his power to prevent the extinction of the innocent. In his mind, Amelia, Brigitte, and the *draculae* were becoming hopelessly entangled.

And why do I want to go back there?

The elders who drove Yanni into the forest years before could have answered him. "Once the *chupacabra* have been allowed to live inside your skull, you are never the same again."

B ob and Yanni Thorne watched a commotion begin near one of the spare rocket engines, while nearby a group of Hendry's men had mounted what was left of the monorail track and were taking measurements.

"Ants," Thorne said. "Just like ants." And in his scientist's mind there was no doubt now, that a new day, a new era had be-gun. "I am seeing the world to come, Yanni. And it ain't pretty."

"And speaking of ain't pretty." Yanni gestured toward Mac-Cready, who was striding toward them at a brisk clip.

"So on a scale of one to ten, how much shit is he bringing this time?"

"Thirteen?" Yanni said.

Once Mac laid out the plan, Thorne realized that Yanni had underestimated. "You want to go *where?*" he said. "Well, this time you've gone too far. And we are not going with you. In fact, I may rat out your plan to Hendry, just to keep your ass off that plateau."

"No, Bob, you will *not* tell Hendry," Yanni countered quickly. "And you are *not* going. I am."

Thorne looked like someone who had been punched in the stomach. "But—"

"We belong to the *chupacabra,* Mac. And we will save them," Yanni said.

Bob was suddenly agitated. "What's with this 'we belong' shit? Who belongs to what *chupacabra?*"

MacCready, who was no less dumbfounded than Thorne, paused for a moment. Although her statement seemed as distant from all prior reality as space-planes and sentient vampire bats, he knew she was right. Deeply intrusive and frightful, there was an intensely personal quality about the song of the *draculae.* Once received, one was apt to obsess.

"Then I am going, too," Thorne announced. "It's settled."

"Well," Mac said, "Hendry *did* order me not to go up there alone."

His friend managed a laugh. "So it seems that now you are only following orders."

M acCready knew that if any of Wolff's men had survived to tie up loose ends, now that the rockets were away, they had at least a full day's lead. So, to shave off several hours, Mac led Bob and Yanni up the same path he had taken during his escape from the *draculae* lair.

The first thing MacCready discovered as they stood atop the forest-capped Mato Grosso Plateau was that he'd been correct about the source of the winds in the caverns below. *It's as if the plateau itself is breathing.*

He encountered the first fissure by accident. A downward gust nearly sucked a map from his hands, even before he saw the deep slash in the ground. The fig trees around its edge had been deformed by the downdraft; trunks leaning into the crevice, while roots clawed in the opposite direction, seeking to anchor the plants against the tug from below.

The second thing MacCready discovered was that Wolff and his mapmakers had done their homework. Underfoot, the tabletop formation was cobwebbed with vertical fissures. The map led him to a second crevice, and in what appeared to be just the right place, someone had planted an explosive device.

"Shit, I knew it. It's a fucking *shaped* charge."

"Which is?" Thorne asked.

"It's designed to channel explosive energy in one direction. So that even a small blast can have a big effect."

"And what direction is this so-called shaped charge pointing?"

MacCready pointed downward. "We're standing on a diamond."

"A what?"

"No time to explain. I need you and Yanni to look for more of these things." He handed them his own hand-drawn version of

Wolff's charge placements and pointed to the forest on the opposite side of the fissure. "And if you find anything—do *not* touch
it. Just let me know."

"No worries, Mac. What do I know from disarming bombs?"

"And keep your eyes peeled. Whoever planted this thing could
still be up here."

Thorne responded with a reluctant nod. Yanni holstered her
sidearm and unslung her blowgun. "Shhhhhhhh," she whispered.

Twenty minutes later, MacCready shimmied out of the crevice, placing the dissected bomb on the ground beside him.
And while it was no longer dangerous, he knew it had taken far
too long to disarm the device.

Mac thought back to Wolff's notebook and the multiple det-
onation points he would now have to deal with (*too many of them
and maybe not enough time*), when Yanni's voice called out.

"Lookee what we found!"

She was walking behind a blond-haired man in his early for-
ties, hands raised over his head.

"My name is Eugen Sänger," he said in accented English.
"And under the articles of the Geneva Convention, I am officially
requesting that you protect me from this savage."

MacCready ignored the comment. "Where are the rest of
these things, asshole?" he said, pointing to the bomb at his feet.

"I have been stranded. Have you seen my guides?"

MacCready winced, reminded of Corporal Kessler's pursuit of
him across the swamp. "Where *do* you guys come up with this shit?"

Yanni responded by poking Sänger hard, in the back of the
head, with the business end of her blowgun. The man staggered
forward a few steps.

"Pally," MacCready said, "if you don't start talking right now, you are going off the side of this fucking plateau."

"My name is Eugen Sänger and under the articles of—"

MacCready unleashed a savage right cross that not only broke the rocket designer's jaw but a bone in his own hand as well. Sänger fell to his knees and looked up with a blood-smeared grimace that turned into a grin.

Mac felt a flutter in the pit of his stomach. Something about the man's expression conveyed a single fact: *It was already so clearly too late.*

He turned to Yanni. "Where's Bob?" And the blood drained from his face when she pointed to the forest on the cliff side of the fissure.

The explosions felt like an insignificant series of muffled pops, compared to their ultimate effect. Wolff and Sänger had indeed done their homework, knowing exactly where, with just a few little taps, they could crack a diamond into a thousand pieces.

"Bob!"

Mac and Yanni sprinted along the plateau side of an ever-widening chain of cracks in the ground. It seemed that new crevices were yawning open every second and in every direction—except one.

"Yanni!" It was Bob's voice and she changed direction, heading into the disintegrating earth.

"Bob!" she screamed, and as she did, Mac grabbed her wrist, yanking it with such force that for a moment he feared he'd dislocated her shoulder.

As if by magic the rumbling stopped and there, in front of them stood Bob Thorne. He was wearing a curious look on his face.

He waved. "Hey, Yanni. Mac."

MacCready looked across the thirty-foot chasm that separated them, and what he saw was heartbreak.

"Hey, Bob." *I'll watch after Yanni,* he thought of saying.

"I know you will," Bob replied.

And then, beginning with a disorienting lurch, a section of the plateau, more than a thousand feet tall, cast off like a ship from a pier. Carrying Bob with it, the ship sank slowly into the smoke and dust of Hell's Gate.

Epilogue

Nostromo Base
April 1946

Only two years had passed, and the forest was already consuming the ruins of *Nostromo* Base. Vines were racing up the monorail supports, while bushes, some of them more than five feet tall, had sprouted from the elevated trackway itself. But the ancient stone-block road upon which the launch ramp had been anchored would survive long after the rail itself was gone.

During the coming decades, pre-Columbian roads and the vestiges of an entire civilization, hidden between *Nostromo* Base and the Mato Grosso Plateau, would become archaeological sites, then tourist attractions.

Irrigation canals dating back over a thousand years were about to be excavated and reactivated—supporting the increasingly expansive cattle ranches. Here and there, careless lumber cutting and agricultural practices were beginning to turn forested regions, through which MacCready had walked, into patches of dry savanna.

The submarine *Nostromo* was being consumed as well—cut apart, hauled away, and sold as scrap. What remained of the boat stood in increasingly open daylight. The Rio Xingu was already dropping, and within two decades it would be reduced to a relative trickle—taking with it the perpetual fog layer that had shrouded the entire valley for millennia.

Though the lack of fog made it easier to haul his heavy welding equipment from town, Hector Uieda hated being out here alone. All of the sheet metal that had covered the labs and other buildings was gone now, leaving only a framework of vine-covered ribs. To Uieda, it wasn't the skeletal appearance of the buildings that chilled him; it was the sounds they made. Normally the occasional breezes rustling through leaves had a soothing effect, but not here, and not now. Beneath *this* rustling was a disquieting undertone, more felt than heard. He'd experienced the odd feeling before, but this evening it seemed stronger than ever. Uieda had to admit, however, that the heat and humidity weren't nearly as troublesome as usual. *It's almost pleasant,* he thought.

Brooklyn, New York

R. J. MacCready and Major Hendry had been able to pull all the necessary strings to expedite the immigration of a war hero's widow to America, especially as she was a war hero herself, albeit a secretly decorated one. Everything about the "*Silverbird* Incident" was being kept so secret that nearly a century would pass before the public learned the full story.

At first sight, Yanni Thorne feared that the concrete wilderness of Flatbush Avenue might prove, as she joked to Mac, "tougher than the one growin' under the plateau."

As always, though, she adapted quickly. Hendry had arranged

living quarters for her near the Brooklyn Navy Yard, on the up-permost floor of a decommissioned factory-warehouse. During the war, the building served as a kind of spare-parts storage box for the navy's Grumman aircraft. By the time Yanni landed in New York, Hendry's two sisters had convinced him that their "crazy" idea about buying the suddenly empty and seemingly useless warehouse at the bargain-basement price of a government auction, then repurposing it into large river-view apartments, "might be just crazy enough to be right."

Yanni was the first to move in, followed by several of the re-gion's bohemian artists, who admired the skill with which she was transforming her glass and concrete cavern into a living, breathing work of art.

Missing Bob and the little house they had shared at the edge of the forest, she brought the forest itself into her new home. With Mac along for the ride, she had scoured every flower shop and nursery from Brooklyn to upper Manhattan for familiar plants. Yanni's indoor replica of the Brazilian tropics thrived under huge factory skylights and windows that ran from waist height all the way up to the ceiling. The furnishings were odd, by most people's standards: a massive rolltop work desk from the 1890s, with a hammock and a little sitting area nearby, all of it surrounded by tropical evergreens and flowering plants. Near what she called her "breathing wall" (a vertical carpet of leafy vines and bromeliads) Yanni had reproduced, as best she could, the kitchen from their home in Chapada.

Mac was a frequent visitor; making sure the apartment was secure and checking out her neighbors with a concern that would have amused Bob. He also contributed a new refrigerator as a housewarming present, but Yanni never plugged it in. She hadn't gotten used to the concept of frozen or prepared foods, preferring to buy fresh meat and produce daily from the local markets. As for the fridge, Yanni removed the door and used the box as additional shelf space for an array of shade-loving plants.

On an exceptionally clear spring morning, Yanni Thorne noticed, during her walk to the Manhattan Bridge, that newspapers were headlining the latest in what were being touted as the "first ever" photographs of Earth from space. They had been snapped by Wernher von Braun's freshly upgraded, suborbital rockets.

"*Second* ever," she said to herself, recalling the ruins of the *Nostromo* lab and the fuzzy-looking photos she and Mac had found. "But they didn't seem so important at the time."

And if Sänger's involved, they'd be wise to keep his ass far away from me, she swore.

As she did every morning—rain, shine, sleet, or snow—Yanni walked the Manhattan Bridge's footpath into the city, and to her job, proudly wearing her Brooklyn Dodgers cap. The span could easily be crossed by train in only a few minutes, but she liked the long stroll across the bridge, because she loved the river. No matter what weather or lighting conditions prevailed on any given morning, the river was beauty, the river was peace.

Upper West Side, New York City

"Who the hell designed this torture device?" MacCready asked himself.

He always had trouble closing the specimen cabinet doors at the Metropolitan Museum of Natural History. The problem was that they slid on tracks located several feet above his head, and would only close if a pair of metal pins on the cabinet frame were precisely aligned with a *supposedly* matching set of grooves on the door itself.

"Can I help you with that, Mac?" came a voice from behind. It was Patricia Wynters, the resident artist in the Department of Vertebrate Zoology.

"Oh, hi, Patricia," he responded, stepping aside. "I think these pins are bent. This one's not going to close anytime soon."

"Let me give it a try," the tiny brunette responded. He'd been associated with the museum, in one capacity or another, since high school and, as always, Patricia was right there whenever he needed a helping hand. Within seconds she slid the four-foot-wide door into place and locked it. "You and prehistoric horses? That's a new one. What's this about?"

"Oh, just a little something I can't stop thinking about," Mac said, smiling. Then he glanced down at his watch. *The band,* he thought. *Dammit, I'm late.*

Mac and Patricia exited the specimen room together. After a "thanks" and a "see you later" Mac bolted down the fifth-floor hall toward the elevators. After a quick jog across Central Park West, then along a tree-lined trail, he stopped outside the Central Park Menagerie. A jazz band was already playing. The "experiment" was under way.

MacCready bypassed the ticket line and headed straight for the bored-looking security guard standing just past the entrance turnstiles.

"Hey, Carl," MacCready said.

"What's cookin', Mac?" the guard responded, waving him through. "Nice to have you back for a change. Oh, and Yanni's a real sweetheart."

"Yeah, thanks. Nice to be stationed in the city," Mac replied. He motioned in the direction of the music. "Sounds like they started without me. Gotta run."

"Better you than me," Carl responded, but by then Mac had already sprinted off, accompanied by the incongruous sound of a jazzy foxtrot.

Mac found a crowd of zoo visitors standing behind the bars of the fenced-off, outdoor portion of the Elephant House. Inside the enclosure stood two elephants, their forelimbs manacled to short sturdy chains attached to pegs that had been cemented into the ground. Standing just out of stomping distance, a mook in a three-piece suit was blowing his trumpet into the trunk of one of the elephants. The animal seemed to be enjoying the attention—gently touching the instrument and rocking back and forth in time with the music.

Looking far less relaxed, the head elephant keeper, who was wearing a long blue jacket and police-style cap, stood close by—alert for any sign of trouble. Completing his ready-for-a-riot attire, the keeper held a cop's baton—this one outfitted with a nasty-looking metal hook. Behind the trumpeteer, another musician played a stand-up snare drum, while a third wrung notes out of a saxophone. Off to one side, several lab-coat types were taking notes. Mac recognized one of them, a Professor Arthur Carrington from Atlantic Tech. At second glance, he could see that Carrington was actually posing for one of the photographers snapping away at the weirdness.

MacCready could also see Yanni Thorne, standing apart from the freak show. She was comforting the second elephant, which looked like a mountain of wrinkles compared to the svelte young lass being serenaded by the band. Still, the tired-looking creature watched the bizarre proceedings with seeming amusement. Yanni, on the other hand, who was stroking the ancient elephant's ear, seemed to be sharing Mac's growing feelings of disgust.

The song ended and one of the scientists hurried over to address the crowd, which was already beginning to wander off. "Ladies and gentlemen, what you have seen here today was a scientific experiment to determine the effect of music on the beasts of the jungle."

"You call that music?" someone heckled, eliciting a burst of laughter from the crowd.

The man in the lab coat, who was *not* laughing, cleared his throat and continued, explaining how the response they had just witnessed was proof that these brutes could remember their days performing with circus band accompaniment.

Mac turned away. "Science experiment, my ass," he muttered to himself. "Definitely a publicity stunt."

Moving along the fence, he could see Yanni and another keeper leading their enormous wards through the barn-size doors of the indoor enclosure. He checked his watch, grateful that she'd be getting out of work soon.

The jazz band had packed up and left, and Mac and Yanni were sitting on a park bench. She was dressed in street clothes now, tight-waisted slacks and a collared cotton top. Her long dark hair was pulled back in a ponytail. "If you think that was a horror show, Mac, be thankful you missed the Monkey House concert."

He flipped a peanut toward a gray squirrel, who was watching their conversation with apparent interest. "So music *doesn't* soothe the savage beast?"

"The monkeys threw their shit at those guys. Pelted them."

Mac laughed. "Well, there's a breakthrough: 'Science discovers a new species of music critic.'"

"Nobel Prize," Yanni replied, "wit outta doubt."

Mac shook his head. "Well, your elephant friend seemed entertained, although Professor Blather had his own ideas about why that was."

Yanni gestured, as if shooing away a fly. "That schmuck? Elephants aren't brutes, Mac. They're as intelligent as you and me. Only different . . . sorta like—"

MacCready suddenly felt uncomfortable—a tightness in his throat. "So, you still like Brooklyn, right?" he blurted. "Your apartment and all."

"What?" Yanni responded, seemingly confused by the abrupt change of topic.

Yanni paused. "Yeah, Mac. Of course, I love it." Now he could see that she knew *exactly* where his thoughts had gone.

"That's . . . good," he said, awkwardly.

"Speakin' of which, I gotta get home," Yanni said, standing. "And you got work to do, I suppose."

MacCready hesitated. "You're right," he said. "I do want to check out those *Parahippus* specimens before I quit for the day."

"I could walk you to the museum, Mac, and then just take the B downtown?"

"No, I'm fine, thanks," he said, with a hint of a smile.

Once again, Yanni managed to impress him with her adaptability, this time leaving him to wonder how a woman from the rainforest had so quickly become an expert on the intricacies of the New York City subway system.

Yanni gave Mac a quick peck on the cheek, then strode off toward Fifth Avenue.

He watched her walking away, let out a long sigh, and headed back for the West Side and the fossils of the extinct horses that he hoped were romping through central Brazil. *I've got an expedition to finalize.*

•   •   •

Major Patrick Hendry had become a frequent visitor to Mac's office at the museum. They'd both been transferred to Fort Hamilton after the war, which actually made it easier for Mac to keep another set of trusted eyes on Yanni and her artsy-fartsy neighbors.

Harder to tolerate was the fact that Hendry was often careless about the way he handled museum specimens, a habit which placed him in what Bob would have called "a somewhat less than positive light" with the curators. Now the major was eyeballing a set of ancient horse fossils that Mac had arranged on a lab bench.

"Here, hold this for a minute," Mac said, intercepting his friend by placing a Civil War–era cannon ball into his hand. "This you can't break."

"What, you don't trust me?" Hendry said, feigning shock. "You're not still busting my balls about *Triceratops*?"

"You mean *Bi*-ceratops?"

"Yeah, well. Accidents happen," Hendry responded, with an embarrassed grin.

Unfortunately, though, Mac also saw something behind the grin that told him this was not one of Hendry's friendly, bull-in-a-China-shop visits.

"So, Mac," the major began, when the phone rang.

"Excuse me, Pat," Mac said, picking up the receiver. "Oh, hi, Yanni. What's going on?"

He noticed with some alarm that Hendry had put down the cannonball and was headed straight for the fossils. "What? You want me to get you a what? Wait a second. Don't touch those, sir!"

Hendry picked up a grapefruit-size skull.

"No, Yanni, I wasn't calling you 'sir.' Major Catastrophe just stopped by. Yeah, Hendry." Now MacCready pointed frantically toward the lab bench, flashing his commander the universal sign for *Put That Down.*

"You bought a what? Yeah, that's what I thought you said. Sure. Right. See you soon, Yanni." MacCready hung up the receiver. Wearing an incredulous look, he turned back toward the major.

"What's the matter?" Hendry asked. "They run out of bananas in the Monkey House?"

"No. Yanni just bought a baritone saxophone."

Hendry laughed. "Why'd she do that?"

"There was this jazz band at the zoo yesterday. I guess the sax guy made a bigger impression on her than I thought."

"You know those musician types. Gotta be careful there, Mac."

"Yeah, don't remind me," Mac said, gesturing toward the horse skull. "You wanna put that down now?"

"Horses, huh? Is this the little filly you ran into in Brazil?"

"That specimen you're holding happens to be about thirty million years old . . . so, unless you want to be offed by curators and have your body consumed by dermestid beetles, I suggest you don't drop it. And the specimen *I* saw was considerably livelier. But I can tell you didn't come up here to talk about fossil horses."

"No, I didn't," Hendry said, carefully placing the skull back on the lab bench. "There's something in the air, Mac, and it just might have your name on it."

"So spill it."

"Like I said, nothing solid yet." Hendry gestured down at the fossils. "Just don't plan any field trips."

"Wonderful," Mac said, rolling his eyes. Wouldn't dream of it."

•   •   •

As spring became early summer, Yanni's indoor forest became filled with what were at first the discordant sounds of a novice saxophone player. But as the weeks passed, her proto-beatnik neighbors, some of whom had become her teachers, were pleasantly surprised at her progress.

Meanwhile, MacCready was working with the renowned natural history artist Charles Knight, to perfect Knight's sketches comparing the anatomy of a trio of prehistoric horses. Knight was intrigued at MacCready's insistence that the artist's prior reconstructions were "a bit off."

"Anatomically, your little hunch makes sense," Knight said. "But what I'd love to know is *how* you're so certain about it?"

And I'd love to show you, one day, Mac thought, just as the phone rang.

"Seven fifteen A.M., this can't be good, Charles. Would you excuse me?"

"Army business, I suppose?"

"'fraid so," Mac replied, watching as the older man exited, grumbling.

"MacCready here."

"Mac, it's Jerry." His friend from the mayor's office sounded edgy.

"Hey, Jerry, everything all right?"

"Not really, Mac. It's Yanni."

Mac felt his heart jump. "Is she . . . hurt?"

"No," Jerry replied, quickly. "It's nothing like that."

MacCready let out the breath he'd been holding. "So what's going on?"

"I'm catching major shit, Mac. The brass at the zoo think Yanni's slipped off the track."

"Look, I told you from the start, Yanni's a little . . . different. And that was *before* I asked you for a favor."

"Yeah, I know you did. But there's still a problem."

Several years earlier, MacCready had mentored the young polymath. Nowadays he was as comfortable cutting diamonds as he was designing lenses for spy plane cameras and flight-testing helicopters. Mac's favorite of Jerry's traits was his talent in the kitchen and the fact that he seemed to know every top chef in New York City. Unlike MacCready, though, Jerry was also quite adept at politics, and had become, at a very young age, a "higher-up" in the mayor's office. Shortly after Yanni's arrival, he'd asked Jerry for a favor—his first, and within hours, the Central Park Menagerie had a new (and exotic) assistant animal keeper.

"So what did she do?" MacCready asked.

"Listen, Mac, I feel bad enough about this. Why not just head over there and see for yourself."

"All right, Jerry. Thanks for the heads-up." MacCready placed the phone's headset on the receiver. Leaving the fossils on the lab bench, he made sure to lock the office door as he exited.

The zoo had not yet opened to the public when MacCready arrived at the large C-shaped building that was the Elephant House. Even before he entered, he could hear Yanni's saxophone, but it was like no music he'd ever heard: a series of jarring, low-frequency blats that never quite came together into a tune. As Mac opened the outer door, a zookeeper brushed past, shooting him a dirty look as he exited.

MacCready followed the atonal auditory assault and was soon standing behind a set of three-inch-wide bars separating the elephants from the curved walk-through that served as the building's public space. On the other side of the bars stood Yanni and the ancient elephant he'd seen during the "jazz experiment."

Taking a deep breath, Yanni blew another series of notes that only the merciful might refer to as music. The elephant responded by caressing the end of the saxophone with the delicate, fingerlike structures at the end of its trunk. When Yanni stopped, the animal paused for a moment, then flattened the tip of its trunk on the sawdust-covered ground.

Yanni smiled at the ancient pachyderm, and Mac could feel a strange vibration running through his body—immediately unnerving him, like another personal message from the dark. He also realized that the scientists had done their experiment wrong. Evidently Yanni had made considerable progress since then, although Mac had no idea just how much.

He cleared his throat.

Simultaneously, Yanni and the elephant turned toward the sound of the intruder. MacCready gave a shy wave, feeling as if he'd interrupted a very private conversation.

"Less than good timing, Mac. I'll be right there," Yanni said, sounding annoyed, before exiting through an inner door.

Moments later they stood watching the zoo's largest inhabitant, as *it* stood watching them.

Mac nodded toward the animal. "So Jumbo here—"

"Her name is Jewel," Yanni corrected him.

"I'm guessing Jewel's preference for music has nothing to do with following a circus band around."

Yanni shook her head. "Nuttin'."

"And you think elephants can talk to each other?"

"It's a bet, Mac. But they're using the opposite end of the . . . what da ya call it?"

"Spectrum?"

"Yeah, spectrum."

"That's why you wanted a baritone sax? Because it produced low-frequency sounds?"

"Bingo!"

"And?"

"Look at her, Mac. Jewel's a prisoner. And she *still* misses her sister."

"But didn't her sister die in—?"

"Nineteen twenty-one. Her name was Hattie. She got sick and they shot her. Right in front of Jewel."

"And she . . . Jewel . . . *still* remembers that?"

Yanni nodded.

MacCready gestured toward a large metal door, behind which a second elephant, Betsy, was trumpeting and rattling its chains. "What about her playmate back there?"

"Jewel says she's an asshole."

"Well that's tough," Mac replied.

"*Very* tough, Mac . . . tough to lose someone so close; to watch them die so horribly. So unexpectedly."

MacCready said nothing, his mind drifting, but Yanni interrupted him. He felt her arm encircle his waist.

"It must have been terrible for Hattie's friends, too," she added, sadly.

M ajor Hendry reached into his desk and withdrew the bottle MacCready knew he kept handy for situations like this. "Well, ain't that a pip?"

Mac sat quietly.

"She talks to elephants, too?" Hendry said, producing his signature shot glasses, before pouring them each a measure of the dark liquid. "Well then here's to . . . Jewel and Hattie."

"And Betsy the asshole," Mac said. He picked up the glass but didn't drink, noticing that Hendry didn't, either. *Here it comes,* he thought.

"I'm thinkin' that little talent Yanni's got might come in handy on this next mission, Mac. And this time you two could be dealing with something bigger than bats."

Mac put down the glass. "What? Yanni's not going anywhere."

"No? Well, maybe you should tell her that yourself," Hendry said, before rapping on the outer wall of his office. Before Mac could settle into rant mode, the door opened and Yanni entered.

"Ya see, it's all been arranged, Mac," Hendry said.

MacCready, still wearing a shocked expression, turned to the woman. "What's all this about, Yanni? What about your apartment? What about Jewel?"

"The apartment will keep, Mac," Hendry answered for her. "Plants watered, et cetera, et cetera."

"And Jewel?"

"She'll be with her sister soon," Yanni said.

"But—"

"I'm going, Mac."

MacCready's eyes ticked back and forth between his friends. Chins raised in assurance, they smiled simultaneously.

"And this calls for another toast," Hendry called out, cheerfully.

"Got that right," Yanni said, taking the whiskey-filled shot glass the major offered her.

This time, R. J. MacCready raised his glass.

Reality Check

T he tale that unfolds in *Hell's Gate,* though fictional, is a convergence of several real and little-known events, including the actual design and partial construction of the world's first manned spacecraft (the antipodal bomber) at the end of World War II. From Eugen Sänger's *Silverbirds* the Nazis intended to release nuclear or biological weapons (on the United States and elsewhere) from an altitude that would be completely indefensible by the Allies. Other weaponry, including the *Wasserfall* surface-to-air missiles and the FA-223 *Drache* helicopter, were also moving off the drawing boards by the end of the war. While the tragic and delusionally blind rocket scientist Maurice Voorhees is fictional, men like him did (and still do) live, and certain historical figures, including Hanna Reitsch and Dr. Ishii Shiro, are real.

As for *Desmodus draculae,* these creatures actually existed in Brazil, Venezuela, and Mexico, perhaps until as recently as the coming of the European explorers. In fact, famed vampire bat biologist Arthur Greenhall (one of author Bill Schutt's mentors) believed that the *draculae* might not have gone extinct at all, and that they or a closely related species could exist even now. We have, however, taken some dramatic and speculative liberties with the taxonomy and biology of our "night demons." In reality, *Desmodus draculae* was not formally described until 1988 (by Morgan, Linares, and Ray). Their fossils, like those of most species that lived in the tropics, are few and far between (given the poor rate of fossilization in environments like rainforests). If, however, the skull fragments of *D. draculae* uncovered by researchers had belonged to juveniles (rather than adults), then their raccoonlike size would be accurate. Nonetheless, most people are surprised to learn how intelligent modern vampire bats have turned out to be. Author Bill Schutt (who maintained two colonies of vampire bats while studying them at Cornell) documented incidents where the sanguivores mimicked the behavior of chicks, coaxing mother hens to let them snuggle under their brood patch—a richly vascularized region, typically used to warm both eggs and chicks. These "chicks," though, used the opportunity to feed on their adoptive mothers. Another vampire bat species figured out how to coax hens to settle down into a mating position, so that it could mount-and-feed. Physiologically, the saliva of living vampire bat species is a cocktail of chemical anticoagulants (like the clot-busting and aptly named desmokinase). These substances are applied to the single, crater-shaped wounds that vampires inflict with their razor-sharp incisors and canines. Since the victim continues to bleed long after the bats have drunk their fill and departed, the scene of a vampire bat attack is only a step down from the one depicted in the stable scene. In reality, the vampire bat's prey eventually dies from either blood loss (smaller species like birds) or infection (an open wound in the tropics is a gateway to disease).

We *have,* however, trespassed on known and suspected aspects of *Desmodus draculae* biology by equipping our creatures with greater brawn and a biological weapon somewhat akin to the lethal bacterial cocktail used by Komodo dragons and other monitor lizards. As for mammals, there are few "venomous" species (e.g., the platypus has a venomous hind leg spur), though the slow loris (*Nycticebus*), a cute-looking primate might fit the bill. Reportedly, it licks an exudate from a gland on its arm, which when mixed with saliva, can trigger a toxic reaction after a bite. Real-life vampire bats do not inject hemorrhagic bacteria into their prey—just a chemical cocktail of anticlotting agents. We hope readers will forgive us this trespass because we have been dreaming for years about penning the proverbial "believable" vampire story. Their ability to use their sono-scans to control the behavior of their prey is also (thankfully) a figment of abstract speculation.

The Hell's Gate region of Brazil is real, and is already so strange in its scenery and biology that we saw no reason to exaggerate the vegetation and the landscapes beyond reality (except for the fog and the occasional "living fossil").

What else in this novel is based on true stories and actual science? Much else, as follows:

Though Eugen Sänger (1905–1964) never brought his antipodal bomber to the level of completion described in this novel, he and his project were real, with research on his *Silbervogel* (or *Silverbird*) carried out in a lab in the small village of Trauen-Fassberg. As the war began, Sänger renamed his project *Raketen-bomber* in an ultimately unsuccessful attempt to prevent funds from being redirected into the Luftwaffe's V-1/V-2 program, and to his rival at Peenemünde, Wernher von Braun. After moving to Egypt in 1961, Sänger spent the last three years of his life helping President Gamal Abdel Nasser to develop missiles capable of striking other countries and especially Israel. Some of Sänger's junior rocket scientists continued to develop his space plane designs in the United States after the war, evolving Sänger's actual engines into the Bell X-1 rocket-plane (the first vehicle to break the sound barrier, with Chuck Yeager at the controls) and the X-15, which, beginning in 1959, became an actual space plane, piloted by, among others, Neil Armstrong, and reaching an altitude of one hundred miles. The X-1 and the X-15 were both launched from beneath airplanes, although a monorail launch system did make an imaginary appearance (based on Sänger's World War II designs) as one of the Academy Award–winning special effects in George Pal's 1951 film, *When World's Collide*. The aluminum oxide powder used in this novel for the *Silverbirds*' solid boosters was based on actual laboratory derivatives of the German passenger airship LZ 129 *Hindenburg*'s doped resin and aluminum powder skin. Aluminum, in essence, is among the most powerful nonnuclear rocket fuels ever invented, though it happened by accident. More than a half century after the *Hindenburg* demonstrated so spectacularly how aluminum, oxygen, and hydrogen can work together (water thrown on burning aluminum enhances the reaction by becoming hydrogen and oxygen), a revised version of the accidental formula powered the space shuttle's two strap-on solid rocket boosters; and it could indeed be said, then, that the post-X-15 generation of space planes flew on *Hindenburg* skin.

Kimura's mentor, Shiro Ishii, actually existed. He was Japan's answer to Germany's Dr. Mengele, Auschwitz's "Angel of Death." The camp known as Unit 731, and the events that took place there under Dr. Ishii, are exactly as described. After surrendering to American forces, Ishii and several of his bioweapons scientists bargained (with the aid of General MacArthur) for immunity from war crimes prosecution. They did so by helping jump-start a U.S. bioweapons program that lasted until the Nixon administration ordered its shutdown. In later life, Dr. Ishii served on the Japanese Olympic Committee and, according to his daughter, built and operated clinics devoted to the treatment and curing of childhood diseases—usually at no charge to their parents. On his deathbed in 1959, he called for a priest and converted to Catholicism, apparently based on the belief that if one repented during the Church's last rites, all sins would be forgiven.

F*lugkapitän* Hanna Reitsch (1912–1979) did indeed exist and did indeed propose and get an endorsement for what our character Voorhees called a suicide squadron. Reitsch joined as one of the squadron's first volunteers while Heinrich Himmler (*Reichsführer* of the dreaded SS) suggested recruiting war-wounded soldiers or condemned criminals to pilot the jet-powered dive-bombs. Though von Braun had been developing increasingly sophisticated guidance systems, Sänger agreed with Reitsch that a human being was the most accurate guidance system that could be acquired, and the only one that had already been mass-produced with unskilled labor. In 1943, Reitsch and engineer Otto Skorzeny demonstrated that they could convert a Vengeance-1 "buzz bomb" (V-1) into a piloted bomb in only five days. The first three test versions were to be landed on sledlike skis, so the craft (and the pilots) could be reused; but of those first three test pilots, only Reitsch survived the landings.

Initially, the plan called for sending Reitsch's Leonidas Squadron against the gathering British and American invading forces, but ultimately it was decided that jet-bomb attacks should be used to slow down the Russian advance. This would be accomplished by destroying power plants, factories, and supply lines as far north as Moscow. Before being accepted into the Leonidas Squadron, volunteers were required to sign the following statement: "I hereby apply to be enrolled in the suicide group as a pilot of a human glider bomb. I fully understand that employment in this capacity will entail my own death." German pilots referred to the concept of flying into their target as "Operation Werewolf" and, though the pilots wore parachutes, their battle cry was "Die for the Führer."

Meanwhile, the Japanese launched two rocket-powered versions of the flying bomb at the American aircraft carrier *Intrepid*. Both were dropped from distant, propeller-driven bombers. The pilots were seated behind a half ton of explosives, with rockets at their backs and steel bullet shields behind their heads. Unlike the German "Werewolves," the Japanese zealots were denied parachutes. Luckily for the Americans, both Japanese rocket-planes were struck by conventional antiaircraft gunfire and detonated far short of their target.

Would-be jet-bomb pilot Hanna Reitsch turned up in Berlin during the last two days of Hitler's command, weaving a small "Storch" plane through Russian antiaircraft fire and landing on a road near the Brandenburg Gate. Her plan was to fly Hitler out of Germany, but she found him in his bunker, refusing to leave and toying with cyanide capsules—one of which he offered to her. On April 28, 1945, Reitsch left Hitler with his cyanide and his new bride-to-be and flew out of Berlin, once again only narrowly avoiding being shot down by the Red Army. Like von Braun, she decided to head west, surrendering to the Americans. She was held and interrogated for eighteen months. By 1952 she was free to enter World Gliding Championships, where she began setting records that are still held to this day. Like the Japanese bioweapons experts and German rocketeers, Reitsch was also spared post-war prosecution. Near the beginning of the space race, in 1961, she was even invited to a White House sit-down with President Kennedy.

SS Sergeant Schrödinger and the legend that followed his capture and escape (after smiling at an interrogator when punched in a bullet wound), are based on a real person, who put a very real scare ("Do you think Hitler has many more like him?") through the U.S. Army's 82nd Engineer Battalion.

I n this novel, the fictional Maurice Voorhees makes several design modifications to Sänger's suborbital space plane—including, finally, extreme measures to reduce the ship's mass. (In all likelihood, the real Sänger design would not have worked without the Voorhees modifications.) During America's Apollo program, scientists encountered the same challenges, with extreme mass reduction strategies directed at the Lunar Excursion Module (LEM). Had the antipodal bomber program progressed to completion, as it does in *Hell's Gate*, the problems addressed at *Nostromo* Base by redesign would likely have resulted in the same simplifications, along with booster-rocket staging. In the case of the Apollo engineers, scraping away every possible gram of mass resulted in a LEM with a hull that was, in places, only as thick as two sheets of newspaper. Under these conditions, far outside the protection of Earth's magnetic field, had solar storms of the intensity experienced during 2003 erupted, the ship's hull could have provided barely more radiation shielding than a silk shirt, and the astronauts would have received lethal doses of radiation within an hour. Since the engineering problems addressed at *Nostromo* Base would have been (and ultimately were) addressed by German rocket scientists during the Apollo program, the solid fuel boosters and other modifications on the original Sänger design have been made in this novel to accommodate reality.

The Battle of the Cherkassy Pocket really did occur in January and February of 1944, in the Ukraine. More than 130,000 exhausted German troops were encircled in a pocket near the town of Cherkassy, and as Soviet forces tightened their pincer operation, the Germans, outnumbered and outgunned, resisted. Incredibly, the German relief force (the 24th Panzer Division) was ordered away when Hitler learned that it had been moved without his approval. Weather became a major factor, as German tanks and trucks became mired in thick mud, and only the horse-drawn *panje* sleds could move supplies. With the Luftwaffe unable to deliver sufficient supplies, the Germans broke out, running a gauntlet through Soviet tanks and artillery. Tens of thousands were slaughtered or captured, but many escaped. For the purposes of our tale, Hanna Reitsch's *Silverbird* attack on Soviet lines facilitated their escape. Coincidentally, this battle was also known as "Hell's Gate." For the Russians it was hell, and worse, with casualties nearly beyond measure. Had they not drawn more than half of the German forces away from Western Europe, through the battle of February 1944, those same forces could likely have overwhelmed the Allied landing force in France, and the Normandy invasion might have failed.

In New York, during World War II, the state-sponsored snatching of children from adoptive parents of German ancestry (the great calamity that turned R. J. MacCready increasingly toward solitude when we meet him at Waller Field) was a little-known but actual occurrence. In the family of one of the author's friends, this happened to Emily H., an adoptive mother who was indeed called "Führer" during a decision that turned out to be anything but a fair hearing. Emily H. survived, as did the real Brigitte, though just barely. Emily's husband, Will, an American World War I veteran doomed by mustard gas exposure, spent his last days barely able to speak, poking an index finger against a photograph of little Brigitte and begging to see her again.

The "Sparrow" seen perfecting a pan drum in Trinidad is based on "Mighty Sparrow," an influential calypsonian (born Slinger Francisco, in 1935) who actually made his professional debut in the 1950s. In 1956, Sparrow won the first Calypso King competition with his song "Jean and Dinah." The Allied base at Waller Field is described as it existed in 1944. World War II for the Trinidadians ushered in American soldiers, their dollars, and their refuse—most notably, fifty-five-gallon oil drums that offered local musicians a large surface area that could produce a far greater range of notes than the paint cans and biscuit tins they had been experimenting with since the 1930s. And while we're on the topic of music, "Junk Ain't Junk No More" was a real jingle—part of a series of public service announcements related to the use of junk and scrap metal for the war effort. See https://www.youtube.com/watch?v=CaD161ENV10.

The downgrading of the fictional Bob Thorne's academic credentials, essentially for being Jewish, came at a time when such actions were common abroad and even in some institutions in the United States. The Manhattan Project was full of Jewish scientists whose degrees had to be reverified under the authority of what later became known as the Atomic Energy Commission. A major New York City university was among the American institutions that, near the start of World War II, downgraded the degrees of Jewish students and limited the numbers of Jewish students who could be admitted. One of those students, Isaac Asimov, would become a famed author. In the first volume of his autobiography, the 1938 graduate recorded that a year later the same metropolitan university announced officially that it would accept no more Jewish students from New York. While moving to Boston Medical School, Asimov discovered that he and other Jewish students had their credentials downgraded to second-class degrees. Asimov wrote: "The thought that even in graduation I was pettily discriminated against irritated me mightily" (Asimov, 1979), and he swore that the only thing the perpetrators would ever be remembered for was what he wrote about them in his autobiography. Additionally, the conversation related by Voorhees to Wolff, between Asimov and Harold Urey, also occurred. Whatever the source of Urey's difficulties with Asimov, they stood apart from religious persecutions of World War II, for until his death in 1981, Urey respected people of all faiths. The problem appears to have been strictly a conflict of personalities, arising from Asimov (a teenage student at the time), who made some dangerously good guesses about what was evolving behind closed doors (with Urey) into the Manhattan Project—and who began publishing science fiction stories with such alarming titles as "Source of Power," "Super-Neutron," and "The Weapon Too Dreadful to Use."

The reality behind the I-400 names: *Nostromo* was the title of a 1904 novel by Joseph Conrad as well as the name of the spacecraft in director Ridley Scott's film *Alien.* The name of the second submarine goes back to the mythical daughter of Kronos and Rhea—and the mother (with Zeus) of Persephone. In his novel *Dracula,* Bram Stoker named his ill-fated ship (which ran aground and was found "mostly" abandoned) *Demeter.* The I-400 submarines themselves were in fact built, as described in this novel. They were undersea aircraft carriers, able to launch a trio of single-engine bombers stored in their enormous hangars.

The vampire catfish, or candiru, is real. Along the Amazon tributaries, the urethra-penetrating abilities of these tiny fish (actually a family of catfishes) is indeed more feared than piranha. In reality, although grisly stories abound, only one person has officially had his urethra invaded by a candiru—an attack that occurred while the man was wading in thigh-high water. While researching *Dark Banquet,* his book on the natural history of blood-feeding creatures, author Schutt asked Stephen Spotte, ichthyologist and the world's foremost authority on the biology of candiru, what the odds of an attack would be if someone were to urinate in a candiru-infested stream. "About the same odds as being struck by lightning while being eaten by a great white shark," Spotte assured Schutt.

The giant turtles inhabiting the swamp near the Mato Grosso Plateau are real, but extinct. *Stupendemys geographicus* lived in South America approximately three million years ago. Its shell was ten feet long, and the animal weighed between 2.0 and 2.5 tons. Although capable of severing limbs and snapping spines in two, it is quite unlikely that this species survived long enough to have encountered humans.

•   •   •

W hence came the *Xavante*: The lost cities of the upper Xingu region of Brazil's state of Mato Grosso are real. Throughout the twentieth century, the remnants of causeways, canals, bridges, and stonework, through which MacCready trekked, existed only as vague and often fantastical descriptions, in local tales told by natives about ancient "ghost cities." (During Schutt's studies on the biology of vampire bats, he also worked in the Mato Grosso.) Although the plateau fortress and its *draculae* tomb remain stoneworks of fiction, the mythical lost cities, pursued by the ill-fated Percy Harrison Fawcett, are proving to be quite real. Until the twenty-first century, with its slash-and-burn farming, the search for dam sites and natural gas, and renewed exploration, most anthropologists and archaeologists believed that the Amazon Basin and indeed all of central Brazil (including the Rio Xingu region) had been pristine and sparsely populated up to and through the arrival of European colonists. Despite stories about lost cities, consensus thinking, by 2003, held that aside from nomadic tribespeople, the land was an archaeological black hole.

University of Florida anthropologist Michael Heckenberger was among the first explorers to take advantage of road building and strip-mine style farming practices to actually roam freely through, and to probe archaeologically, a world that had remained hidden from Percy Fawcett nearly a century earlier. Canals, farming settlements, building foundations, and terra-cotta cooking pots (unearthed from ancient settlements and studied for traces of their former organic contents) revealed that carefully rotated crops and great quantities of farm-raised fish supported towns approaching the population of modern-day Ithaca, New York (30,000 people). From everything we now know, the mythical Golden City of Eldorado might actually have existed.

Heckenberger spent more than two years living with the Kuikuro tribe and reported that the people are familiar with the earthworks and other peculiarities of the landscape. The upper Rio Xingu region, he reported, "[h]ad an economy that supported a large number of people in multiple large villages integrated across the region into a grid-like system. Their rotational [fishery]-agricultural and settlement cycle essentially transformed the entire natural landscape" (Heckenberger et al., 2003). The agricultural methods at the base of intervillage commerce were evidently more sophisticated than, and very unlike, modern slash-and-burn farming practices. The towns were arranged in a "galactic" pattern around a central hub. Nineteen such agricultural cities, in two large clusters, were connected by roads. "Virtually the entire area between major settlements was carefully engineered and managed," Heckenberger wrote. His team found linear mounds or "curbs" positioned at the margins of major roads—"and circular plazas and bridges, artificial river obstructions and ponds, raised causeways, canals, and orchards." The earliest construction phases began about A.D. 800, and the civilization lasted until A.D. 1600. A hundred years later, all of these structures had been swallowed by the forest, and the civilization lived on only in mythology. The upper Rio Xingu region of Mato Grosso and Hell's Gate is so remote that Europeans did not reach the area until about 1750, more than two hundred years after the first colonists established a foothold in Brazil. The disappearance of the canal and bridge builders was likely the result of newly introduced diseases (including influenza) that moved along native trade routes ahead of the people from the east. Current estimates suggest that up to 90 percent of the population was felled by diseases to which the Europeans had long ago become virtually immune. Today's Kuikuro,

Xinguano, and Xavante tribes are descended from the disease-resistant survivors of the people who built the cities.

The jazz band's visit to the Central Park Zoo (referred to in our story as the Central Park Menagerie) was a real event (as were the elephants), though the actual event took place in 1921. The poorly executed "experiment" (read, "publicity stunt") scared some of the animals and enraged others. According to a reporter from the *St. Petersburg Times*, "Betsy and Jewel, the elephants, seemed to enjoy the music immensely, but Professor E. L. Davis of Columbia, pointed out that the pachyderms had probably followed a circus band. So there was a reason for their enjoyment that could be easily explained." Modern zoo experts knew that, at only six acres, the zoo was too small to house large animals like elephants, rhinos, and lions, and so most of the larger animals were removed (although sea lions and bears remain). A major renovation in the 1980s transformed the Central Park Zoo into the beautiful, and essentially cageless, institution that exists today.

Finally, the discovery that elephants can communicate by producing low-frequency sounds is absolutely true . . . although it wasn't determined until decades after Yanni's fictional work with a baritone sax.

Acknowledgments

From Bill Schutt and J. R. Finch

The authors would like to thank Gillian MacKenzie for her hard work, great advice, and perseverance in getting our nightmares off the ground. Thanks also to Kirsten Wolff and Allison Devereux of the Gillian MacKenzie Agency.

We also thank Rebecca Lucash, Tom Pitoniak, and the entire production team at William Morrow.

Both of us are extremely grateful to Patricia J. Wynne for the amazing figures of Brazilian wildlife that grace our novel.

Special thanks also go out to James Cameron for his encouragement and kind words, and for *The Years of Living Dangerously,* his excellent documentary series about rainforests and other habitats threatened by human activity.

For their firsthand knowledge of the German WWII rocket programs, rocket-planes, and the world's first true "space ship" (the Apollo lander), we thank Tom Kelly, George Skurla, and Al Munier (Northrop/Grumman), General Tom Stafford, Fred Haise, Jr., Alan B. Shepard, Jr., Harrison Schmitt, and Michael Collins.

Finally, we owe much to our talented editor, Lyssa Keusch at William Morrow, who had faith in us and contributed much to improving our tale. We knew that someone would fall in love with this story and we're thrilled that it was you. See you in Tibet.

From Bill Schutt

I owe a huge debt of gratitude to my friends and colleagues in the bat research community and at my favorite place in the world, the American Museum of Natural History. They include Ricky Adams, Wieslaw Bogdanowicz, Frank Bonaccorso, Mark Brigham, Patricia Brunauer (RIP), Deanna Byrnes, Catherine Doyle-Capitman, Betsy Dumont (who was there in Hell's Gate with me), Neil Duncan, Nicole Edmison, the late Art Greenhall (whose hunch that *Desmodus draculae* might still be alive today served to fire his student's imagination), "Uncle" Roy Horst, Tigga Kingston, Mary Knight, Karl Koopman (RIP), Tom Kunz, Gary Kwiecinski, Ross MacPhee, Eva Meade and Rob Mies (Organization for Bat Conservation), Shahroukh Mistry, Mike Novacek, Stuart Parsons, Scott Pedersen, Nancy Simmons (It's good to know the Queen), Elizabeth Sweeny, Ian Tattersall, Merlin Tuttle, Rob Voss, and Eileen Westwig.

I've been incredibly fortunate to have had several incredible mentors in my educational and professional life. None was more important than John W. Hermanson (Cornell University, Field of Zoology), who took a chance in 1990 by taking me on as his first Ph.D. student. John not only taught me to think like a scientist but also the value of figuring things out for myself.

A very special thanks to my close friend and coconspirator, Leslie Nesbitt Sittlow.

My dear friends Darrin Lunde and Patricia J. Wynne were

instrumental in helping us develop this project from a vague idea into a finished novel.

A special thank-you goes out to my teachers, readers, and supporters at the Southampton College Summer Writer's Conference, especially Bob Reeves, Bharati Mukherjee, Clark Blaise, and Helen Simonson.

At Southampton College (RIP) and LIU Post, thanks and gratitude to Ted Brummel, Scott Carlin, Matt Draud, Gina Famulare, Paul Forestell, Art Goldberg, Katherine Hill-Miller, Jeff Kane, Howard Reisman, and Steve Tettlebach. Thanks also to my LIU graduate students (Maria Armour, Aja Marcato, and Megan Mladinich), who often found themselves along for this sometimes bumpy ride.

Thanks and love also go out to Bob Adamo—my late best friend and the inspiration for the character Bob Thorn. Rock on, Dimi!

To my cousin Richard, who wanted to die in my novel, and to LK and MV, who may not have, but did anyway.

Sincere thanks goes out to John E.A. Bertram, John Bodnar, Chris Chapin, Alice Cooper, John Glusman, Chris Grant, Kim Grant, John Halsey (Peconic Land Trust), Gary Johnson, Kathy Kennedy, Bob Lorzing, Suzanne Finnamore Luckenbach (who predicted it all), Deedra McClearn, Elaine Markson, Carrie McKenna, Farouk Muradali (my mentor in Trinidad), Ruth O'Leary, the Pedersen family and various offshoots, Gerard, Oda and Dominique Ramsawak (for their friendship and all things Trinidadian), Isabella Rossellini, Jerry Ruotolo (my great friend and favorite photographer), James "Camuto Jim" Ryan, Laura Schlecker, Richard Sinclair, Edwin J. Spicka (my mentor at the State University of New York at Geneseo), Katherine Turman (*Nights with Alice Cooper*), and Janny van Beem (the *real* inspiration for Yanni). Special thanks also go out to Mrs. Dorothy Wachter—for listening patiently, nearly forty years ago, when I told her I wanted to write a thriller. I think she would have loved the story that J. R. and I came up with.

Finally, my eternal thanks and love go out to my family for their patience, love, encouragement, and unwavering support, especially Janet Schutt, Billy Schutt, Chuck and Eileen Schutt, Bobby and Dee Schutt, my grandparents (Angelo and Millie Di-Donato), all my Aunt Roses, and of course, my late parents, Bill and Marie Schutt.

Selected Bibliography

Altenbach, J. S. "Locomotor morphology of the vampire bat *Desmodus rotundus.*" *American Society of Mammologists Special Publication* 6 (1979): 1–137.

Asimov, Isaac. *In Memory Yet Green.* New York: Doubleday, 1979.

Brown, David E. *Vampiro: The Vampire Bat in Fact and Fantasy.* Silver City, NM: High-Lonesome Books, 1994.

Duffy, James P. *Target America: Hitler's Plan to Attack the United States.* Guilford, CT: Lyons Press, 2012.

Emmons, Louise, and François Feer. *Neotropical Rainforest Mammals: A Field Guide.* Chicago: University of Chicago Press, 1990.

Fleming, Peter. *Brazilian Adventure.* Evanston, IL: Northwestern/Marlboro Press, 1999.

Garlinski, Jozef. *Hitler's Last Weapons.* New York: Times Books, 1978.

Georg, Friedrich. *Hitler's Miracle Weapons.* Solihull, England: Helion, 2005.

Greenhall, Arthur M., and Uwe Schmidt, eds. *Natural History of Vampire Bats.* Boca Raton, FL: CRC Press, 1988.

Griehl, Manfred. *Luftwaffe Over America.* New York: Barnes & Noble, 2004.

Harris, Sheldon H. *Factories of Death.* London and New York: Routledge, 1994.

Heckenberger, M., et al. "Amazonia 1492: Pristine forest or cultural parkland." *Science*, September 22, 2003.

Herwig, Dieter, and Heinz Rode. *Luftwaffe Secret Projects: Strategic Bombers, 1935–1945*. Leicester, England: Midland, 2000.

Hogg, Ian V. *German Secret Weapons of the Second World War*. New York: Fall River Press, 1999.

Hyland, Gary, and Anton Gill. *Last Talons of the Eagle*. London: Headline Books, 1998.

Middlebrook, Martin. *The Peenemünde Raid*. New York: Bobbs-Merrill, 1982.

Morgan, G. S., O. J. Linares, and C. E. Ray. "New species of fossil vampire bats (Mammalia: Chiroptera: Desmodontidae) from Florida and Venezuela." *Proceedings of the Biological Society of Washington* 101 (1988): 912–28.

Myhra, David. *Sänger: Germany's Orbital Rocket-Bomber in World War II*. Atglen, PA: Schiffer Military History Books, 2002.

Nash, Douglas E. *Hell's Gate: The Battle of the Cherkassy Pocket*. Southbury, CT: RZM Imports, 2001.

Neufield, Michael J. *The Rocket and the Reich*. Washington, D.C.: Smithsonian Books, 1995.

Piszkiewicz, Dennis. *From Nazi Test Pilot to Hitler's Bunker: The Fantastic Flights of Hanna Reitsch*. London: Praeger, 1997.

Rhodes, Anthony. *Propaganda—The Art of Persuasion: World War II*. New York: Chelsea House, 1993.

Schutt, Bill. *Dark Banquet: Blood and the Curious Lives of Blood-Feeding Creatures*. New York: Crown, 2008.

Schutt, W. A., Jr. "Chiropteran hindlimb morphology and the origin of blood-feeding in bats." In T. H. Kunz and P. A. Racy, eds., *Bat Biology and Conservation*. Washington, D.C.: Smithsonian Books, 1998.

————. "Functional morphology of the common vampire bat, *Desmodus rotundus,*" *Journal of Experimental Biology* 200, no. 23 (1998): 3003–3012.

Smith, Anthony. *Mato Grosso.* New York: Dutton, 1971.

Wilkinson, G. "Reciprocal food sharing in vampire bats." *Nature* 308 (1984): 181.

Ziemke, Earl F. *The Soviet Juggernaut.* Alexandria, VA: Time-Life Books, 1980.

About the Authors

J. R. Finch is the pen name of a painter, history buff, and cave explorer. He lives in New York with three cats.

Bill Schutt is a vertebrate zoologist and author. He is a research associate in residence at the American Museum of Natural History and a professor of biology at LIU Post. Bill's first book, *Dark Banquet: Blood and the Curious Lives of Blood-Feeding Creatures,* was critically acclaimed by E.O. Wilson, the *New York Times,* and Alice Cooper. His next nonfiction work will explore the natural history of cannibalism. Bill lives with his wife and son on the East End of Long Island, and he is currently working on a sequel to *Hell's Gate* with J. R. Finch.

ML   6-16